Dee Williams was born and brought up in Rotherhithe in East London where her father worked as a stevedore in Surrey Docks. Dee left school at fourteen, met her husband at sixteen and was married at twenty. After living abroad for some years, Dee moved to Hampshire to be close to her family. She has written fourteen previous sagas including PRIDE AND JOY, HOPES AND DREAMS and A RARE RUBY.

Also by Dee Williams

Carrie of Culver Road
Polly of Penn's Place
Annie of Albert Mews
Hannah of Hope Street
Sally of Sefton Grove
Ellie of Elmleigh Square
Maggie's Market
Katie's Kitchen
Wishes and Tears
Sorrows and Smiles
Forgive and Forget
A Rare Ruby
Hopes and Dreams
Pride and Joy

Love and War

Dee Williams

headline

First published in 2004
by HEADLINE BOOK PUBLISHING

First published in paperback in 2005
by HEADLINE BOOK PUBLISHING

1

ISBN 0 7553 2210 X

Typeset in Palatino by Avon DataSet Ltd,
Bidford-on-Avon, Warwickshire

Printed and bound in Great Britain by
Mackays of Chatham plc, Chatham, Kent

Headline's policy is to use papers that are natural, renewable and recyclable products and made from wood grown in sustainable forests. The logging and manufacturing processes are expected to conform to the environmental regulations of the country of origin.

HEADLINE BOOK PUBLISHING
A division of Hodder Headline
338 Euston Road
London NW1 3BH

www.headline.co.uk
www.hodderheadline.com

This is for all those who suffered in the London bombings. Everybody was so brave.

Chapter 1

August 1939

EILEEN WELLS, LIKE every other housewife in Perry Street, stood looking up the road at the men on open-backed lorries piled high with huge silver corrugated sheets of metal that glistened in the bright morning sunshine.

The noise was incredible. Men were yelling orders to one another and throwing the large sheets off the lorries; with an ear-splitting clatter they hit the ground, sending up clouds of dust. Other men picked them up and stood them against the small wall that ran along the fronts of the houses. Slowly the lorries and the gang of men moved towards Eileen.

'What's your old man think of this lot then?' shouted Nell Drury, trying to make herself heard above the din.

Nell lived opposite Eileen; they had been friends for many years. They went shopping together, then on two afternoons every week, went off to the Gaumont to see the latest pictures.

Nell winced when another sheet hit the ground as she made her way across the road.

'Reg thinks we could be in for it if this bloke Hitler carries on. And seeing this lot don't help,' said Eileen, waving her hands towards the lorries as her friend came within hearing distance.

'My Fred reckons Chamberlain's too weak to stand up to him. Please God we don't have another war. Lost me dad in the last one.'

'So did I. Reg was saying at least being in the docks should make him and your Fred exempt.'

'S'pose that's gonner be the one good thing about working at the Surrey then. Mind you, you're lucky, your old man don't come home covered in lamp black one night and flour the next. Never know what colour he's gonner be when he walks in,' laughed Nell.

Eileen smiled. Her Reg had been in the Surrey docks all his working life and slowly worked his way up. Now he was a stevedore, which sometimes meant getting the right men for the right jobs. They were comfortably off: money wasn't a big worry for them, not like some of their neighbours round here. 'And I'm glad I've got daughters as well.' As soon as the words left her lips Eileen wanted to snatch them back. 'I'm sorry, Nell. I didn't think.'

'S'all right. Me and Fred have been talking about it. It'll be bloody rotten if Dan gets called away now, just as he's finished his apprenticeship and is earning a few bob. This is one time when you hope he's got flat feet or something.'

Eileen knew how proud Nell and Fred were of their only child. Dan had got a scholarship and had gone on to become an engineer. It had been a struggle for them and for a while Nell had had to get herself a cleaning job, but they were determined to do all they could for him.

Eileen and Nell had lived in Perry Street all their married lives. Eileen already had Ann, her eldest, when Nell and Fred moved in opposite. Their children had grown up together.

Nell turned to the bloke who had just stacked some of the sheets against Eileen's wall. 'What's gonner happen now?' she asked.

'There'll be some blokes round in a couple of weeks to dig the holes in your back yard.'

'How deep they gotter go?' asked Nell.

'Three feet.'

'Three feet?' repeated Eileen.

'They then bolt 'em together and your old man'll have to put all the earth back over the roof to act as a sort of camouflage.'

'What if we don't have a war?' asked Nell.

'Then I expect the government will take 'em back.'

'All that lot gotter come through the house?' asked Eileen.

''Fraid so, missis, as you lot in this street ain't got back alleys.'

'More bloody mess,' said Nell. 'Takes me all me time to clear up after the coalman's been. He chucks more over the floor than under the stairs. That's without the dust flying everywhere.'

Eileen sighed. 'I know. I'd love to have things like the coal stored in a back garden and not have it under the stairs.'

'Ain't many of 'em got gardens round here. Can hardly call our back yards gardens, can we?'

'Always been me dream that has, a house with a garden, but it looks like that's all it will ever be: a dream,' said Eileen, watching the lorry as it moved slowly along the road.

'No harm in dreaming, ducks,' said Nell. 'I'm off up the Blue in a tick, fancy coming with me?'

'Why not. I'll just get me hat and coat.'

Eileen and Nell went to the market that was named after the Blue Anchor pub two or three times a week.

They wandered around the stalls buying a bit of veg here and a reel of cotton there. The banter with the stallholders was a laugh as usual, but this morning as they walked home the two friends were unusually quiet. As they passed the huge silver sheets of metal both were reflecting on all that was going on around them. They couldn't help but worry about their future. If there was a war, what it would mean to them and their families?

* * *

Eileen looked up at the wooden clock sitting on the mantelpiece. It was almost six: soon the house would be full of laughter and chatter when the girls and Reg came home from work.

'Cor, Mum. What's that lot outside? What's going on?' asked Shirley, her youngest, as she burst into the kitchen. At sixteen she was a stunner like all of Reg and Eileen's three daughters. Slim, with short dark hair and sparkling brown eyes, Shirley was the shortest of the three, full of devilment and always smiling.

'Shirley, take that bag off the table, can't you see I'm trying to lay it?'

'Sorry, Mum.'

'Why do you do that every night? You know it makes me cross.'

'Sorry, Mum,' Shirley repeated, picking up her handbag and clutching it close to her. 'Anyway, what's all that outside?'

'It's for the Anderson shelter we're having put in the yard.'

'That sounds exciting.'

'Won't be if we have a war and we have to live in it. Be like bloody rabbits stuck down a hole.'

'Mum!' Shirley was shocked to hear her mother swear. 'Don't often hear you use naughty words.'

'Well, it's enough to make anybody swear.'

Shirley, still clutching her handbag, pulled a chair from under the table and sat down. 'We won't have to live in it, will we?'

'I hope not.'

Eileen told Shirley what the delivery men had told her about what having a shelter meant. Shirley was very interested and asked plenty of questions, but in truth, nobody really knew that much.

Shirley worked behind the cosmetic counter at Woolworth's and, despite being on her feet all day, enjoyed her job. She loved bringing home new make-up for her and her sisters to experiment with. Eileen would smile at the laughter that spilled down the stairs when her daughters were all together. She was very proud of her girls and although she knew it was selfish she knew she wouldn't be happy when the day came for them to fly the nest. She loved them so much she didn't want them to marry and leave home.

Half an hour earlier, it was time for Ann and Lucy Wells to leave the tea factory where they worked. Lucy was in an office with three other typists, which she enjoyed, though Ann had the better job. She had gone to night school to learn shorthand and typing and now she was secretary to Mr Harry Fisher.

Ann came into the room and pulled her sister to one side away from the other chattering women as they cluttered past. 'Luce, d'you want a lift?' she whispered. 'Harry's taking me home.'

Lucy smiled and placed the cover over her type-writer. 'Course. Got to be better than waiting for a bus.'

'I'll see you outside.'

Ann at twenty-two was the eldest of Eileen and Reg Wells's daughters. Her dark eyes were wide and alert and her short dark hair had coppery tints in the summer. Ann was the tallest and most striking; she had been going out with Harry for a few months now. Harry was a smashing bloke and Ann had told Lucy that she was very fond of him, but she had tried to keep her feelings for him from her mother, just in case Eileen jumped to the conclusion that he was stringing her along. Ann knew he wasn't. She would have to bring him home soon as her mother had been asking questions about him. Although Eileen knew Ann had a boyfriend she had met at work, she didn't know it was her daughter's boss. Ann had been Mr Potter's secretary for years and when he'd retired a year ago Harry Fisher had taken his place and they had hit it off right away.

Harry was just like a film star: tall, dark and handsome, and the girls in the office were always looking at him and making very complimentary comments behind his back. Ann laughed when Lucy told her that. Lucy couldn't understand why her sister was against bringing him home. Was she worried that they weren't good enough for him?

Harry had a car and sometimes he and Ann would go out for a meal or to the pictures. They always acted very professionally at work and none of the girls in Lucy's office suspected anything.

Ann and Lucy left Harry behind in his car at the top of their road. A car in Perry Street would have started all the tongues wagging and that was the last thing Ann wanted; she didn't want all the neighbours to know her business, she was a very private person. The girls walked silently down the street looking at the sheets of metal: all-too-real evidence of the threat of war.

In the kitchen Ann took off her navy-blue beret and threw it on the chair. She ran her fingers through her dark hair. 'I see it's started,' she said wisely, inclining her head towards the passage. 'They reckon every home in London has got to have an air-raid shelter in their garden.'

'Hope they send some good-looking fellers round to put 'em in,' said Lucy, taking off her coat to reveal her round figure. The long-sleeved, sensible navy wool frock she wore for the office hugged her body; she wasn't as slim as her sisters and her hair and eyes were slightly lighter. But she had a wonderful sense of humour and nothing seemed to get her down. 'Could do with some handsome blokes to goggle at.' Her one wish was that she had a boyfriend. She was very fond of Dan Drury, Nell's son, who lived opposite; they had grown up together but he had only ever looked on her as a mate.

Eileen Wells smiled at the banter. 'Now take your things upstairs before your father gets home.'

The girls traipsed out of the kitchen still all talking at once.

Eileen tutted and raised her eyes to the ceiling. She was so lucky; her 'girls' as she always called them got on very well and often went out together. As far as their money allowed they were very fashionable and apart from the odd argument about who was wearing whose blouse or skirt there weren't too many skirmishes between then.

Upstairs the girls went into their rooms. Lucy and Shirley shared the back bedroom while Ann had the small front box room to herself. The third bedroom was their parents'.

'Came home in Harry's car today,' said Lucy. 'It seems funny calling him Mr Fisher at work – not that I see a lot of him – and Harry when I'm in the car.'

'Luce, d'you think our Annie will marry Harry?' asked Shirley.

'Don't know. He's a nice enough bloke but a bit too staid for my taste.'

'But that sort would suit Annie. I don't know how you two can work in that stuffy office all day.'

Lucy smiled. 'Cos we're the brainy ones, that's why.' She sat at the dressing table and ran a comb through her mousy-coloured hair. 'Could never understand you wanting to work behind the counter in Woolies.'

Shirley laughed. 'At least we have a few laughs. Perhaps I should have paid more attention when I was at school. But I'm happy enough.'

They heard the front door shut.

'Sounds like Dad's home,' said Lucy. 'Better get downstairs.'

Reg Wells went into the scullery where Eileen was putting mashed potatoes on the plates. He kissed the back of her neck. 'See we're being blessed with that lot outside. Did they say when they'll be back?'

'No, love. Had a good day?'

'Not bad. We had a Russian ship loaded with timber. Funny blokes, those Russians.' The docks where Reg worked was only a short distance from Perry Street.

'Why?' asked Eileen.

He laughed. 'Can't speak a bloody word of English. We spend all our time waving our arms about and shouting at 'em.'

'Oh Reg, you didn't?'

One after the other the girls came into the kitchen.

'Hello, Dad,' they said as they sat at the table.

'All right then, girls?'

'Not bad,' said Ann. 'What d'you think of that lot outside?'

'Not much. Seems the government's determined to get ready just in case.'

'D'you think we will have a war?' asked Eileen as she put the last plate of meat pie, cabbage and mash on the table.

'Wouldn't like to say, but I hope not. Mind you, they was saying in the papers that they're going to be issuing us gas masks and identity cards next.'

Lucy looked up. 'Can't say I fancy wearing a gas mask.'

'You'd have a bit of a job kissing your boyfriend,' laughed Shirley.

'It won't be a laughing matter if there is another war,' said Ann seriously.

'I don't want another war,' said Eileen.

'Neither does anybody who's got any sense.'

After that Ann, Lucy and Shirley sat very quietly. They could see the worry on their parents' faces and it unnerved them.

It was a week later before they had any further news about the shelters.

Nell called out as she pushed open Eileen's front door: 'Ooh, ooh, Eileen, it's only me.'

Eileen came out of the kitchen. 'Hello, Nell. I've just made meself a cuppa, fancy one?'

'You should know me be now. Never say no.' Nell sat at the table. 'Just popped over to tell you that Mrs Jacobs in the newsagent's says the blokes who're supposed to be putting them shelters in, they was in there for their baccy, well, they reckon they should be starting in this street early next week.'

Eileen pushed a cup of tea and the sugar bowl towards Nell. 'Christ, I hope it ain't on Monday, wash day. What'll we do about the washing? We won't have anywhere to hang it.'

Nell put a spoonful of sugar in her tea and slowly

stirred the contents. 'That's true. Let's hope it don't rain. Think of all the bloody mud they'll be bringing in and out.'

'Oh don't, Nell. I hate mess.'

'So do I. Not a lot we can do about it though, is there?'

'What if we don't have a war? All this will be for nothing.'

'Do you honestly think the government would be spending all this money if they thought that?'

Eileen shrugged. 'I don't know. All I know is that I don't want a war.'

Chapter 2

LUCY GOT OFF the bus at her stop and turned when she heard her name being called.

'Hello, Dan.' Lucy's heart gave a little flutter. 'What was you doing on the bus? You always use your bike.'

'Got a puncture. I was upstairs having a smoke.'

'There was standing room only when I got on so I had to stay downstairs.'

'Should have come up and you could have sat on me lap.'

'No thanks. But I'm glad to see you took your old overalls off, wouldn't fancy sitting next to you covered with oil.'

Dan grinned. He was two years older than Lucy and they had played together all their lives. He had gone from being a gangly kid to a spotty youth, and now he was a tall, fair-haired, good-looking young man with twinkling blue eyes. Lucy had always had a soft spot for him but knew he didn't lack girlfriends.

'So, how's work?' asked Lucy.

'Great. I don't know what I'll do if there's a war though,' he said as they walked past the lumps of steel that were waiting to be put into the back yards. 'Could find a job that would make me exempt, I suppose, but I'd fancy doing me bit.'

'What, going off to fight?'

He nodded and, pushing a lock of hair from his eyes, asked, 'What uniform d'you reckon would suit me?'

'Dunno. Air force or navy, I reckon. What's your mum got to say about it?'

'Ain't said nothing to her yet, so don't say a word to your mum, you know how they gossip when they're together.'

'Shouldn't you tell her and your dad what you're thinking of doing?'

'Not yet. Let's wait till it all happens. See you,' he said, arriving at his house and pushing open the wrought-iron gate.

'If it happens,' said Lucy as she crossed the road and walked through her own gate. Lucy was deep in thought as she pulled the key through the letterbox and opened the front door. If there was a war all the young men like Dan would have to go away. And a lot of them wouldn't come back. Although it was a warm evening she still shuddered at that thought.

'Hello, Mum,' she called out when she went into the kitchen.

'Mum's in the lav.' Shirley was sitting in the armchair

and she looked up from her magazine when Lucy walked in. 'What's wrong? You look like you've just lost a shilling and found a tanner.'

'Nothing.' She threw herself down in another armchair. 'Walked home with Dan. He had a puncture and had to use the bus.'

Shirley grinned. 'So what did he say to make you look so miserable? He gonner take you out?'

'No, course not, you daft ha'p'orth.'

'He's a good-looking bloke now.'

'Yes, I know.' Lucy looked at the scullery door; she didn't want her mother to hear what she was going to say. 'We was talking about if there's a war. It ain't gonner be a bowl of cherries, you know.'

Shirley put her magazine down. 'Don't, you're making me nervous. Does Dan think there's gonner be one?'

Lucy shrugged. 'Dunno.'

'I don't want any more talk about a war,' said their mother as she walked in.

'Can't stop talking about it when you see the newsreels and that lot outside,' said Lucy, going out of the kitchen.

'What's got her goat?' asked her mother.

'Dunno. She came home with Dan. It seems they've been talking.'

'I hope Dan ain't thinking of doing anything silly,' said Eileen. 'That would break Nell's heart.'

'He might not have a lot of choice.'

'Don't say that.' Eileen went back into the scullery. She rested her hands on the deep white sink and stared out of the window at the back yard. She tried to imagine one of those shelters out there; the yard wasn't very big. Would it take up all the room? She didn't like all this talk that was filling the newspapers, the news, the newsreels and was on everyone's lips. The thought of all these young men going off fighting upset her. The sound of the potatoes boiling over on the gas stove brought her back. She quickly lifted the saucepan off the stove and plonked it on the wooden draining board next to the sink. 'I really should keep me mind on me work,' she muttered.

The following Monday the men arrived at the bottom of Perry Street to start the digging. Eileen and Nell, like many of their other neighbours, stood at their doorways watching the proceedings as the large silver sheets began to disappear inside the houses.

Above the din there was suddenly a blood-curdling yell from Mrs Conner who lived a few doors down. She came running up the road clutching a bundle that was wrapped in an old towel. 'They've killed him,' she shrieked. 'They've bloody well killed him.'

'Who?' asked Eileen. 'Who's killed who?' Fear filled her. Mrs Conner had two young boys.

'Me cat. Jimmy me cat. Clumsy sods. They've killed me cat.'

'How did they do that?' asked Eileen, relieved.

'Trod on him, that's what, then threw one of those sodding sheets on him. Look. They've squashed the life out of him.'

Eileen didn't want to look at the squashed cat. What if it was all bloody? But Mrs Conner was gently unwrapping his head. With his staring eyes, he did indeed look very dead.

'I'm so sorry,' said Eileen. 'What you gonner do?'

'I'll have to bury him. I loved him, you know,' she said with a sniff.

'But you've got others,' said Nell.

'I know. But even with six you still get upset when you lose one.'

Mrs Conner's cats were the bane of Perry Street, even if they were good mousers. They used everyone's yard for their toilet.

Mrs Conner walked away clutching her bundle.

'I thought it was one of the kids be the way she was carrying on,' said Nell.

'So did I.'

'I'm surprised those cats stay in that house with those boys. Have you seen what they get up to?'

'I can guess,' said Eileen as the lorry came closer.

'Mind you, I ain't sorry to see one go,' said Nell. 'I forgot to tell you, the other night Fred went out to the lav for a pee, he didn't have any shoes on, well, you can guess what happened.'

'Oh no. He didn't . . . ?'

Nell nodded. 'You should have heard him hollering.

I'm surprised the whole street didn't hear him yelling and carrying on.'

Eileen laughed. 'Sorry, Nell, I shouldn't laugh.'

Nell laughed with her. 'Don't worry, me and Dan had a good giggle. I wouldn't let him in the house till he'd washed his feet.'

Eileen was looking at the lorry. 'Look, I'm going in to take me runners up then I'm gonner put newspaper all up the passage.'

'D'you think that'll help?'

'Dunno, but we've gotter try to keep the place up to scratch.'

'It's gonner be hard work. Look at the state of their boots.'

Eileen shuddered at the thought of all that mud and mess being brought through her passage.

'Right, missis, your turn,' yelled one of the men as he pushed open the front door. 'Don't reckon that paper's gonner be a lot of good.'

'P'r'aps you can try to walk on it,' said Eileen.

She stood and watched as pickaxes and shovels were brought along the passage and out into the yard. Eileen followed them through the kitchen and scullery and stopped at the scullery window to watch the men start to break up the yard, piling the earth and rubble in a corner.

Perry Street consisted of a row of back-to-back houses. The sculleries had been added on and from the upstairs windows looked like a row of carbuncles protruding into the yards. As the morning went on the hole gradually got larger and deeper, until one of the men with a pickaxe had jumped down into it.

Suddenly there was a shout and water began to shoot up into the air. The man down the hole scrambled up.

'Bleedin' hell,' he shouted. 'We've hit a water main.'

Eileen looked at the water spurting upwards and filling the yard. 'What you gonner do?' she screamed through the open scullery window.

'Bert. Quick, turn the water off in the street.'

Bert ran through the house with his wet muddy boots and out into the street.

Eileen stood watching as the plume of water gradually subsided. Tears filled her eyes at the mess.

'What's happening over here?' said Nell as she came through the house. 'Bloody hell,' she said as she too looked through Eileen's window at her flooded yard. 'What's gonner happen now?'

'Well, you can't have an Anderson, that's for sure,' said the bloke who had been down the hole. The water was running off him.

'Why?' asked Nell.

'Water main. Can't go down deep enough.'

'So what happens now?' asked Eileen.

'Have to fill it all in again when they mend the pipe.'

'How long will I be without water?'

'Not long. We've got a gang with us.'

'This happened before?' asked Nell.

'A couple of times. We thought these pipes was deeper than that.' With that he threw his pickaxe over his shoulder and went to leave the scullery. As he turned the pickaxe caught the lace curtain and pulled it out of his hand and straight through the window.

The tinkling of glass brought a gasp from Nell. 'Bloody hell.'

Eileen stood transfixed, her face a deathly white.

'Sorry, missis. I'll send the winder bloke round.' With that he left the kitchen very quickly.

'From the state of your yard it looks like the war's already started,' said Nell.

Eileen looked round her scullery and back yard. 'Look at this mess. Where do I start?'

'You can't do much till they've mended the pipe and the window, then I'll give you a hand to clean this lot up,' said Nell. 'Give us your dustpan and brush and I'll clear this glass up for now.'

In a daze, Eileen took the dustpan and brush from under the sink and handed it to her friend. Then she took the torn piece of curtain down from the window. 'Good job I've got another one I can put up. Don't like to think that lot over the back can nose in.'

By the time the family came home at six-thirty the water had been put back on, the window repaired and the hole filled in. Eileen and Nell had spent the afternoon clearing the mud from inside the house.

When they were sitting round the table Eileen told

the others what had happened, from Mrs Conner's cat to the broken window and the burst water pipe.

'Sounds like you've had a busy day, Mum,' said Shirley.

'A day I could have well done without.'

'So we can't have an Anderson then?' asked Reg. 'I hope the government's got some other ideas.'

'The blokes told us we could be having a brick one. That means more mess being brought through.'

'What about Nell? Will she be having one of those underground ones?' asked Ann.

Eileen shook her head. 'No. They reckon the water pipe runs along her back so they ain't taking any chances. All along the road from us up are gonner have to have these brick ones as well.'

Reg sat back and grinned. 'Well, if we don't have a war looks like I could end up with a very nice workshop. It'll be nice to have a work place.'

'Thanks,' said Eileen. 'What would you do in a workshop?'

'Could get a few tools in there and make things.'

'Is that all you can think about? Remember it's me that'll have to clean up after 'em.'

Reg stood up and collected the plates. 'Don't worry about the mess, love. I'll give you a hand.'

Eileen tutted. 'Now that's something I'd like to see, you on your hands and knees scrubbing the floor.'

'Have to get the camera out for that picture,' said Lucy.

'Saucy cow,' said her father laughing as he went into the scullery with the dirty plates. He was trying to ease the tense situation, but at the back of Reg's mind was the thought that the government wouldn't be spending all this money and going to all this trouble if they weren't sure there was going to be a war.

Late one Monday afternoon at the end of August, Eileen and Nell were in the grocer's, busy chatting, when Mrs Conner walked in. They could see she had been crying.

'Another cat must have kicked the bucket,' whispered Nell.

'Shh,' said Eileen. 'Got problems?' she asked Mrs Conner.

She nodded and blew her nose. 'Just had a letter from the school. All the schoolkids over five have got to be evacuated out of London.'

'No,' said Eileen.

'What about those under five?' asked Nell.

'Their mothers can go with 'em.'

'I wish my Charlie was still only five. Him and Ronnie thinks it's great going off on their own. They're only six and seven. It's gonner break me heart.'

'Where they sending 'em?' asked Eileen.

'Don't say. Just that we've got to go to the playground at eight o'clock on Sat'day morning and the buses will take 'em to the trains.'

'That's awful,' said Eileen.

'The war ain't even started yet,' said Nell.

'I know.' Mrs Conner wiped her nose.

'And you don't know where they're going or who's gonner look after 'em?' asked Eileen.

She shook her head. 'No. I don't want me boys to go.'

'Can you refuse to send 'em?' asked Nell.

'The letter said all the schools will be closed and if the war comes London will be the first to suffer. So what do we do? Let 'em stay and be killed, or let 'em go?'

'I can't answer that,' said Nell softly.

Eileen swallowed hard. The threat of war was getting ever closer.

That evening, as the family sat round the table, Eileen told them about Mrs Conner's boys, then added, 'There's some more of those government leaflets on the dresser. There's one telling us about the gas masks we've got to be fitted with – they're coming round every night this week – and there's another telling us about the identity cards we've all got to carry and about these blackout curtains we've got to have up at the windows.'

Everybody was very quiet. They each had their own thoughts, but they all hoped that Mr Chamberlain would come back from Munich with good news, like they thought he had a year ago when he promised 'Peace for our time' after his previous meeting with Adolf Hitler. But that was a year ago. Things were very different now.

Chapter 3

THE MORNING OF Saturday 2nd September saw most of the inhabitants of Perry Street standing at their front doors. Those that didn't have children being evacuated watched with sympathy as the sad little ones, like many of their mums, shed tears. The small ones walked along clutching their parents' hands. One or two of the older ones were excited. They thought this was going to be a great adventure and waved happily goodbye to the neighbours they had known all their lives. The brown luggage labels with their name and address on tied to their coats made them look like parcels waiting to be delivered. Some of them carried small attaché cases with their few bits of clothing inside, while others only had a brown paper bag to carry their meagre belongings. Many were clutching their favourite toy close to them, their eyes wild and bewildered. Over their shoulders on a length of string was a brown square cardboard box that held their gas masks. The schoolchildren had been the first to be fitted. Next week the rest of the country would have theirs. It was heartbreaking to watch and Eileen, like most women, stood quietly dabbing her eyes.

'I think it's all wrong sending these little 'ens away when we ain't even at war,' said Eileen. 'Perhaps it's just a precaution,' she added hopefully.

Nell sniffed as the Conner boys gave them a wave. 'I feel so sorry for their mum and dad. Fancy sending your kids off to Gawd only knows where.'

'And will they be wanted and properly looked after?' asked Eileen.

'This street's gonner be like a graveyard with no kids running about,' said Nell. 'And I bet some of the blokes whose wives are going are secretly saying that they can't wait for 'em to go.'

'I bet they won't be saying that in a few weeks' time when they can't find a clean shirt or their socks want darning,' said Eileen.

As the last of the children waved before they turned the corner, Eileen whispered almost to herself, 'Let's hope they'll all be home next week when Mr Chamberlain comes back from Germany with good news.' She looked up at the sky at the large silver barrage balloons bobbing about on their long strong wires. They could now be part of their life as would be the sandbags that were being stacked in front of every important building and hospital if Mr Chamberlain didn't come back with the right promise. She gave a long sigh.

'All right, Eileen?' asked Nell.

'Not really, but we can't do anything about it, can we?'

'No. But we must all stick together.'

Slowly, one by one, the women in Perry Street went quietly indoors. None of them really knew what to believe any more.

The following morning, Sunday 3rd September, at eleven o'clock, like most of Britain, the Wells family sat quietly listening to the wireless. Mr Chamberlain was telling the world that they were now at war with Germany.

'What happens now?' asked Eileen.

'I don't know, love. Carry on as usual, I suppose, till we're told to do otherwise.'

'I'm frightened,' said Shirley.

'We all are,' said Ann.

'Dad, do you think he'll bomb us?' asked Lucy.

'I don't know, love. As Mum says, I think we should try and carry on as usual. Now, who's going to the creamery for the cream?'

Every Sunday morning one of the girls would go to the factory under the arches to collect the cream for their afters. Some of the arches were very low and Shirley hated it as the trains rushed across almost on top of their heads.

'I'll go,' said Lucy. 'I need to get out.'

Eileen gave her the pretty bone china jug that had belonged to her mother. It was one they always used and every Sunday she always added, 'Don't drop it.'

To Eileen it was precious; she loved to see it in pride of place on the table at dinnertime. It was one of the few things she had from her mother. They had been very hard up after the war and most of their belongings had been pawned or sold.

As Lucy walked along, she looked constantly about her. She was frightened to be alone; she should have made Shirley come with her. She was almost expecting a German to run round the corner with a bayonet on the end of his rifle.

When she went into the factory she was surprised and pleased to see Dan there.

'Don't normally see you here,' said Lucy, trying to sound light-hearted and brave. 'Is your mum all right?'

'She's worried now the war's started. She didn't want to go out, she thinks Hitler's gonner send his bombers over right away. So I said I'd get the cream. Must have cream on me apple pie.'

Lucy smiled. She didn't tell him she too was scared.

As they were walking home from the creamery, suddenly the mournful sound of the air-raid warning filled the air. They had been told about the up and down sound that would herald the start of an air raid.

Lucy screamed and, dropping the jug, flung her arms round Dan's neck.

'Don't worry. I expect they're just trying it out,' he said, holding on to her.

Tears ran down Lucy's face. 'What if he's going to bomb us?' she yelled out. 'Quick, let's get home.'

'No. Stand here.' He held her close. 'We should be safe under the arches.'

Lucy stood shaking. She looked at the ground. The precious jug was in pieces and the cream had spilled all over the pavement. She began to sob.

'Here, come on,' said Dan, lifting her chin. 'No good crying over spilled milk.'

'I've broke me mum's jug.'

'It ain't the end of the world.'

'It is for me mum.'

Dan smiled as the all clear sounded. 'See. I told you they was only trying it out.'

'I'm glad you was here with me,' said Lucy. 'I was ever so frightened.'

'You don't have to be frightened when I'm around.'

'What can I tell me mum about the jug?'

'She'll understand. Tell her it's the first casualty of the war.'

Lucy wiped away her tears and smiled. 'Let's hope it's the last.'

They both knew that wasn't going to be.

Eileen was at the front door when Lucy turned into Perry Street. She rushed towards her daughter.

'I'm so sorry, Mum, but I dropped the jug. The air-raid siren frightened me.'

Eileen held her daughter close. 'Don't worry about it. It's only a bit of china.'

'But it was your mum's.'

Eileen gently stroked Lucy's hair and kissed the top of her head. 'You're far more precious to me than a jug. I was so worried about you out there on your own. What did you do?' she asked as she ushered Lucy into the kitchen.

'Me and Dan stood under the arches.'

Reg quickly looked up. 'Was that wise?'

'Didn't know what else to do.'

'Good job Dan was with you,' said Shirley.

'I know.'

'I don't like it,' said Eileen.

'Nobody does, love.' Reg could not hide his concern. What was going to happen to them?

For the rest of the day they listened to the wireless, hoping for any scrap of news that would lift their spirits. Today's date, 3rd September 1939, would certainly go down in history.

As the month went on it seemed that every day government leaflets were delivered offering advice and warnings of what could happen in a gas or bomb attack. They were told not to talk to strangers and what to do if they saw a parachutist; rumours were flying about all the time. There was even talk that there would be cardboard coffins available.

'I don't like the sound of that,' said Nell as she and Eileen stood in the grocer's.

'Always wanted to be buried with me mum and dad,' said Mrs Toms as she sliced up some bacon.

'It's this talk about rationing that worries me,' said Eileen.

'Don't know how we'll manage sorting out the books and all that,' said Mrs Toms. 'We'll have to be strict when they do start. They've told us that the inspectors can come and check at any time.'

Eileen looked at Nell and smiled. She knew that what the woman was saying in a roundabout way was: Don't ask for more than your allowance.

When the identity cards appeared Reg decided to give the girls a bit of a talking to. He thought they were taking things too flippantly.

'Now then, you've got to remember your identity number and carry these about all the time.' Reg waved the blue card at them. 'And if a policeman or warden asks to see them and you ain't got it, well, you could finish up with a big fine or even be sent to jail.'

'I don't like sitting on a bus with no lights,' said Shirley. 'You never know who's sitting next to you, could be some dirty old man with wandering hands.'

'I'm afraid our lives are going to be very different from now on,' said Reg.

Carrying gas masks about with them was something everybody quickly adapted to. There had been a great deal of merriment in the Wells household when they were being fitted.

'What do I look like?' asked Shirley, her voice muffled.

Lucy was laughing, which made the visor steam up.

Eileen quickly took hers off. 'Don't think I'll ever get

used to wearing that,' she said, wiping her brow. 'Look, it's made me all sweaty.'

'You'll have to if there's a gas attack,' said Reg.

'Don't say things like that, Reg.'

'We have to be prepared.'

'Don't even think about it, Mum,' said Ann.

Eileen and Nell had been to the market to buy blackout material and had been busy making new curtains. Every night they had to be drawn and someone had to go out and check that there wasn't even a small chink of light shining through, otherwise hefty fines would be imposed.

Without too much trauma the brick shelter had been put up in the yard and Reg had busied himself making it as comfortable as possible. He had put a door on the opening, bought a couple of cheap armchairs, put up a shelf for a torch and some candles and fixed up a hurricane lamp.

'Looks like home from home,' said Nell when she came over to examine it. 'Dan and Fred have made a good job of ours as well. Well, it gives 'em something to do.'

'I'm a bit worried about those old chairs though,' said Eileen. 'I hope they ain't got any bugs or fleas in 'em.'

'D'you think we'll ever have to use these things?' asked Nell, sitting herself down.

'Dunno. I hope not. Can't say I fancy staying in here for long.'

'I'll be glad when things settle down and they open the pictures again. I really miss our little trot up the Gaumont,' said Nell.

'Reg said it'll all take time.'

'I'm still worried about when they start the rationing. We'll only have three books, of course. How will you manage?'

'Shouldn't be too bad. Reg reckons it'll be a good thing having some things on ration. It'll stop people stock piling.'

'That's true.'

Eileen gave a little smile.

'What's funny?'

'Us. Here we are sitting in a brick air-raid shelter talking about rations, as if it was all normal.'

'We ain't got a lot of choice. Mind you, I hope we don't ever have to wear those rotten gas masks.'

'So do I. I hate the smell of rubber.'

'Eileen, I'm worried about our Dan. I don't think his job makes him exempt.'

'Oh Nell. I'm so sorry.' Eileen felt full of guilt. She couldn't find any words of comfort for her friend. She was so grateful she had daughters and knew they wouldn't be made to go off and fight. 'When will he know?'

'Fred said he'll hear soon enough. I don't want him to go.'

'Course you don't.'

'I was talking to Mrs Conner yesterday,' said Nell.

'She was telling me about her boys. They're down in Sussex. They seemed to have settled in all right.'

'She must miss 'em,' said Eileen.

'She was saying she might bring 'em home for Christmas.'

'Is that wise?'

'She said she wants to have 'em round her at Christmas, it's only natural. After all, not a lot's happened, has it?'

'Not yet it ain't.'

'You're a right Jonah. We've all gotter have something to cheer ourselves up.'

'That's true.' Eileen sat thinking about Christmas, although it was still weeks away. Not everybody would have the heart to enjoy it, but she thought they had to make the most of it. 'I'm glad I got a bit of dried fruit in for me pudding and cake. Mrs Toms said she's having a job to get stuff.'

'It's funny to see nearly all the shelves in the shop empty.'

'She was saying she's only got empty boxes to put on display.'

Nell laughed. 'I wonder what else will disappear under the counter?'

'Dunno. Let's hope she remembers us when something comes in that ain't on ration.'

The girls had been listening to the news before going up for their Friday evening chinwag. As the advert on

Radio Luxembourg told them: Friday night was Amami night when all women should stay in to wash their hair. They were sitting on Ann's bed painting their nails and doing one another's hair. They were a lot quieter than usual.

'You look a bit down tonight, Ann. What's up?' asked Lucy.

'Harry got his calling-up papers this morning.'

'The girls in the office were saying that some of the blokes on the shop floor have got theirs as well. What's gonner happen to them?'

'I don't know. I will miss him. I promised that I'd write to him.'

'I ain't got no one to write to,' said Shirley. 'What about you, Luce, you got anyone?'

'No.' She didn't want to add that if Dan went away she would be more than willing to write to him.

'There won't be anyone left round here if they all get called up,' said Shirley, drying her hair on the towel. 'Can I borrow your curling tongs?' she asked Ann.

'Yes, but be careful, you left them on the gas too long the last time you used them and you nearly lost a lump of hair.'

'That's cos Mum was talking to me and I forgot about 'em. So what's this Harry like?' Shirley went on.

'He's very nice.'

'Lucy said he was your boss.'

'Yes, I do work for him.'

'Is he old?'

'Of course not.'

'Do you like him in a lovey-dovey way?'

Ann didn't answer and looked away. She didn't want her young sister to see feelings that might be written in her face.

'So do you like this Harry then?' Shirley persisted.

'Yes I do. He's very nice.'

Shirley giggled. 'When we gonner see this mysterious man?'

'I don't know.' Ann gave a little smile. She could never get cross with her youngest sister even if she was a scatterbrain. Her thoughts went to Harry; she was going to miss him. She had been out with him quite a few times now and she really did like him a lot, but hadn't mentioned that to any of the family; even Lucy didn't know the depth of her feelings for him. Before he went away Ann was going to invite him round to tea, then all the family would see what a nice person he was and how he wasn't that posh.

Chapter 4

IT WAS JUST two weeks to Christmas and Eileen was smiling. She had never seen her sensible eldest daughter look so flustered and tongue-tied. And the tall good-looking young man who was causing all this was sitting opposite her. As soon as Harry Fisher had come into the house he'd been at ease with the family, happily joining in the conversation. Shirley was almost drooling over him and Lucy was enjoying his company even though he was her boss at work. When he'd first arrived Reg had stood at the front-room window admiring his car.

'So how's petrol rationing affecting you then, Harry?' Reg had asked when he walked in.

'Well, at the moment it hasn't as I only use it for work.' He smiled at Ann and ran his fingers through his unruly dark hair. 'I might have to put Nancy in a garage when I go, that's if I can't take her to wherever I finish up.'

Ann smiled back at Harry. His smile gave her a thrill.

'Ann said you've got your call-up papers?' said Reg.

'Yes. Go next week.'

Ann was getting a little fidgety. She wanted him to talk to *her*.

'Do you fancy a little spin before it gets dark?' Harry asked Reg.

'I should say so.'

Shirley giggled. 'Nancy? Is that what you call it?'

'Please,' said Harry with a mock pained expression. 'Don't let her hear you call her "it".'

Everybody joined in the laughter.

'You don't mind, do you, Ann?' asked Harry gently.

'No. No, that's all right,' she answered with a false smile.

'We won't be long.' He gently squeezed her arm, which sent shivers down her spine. Soon they were all standing at the window watching as Harry and Reg climbed into the little dark-blue Morris.

'I bet there's a few curtains twitching,' said Lucy.

'Well, we don't see that many cars round here,' said Eileen proudly. 'Why didn't you say he was your boss?'

'I don't know. I suppose I didn't like to just in case you thought he was an old man. I wasn't sure how he would feel when he saw us either.'

'D'you know, you can be such a daft ha'p'orth at times.'

'Well, I like him. I think he's ever so nice,' said Shirley.

'Yes, he is.' Ann was still gazing out of the window even though the car was out of sight.

'When's he got to go off?' asked Eileen.

'He has to report to a camp somewhere up north next week.' They were trying to make the most of every moment they had left as the war had suddenly hastened things up.

'Will you write to him?' asked Shirley.

'If he wants me to,' said Ann as they wandered back into the kitchen.

'I expect he will,' said Lucy. 'He's a lot different at work, but he's nice and all the girls like him.'

'Where does he live?' asked Eileen.

'Southwark Park Road.'

'Cor, there's some really posh houses over there,' said Shirley. 'Does he live in a posh house?'

'I think so. That sounds like them,' said Ann as the front door slammed.

'That was great,' said Reg. 'When this lot is over that's what I'm gonner get. It'll be smashing being able to pop down to the seaside for the day.'

Nobody answered. This war had only just begun and none of them knew what was in store for them.

Tea was a huge success and Ann's eyes had never stopped sparkling. Eileen could see her daughter was in love with this young man. Would Ann be the first of her daughters to get married and leave home? They were such a happy family that the thought of her and Reg finishing up alone frightened her – but that was life. She knew she had to accept it. Then what about when there were grandchildren? She smiled at the thought of that.

In the middle of December everybody was elated and surprised when the news came through that the German ship the *Graf Spee* had been scuttled by its crew. It had been hounded by the Royal Navy and its captain was determined his ship wasn't going to be sunk by the British. But that would never compensate the loss of the navy's battleship the *Royal Oak*, which had been torpedoed a few months before.

Up until Christmas most shops still had limited stock so the festivities weren't going to be as bleak as some had predicted.

A few days before the big day Eileen met Mrs Conner in the grocer's; she was full of how wonderful it was to have her boys home for the holiday. The two young ones grinned at Eileen. They appeared taller and fitter and had acquired rosy cheeks to banish that pale pasty look. They also seemed to be better behaved. Their mother told Eileen that the woman they were billeted with was very strict and she thought she might have a job getting them to go back there.

'You wouldn't keep them here, would you?' asked Eileen.

'Dunno. Nothing's happened so far – well, not here anyway. It's awful that ship being bombed with those evacuees on. You think you're doing the right thing for your kids and that happens.'

'Those poor parents, they must be heartbroken,' said Eileen. 'I can't imagine the grief at losing your child.'

By this time the boys had got restless and gone home.

'I don't know what to do, but as my Tommy says, if none of the schools is open what're you gonner do with 'em all day?' Mrs Conner looked out of the door. 'Don't want 'em listening to what I'm saying or running wild with no school to go to. Most of the teachers that ain't been called up went with the kids. My Ronnie said his class has got a lot of London kids in it and the locals take the mickey out of the way they talk. I think they've been in a few scraps. But there you go, that's kids for you and what the eye don't see the heart don't grieve over.'

Eileen smiled and nodded in agreement.

Ann had been thrilled when she received a Christmas card and her first letter from Harry. Ann often thought about that Sunday when he'd come to tea, she had been so proud of him. He always looked smart and his car had caused a few eyebrows to lift in Perry Street. All the family liked him and he had quickly made himself at home. Shirley was still talking about his good looks, dark hair and smouldering brown eyes. Remembering his good looks even made sensible Ann behave like a schoolgirl and she read his letter over and over again. She was sitting on her bed doing so when Shirley poked her head round the door.

'Well, what does he say?'

'Just that he's been doing a lot of square-bashing.'

'What's that?' Shirley asked, coming in and plonking herself next to her sister.

'Exercise on the parade ground. You know, marching and that sort of thing.'

'Sounds dead boring.'

'He says he wants to train to be aircrew.'

'Wow. Does that mean he'll be flying a plane?'

Ann was almost bursting with pride. 'I don't know, I suppose it could be.'

'They have better uniforms than the blokes in the army have. I bet he looks really handsome.'

'I think he must.'

'Ann, do you love him?'

Ann moved over to her dressing table and, peering in the mirror, fiddled with her hair. 'That's an impertinent question.'

'Well, do you?'

'I don't know. Why?'

'No reason. Just wanted to know, that's all.'

'Scram, you nosy little whatsitsname.'

Shirley left the room laughing, but once outside her mood changed. She was worried about her sister. What if she did love Harry and anything happened to him? They were beginning to hear about some of the boys they had gone to school with being killed or injured. She didn't want her sister ever to be unhappy.

On Christmas Day the Wells family felt blessed and lucky to be together and to have all the usual goodies.

Reg even managed to get them a tree; it was a lot smaller than they were used to, but the front room looked really Christmassy with the paper decorations hanging from the ceiling and the fire burning brightly: festive, warm and inviting. When they finished tucking in to their dinner and after the girls had done the washing up they all sat around in the front room. Reg had handed each of them a small glass of port. He stood up.

'To all those that are parted from their loved ones.'

They raised their glasses.

Eileen looked at Ann and thought she saw a tear glistening in her eye.

In the New Year, strict rationing began. The weather had also turned very cold and Reg was worried that the ships might not be able to get into the docks as part of the Thames had frozen over and no ships meant no wages.

Dan was waiting at the bus stop for Lucy.

'What're you doing here?' she asked when she saw him leaning on his bike as she got off the bus.

'Waiting for you. Where's Ann?'

'She's staying on to help Mr Potter. Now Harry's gone the poor old bloke's finding it a bit hard.'

'Luce, I reckon I'll be getting me call-up papers soon.'

'So your mum was saying. She ain't all that pleased about you going, you know.'

'What about you?'

Lucy stopped. 'Me? Well, I won't be that happy to see you go.'

'That's nice. D'you know I've always liked you?'

Lucy laughed. 'I should hope so!'

He fell into step beside her, looking around. 'I'll miss all this. I was wondering. Do you think . . . Luce, as I ain't got anyone to write, would *you* write to me?'

Lucy was thrilled. 'If you want me to.'

'I'd like that. We've been mates a long while, ain't we?'

'Yes.' She wanted to add: I'd like to be a lot more than just a mate.

'That's great. Got to go, Mum'll have the dinner on. See you at home.' With that he jumped on his bike and pedalled away.

Lucy watched him go. Did he want her to be more than just a mate?

Dan *had* wanted to say more, but didn't feel this was the right time.

When Nell came over to see Eileen early the next cold Wednesday morning, her eyes were red and Eileen quickly guessed the reason.

'Dan's got his call-up papers,' sniffed Nell.

'Nell, what can I say?'

'There's nothing to say. Please God that this is all gonner be over soon. Me heart'll break if anything happens to him.'

Eileen swallowed hard. 'When's he gotter go?'

'End of next week. Fred's really cut up about it. He had a bit of a row with him. He reckons he could have got a job that would have made him exempt. But you know what these boys are like. Can't wait to have a go.'

Eileen nodded. This was something they were hearing all the time.

'Dan said your Lucy's gonner write to him.'

'That's nice.'

'I think he's got a soft spot for her.'

'Well, they've always played together, almost like brother and sister.'

They sat for a while reminiscing about their families and when the children were young.

'They were good times,' said Eileen.

'Yes, they were.'

When the girls came home that evening they were all sad to hear that Dan had been called up.

'So you're gonner write to him?' Eileen asked Lucy.

'Course.' She went up to her bedroom. She wanted to cry. Although she'd known this was coming she didn't want the others to see how much the news had upset her. She was very fond of Dan and she hoped that in time he could feel the same way about her and not just as a mate who wrote letters.

Later Eileen, who was busy with her knitting, sat with Reg quietly listening to the wireless. The girls were all out at the pictures. Lucy hadn't wanted to go after she'd heard Dan was going away, she wanted to be with him, but she had promised her sisters.

'That's sad about Dan,' said Eileen. 'Nell was really upset.'

'I expect she was. I'm glad we've got girls.'

'So am I. I don't think I could stand them going away.'

Reg leaned over and patted her hand. 'We've got nothing to worry about on that score.'

Eileen smiled. 'I'm glad they've opened the cinemas again,' she said.

'Yer. Although it does make you wonder what's gonner happen next.'

'Reg, do you think it will get worse?'

'Don't know, love. The way he's marching through Europe let's hope the Channel'll stop him.' But Reg was worried none the less.

On Saturday evening Dan came over and sat at the Wellses' table.

'So you gonner write to me then?' he asked Lucy.

'I said I would, didn't I?'

'All right, keep yer hair on. I only asked.'

'Sorry. It's just . . .' How could she say: I want to see you alone without all the family around.

'Look, fancy coming out tomorrow night?'

'Where?'

'Dunno. D'you fancy the pictures? It's the warmest place.'

'I went on Wednesday.'

'Well, you can go again.'

'Cor. Listen to this. Dan wants to take our Luce out on a date.'

'Shirley, shut up,' said Lucy, glaring at her sister.

'Sorry.'

'All right, I'll come to the pictures with you.'

'D'you wonner come as well, Shirl?'

Lucy could have thumped Dan. She wanted to be with him on her own.

'No, but thanks all the same. I'm going out with a girl from work.'

'Who's that?' asked her mother. 'You didn't say. What time you going out and where are you going?'

'I'll tell you later.'

Lucy smiled. She knew this wasn't true. She mouthed a silent thank you to her sister when she knew nobody was looking. She was going on a proper date with Dan.

On Sunday evening Lucy waited in the kitchen for Dan to collect her. Shirley and Ann had decided to go out together to make Shirley's little fib sound right.

'Shirley, what about your friend?' asked her mother as the two girls gathered up their handbags and made for the door.

'We was going out with another mate, but Ann said she fancies seeing *The Great Ziegfeld*, so I said I'd go with her.'

'I see,' said Eileen with an 'I don't believe you' look. 'Won't they be waiting for you?'

'I told 'em not to hang about if I wasn't there be seven.'

Eileen looked up at the clock on the mantelpiece: it was almost seven now. 'Well, I hope they don't wait around too long in this weather. You shouldn't make promises you can't keep, young lady. And you, Ann, shouldn't encourage her.'

Ann only smiled silently.

'Bye,' they called as they left.

'So what are you going to see?' Eileen asked Lucy who was straightening her stockings.

'Don't know.'

'You look very nice,' said her mother as she picked up her knitting bag and settled herself down in the armchair.

'Thanks.'

'But do wrap up. That was nice of Dan to invite Shirley to go with you.'

'Yes, it was.'

'Lucy, don't get too fond of Dan.'

Lucy laughed. 'Course I'm fond of Dan. Known him all me life.'

'I know. But you know what I'm talking about. He is going off to fight.'

'I know.'

'I don't want you to get hurt and upset if—'

'Mum, how can you even think like that? None of us knows what's gonner happen. Look, he's late, I'm going over to meet him.' She turned at the door. 'And,

Mum, don't let Dad or Mrs Drury hear you talk like that.'

'I'm sorry. I didn't mean . . .' But Lucy had gone.

As Lucy carefully picked her way across the road, trying to avoid the puddles that would no doubt freeze over again tonight, she was thinking about what her mother had said. She knew she could easily get very fond of Dan. But what did he really think of her?

Dan was full of apologies when he answered the front door. 'Sorry I'm late.'

'You did say seven.'

'I know. Don't nag.'

'Hello, love,' said Mrs Drury when Lucy walked into the kitchen.

'Right. I'm ready.' Dan kissed his mother's cheek. 'Don't wait up.'

'Bye,' said Lucy as they left.

'You don't seem very happy,' said Dan.

'I'm all right.'

'You didn't have to come out with me, you know.'

'I wanted to.'

'That's good. Now what we gonner go and see?'

'I don't mind. Shirley and Ann have gone to see *The Great Ziegfeld*.'

'Don't fancy that. There must be a cowboy or murder film on somewhere.'

As most of the cinemas were close to one another it

wasn't long before Dan found one he wanted to see: *The Prisoner of Zenda*.

Lucy didn't care what she saw. She was just excited to be out with Dan on a date. A proper date – but Dan didn't put his arm round her during the film even though she tried to snuggle up to him.

As they walked home, however, he held her arm. She gave a little smile, pleased that Dan appeared to be the proper gentleman, always walking on the outside.

'It's bloody cold,' he said, his breath forming little clouds.

'I hope they give you enough blankets where you're going.'

'So do I. Mind you, I don't fancy all that square-bashing on those wide-open spaces.'

'Go on, it'll make a man of you.'

'What if we have to do it in a vest and shorts?'

'I've seen your legs, they ain't that bad,' laughed Lucy.

Dan suddenly stopped.

'What's that matter? What is it?'

'Luce, I'm glad you came out with me tonight. You know I've always liked you, but I've never been able to tell you. I was glad Shirley didn't want to come with us, but I had to ask as we're all mates.'

Lucy stood shivering; she wasn't sure if it was with the cold or with anticipation at what Dan was going to say.

'Lucy, will you be my girl and wait for me?'

She looked up at him. It had started to snow again. The snow gently landed on her lashes. 'I'd love to be your girl, Dan.'

He bent down and kissed her lips.

She couldn't feel her feet, but that didn't matter. She was floating on air.

'You will wait for me?' he asked, breaking away.

'If you want me to,' she whispered as he kissed her again with a force she'd never known.

No matter what lay in store for them, Lucy knew this was something she had always wanted. The plain plump one who had never had a proper boyfriend was going to be tall, good-looking Dan Drury's girlfriend and he had asked her to wait for him. She would wait for ever, no matter how long that was.

Chapter 5

EILEEN LOOKED UP at the clock when she heard the front door shut. Reg was the first home. Eileen had been pleased that he'd been for a drink with Fred; she knew how down their neighbour was that his son was going into the army. She put her knitting on the floor when he walked into the kitchen.

'It's bloody freezing out there,' he said, standing in front of the fire to warm his backside. 'I hope those girls have gone out wearing something sensible.'

'They looked quite well wrapped up. How was Fred?'

'Still upset about Dan.'

'Reg, I'm a bit worried about our Lucy.'

'Why?'

'She's very fond of Dan, you know.'

'I expect she is. We all are.'

'I think she thinks a bit more of him than we do.'

Reg grinned. 'So is that such a bad thing?'

'What if he wants to get engaged or something?'

'What's wrong with that?'

'He's in the army. What if anything happened to him?'

'Bloody hell, love. Don't start thinking like that.'

'I can't help it, I don't want to see the girls hurt.'

Reg moved away from the fire and sat in the armchair. 'What about these young blokes' mothers? Look, whatever you think, the girls have got their own lives to lead and they won't have a lot of choice who they go out with as most of the lads will be in the forces soon.'

'Yes, I know you're right.'

Reg lit a cigarette. 'Remember, they'll be getting married and leaving home one day with or without your blessing.'

She could see Reg was getting a little cross with her. 'I'll go and make us a cup of cocoa,' she said light-heartedly, trying to ease the situation.

'That'll be lovely,' he said, holding his hands out to the fire.

While Eileen was in the scullery her thoughts went to Ann and Lucy. She wanted them to be happy, but she didn't want them to be hurt. If they were married and the worst did happen . . . She shuddered. She mustn't think like that.

Reg and Eileen were sitting quietly drinking their cocoa, each with their own thoughts, when Lucy came in. Her cheeks were flushed and her eyes shining and Eileen didn't think it was just from the cold.

'See a good film, love?' asked Eileen.

'Wasn't bad. It was more Dan's choice.'

'Kettle's boiled if you fancy a cup of cocoa.'

'Thanks. I'll take it up with me. The others home yet?'

'No, not yet.' Just as Eileen spoke the giggling from the passage told them that Shirley and Ann had arrived.

'You two, watch that blackout,' Reg called out. 'Don't want old Charlie coming round here shouting at us.' Charlie was the local ARP warden and took his job very seriously.

The girls burst into the kitchen.

'Sorry, Mum, but Ann got all wrapped up with the blackout curtain and she lost her hat in the middle of it.'

'I wouldn't mind,' said Ann, 'but I've lost me hat pins too, so, Mum, be careful when you pull 'em back tomorrow.'

Eileen smiled. At least this family had something to laugh about.

The day Dan left Perry Street, Nell sat in Eileen's kitchen all day. She was almost in a trance. 'What am I gonner do without him around?'

'I don't know,' said Eileen as she pushed another cup of tea towards her friend. No words could compensate for her son being sent away.

Nell knew she would just have to endure it as best she could. She tried to put a brave face on, but couldn't help fretting, as she and Eileen made their way to the market one frosty morning: 'I worry about my Dan in this weather, I don't like the idea of him doing all these silly exercises out in the open. I reckon he'll end up catching a cold. Where will the army be if all the lads finish up with the flu?'

Eileen grinned. 'Well, if they all sneeze over the Germans then the war will be over quick.'

'Silly cow,' said Nell, but she was grinning too.

'Just look at the price of those potatoes,' said Eileen as they joined a queue at the greengrocer's stall. 'And they've got enough mud on 'em to plant 'em again.'

'Bloody take on, if you ask me,' said Nell.

'Look, missis,' said the stallholder when they got to the front of the queue, 'would you like to be bent over in a field in this weather just to bring you a few taters? I tell you, standing here in the cold's bad enough trying to please you lot, let alone digging 'em up. Now, do you want any or not, cos if not there's a bloody great queue behind you that does.'

'I'll have five pounds then,' said Eileen.

'You'll have three and like it. Gotter give everybody a chance.'

'But I've got five mouths to feed.'

'Well in that case send one of them round to join the queue.' He weighed up some more potatoes and called out, 'Next.'

Eileen and Nell got their purchases and moved on.

Nell looked in her bag and tutted. 'And I bet when we've washed off the dirt, peeled 'em and took all the eyes out we'll be left with just about a mouthful.'

'Three pounds ain't gonner go far in my house,' said Eileen. 'It's all this talk about meat going on ration that's worrying me. My Reg does like his Sunday joint and a stew and a steak and kidney pie in the week.'

'They're manual workers, they need a good meal and they can't do their sort o' work if they ain't got meat inside 'em.'

'It is a worry.'

'I know, 'specially with just the two of us. I'm finding it hard to manage with just two ration books. Run out of butter last week, Fred had to have marg on his sandwiches. I can tell yer he wasn't none too happy about that.'

As they walked home Eileen thought about her family: they meant so much more to her than just five ration books. Although her two daughters were sad that their friends had been sent away, a ray of sunshine in their lives came when they received letters from Harry and Dan, but neither boy could tell them where they were or how long they would be away.

The weeks moved on and everybody was getting worried at Hitler marching through countries in Europe. British ships were being sunk and every day seemed to bring more and more shortages.

Ann and Lucy continued to look forward to the letters

they received and spent many hours writing long letters back to Harry and Dan telling them everything that was happening. While Harry's letters were loving, Dan's were short; he just told Lucy about the blokes he was with and what they did. But she didn't mind, he was writing to her and that was the important thing.

It was a Friday night, the Wells family was relaxing after finishing their meal and the girls were discussing hairstyles and the problem of getting their favourite shampoo when they heard someone banging on the front door. They all looked up.

'I'll go,' said Reg.

Lucy was over the moon when Dan walked in. She threw her arms round his neck and kissed him. She didn't care that the family were watching.

'What a lovely surprise,' said Eileen. 'I bet your mum's pleased.'

'Yes, she is.'

'When did you get home?' asked Lucy.

'About four.'

'How long you got?'

'Twenty-four hours.'

'Twenty-four hours!' repeated Eileen. 'Is that all?'

' 'Fraid so. I reckon we'll be shifted out somewhere pretty soon.'

'What, abroad?' asked Lucy.

He nodded. 'I thought I'd come over and see you. Dad wants me to go up the pub with him and he wanted to know if you'd come, Mr Wells.'

'I'd love to, mate, but what about Luce here?'

'She can come too – is that all right, Luce?'

She nodded. 'I'll just get me coat.' As much as she wanted Dan to herself she knew he had to be with his dad. Twenty-four hours was such a short time.

In the pub Dan sat with Lucy while their fathers propped up the bar.

'I'm sorry about this,' said Dan. 'But I couldn't say no to Dad.'

'That's all right. I understand.'

'Lucy, I love your letters, you will still keep on writing to me, won't you?'

'Course I will.'

'I might not be able to answer your letters, but don't ever give up.'

'Do you really think you'll be sent abroad?'

'I think it's on the cards,' Dan replied. He wanted to tell her that her letters meant everything to him, he wanted them to be more than just good mates, but he was finding it hard to put his feelings into words.

Lucy huddled closer to him. 'It's funny, all these years we've known each other and you used to tease the life out of me and here we are sitting in a pub talking about you going to war.' She choked back a sob.

'I know. I've been doing a lot of thinking while I've been away.' He took hold of her hand. 'Lucy, I do like you. I like you very much and perhaps one day, when all this is over we might . . . you know?'

Lucy felt a thrill run up her spine when he squeezed her hand.

'All right, you two,' said Fred Drury, coming over and sitting with them. 'It's good to have him home again, ain't it, gel?'

Lucy was upset at the interruption and quickly moved away from Dan, but she smiled and nodded.

'Pity it's just for a day. Want another drink, son?'

'Yes please, Dad.'

'Better make this the last as I'll have yer mother having a go at me for keeping you away from her.' Fred walked up to the bar.

'Will I see you tomorrow?' asked Lucy.

'I'll pop over before I leave. I'll be going about four.'

Lucy wanted to hold him close and smother him with kisses. 'I'll be in all afternoon,' she said softly. But they wouldn't be alone. Lucy knew the rest of the family would be there. She was disappointed but what could she do?

On Sunday Lucy finally confessed to Ann that her feelings for Dan had grown. 'D'you think I'm daft?'

'No I don't. I know how I feel about Harry. I was slightly always in awe of him when he first took me out, but since he's been away, somehow you can put things on paper you can't always say face to face.'

Lucy smiled. 'I really do like Dan and he says he likes me. But I'm not sure how much.'

'Course he does,' said Ann as she polished her dressing table.

'I'd like him to like me more than just as a friend.'

'Move that hairbrush a minute. I reckon when he's away he'll be thinking about you all the time. He'll be very different when he gets back home, you'll see.'

Lucy held the hairbrush close to her chest. 'I hope so. I really do hope so.'

Shortages were beginning to bite and Shirley was very popular when one evening and with a great flourish she brought out of her bag two pots of Pond's cold cream.

'You clever girl,' said Lucy. 'Is one for me? This weather's making me skin all dry.'

'Wait a mo. I'm nearly out, I've been everywhere trying to get some more,' said Ann, almost caressing the jar.

'They would only let the staff have two pots, so if you've got any room in an old one, you and Lucy can have half each.'

'Thanks. I bet a lot of things will disappear under the counter now. Good job we've got you to keep us supplied.' Ann kissed Shirley's cheek.

Shirley giggled. 'See, you're all glad now I'm working at Woolies. Looks like I'm going to be the most popular member of this family.'

'Not for me, I won't be using any of that stuff,' said her father with a grin.

'Not yet you don't, but if I was you I'd stock up on shaving soap, bootlaces and shoe polish. Things like that are going very fast and we ain't getting much new stock.'

The knocking on the front door made them all look up.

'Who can that be at this time of night?' asked Reg.

'Did you check the blackout?' asked Eileen anxiously as Reg left the room.

They sat listening to voices in the passage and were surprised to see Charlie the warden behind Reg when he pushed open the kitchen door.

'Hello, Eileen, girls,' he said, removing his tin hat and nodding at them.

Eileen looked worried. 'What is it, Charlie? We ain't showing any light, are we?'

'No.' He smiled. 'Come to ask Reg here if I can call on his services sometime in the future.'

'Depends,' said Reg.

'It's only rumours at the moment but they're talking about having blokes to be fire wardens.'

'Why? We gonner have an air raid?' asked Eileen, her voice full of panic.

'Not yet, but . . . it could be.'

Reg pulled a chair out from under the table. 'Have a seat, Charlie. What will I have to do?'

'Well, you'll have to do shifts every night at a set time. The first'll probably be up to midnight and the second shift up till daybreak. You'll have to wander round looking for incendiaries.'

'He'll have to go out in a raid?' asked Ann with alarm.

'That's the general idea.'

'Don't like the sound of that,' said Eileen.

'Don't worry, he'll have a tin hat.'

'Thank Gawd for that,' said Reg.

'Been and seen Fred, so you'll have company, you can work as a pair. Now I must get on, got to find some more recruits.' Charlie gathered up his papers. 'And if I don't get enough then they may have to start to conscript 'em. I'll let you know what shift you'll be on when the paperwork's sorted out.'

When Reg returned from seeing Charlie out he sat down in his chair with a sigh. 'Well, that's a turn-up for the books.'

'I for one don't like it,' said Eileen. 'I don't like the idea of you standing around while the bombs are dropping all around you.'

'You must be joking. I won't be a warden or being paid for the job so there's no way I'll be outside if and when that happens. I'll be in the shelter with you lot.'

Eileen smiled. 'That's all right then.'

'With a bit of luck we might not get any raids round here,' said Ann.

'Don't know about that, love,' said her father seriously. 'With the docks only up the road and the Thames the shape it is, I'm afraid we're gonner be pretty vulnerable on a moonlit night.'

'Reg, don't say things like that. You're frightening the life out of me,' said Eileen.

Reg looked at his wife and daughters' pale faces; he had a feeling that this was going to be a long, hard battle. Although he wasn't a religious man he could only hope and pray they would all come through this together.

Chapter 6

IT WAS EARLY May and a bright Sunday morning. Everything in the Wells household was quiet as the girls were all having a lie-in. Ann had heard her father go downstairs; she knew he would be up soon with tea for all of them. As she stared up at the ceiling she started thinking about Harry. He had been away for weeks now and his letters told her that he was hoping that when he finished his basic training he would get some leave before he was moved on. His letters were very romantic and she knew that he loved her. She also knew that she was deeply in love with him. She turned over and hugged herself. She wanted to be with him so much. In three weeks' time it would be her twenty-third birthday; it would be wonderful if he was home for that. But what did the future hold for her and Harry? What did the future hold for anyone? She knew that there was talk of the government beginning to conscript women. Ann suddenly became aware of the sound of a car coming up the road; they didn't see many cars in Perry Street – even fewer since petrol rationing –

especially on a Sunday morning. When it stopped outside their house and she heard the car door shut she jumped out of bed and lifted the lace curtain. She couldn't believe her eyes. Harry was getting out of his car. He looked up and waved.

She screamed out his name and grabbing her dressing gown rushed down the stairs like a silly schoolgirl. Throwing open the front door, she fell into his arms.

'What's going on?' asked her mother, coming out of her bedroom and seeing Lucy and Shirley standing at the top of the stairs.

'We heard the racket she was making and came to have a look,' said Lucy.

'Looks like Harry's home,' said Shirley. 'Wait till she catches sight of herself in the mirror, she'll go mad that she ain't done her hair and got herself all dolled up.'

'I don't suppose Harry minds,' said Lucy as they hung over the banisters watching their big sister locked in Harry's arms. When Dan comes home, she thought, I won't mind if I'm in sackcloth and ashes.

'Don't he look handsome in his uniform?' said Shirley as she watched Ann drag Harry into the kitchen and the rest of the Wells family followed behind.

'Hello, Dad,' said Ann. 'Look, Harry's home.'

'I can see that. How are you, mate?' said Reg, going up to him and shaking his outstretched hand.

'Not too bad.'

'Cuppa? I've just made it, was going to take the girls and the missis up one, but I see they've all come down.'

Harry turned round. 'I'm so sorry. I hope I didn't wake you. I know it's a bit early, but I've only got today and I did so want to see Ann.'

'No, that's all right,' said Eileen, beaming. 'I was getting up anyway.'

'When you got to go back?' asked Ann.

'Tonight. I could only get a forty-eight-hour pass. I spent yesterday with Ma and Dad so that I could spend all day with you. That's if you haven't got anything else planned?'

'No. No. I'm free all day.' Ann's eyes were shining. Despite her tousled hair and no make-up, she was glowing.

Shirley gave Lucy a sly nudge.

'So where're you stationed?' asked Reg.

'Dad, remember careless talk costs lives,' said Shirley seriously.

They all laughed. Everybody knew all the slogans that told them to be careful whom they talked to.

'Now I've finished my basic training I'm being moved. Can't say where I'll finish up, not till I get back. I hope it's not too far away and I can take Nancy with me.'

They sat round the table drinking tea. Eileen looked like a cat that had got the cream. In peacetime he would definitely have been the sort of young man she would have chosen for one of her daughters; what a pity the war was on.

When Ann finished her tea she ran upstairs to get

herself ready. She was going out with Harry. Her heart was beating so fast, she was sure everybody could hear it.

Harry stood up when she returned to the kitchen. 'You look very nice,' he said.

'Thank you. Where shall we go?' she asked as Harry helped her on with her coat.

'I don't mind.'

'Don't worry about dinner for me, Mum, we'll get something out. Is that all right?' she asked Harry.

'Of course.'

Ann thought she was floating on air as she got into the car. 'This is such a lovely surprise,' she said as he started the engine.

'Ann, I wanted to come and see you yesterday, but you know how it is. I had to have one day at home.'

'That's only as it should be.'

They turned out of Perry Street. 'Is there anywhere special you want to go?' she asked.

'Not really. How do you fancy Greenwich?'

'That sounds lovely.' Ann would have been just happy sitting in the car in the street. Anywhere was fine; she didn't care, she was with Harry.

They walked hand in hand up to the observatory.

'I've been dreaming about this moment,' said Harry.

'Have you? Have you really?'

'Ann, as you know I've put in to be aircrew.' He stopped and pulled her round to face him. 'I do love you. You will wait for me, won't you?'

Ann looked up at him.

'What I'm asking is for us to be engaged.'

'Engaged? Are you sure?'

'As sure as I'll ever be. I don't want anyone else stealing you while I'm away.'

'There's no fear of that,' she said, smiling.

'So, what do you say?'

'I'd like that very much.'

He took her in his arms and kissed her. It was a long hard kiss and she didn't want it to end. When they eventually broke apart Harry took her hand and led her to a seat under the trees. Even though it was Sunday church bells weren't allowed to ring. As most children had been sent out of London, there weren't any kids playing. Ann was aware of the birds singing their little hearts out. Only the odd person walking their dog disturbed the scene, it was all so quiet, almost unreal.

'As soon as I get settled I'll write and on my next leave I'll take you home to meet my parents and we can get your ring.'

Ann felt she was in some kind of dream. 'Harry, are you sure your family will approve of me?'

'Of course. I've told them all about you and they can't wait to meet you. I only wish we had time now, but for these few hours I didn't want to share you with anyone. Besides, it's not them that want to spend the rest of their life with you.'

Ann shuddered. How long did they have? How long would the rest of their lives be?

He put his arm round her shoulder and drew her close. 'Ann, as soon as I saw you sitting behind your desk I knew I wanted to get to know you, really know you. My biggest regret is that I didn't do it earlier. I don't want to rush you. I just want you to be sure this is what you want. Now kiss me, just to make sure you are really here with me.'

Ann was letting her heart rule her sensible head. She didn't mind about being rushed, even though they hadn't been courting for that long and she'd never met his parents. She didn't care, she just wanted to be with him.

'You have told your parents all about me, haven't you?'

'I've told them that you're the most wonderful girl I've ever met and they can't wait to meet you, but not today. I want you all to myself today.'

Harry went to kiss her but she gently pushed him away. 'They do know our lives are very different?'

Harry kissed her nose. 'Yes. Don't worry about it. They'll love you as much as I do.'

'They do know where I live and that my father's a stevedore?'

'What difference does that make? It's you I want to marry.'

Ann settled comfortably in his arms and smiled. This was where she belonged.

They sat all morning talking about how they hoped their future would work out.

'Now, how about us trying to find somewhere where we can eat? I'm starving.'

To Ann, food was an afterthought. She felt that at this moment she could live on love.

Eileen was singing along with the wireless as she prepared the dinner.

'You sound happy, Mum,' said Shirley.

'Yes I am. We've got a decent bit of beef today.'

Shirley laughed. 'Is that all that makes you happy?'

'It is when you have to queue up for hours only to be told they've sold out.'

Shirley went up to her mother and kissed her cheek.

'What was that for?'

'Dunno. Nothing really. I'm just glad that we're all here together.'

'So am I, love. So am I.'

'D'you realise that nearly every house in this street has got someone away?'

'I know. If it's not in the forces it's kids being evacuated. Now you can get on and make the batter.'

'You mean to say we've got an egg as well?'

Eileen looked around her. 'Ssh,' she said, grinning. 'Careless talk and all that.'

They laughed together. But deep down both were afraid that this happiness might not last.

It was dark when Harry pulled up outside Ann's house.

'Look, if you don't mind I'd rather not come in. I've

got to catch a late train, I have to be back in camp very early tomorrow.'

'No, that's all right.'

He kissed her. 'As soon as I get settled I'll let you know. Ann, I do love you.'

'And I love you.'

They kissed again.

'Please take care,' she whispered.

'I will. I promise.'

Ann stood and watched as the car disappeared. This was the happiest day of her life. She was going to marry Harry Fisher. What would the family say about that? She knew how much her mother worried about Lucy getting too fond of Dan. But she had to realise that all the eligible young men would soon be in the forces and life was being accelerated even though everybody was hoping this war would be over soon. Although she wanted to cry at saying goodbye to Harry, Ann painted a smile on her face and pulled the key through the letterbox.

Chapter 7

'YOU LOOK LIKE you've had a good day,' said Eileen, looking up from her knitting when her daughter walked in.

'Yes, I have.' Ann's face was full of happiness.

'Go anywhere exciting?'

'We went to Greenwich.'

'I like it there, it's nice,' said Shirley. 'Was the observatory open?'

'No.'

'Probably because of the war,' said their father. 'Your Harry's not a bad lad. In fact I quite like him.'

Ann beamed. He had called him 'your Harry'. 'That's good because, Mum, Dad, Harry wants us to get engaged on his next leave.'

'Wow,' said Shirley. 'Can I be your bridesmaid?'

'I said engaged, not married.'

'I know, but one should lead to the other,' said Shirley.

'What do you mean, get engaged on his next leave? Is that wise?'

'I'm sorry, what d'you say, Mum?' asked Ann.

'Well, with all this unrest, what if he gets—'

'Don't you say it. Don't you dare say it,' whispered Ann.

'Hold on,' said Reg. 'What was your answer?'

'I would have thought that was obvious,' said Lucy. 'Look at the grin she's got stuck on her face.'

Despite her disappointment at her mother's reaction Ann couldn't stop smiling widely. 'I said yes, of course. So, is that all right?' She looked at her mother and father.

'You're old enough to make up your own mind,' said Eileen, but it was said disapprovingly as her knitting needles clicked away.

'Mum.' Ann squatted on the floor beside her mother and took hold of her hand. 'I thought you liked Harry?'

'I do. But is it wise to promise yourself to someone in this day and age?'

'We can't stop loving people just because there's a war.' Ann stood up; all the joy had gone out of her.

'I was only going to say what if he gets stationed far away and meets someone else. There's a lot of young women joining up now and after all, he's only human.'

'I love Harry and he loves me.'

Lucy and Shirley looked at each other. The thought that was racing through Lucy's mind was: Would I get the same reaction if Dan asked me to marry him when he was home again?

'You haven't been out with him that many times.'

'I know, but I've known him a long while. Don't forget I've worked at the office with him.'

'Work's different. What about his parents? Have you met them?' asked Eileen. The clacking needles got louder and faster.

'No. Not yet, but I'm not going to marry his parents, am I?' Ann said curtly.

'Now calm down, Ann,' said her father. 'I'm sure your mother didn't mean anything, it's just that she's worried about you and don't want to see you get hurt.'

'We've got to grab the moment. We don't know how long this war is going on for or where he'll be sent. All I'm doing is getting engaged, I'm not bloody well running away with him.'

'Watch your language,' said her father disapprovingly. 'Of course you can get engaged. You're over twenty-one and don't need our approval. What you do with your life is up to you.'

'Just as long as she knows the pitfalls. Anything could happen and I don't want to see her hurt,' said Eileen.

Ann rushed to her mother and held her close. 'Oh Mum. You know I wouldn't upset you for the world, but I love Harry.'

Lucy stifled a sob. She was still under age.

'When you're in love you can't see any pitfalls; besides, it'll be nice to have a wedding to look forward to,' said Shirley.

'Hark at the wise one,' said Lucy trying to make light of the situation.

For the rest of the evening the atmosphere was very strained and everybody listened to the wireless without too many comments. They were all pleased when it was time for bed.

'Well, that was a turn-up for the book,' said Shirley as she climbed into bed.

'It certainly was,' said Lucy. 'I knew they liked each other but I never thought it was that serious. Wait till they find out at work.'

'Should you say anything?'

'No, s'pose not. I'll leave that to Ann.'

'I wonder when they'll get married?'

'Dunno. Got to wait and see where Harry finishes up, I suppose.'

'Poor old Ann. It wasn't the sort of reaction she expected from Mum.'

'I know. But Mum's gotter remember that all's fair in love and war.'

Shirley giggled. 'Cor, hark at *you* now, you're a proper little poet.'

'I have me moments. Now go to sleep.'

Ann, however, was tossing and turning. She knew that sleep wasn't going to come easily. She had been so happy; now because of her mother's cool reaction she felt deflated. She loved Harry so much, surely her mother could see that there being a war on didn't stop people falling in love; they had to make the most of every moment. She wondered what Harry's parents' reaction would be to the news, especially as they had never even met her. Had he told them? She couldn't wait for his next letter. 'Please don't let him be sent too far away,' she whispered.

The following morning Eileen told Nell Ann's news.

'And be the sound of it you ain't none too pleased.'

'Well, what if anything happened to him?'

'Look, mate, you can't stop 'em falling in love. And you can't keep thinking "what if". Christ, if we all thought like that then we might as well put our heads in the gas oven now and be done with it.'

'Nell, that's a dreadful thing to say.'

'Well, you are keeping on. Give the kids a chance to live their own lives, and for Gawd's sake, cheer up.'

Eileen gave a faint smile. 'I suppose I am being a bit of a moaner.'

'I can understand how you feel, but just think of us mums who had to let our boys go.'

'Yes. I'm sorry.'

'Now come on, put your hat and coat on and let's go and see what queue we can join.'

'It would be nice if we could get some sausages or a bit of liver.'

'I think to get them you might have to sleep with the butcher.'

'No, as much as I love my lot, I wouldn't fancy that,

not sleep with old Alfie Stewart. I don't know how his wife puts up with his big fat belly and loud voice.'

Nell laughed. 'He must have something, apart from plenty of meat and offal.'

They spent the morning queuing and joining in with everyone else's grumbles and laughter. The word went round faster than jungle drums when someone said the greengrocer had oranges. But Nell and Eileen were too late.

'Better luck next time,' said Nell as they made their way home.

Eileen said nothing more about the forthcoming engagement and Ann did not mention getting another letter from Harry, which told her that he had told his parents about their agreement and they were pleased for him and couldn't wait to meet her. Lucy, however, had seen the envelope when it arrived, and she became upset, because she hadn't heard from Dan for weeks. She told Shirley she was worried that he might be abroad.

'Has Mrs Drury said anything to Mum?' Lucy asked her sister.

'I don't think so. Mum would have told us.'

'D'you think I should go over and ask? It wouldn't look too forward, would it?'

'Course not. She knows you two are writing to each other. I like Dan's mum, she's nice.'

'Right, I'll go over on Sat'day. P'rhaps be then I might get a letter.'

Shirley also hoped her sister would hear from Dan soon. Although she was the youngest it didn't stop her taking note of all she saw on the newsreels. She knew that a lot of their soldiers were fighting in France and she hoped for her sister's sake that Dan wasn't with them.

'Hello, Lucy love,' said Fred when Lucy went over to see them on Saturday afternoon. 'Come on in. What can we do for you?'

'I was wondering if you've heard from Dan lately?' asked Lucy as she made her way down the passage.

'Not for weeks, how about you?'

'The same. You don't think he could be in France, do you?'

Fred pulled on her arm and lowered his voice. 'Don't say too much to Nell. I've been trying to make out he's not over there, but now I'm beginning to have me doubts.'

'Fred, who you talking to?' Nell Drury opened the kitchen door. 'Lucy, it's you. Come on in, love. Have you heard from Dan?'

'Not for a while. I was wondering if you'd had any letters.'

'No, the little bugger.' She smiled. 'I'll give him what for when he does write.'

'I expect he's busy.'

'Well yes. I'm also worried that he might be fighting in France.'

Lucy looked up at Fred. So much for him trying to keep it from her.

'I know Fred here don't think I read the papers, but me and yer mum goes to the pictures enough times and the newsreels tell us all we want to know.'

'So what do you think, Mr Drury?'

'I don't know, love. I really don't.'

'Yer mum was saying that Ann and her bloke's gonner get engaged on his next leave,' said Nell, deliberately taking the conversation away from her son.

Lucy nodded and smiled. It would be wonderful if Dan wanted to do the same when he came home.

After a cup of tea and general chitchat, Lucy made her way back home, her mind still on Dan. She did so want to know where he was and if he was safe.

By the end of May things were very bad in France; the British army was losing ground every day.

The girls had gone to the pictures and Reg and Eileen were sitting quietly alone for a change.

'Don't like the look of things,' said Reg, looking up from his newspaper.

'Poor Nell is at her wits' end worrying about Dan,' said Eileen.

'So she should be if Dan's over there with this lot.'

'What will happen if France surrenders?'

'They're trying to get the lads back. Must be a bloodbath.'

'Don't say that, Reg. Poor Nell. D'you think we might be next?'

'Wouldn't like to say, let's hope the Channel'll keep 'em at bay.'

'You don't really think he'll invade us, do you?'

'It could be a possibility, but now Churchill's in charge he'll rally everybody.'

'I hope so. I really do.'

Excited noise in the passage told them the girls were home; they were all talking at once.

'Mum. Mum. You'll never guess. I'm sure I saw Dan on the newsreel. He had a cup of tea in one hand and a fag in the other and a big grin on his face. They were showing the boys coming back from France.'

'You should have heard her scream out. Everybody in the cinema thought she was having a fit,' said Ann.

'And they told her to shut up,' said Shirley, plonking herself in the chair.

'I'm going again tomorrow night. I'll ask Mrs Drury if she wants to come with me.'

'Was it Dan?' asked Reg.

'It could have been. It was only a quick shot; they all looked the same to me: dirty and needing a shave,' said Shirley.

'They'd just come over from France, they'd been fighting,' said Lucy. 'I know it was him, I just know it.' Her face was glowing. 'It's too late to go over and tell them now.'

'I'll tell Nell in the morning. But I don't want to get her hopes up if you're not sure,' said Eileen.

The following morning when Eileen told Nell what Lucy thought she'd seen at the cinema, Nell dragged Eileen along with her to the pictures as soon as they could that afternoon. 'I'm that nervous I need you to hold me hand.'

Eileen only smiled.

They had just missed the news so they had to sit through the B film, the main film, the adverts and forthcoming attractions. Then at long last the news came on. Nell sat on the edge of her seat. To see all these young men smiling and drinking tea brought tears to Eileen's eyes.

Suddenly Nell grabbed Eileen's hand. 'It's him. Look. It's him,' she screamed, pointing at the screen.

The woman in front tutted and, turning round, 'Shh'd' them, but Nell ignored her, shouting out, 'That's my son.'

Eileen looked at the grinning faces as the camera slowly made its way along the line of men. It certainly did look like Dan, but it was such a fleeting glance.

Nell sat back and cried.

They left the cinema and all the while Nell was dabbing at her eyes and blowing her nose.

'I wonder how old those newsreels are? I wonder when my Dan will be home?'

'I don't know,' was the only answer Eileen could come up with.

'If Lucy wants to come again tonight I'll come with her.'

'I'm sure she will. Mind you, those films were a right load of rubbish.'

Nell gave her a smile. 'To tell the truth I don't remember what they were about.'

Lucy, Nell and Fred went to the pictures again that evening and once again they sat and waited for the newsreels.

'Well, was it him?' asked Shirley when Lucy got home.

'We think so. Now we've got to wait for him to get some leave.'

Eileen noted the look on Lucy's face. This wasn't the look of a girl who was just a friend of a neighbour. Was she going to have another of her girls promising herself to someone?

Chapter 8

IT WAS A warm Thursday afternoon and just two days after Nell had seen Dan in the newsreel. She was still in a dream and couldn't stop talking about it and wondering how long it would be before she saw him again.

She had spent the morning with Eileen queuing at the shops. They had been really pleased when they managed to get half a rabbit each.

'What you gonner do with your half?' she asked Eileen.

'Gawd only knows. It'll be just about a mouthful each. Better put it in a stew, I suppose. A few dumplings and plenty of veg will help fill 'em up.'

'I'm gonner make a pie and a stew. That'll please Fred.' Nell had a self-satisfied look on her face. 'Good thing old Alfie chops 'em longways. I reckon there'd be a riot if one had the back and the other the front half.'

'Could have done with a whole one,' said Eileen, feeling a little disgruntled. That was one of the advantages of only having two to feed, thought Eileen. Half a rabbit wouldn't go far between five.

Nell was busy making her pie when she heard the key being pulled through the letterbox. She looked up at the clock: it was only four o'clock. What was Fred doing home this time of day? She always worried when he came home early as short time meant short money. He'd said only that morning that they would be all day unloading this one. She was still puzzling about Fred when the kitchen door opened.

'Hello, Mum.'

Slowly she wiped her floury hands on the bottom of her pinny. It took her a moment or two to realise her son was filling the doorway and grinning at her. She screamed out his name and hugged him as close as she could. He was carrying some of his kit. 'Dan. Dan. How are you? Are you all right? Was you injured? How long will you be home?'

'Hang on, Mum. Let me get me breath back. Can I come in?'

She laughed. 'Course. Oh son, it's so lovely to see you safe. You've lost a bit of weight, was you injured at all?'

'No. I was one of the lucky ones.'

Tears were streaming down Nell's face as she closed the door.

'Don't cry.'

'Why didn't you let me know you was coming home? I would have made a cake or something,' she said.

'Didn't have time.'

'No, course not. Sorry, I'm being silly.' Nell was

overcome with happiness and dabbed at her eyes with her pinny. 'We saw you on the newsreels.'

He grinned. 'You didn't, did you? That must'a been when we got off the boat. I don't think I was looking me best.' He rubbed his chin and laughed. 'And I definitely needed a shave.'

'Was it bad?'

'It wasn't good. I'm surprised you could tell it was me. We all looked alike, dirty and war worn.'

'It was Lucy who saw you first. I went to the pictures twice, just to make sure it was you.'

'How many times did Lucy go?'

'Twice.'

That pleased Dan. He was trying not to think about Lucy – well, not just yet. There was so much he wanted to say to her. 'How about a cuppa? I've got me ration card.'

Nell was grinning fit to bust. 'I just want to look at you. I can't believe you're home. Oh Dan, I've missed you so much and been that worried about you.' Once again she hugged him and let her tears slip slowly down her cheeks.

'Mum, don't cry.' He held his mother close. There was no way he was going to tell her what hell he'd been through. The bombs, the guns, the incessant noise day and night. Marching for days and diving into ditches to avoid the German machine guns. Planes swooping down and bombing them as they queued to get on the boats. Seeing mates gunned down and rotting bodies all around you and being waist deep in water for hours on end, only to see the boat you were waiting to get on go away or get bombed. It had all been very orderly and very British, but he too had felt like crying. Dunkirk had made him grow up – brutally. Had made him think about the future and whether he had one. 'It's good to be home,' he whispered. 'Now how about that tea?'

'Come in the scullery with me. I don't want to let you out of me sight.'

Dan laughed. 'I can remember the time when you used to shout at me for getting in the way and under your feet.'

'That was a lifetime away.'

'How's Dad?'

'He's fine, he's a fire-watcher now. Not that we've had any fires for him to watch. Him and Reg over the road go out patrolling together. You should see his tin hat. Talk about a pimple on a piecrust. If you ask me it's just a good excuse to go to the wardens' post for a few beers and a game of cards all evening.'

'Sounds like Dad's enjoying himself.'

They sat at the table drinking tea. 'What time does Dad get home?' said Dan, looking at the clock.

'About six, that's if there's a ship in. It's been a bit hard scrounging for jobs as a lot of ships are being sunk. Good job Reg is in charge of hiring.'

Dan looked at the clock again. He knew Lucy would be home soon. He had to see her.

'I'm glad you've got two weeks' leave,' said his mother, interrupting his thoughts.

'Yer, it'll give them time to get our new kit.'

'Mind you, I reckon you should have more than just two weeks after all you've been through.'

'Well, they've got to gather us together, get us kitted out and then, who knows. Got to see how many of us are left, I suppose.'

'I hope they don't send you away again.'

'Got to go where we're sent.'

'Bloody war. I'd like to see some of those toffs higher up go off and fight.'

Dan didn't want to talk about it; he knew that when his father came home he would have to go through it all again. 'Mum, I'm just going over to see if Lucy's home.'

'Wait till you see yer dad first. He should be here in a tick.'

The next half-hour was agony for Dan. He didn't want to upset his mother but he did so want to see Lucy. He wanted to meet her bus and hold her in his arms. She had filled his thoughts most of the time when he wasn't fighting or running scared for his life. He knew now that he loved Lucy and wanted her so badly.

When Fred walked into the kitchen he stood speechless for a moment or two before grabbing his son and holding him close, patting his back as he had done when he was a baby. 'It's so good to see you, son. We were all a bit worried when we didn't hear from you. How was it?'

Dan looked at his mother before he answered his father. 'Not good.'

Fred picked up on Dan's concern and didn't labour the point. 'So you've got two weeks' leave. That's great. Nothing much's happening over here, I'm glad to say.'

'Not yet it ain't,' said Dan.

'You think it could then?'

Dan shrugged. 'He ain't gonner let it go, not now he's in France.'

'Now, I don't wonner hear any more talk about war,' said Nell.

'Right, son, how about a drink tonight?'

'What about your fire-watching?'

'Not on duty tonight. That all right, Nell?'

'He was going over to see Lucy.'

'She's a great girl. Did your mum tell you about us seeing you at the pictures?'

Dan laughed. 'Seems I'm quite the film star.'

'She was the one who told us about it.'

'So Mum said.'

'Pop over and tell her and Reg to come out with us,' said his father, grinning fit to bust.

It was Mrs Wells who opened the door. 'Dan!' she yelled out. 'Come on in, love,' she added. 'She's in the kitchen. I was just going to dish up the dinner.'

'I'll come back later.'

'No, that's all right. Lucy,' called Eileen. 'Look who's here.'

Lucy opened the kitchen door and was down the passage in a flash. 'Dan. Dan. It's smashing to see you.' She threw her arms round his neck and kissed him on the lips, leaving a lipstick smear that he wiped away with a grin.

'Now that's what I call a real welcome.'

'Come in the kitchen,' said Eileen, noting Lucy's joy.

The rest of the family was waiting for him and they bombarded him with questions about France and how he'd got back. Had he lost many friends? Dan just skirted round the answers, as he didn't want to keep repeating his experiences; it was too painful.

'Dad wants me to go for a drink with him tonight. Will you come, Luce, and you, Mr Wells?'

'I'd love to,' said Lucy.

'Give us time to finish our dinner then we'll be over,' said Reg.

'I'll just go and tell Dad.'

Lucy walked up the passage with Dan. 'It's really smashing to see you. Did your mum tell you we saw you on the newsreels?'

'Yes, she did and she said you went to see it twice.'

Lucy blushed. 'Well, I wasn't sure the first time.'

Dan hugged her close. 'I've really missed you.'

'And I've missed you.'

They kissed long and hard.

'Lucy, your dinner's getting cold,' yelled her father.

'I've gotter go.'

'I'll see you a bit later. I've got two weeks' leave and I'm hoping we can go out a couple of times. There's a lot we've got to talk about.' He kissed her lips again and she felt all sorts of strange feelings rush round her body. She wanted to be with him so much. 'See you later,' he said.

Lucy stood and watched him cross the road. This was going to be the best two weeks of her life.

She went back into the kitchen.

'He don't look bad considering what he's been through,' said her father.

'He looks older,' said Shirley. 'You still gonner go out with him?'

Lucy looked away. 'Course.' She knew she was blushing again.

Lucy couldn't wait to finish her dinner and get ready. After she'd done her hair and put on her make-up she found Ann standing outside her bedroom. 'Lucy, if you and Dan want to be more than just friends I'll do everything I can to help smooth the way.'

Lucy smiled. 'Thanks,' she said, walking down the stairs with a spring in her step.

All evening they sat next to each other. Lucy could feel his leg close to hers and even though his uniform was rough, she didn't care. She wanted to be alone with him. When he smiled at her it seemed to have hidden depths, or was she just being silly and reading something that wasn't there?

When both dads were up at the bar Dan moved even closer to Lucy. 'Look, tomorrow can we go to the pictures?'

'I'd like that. I can come straight from work, I'll meet you outside the Odeon if you like.'

'That'll be great. We can have a cuppa and something to eat in Lyons first.'

'All right.' Lucy could feel her cheeks burning. Their letters had been friendly, nothing more, but somehow now he was here it was different. He seemed grown up. She no longer looked on him as a mate or as someone she just liked, she knew that she loved him. She desperately hoped that he might feel the same way about her. Tomorrow would be a long time coming.

Chapter 9

BEFORE LUCY LEFT work that evening she took extra time making up her face and doing her hair.

'You look great,' said Ann as she waited for her. 'And you smell nice.'

'It's that Evening in Paris scent you gave me last Christmas.'

'You've still got it?'

'I only use it very sparingly. Besides, I didn't have anyone to smell nice for.'

Ann laughed. 'And now you have. I always thought you had a soft spot for Dan.'

'I did, but I knew he didn't think of me in that way. I was always the chubby jolly one, remember.'

'Not now you're not. Quite the little stunner now and especially tonight.'

'Thanks.'

They laughed and, linking arms, left the factory together.

Lucy said goodbye to Ann at the bus stop.

'Have a good time,' said her sister as Lucy walked on towards the cinema.

Lucy was trembling with anticipation, but she was cross with herself too. What was she expecting? After all, she was only going to the pictures with a mate . . . but to her he was more than that.

When Dan caught sight of her he ran up to her and after kissing her full on the mouth, held her tight. It was broad daylight but she didn't care who saw them.

'God I've missed you,' he said in her ear.

'And I've missed you,' she replied, taken aback by his kiss. She had prayed that Dan would think of her this way.

'Do you really want to go to the pictures?' asked Dan half-heartedly as they walked along.

'Not fussed. What about you?'

'Not really,' he said, taking hold of her hand.

'That's all right by me.'

'Good.'

'I've had a lot of time to think about you,' he said suddenly. 'I know we've always had a laugh together. By the way, I really liked your letters.'

'Thank you. So, you want me to be your secretary when you start your own business?'

He looked at her blankly. 'What you on about?'

'You said you liked my letters, so I don't matter.'

'Lucy Wells,' he laughed. 'D'you know you can talk a right load of old tosh at times. I liked your letters because I felt near to you. And I want you to know that I like you very much. You're a bit special and I missed you.'

'And I've missed you. I was so happy when I saw you on the newsreel, I knew then that you were safe.' Lucy stopped. She knew she was rambling on but he *had* said she was special.

Dan kicked a stone. 'Luce, while I was lying in a cold, wet trench you was never out of my thoughts and I was thinking, what if another bloke comes along and wants to whisk you away?'

Lucy laughed. 'Now, who would want to do that?'

'You never know. You're not a bad looker now.'

'Well, thank you kindly, sir.'

'Luce, I know this might come as a bit of a shock, but what would you say if I asked you to marry me?'

Lucy stopped dead in her tracks. 'What did you just say?' she whispered.

'I said, I want to marry you.'

'I didn't think you thought of me like that. Not to be your wife.'

'Well I do. So, what d'you say?'

'I don't know. I can't think. What would our mums say?'

Dan looked at her. 'I'm sorry, I'm rushing you.'

'I thought we was just mates,' she said softly.

'We are, but I want us to get married – that's if you want to. I've always liked you, and I've come to realise just how much I missed you. Lucy, I do love you and if you think you could love me, well, I'm sure it'll work out fine.'

'Dan, I've loved you for years. And yes, it was a schoolgirl crush before, but not now. I'd love to marry you one day.'

'Yippee,' he shouted and, grabbing her, kissed her long and passionately.

'Go on, mate, get stuck in,' yelled a passerby.

As both Dan and Lucy held each other tight they were completely oblivious to their surroundings.

'Let's go into Joe Lyons,' said Dan when they broke away. 'We can talk in there.'

Lucy was smiling and nodding. She couldn't believe this was happening to her. Dan Drury wanted to marry her and be with her for the rest of their lives. She wanted to pinch herself. This sort of thing only happened in books. Although when he first went away she'd said she would wait for ever, she hadn't really thought he meant it.

They sat at the table and Dan took hold of her hand. 'I really do mean it, Luce, I really do want to marry you.'

'I never thought you thought of me as a proper girlfriend. You never gave me any hint in your letters.'

'I think it all started when that first siren went off and we was under the arches. I held you cos you was frightened and I wanted to protect you. Then when I had time to think it was you that kept filling me thoughts and all the laughs we had together as kids. I knew then that I wanted to marry you, to spend time with you. I don't want anybody else to have you.'

Lucy squeezed his hand as the waitress put their teacakes and pot of tea in front of them. 'It's funny,' Lucy said, putting the tea strainer in the cup. 'We've grown up together, and here we are talking about getting married. I think our mums and dads will be pleased when they get used to the idea.'

'Lucy, do you think you can love me?'

She blushed. 'As I said, I've always loved you even though you only ever treated me like just one of the gang.'

He smiled. 'Well, you was always a good sport and you never ran home crying when you fell over.'

'Or got pushed, if I remember right. Is that why you want to marry me?' she asked laughing. 'Cos I don't go running to me mum crying?'

'I can remember the number of times you fell over. You always tied bits of rag round your knees.'

'It wasn't rag, it was me hankie. Me knees were always bleeding and it didn't half hurt. I must have had two left feet.'

Dan kissed her hand. 'See what I mean? My brave little soldier.'

Lucy picked up the tea strainer to transfer it to the other cup.

'It seems as if we've grown up all of a sudden. I know when we had to put down who was our next of kin, how I wished I could write Lucy Drury, wife.'

'Oh Dan, that's a lovely thing to say. It will be one day.'

'That's if we live that long.'

'We mustn't think like that.'

'Lucy, we're not kids anymore. I can get a special licence and we can be married next week.'

Lucy dropped the tea strainer with a clatter. 'What did you just say?'

'We can be married next week.'

Lucy felt her knees go weak. 'We can't! For one thing I'm under age.'

'Your mum and dad will let me marry you. After all, they know all about me.'

'I know, but you're in the army.'

'That's all the more reason we should get married and have a few days together. We don't know what's round the corner. We must live for the moment.' He wanted Lucy so much, to hold her and make love to her; he wanted her to be his *wife*.

Lucy's mind was racing. She was thinking of how upset her mother had been when Ann said she was going to get engaged and she was over twenty-one. 'Have you said anything to your mum about this?'

'No. I had to ask you first, just in case you said no.'

'I can't get married next week.'

'Why not? I'll get a special licence.'

'What can I wear? Oh Dan, let's be sensible about this. I don't think me mum or dad will give their permission.'

He sat back. 'Is this your way of letting me down gently then?'

'No. No, course not, I do want to marry you, but I want to get married properly. You know. The long frock, flowers, friends and family all in the church.'

'We can still ask friends and family.'

'But it won't be the same.'

Dan lit a cigarette. 'Lucy, I don't think we'll have time for a long engagement. I don't know where I'm gonner finish up.'

Lucy quickly put her hand to her mouth. 'Dan, don't say things like that. You're frightening me.'

'I'm sorry, but we have to be realistic and grab the moment. I want you, Luce. I want us to be together.' He couldn't say for ever because he didn't know how long their for ever would be. This war was going to go on for a long while and who would be left at the end was anybody's guess. 'Besides,' he continued, 'I don't want any other Tom, Dick or Harry coming along and whisking you away.' He drew long and hard on his cigarette. He could never tell her the suffering he'd witnessed, and how that had made him see that this might be their only chance to be together, no matter for how short a time. He had envied men who talked about their wives and how much they loved and missed them. He was sure that was what had kept some of them alive and determined to get back home.

Lucy sat stunned; her mind was churning over and over. She couldn't think straight. This wasn't what she had been expecting. She did love him and wanted to marry him, but it was all so sudden. What should she do?

'Tomorrow we can go and get you an engagement ring and your wedding ring,' said Dan, interrupting her thoughts. 'I've got a bit saved.'

'I'll have to tell Mum and Dad first. What if they say no?'

'We'll go back and tell them now.'

'Dad's on fire-watching duty tonight. Him and your dad are on early shift and they don't finish till midnight.'

'That's all right. We can wait for him. Lucy, you do want to marry me, don't you?'

She nodded, but although she was bursting with happiness she knew this was going to cause a lot of problems.

'We can get married as soon as I get the licence.'

'Do we have to? Can't we wait till you get some leave?'

'I don't think so. The next leave I get will probably be embarkation and then we can be shipped out at very short notice.'

'They won't send you abroad again so soon, will they?'

'I don't know. All I know is that I'd like to spend a couple of nights as man and wife then when I do get some leave we can spend all the time together. Please say yes, Luce.'

'I do want to marry you, but I'm all bewildered. I came out tonight expecting to go to the pictures and here we are talking about getting married next week. I'll say this for you, Dan Drury, you certainly know how to sweep a girl off her feet.'

He smiled and kissed her hand again, which made Lucy's legs wobble.

'Just you remember what a fine catch you're getting, young lady. See, I can woo anyone I like, but I happen to like, no, love you.'

'Go on with you. Woo anyone you like. Don't you let me mum hear you talk like that.'

'D'you know what I wonner do right now?'

She shook her head.

'I want to hold you close and kiss you and kiss you till you yell for me to stop.'

'I don't think I'll ever ask you to stop.'

'Come on, let's go then I can kiss you all the way home.'

Lucy gathered up her handbag. 'Now that's an offer I can't refuse.'

'You're home early, wasn't the film any good?' asked Eileen when they walked into the kitchen.

'We didn't go to the pictures,' said Lucy, taking off her hat and coat.

Dan sat at the table. 'All right then, girls,' he said to Ann and Shirley who were sitting with their hair rolled up in pipe cleaner curlers. 'You both look very beautiful.'

'We hope we will tomorrow,' said Shirley. 'We have to suffer for our beauty, you know.'

'And as far as I can see, it's all worth it.'

'He's such a smooth talker, Luce,' said Shirley, grinning.

'I know.'

'D'you fancy a cuppa?' asked Ann.

'No thanks,' said Lucy. 'We've just had one in Lyons.'

'So why didn't you go to the pictures then?' asked Eileen, her knitting needles clicking faster. She was worried. There was something about these two that she couldn't put her finger on; her daughter had a glow about her. I only hope Dan has been behaving himself, was the thought that was running through her mind. She couldn't bear it if he went off and Lucy found she was pregnant. The shame of something like that happening to one of her girls!

'Mrs Wells.' Dan took a breath. 'I know I should wait till Reg is home, but I think I should ask you before I burst with happiness.'

Ann and Shirley sat up. Eileen put her knitting in her lap and turned down the wireless. She could sense this was something important.

'Mrs Wells, I've asked Lucy to marry me and she's said yes.'

'Congratulations,' said Ann who quickly came over to her sister and held her close.

'Another wedding,' said Shirley who had been filing her nails. 'Looks like I'll have to go out and find meself a bloke if I'm not gonner be left on the shelf.'

'That's not the reason to get married, young lady,' said Eileen. She looked up at Dan. 'What does your mother have to say about this?'

'She don't know yet. We thought we should ask you and Reg's permission first as Lucy is under age.'

'So are you, young man.' Eileen's tone was a little abrasive.

He grinned. 'I know. But I don't think she'll mind.'

Lucy wanted to throw her arms round his neck and smother him with kisses. 'So, can we?' she asked her mother.

'Well, it's a bit sudden. You'll have to wait and see what your father says.' Eileen picked up her knitting again.

'Is that it? Ain't you gonner ask me when?'

'I assume, if we do give permission, it'll be sometime on Dan's next leave.'

Dan took hold of Lucy's hand. 'Well, no, Mrs Wells. You see, we want to get married next week.'

For a second or two there was complete silence. Only soft music in the background from the wireless disturbed the air. Then Ann, Shirley and Eileen all spoke at once. They yelled out, 'What?'

'What did you just say?' asked Eileen.

'I want to marry Lucy next week.'

'Don't talk such nonsense.'

'Mrs Wells, I don't know when I shall be home again. We've got to make the most of the moment.'

'Rubbish.'

'Mum,' shouted Lucy. 'We don't know when Dan will be sent away or to where.'

'I was lucky this time—' Dan added.

'So you want to make my daughter a widow before she's much older?'

'Mum, that's a dreadful thing to say,' said Ann.

'Mrs Wells, I don't intend to get myself killed, but I ain't got a lot of say in the matter.'

Tears were falling down Lucy's cheeks.

Dan put his arm round her shoulders. 'Come on, love, let's go and face the music the other side of the road.'

Shirley jumped up and gave her sister her coat. The look in her eyes gave Lucy hope. She knew that as soon as they walked out of the door both Ann and Shirley would have a go at their mother. But would it do any good?

Chapter 10

SHIRLEY LOOKED AT Ann.

'Why are you being like this, Mum?' asked Ann. 'She's too young to be thinking about getting married next week. Has she had time to think about it and what it means?'

'It ain't as though she's just met Dan. We've known him all our lives, they've grown up together,' said Shirley.

'So why this hurry to get married all of a sudden?'

'Well, I would have thought it was obvious. He's damn well nearly been killed fighting for his country and he wants to know what love is all about before he's shipped out again.' Ann was getting very angry.

'If that's all he wants he could find that out with any girl.'

'Mum, I don't think that this is what this is all about. If that's all he wanted then they could have done it in any shop doorway.'

Shirley giggled.

'He loves Luce and wants to be with her. They want a commitment and to start a life together.'

'And what sort of life will that be with him off fighting somewhere and her sitting here knitting and waiting?'

'Lucy don't like knitting,' said Shirley.

'Shirley, stop being silly,' said Ann. 'None of us knows what's going to happen. We've got to make the most of every day while we can.'

Eileen sat staring at her knitting pattern but she couldn't see what she should be doing. She couldn't concentrate. She wanted her daughter to be happy but this was too sudden. Lucy was too young. Why couldn't they wait? What if after they were married they met someone else? Eileen's head was pounding. This bloody war was sending common sense out of the window.

'Surely, Mum, you can let them have a bit of time together as man and wife?' Ann was thinking that she wished it were her and Harry that could be getting married next week. She had written and told him her thoughts and when Harry did come home perhaps it could be for their wedding.

'And what if she finds she's gonner have a baby after he's gone off?'

'That's all right, there's plenty of women that are having babies.'

'She's only nineteen.'

'Mum, there's a war on.' Ann was getting cross with her mother.

'That's no excuse for acting silly.'

Ann sighed. 'Well, you've made up your mind. But just remember all the young women that were left after the last war.'

'That's just what I am thinking of. I don't want her to be a widow.'

'You mustn't think like that. If this war gets worse we could all be dead.' Ann was angry now, realising she was fighting a losing battle. Perhaps their father would have a different view.

'Don't talk like that.'

'Well, it's true,' mumbled Ann.

'I wonder what Mrs Drury will say about it?' asked Shirley, trying to ease the situation.

'Knowing Nell, she'll go all soppy.'

'Shame though; if they do get married next week she won't have time to get a wedding dress or have bridesmaids,' said Shirley, disappointed about that.

'Is that all you're worried about?' said Ann.

'No, course not.'

Eileen stood up. 'I'm gonner make some cocoa, d'you want a cup?'

'Yes please,' they said together.

'And Shirley. You don't have to worry about not being a bridesmaid as there ain't gonner be a wedding.'

'Ann,' whispered Shirley, casting a furtive glance at the scullery door, 'what we gonner do to make Mum change her mind?'

'I don't know. Let's hope Dad will give his consent and talk her round.'

'Poor Luce.'

'I wish it was me getting married,' sighed Ann.

'At least you're old enough to go off and do what you want.'

'I know. But I'd still like Mum and Dad's blessing.'

Eileen pushed open the door with her bottom. 'What do you want our blessing for?'

'When I get married,' said Ann as she cleared enough room on the table for the tray her mother was carrying.

'Well, I don't think that'll be for a while yet. At least Harry's a sensible lad and we'll have plenty of time to get used to the idea.'

Ann smiled. Not if she had her way.

As they crossed the road Lucy gripped Dan's hand. 'I'm really worried about me mum. I don't think she'll give us permission.'

'Don't worry. I'm sure my mum will make her see sense.' Dan turned and kissed her cheek.

Lucy smiled. But she wasn't so sure.

'Hello, love,' said Nell when they walked into her kitchen. 'Was the film any good?'

'Didn't go to the pictures,' said Dan. 'Have a seat, Luce.'

'I'll make some tea,' said Nell.

'Mum, sit down.'

Nell looked at her son and was filled with fear. What was he going to say? She knew by his tone that it was going to be something awful. Had he had a message to say he had to go back to camp immediately?

'I know we should wait for Dad to get home, but you see Lucy and me, we wonner get married.'

Nell jumped out of her chair and, grabbing first Dan's face then Lucy's with both hands, kissed them both. 'I'm so pleased. That's always bin me dream that you two would get married some day. I'm so pleased for you. We'll have to have a drink to celebrate this when yer dad gets home. Have you told Eileen?'

Lucy nodded. Although this was the sort of reaction she'd expected from Mrs Drury she wasn't sure how she would feel about the next bit of news.

'We've just come from there,' said Dan.

'Oh dear,' said his mother. 'And by the look on your faces I don't suppose she's very happy about it? I know the fuss she made when Ann said she was going to get engaged. I'll have a word with her tomorrow.'

'Mum, we want to get married next week by special licence.'

Nell Drury plonked herself down in the armchair. 'What did you just say?'

'We want to get married next week.'

Nell sat staring at them for a while almost as if she was letting the news sink in.

Lucy was willing her to speak.

'I know I'm under age, but I don't think you'll stop us,' said Dan, standing in front of the fireplace fidgeting with a box of matches.

'I don't know what to say, son. This is a bit of a shock. Did you tell Eileen?'

Lucy nodded.

'Well, I can guess her reaction.' Nell stood up, obviously taken aback at their news. 'You'll have to wait till your father gets home and we'll talk about this.'

Dan put his arm round his mother's shoulders. 'I knew you wouldn't let me down.'

'Yes, but you've got to wait for your father. You're both very young and he'll have to have the last word on this. Then you've still got to get round Eileen.'

Lucy sat pleating then smoothing out the dark green chenille tablecloth. She couldn't believe this was happening. They were talking about her wedding. This time next week she could be married.

It was midnight. Lucy looked at Dan when they heard the front door being shut. She took hold of Dan's hand.

'Don't worry,' he whispered. 'Hello, Dad. All right then?'

'Yes thanks. Hello, Lucy. Didn't expect to see you here at this time o' night.'

'You'd better sit down, Fred. They've got something to say,' said Nell.

Fred placed the tin hat he was carrying on the table and took off his cap and jacket. He then settled himself in the armchair next to the fireplace. 'Well, what is it?'

Dan went on to tell his father what he had in mind.

'Bloody hell.' Fred sat up. 'What do Eileen and Reg have to say about it?'

'Dad don't know as he was with you,' said Lucy. 'Mum said she won't give us permission.'

'That's gonner be a bit of a problem,' said Fred.

'Will you give us consent?' asked Dan.

'Well, me lad. If you're old enough to fight for your country then I should think you're old enough to get married if that's what you want.'

'That's what we both want. Thanks, Dad,' said Dan, shaking his hand.

Fred took hold of Lucy and hugged her. 'Welcome to the family, Luce, although I think you've been part of it all your life.'

Lucy had tears rolling down her cheeks as Fred held her tightly. 'I only hope Mum can be persuaded,' she whispered.

'Don't worry, love,' said Fred. 'We'll work on her. Now I think this calls for a toast.' He rummaged in the dresser next to the fireplace and produced a bottle of port. 'For medicinal purposes as well as for drinking a toast. Get the glasses, Nell.'

Nell Drury was all smiles as she brought out four glasses.

'To the happy couple,' said Fred. 'So when's the happy day gonner be?'

Dan raised his glass and kissed Lucy. 'As soon as I can sort it all out.'

Lucy was smiling but in her heart she knew it was going to take a lot to make her mother change her mind.

'Hello, you lot still up?' said Reg when he walked into the kitchen.

'There's a reason,' said Eileen, her face set in a grim fashion.

'Oh dear,' he said, grinning. 'Looks like I'm in the doghouse. What've I done?'

'It's not you, it's our Lucy and Dan across the road.'

'What they done? Oh God, they've not been involved in an accident, have they?'

'No. Course not.'

'Well, what is it then?'

Once again the news was blurted out.

Reg laughed out loud. 'Is that all? Well I reckon that's been on the cards for years.'

'It ain't funny.'

'Come on, love. I think it's a good thing.'

'So do I,' said Shirley.

'Shirley, be quiet. Reg, you ain't heard the worst bit. They want to get married next week.'

'Bloody hell. I must say that is a bit of a shock. What did you say, love?'

'I said no.'

Without saying a word Reg took his tobacco pouch from his jacket pocket and went through the ritual of rolling a cigarette. They sat watching as he licked the edge of the paper. After lighting it with a match he took a long draw and said, 'We've got to think very carefully about this.'

'Is that all you can say?'

'Eileen, there's a war on. Things are different to what they was a year ago. The lad's a fighting soldier.'

'I know and that's what worries me. What if he gets killed?'

Reg sat up. 'What if any of us gets killed? Can we honestly stop them having a few days of happiness?'

Shirley went to speak but Ann nudged her to silence her. Ann didn't want to stop her father making his point and hopefully it would make her mother see sense.

'It ain't as though he's a stranger. We've known the boy all his life.'

'I know.'

The front door shut and everybody waited for Lucy to come into the kitchen. When she walked in Dan was behind her.

Ann could see that her sister's mascara had run, so she must have been crying. Had his parents refused permission as well?

'Hello, Dad. I expect Mum's told you?' Lucy looked at the clock: it was well past midnight.

'So what have Nell and Fred got to say about this then?' asked Reg.

'They gave us their blessing.'

'Good,' screamed out Shirley.

Everybody looked at her.

'Sorry,' she said sheepishly.

'Now it's up to you,' said Lucy.

'You know how I feel about it,' said Eileen with her lips pursed.

'What about you, Dad?'

'Well, I think you're a bit young, but then times are different now.'

Lucy rushed to her father and held him.

'Steady on there.'

Dan went and shook Reg's hand, then he was kissed and held tight first by Ann and then Shirley.

'I'm sorry, Mum,' said Lucy, squatting on the floor next to her mother. 'I don't want to hurt you, but I love Dan very much.'

'We'll talk about this in the morning,' said Eileen, standing up abruptly. 'Goodnight.'

When her mother left the room Lucy began to cry.

Dan went and held her close. 'Don't worry, love,' he said as he gently brushed her hair from her face. 'I'm sure it's all gonner work out all right.'

'Lucy, don't upset yourself. I'm going up as well and as Dan said, it'll all work out all right, you'll see.' Her father gave her a wink and kissed her cheek, then left the room.

'Wow. What a night,' said Shirley.

'I think it's time we went to bed as well,' said Ann. She too kissed her sister. 'And don't worry.'

As soon as Dan and Lucy were left alone he held her tight and kissed her passionately. 'Do you realise that this time next week you could be Mrs Drury?'

'I hope so. I really do hope so.'

'I love you, Lucy Wells.'

'And I love you, Dan Drury.'

But Lucy was worried. The last thing she wanted was to cause a rift between her parents. But she did love Dan so very much and knew that this would be for life.

Chapter 11

THE FOLLOWING MORNING after pulling back the blackout curtains Lucy jumped straight back into bed. Did all that really happen last night? Could she really be getting married next week if her mother gave her permission? Lucy should be going to work today but she'd told Dan she'd take the morning off as they were going to buy a wedding ring. Lucy had told him not to waste his money on an engagement ring, that could wait. But what if her mother wouldn't give her consent? Surely she must see that in wartime everybody had to make the most of every day. She didn't know what Dan had been through at Dunkirk but the newsreels and the wireless had told them as much as they were allowed and that was bad enough. It must have been horrible. Thank God he'd come back safely. She truly loved Dan and wanted to be his wife and be with him for ever. This wasn't just a silly girl notion: they had to seize the day. She closed her eyes; she wouldn't think about the future or what was in store for them, any of them.

'Glad you're awake, Luce,' said Shirley, easing herself up on her elbow. 'What you gonner do if Mum won't say yes?'

'I don't know.'

'Could you run away?'

'I don't think that would work. I'm just hoping that Dad will talk her round. I don't want there to be any bad feelings.'

Shirley lay back down. 'I'm really glad you're going to marry Dan. I think he's something special. I really like him.' She chuckled. 'And if you hadn't got there first, well, who knows.'

'Shirley Wells, I didn't know you had a soft spot for him!'

'Always have had. And if you don't hang on to him then I'll certainly try my hardest to get him to like me.'

Lucy also lay back down and, smiling, said, 'Over my dead body.'

They heard the front door slam.

'That's Dad going to get his paper. I suppose we'd better get up. Remember you've got to go to work.' Lucy sat up.

'Don't remind me. Shouldn't you be getting up?'

'No. I'm taking the morning off. We're going to buy my wedding ring.'

Shirley looked at her sister. 'Don't you think you'll be pushing your luck?'

Lucy shrugged. 'I hope not. Now come on, up.'

'I often wish I didn't have to work on a Sat'day,' said Shirley as she got out of bed.

'I do so hope Dad's managed to talk Mum round,' whispered Lucy as she put her feet to the floor, almost as if in prayer.

Across the road Dan was also awake and as he got dressed he gazed out of the window. He wished his bedroom was at the front of the house then he would have been able to see if Lucy was up. He knew she was taking the morning off, but the thought that was continually running through his mind was that he hoped Mrs Wells had changed her mind. He did so want to marry Lucy. He wanted to spend a few days with her. God only knew where they would be sent next. He could be away for years. He wanted her to be his wife. He wanted her next to him whenever he was on leave. Was he being selfish only wanting to fulfil his own desires?

'Cup of tea, son,' said his father as he pushed open the bedroom door. 'Oh, you're up and dressed.'

'Thanks, Dad. I want to get out early.'

'Can't do a lot today, son, all the offices will be shut.'

'I know, but I can get the ring.'

Fred Drury sat on the bed. 'Now, look, I ain't gonner give you a lecture—'

Dan grinned. 'If you're gonner tell me about the birds and bees, well, Dad, I think yer a bit late for that. I learned most of it at school and with what the army's been telling us, well, you wouldn't go near any old tart with a barge pole.'

'No, you silly sod, I ain't talking about that. If you don't know what's what be now, well, you ain't no son of mine. All I'm worried about is that you're sure you're doing the right thing. We love Lucy, always have done. Just as long as you're sure she's the right one for you and you ain't just stringing her along.'

'I'd never do that, Dad. I love her.'

'What if you meet someone else while you're on your travels?'

'I don't reckon there's many girls fighting. Well, not on the front line anyway.'

'Not yet there ain't, but who knows? And you must get some time back from the front line.'

'Thanks for your concern, Dad, but as I said I really do love Luce, always have done, and I don't want anyone else coming along and snapping her up.'

Fred Drury squeezed his son's shoulder affectionately. 'That's all I wanted to hear, son. Now come on down, yer mother's got yer breakfast ready.'

Lucy sat on the bed and waited for her father to return from collecting his newspaper before she went downstairs. She didn't want to face her mother without his support. When she heard the front door close again she knew he was back. She took a deep breath ready to face the music.

As she got to the bottom of the stairs, Shirley was

just going out of the front door. She took the toast from out of her mouth. 'Good luck,' she said.

Ann was sitting at the table reading a letter. She looked up and smiled. 'Just got one from Harry.'

'I gathered that by the grin on your face,' said Lucy, sitting next to her. 'Everything all right?'

Ann nodded. She couldn't tell her sister that this letter was in answer to her asking Harry if they could get married on his next leave and not just get engaged. His answer had been yes. He told her to start having the banns read in her church, as he wanted everything to be ready for when he got home. Ann wanted to shout it from the rooftops, but how could she tell anyone with this air of despondency hanging over them?

'When's he coming home?' asked Lucy.

'Soon as he's finished his training. He hopes to be aircrew.'

'That sounds a bit dangerous,' said Eileen coming in from the scullery and putting the teapot in the middle of the table. 'Pop the cosy over that, love,' she said to Lucy as she went back into the scullery.

Lucy went to mouth something to Ann but she quickly shook her head. 'I'd better be off as well. What do you want me to tell Miss Leonard?' she whispered to her sister.

'Just tell her I'm not feeling too good.'

Their father was sitting in the armchair studying the paper so he wasn't listening to the girls.

'What's the news, Dad?' asked Lucy.

'Not good. In fact it's bloody awful all round. Churchill's told Parliament that we now stand alone. Mind you, I never did like those Frenchies.'

'You don't know any,' said Ann.

'No I know, but I still don't like 'em.'

Lucy grinned. She knew her father was trying to ease the strained atmosphere.

'Are you girls going out this afternoon?' Eileen asked when she walked back into the kitchen.

'I'm not going out,' said Ann.

'I'm not going in to work this morning.'

'Why not?'

'I shall be going out with Dan,' said Lucy, looking at her father. 'But I'm not sure what time.'

'I see,' said Eileen. 'Anywhere in particular?'

Lucy took a deep breath. She didn't see any point in telling lies. 'We're going to get my wedding ring.'

Reg looked up from his newspaper.

Ann stood at the door ready to leave, waiting for the explosion, but it didn't come. 'I must go. Mustn't miss me bus,' she said reluctantly as she left the kitchen. She did so want to hear the outcome.

'Where're you going?' Eileen asked Lucy.

'Probably Peckham.'

'I see,' repeated Eileen as she poured out the tea. 'Reg, come and sit up at the table. I'll just bring in the toast. By the way, that's the last of the marmalade till Mrs Toms gets some more in.'

Lucy was dying to ask her mother if she had changed

her mind but the opportunity didn't arise. Every time she looked at her father he just quickly shook his head and silently shhed her. Had he talked her round? Was he waiting for her mother to broach the subject?

When Dan knocked on the door Lucy still didn't know if she was getting married or not next week. 'That'll be Dan,' she said, pulling on her coat. She picked up her handbag and made for the door.

'Ain't you gonner ask him in?' enquired her mother.

'No. Ain't any point as I'm all ready.'

'I think you'd better,' said Eileen.

Lucy almost froze to the spot, but she forced herself to walk calmly to the door. When she opened it Dan kissed her cheek. 'I see you're ready, love. Everything all right?'

She shook her head. 'You'd better come in.'

They went nervously back to the kitchen and Lucy sat at the table, her face pale and her eyes filled with tears.

'What is it? What's happened?' Dan guessed from the look on her face that now they wouldn't be getting married next week.

'Well, now Dan's here you can both hear what we've got to say. Go on, Reg, tell 'em.'

Lucy took a breath, surprised that her mother didn't sound angry.

Reg cleared his throat. 'Me and your mother had a long talk last night and we both think that, under the circumstances, we'd better give permission for you two to get married. As you know, your mother ain't that happy about it, but things are a bit different these days.'

Lucy couldn't believe it. She felt the tears run down her cheek when Dan hugged her. Then Dan was shaking her father's hand and thanking him.

Lucy went to her mother and hugged her tight. 'Thank you. Thank you so much,' she sobbed.

'Well, I would only have had Nell carrying on at me. She wouldn't have given me a minute's peace.'

Lucy held her father close. 'Thank you, Dad,' she whispered.

'I know you're doing the right thing,' he said, kissing her cheek.

'I think we'd better pop over and tell Mum and Dad before we go out, Luce,' said Dan, who was beaming.

'Tell 'em we'll all go up the Beak for a drink tonight,' said Reg.

'Why not.' Dan took hold of Lucy's hand and they made their way out of the house.

'I know that was hard for you, love,' said Reg after they'd left.

'I can't help it, but as you rightly pointed out, they won't be leaving home, not till this war's over. Besides, I realised I was being very selfish just thinking of meself.'

Reg gave her a cuddle.

'What's this for?'

'Just that I love you and I hate it when we can't sort things out.'

'Well, it's all sorted now. I'll make a cup of tea.'

Eileen stood looking out of the scullery window at the air-raid shelter, which took up most of their little yard. She felt tired; she hadn't had a lot of sleep. When they first went to bed Reg had spent a long while trying to convince her she was wrong not to let them get married. He insisted that they should be allowed a little bit of happiness. What if they didn't get married and Dan never came back, could she live with that? Would Lucy ever find someone else to marry? Eileen had lain awake for many hours pondering. After all, she herself was happily married to the man she loved. She couldn't deny her daughter the same chance.

Dan and Lucy were laughing when they left Nell and Fred Drury. As Lucy had guessed they were delighted that her mother had come round.

'Knew she wouldn't hold out for long,' had been Nell's comment as she gave Lucy a hug. 'She knew I would have made her life a misery,' she'd chortled.

As they made their way to Peckham, Lucy couldn't stop smiling. 'I'll have a look in the clothes shops to see if I can find something to wear. It's a shame I can't have all the trimmings.'

'It's a pity we can't get married in church, but not to worry. I can sort it all out on Monday.'

'I'd like to get married on Sat'day, if that's all right?'

'You mean I've got to wait a whole week before I can have me wicked way?'

Lucy giggled. 'Shh, you'll have everybody looking at us.'

'I don't care. I want to stand on a street corner and shout out to everyone that I'm marrying the most wonderful girl in the world.'

'If you start doing things like that, I'll walk away.'

'Luce, I do love you.'

'And I love you.'

They stopped and kissed. It was a long, passionate embrace. Lucy didn't care who saw them and at that moment she didn't want to wait till Saturday to be Mrs Drury, she wanted him now.

When they broke away Dan took her hand. 'Come on. At this rate we'll never get a ring for you and we can't get married without a ring.'

Together they wandered round the shops. Buying the ring wasn't hard but when it came to getting something for Lucy to wear she wasn't happy with anything she looked at. As the afternoon wore on she became more and more despondent: whenever she saw something she liked, they didn't have her size.

'I wish me sisters was here,' she said as she came out of yet another shop, shaking her head. 'Why can't I get what I want?'

'Could be you're a bit too fussy?'

'Course I'm fussy. It's me wedding outfit.'

'Sorry, love. Don't get upset. I'm sure you'll find something nice.'

But Lucy *was* upset. This was going to be the happiest

day of her life and she couldn't get married in any old thing.

Dan put his arm round her waist. 'Come on,' he said, kissing her cheek. 'Cheer up. It ain't the end of the world.'

But to Lucy it would be if she couldn't find what she wanted.

By the time Lucy arrived home she felt really sad.

'I'll be at work all week,' she wailed. 'There's no way I can get out to get a new outfit.'

'Cheer up,' said Ann. 'I'm sure we can sort something out.'

'How?'

'Look, why don't you go over to Brick Lane in the morning,' said Eileen. 'They're always open on a Sunday morning and I'm sure you'll find something there.'

Lucy brightened up. 'I'd forgot all about that. Thanks, Mum.'

'Tell you what,' said Ann. 'Me and Shirl will come with you. We won't let those old boys fob you off with any old rubbish they can't get rid of.'

Lucy was over the moon. This was what she'd wanted. Her mum was being helpful and she was going shopping with both her sisters. She knew that things could only get better from now on.

Chapter 12

It was well past eleven o'clock when the Wellses and the Drurys left the pub. Dan was having difficulty walking as everybody had been congratulating him and buying him drinks. Lucy had been smiling so hard all evening she felt sure her face had stuck, but it was a lovely feeling. She was so lucky: she had her family, the man she was going to marry and his family round her, people she had known and loved all her life. She wanted to cry she was so happy.

'You all right?' asked Ann, taking her arm.

Lucy nodded. 'I'm so lucky. I don't want this week to ever end.' She looked up; the clear dark sky had thousands of stars twinkling high above them, the large silver barrage balloons silhouetted against the night bobbed about on long wires. 'And if Hitler thinks he's gonner spoil my day, then he's got another think coming.'

'That's right, sis, you tell 'im,' said Shirley, linking arms with her sisters. 'I'm really looking forward to going shopping in the morning.'

'Me too,' said Lucy. 'Wait till we go shopping for your wedding outfit,' she said to Ann.

Ann smiled. 'Hopefully that won't be too far off.'

'Why? What d'you mean?' asked Lucy.

Ann looked behind her at her parents who were enjoying their own conversation, laughing along with Nell and Fred Drury. Fred was helping his son walk home.

'When Harry comes home, we're hoping to get married.'

Shirley and Lucy stopped.

'I thought you was just gonner get engaged,' said Shirley.

'We were, but then we changed our minds. Like you and Dan we don't know how long Harry will be in this country.'

'You're a bit of a dark horse,' said Lucy. 'You didn't say anything.'

'I know. You see I didn't want to upset Mum and I thought I'd wait till you were married before I put the banns up.'

'You gonner get married in a church?' asked Lucy in surprise.

'We hope to.'

'Lucky old you.'

'Oh come on, Luce, don't get down. Just think, this time next week you could be a married woman,' Shirley was holding on to her sister's arm.

'I ain't down, but I wish you'd told me, Ann.'

'Why? What difference would it have made?'

'Dunno.'

'How long before you can get married, Ann?' asked Shirley as they turned into their gateway.

'I don't know. But once the banns have been read they last for a little while. So till I know when Harry's coming home I'll have to be patient and wait. Luce, and you, Shirl, don't say anything to Mum. I want Lucy to have all the attention. After all, it's going to be her big day.'

Lucy whispered her thanks and went over to Dan. 'I hope you'll be in a fit state to take me out tomorrow evening.'

He put his arms around her.

'Phew, you smell like a brewery.' Lucy screwed up her nose.

'Don't worry. I'll be over as soon as you get back from your shopping expedition. I do love you, Lucy Wells.'

'And I love you, Daniel Drury.' They kissed and parted company.

As Lucy made her way into the house she was still thinking about Ann. She might be getting married in a church but how long would she have to wait till Harry came home? She smiled to herself. She was getting married next week.

The following morning everybody except Reg Wells was up and about bright and early.

Eileen smiled when her daughters came into the kitchen. 'Try not to make too much noise, your father's got a bit of a headache.'

Lucy laughed. 'If he's like this when I get engaged, what's he gonner be like when I get married?'

'Don't worry. I'll make sure he behaves himself.'

Lucy couldn't help but go to her mother and hold her tight. 'Thanks for everything.'

'Oh, go on with you. I'm only sorry I made such a fuss.' Eileen smiled, but deep down she was still against her daughter marrying so young.

Ann was more than happy with the situation. She would wait till after Lucy's wedding before she sprung her news on her parents.

Later that morning the three Wells girls made their way round Brick Lane. They wandered along and peered in the shops. Although they were looking for something for Lucy to wear Ann was also quietly looking at wedding dresses; she was going to get married in a church with all the trimmings, but today she had to be discreet. She wished she was getting married before Lucy then her sister could have borrowed her frock.

It took a while but at long last Lucy found what she was looking for: a beige linen dress and matching coat topped off with a small smart dark brown hat that had a saucy spotted eye veil. With beige gloves and new shoes the whole outfit looked lovely.

'That's really nice,' said Eileen when they arrived home and Lucy paraded round the kitchen.

'You should have seen some of the rubbish they wanted to palm her off with,' said Ann.

Reg laughed. 'You three must have been a frightening force when you marched in the shops.'

'Well, we wasn't gonner stand for no old nonsense, I can tell you,' said Ann.

'I saw a dreamy frock, but I can't afford it,' said Shirley. 'Looks like I'll have to make do with one of me old 'ens. Would have liked a new frock for me birthday next week.'

'Don't,' said Reg. 'You're tearing me heart strings out.'

Lucy put her hand to her mouth. 'Shirley, I'm so sorry, but with all the excitement I completely forgot about your birthday.'

'Thanks.'

Ann went to her handbag and took out a ten-shilling note. 'Look, take this and put it towards a new frock.'

'Thanks,' Shirley said again, but with a big smile on her face. 'What about you, Dad, you gonner contribute to the help-Shirley fund?' She waved the money in front of him.

'I reckon I can find a few bob.'

'I'll give you some money as well,' said Lucy. 'But you'll have to wait till pay day as I've spent all me money today.'

Eileen laughed with her family then went into the scullery. Despite her early misgivings she was truly happy for her daughter.

'It's not as though there'll be a lot of guests at the wedding so you don't have to worry too much about what you're wearing,' said Lucy. 'And besides, we all know each other pretty well.'

'Right, dinner's ready,' called Eileen.

'Have I got time to pop over to Dan's?'

'No, have your dinner first.' As Eileen was dishing up she said, 'Last night me and Nell was wondering what to get you for wedding presents.'

'Don't know. Ain't thought about that. It ain't as though we'll have a home of our own.'

'You should start collecting for your bottom drawer though.'

'I suppose so.'

'Nell was saying her and Fred are gonner let you have a bit of time on your own. They're gonner let you stay at their place on your wedding night.'

Lucy blushed at her mother talking about her wedding night. 'Where're they gonner go?'

'Last night Fred asked Bill in the pub if they could stay the night there. Bill does bed and breakfast sometimes,' said Reg.

Lucy swallowed hard. Everybody was willing to put themselves out. 'I'll have to go over and thank them.'

'Finish your dinner first.'

Dan opened the door and straight away kissed Lucy. 'I'm so pleased. You'll never guess what Mum and Dad are doing? They're going to spend our wedding night at the pub. We'll be on our own all night. So I'll be able to have me wicked way without anybody hearing us.'

Lucy could feel herself reddening at the thought. 'That's ever so nice of 'em.'

'Yer, but I think Dad's more than pleased to spend the night in a pub, he reckons that'll be the best part of it. He said he might even do a bit of sleepwalking – he could finish up in the cellar.'

Lucy laughed as they made their way down the passage. 'What did your mum say to that?'

' "Over my dead body." ' Dan pushed open the kitchen door.

'Hello, love,' said Nell when they walked in. 'Did you manage to get your outfit?'

'Yes I did.'

'That's good. Your mum was saying last night you was worried about it. Usually manage to get something over Brick Lane.'

'That's nice of you to spend the night in the pub,' said Lucy.

'I can tell you it ain't no hardship for Fred. He reckons it could be like going to heaven with all that booze round him. Now, what we gonner get you two for a wedding present?'

'I don't know. I ain't thought about that.'

'What about a pair of sheets? That way when Dan gets home you'll be able to use yer own linen.'

'That'll be very nice. Thank you.' Lucy's mind was in a whirl: all this talk about wedding presents, her wedding night and a new outfit was something she had only been able to dream about a few days ago, now it was all happening.

'Me and your mum are going to discuss what to do about your wedding breakfast just as soon as you let us know how many will be coming.'

'I don't know,' said Lucy. 'I ain't had time to think about that.'

'Mind you, it can't be nothing fancy, it'll have to be whatever we can get hold of, but I'm sure Mrs Toms and the butcher will help us out.'

'This is very kind of you.'

'Don't worry about it, me and your mum will sort it out.'

'All right if we go for a walk?' Dan asked Lucy.

'I don't mind.'

As they walked to the park Dan held on to her arm. 'Tomorrow I'm gonner get the licence. Then I'll go along to the register office. Is there any special day or time you fancy getting married?'

'No. I'd really like it on Sat'day, but not too early. I've got to make time for me beauty treatment.'

'That shouldn't take you long. You're lovely already.' He kissed her cheek.

Lucy laughed. 'I never thought of you as being such a romantic.'

'You wait and see what I can do.'

Lucy blushed again. Although she loved Dan and couldn't wait to be his wife she was still a bit apprehensive at what was going to happen.

They talked at length about the wedding and when they returned home all their plans were ready.

Today was the big day. Friday 21st June was Lucy and Dan's wedding day. Lucy had been disappointed at not getting married on Saturday, but the slots were all booked up. A lot of people were getting married in a hurry these days.

At two o'clock they stood in front of the man who was going to marry them. It was a very plain room and all over so quickly that to Lucy it didn't seem a proper wedding. Was that it? Was she really married?

'That went well, didn't it?' said Nell to Eileen when they were back at Eileen's house.

'As well as could be expected, though she would have loved a white wedding with all the trimmings.' Eileen looked over at her daughters all laughing together.

'I know. But she looked lovely and as long as they're happy, that's the most important thing.'

'Yes. Yes it is,' said Eileen quickly.

'Right. Let's get this food sorted out,' said Nell. 'What there is of it.'

'I think we've done 'em proud.'

Eileen smiled. 'Thanks for all your help.'

'Well, we're related now, and we've got to stick together,' said Nell.

They wandered into the scullery and looked at the plates of sandwiches.

'At least old Alfie Stewart came up trumps with that sausage meat,' said Nell. 'And that cake looks good.'

'Pity we couldn't get any icing sugar.'

'I don't suppose anybody'll be too worried about that. It was nice of Mrs Toms to give 'em that as a wedding present.'

Eileen nodded. 'She said she got it from her baker.'

'As I said, all in all, given the short notice, I think we've done 'em proud.'

Again Eileen nodded.

'I'm so glad everyone could get the time off,' said Lucy to her sisters when they were gathered in the Wellses' front room.

'So am I. If not I would have told the manageress what to do with her job. As it is now I'm seventeen I'm thinking of going into a factory,' said Shirley as she took a sausage roll from the plate that Nell had put on the table.

'What?' said Ann.

'You can't,' said Lucy.

'I can. They get a lot more money than shop workers and besides the country needs women in the factories.'

'I know. But a factory. All that noise. Mum won't like it,' said Ann as she too helped herself to a sausage roll.

'It won't be Mum working there. These are ever so nice,' said Shirley as she grabbed another sausage roll.

'Mum and Mrs Drury have done a wonderful job with the food,' said Ann with a mouth full of food.

'I wonder what they had to bribe the butcher and Mrs Toms with,' laughed Lucy.

'I dread to think. Now, Shirley, you've got to think very carefully about this factory lark. Mum really won't like it, you know,' said Ann.

'Well, don't tell her, not till I've sorted it out.' Shirley grabbed another sausage roll and walked away.

'Mum ain't gonner be pleased about that,' said Lucy.

'Poor Mum. She's got one thing after another to worry about. Who'd have kids?'

'I would,' Lucy said wistfully.

'Would you? Would you really want to bring up a kid in wartime?'

'Yes. Dan and me have talked about it and if anything, God forbid, happened to him, I'd have something of his to remember him by.'

'Do you need anything to remember him by?'

Lucy looked across the front room at her husband who was deep in conversation with his father and hers. 'No, I don't suppose I do.'

That night as Lucy lay in Dan's arms she felt a tear slowly trickle down her cheek. It was a tear of joy and sadness. She loved him so much. Dan had been so gentle with her and their lovemaking had been perfect. She knew she would die if anything ever happened to him. They knew they only had five days together. Next Thursday her husband – she gave a little smile: her husband, those words sounded so wonderful – had to go back to camp and God only knew where he would be sent. She fingered her wedding ring. It was new, bright and shiny, like their love for each other. It was put there with love and would never be off her finger. Like their love, it was going to be there for ever.

Chapter 13

AFTER DAN WENT back to camp Lucy's life went on just the same as before she was married. She went to work, came home and went out with her sisters. The only joy she had was getting Dan's letters, which were full of love. She often thought that getting married and being in Dan's arms for those few nights had only been a wonderful dream. Lucy's biggest disappointment was that she wasn't pregnant. That was her dearest wish, to have Dan's baby.

Ann's letters from Harry were also full of love. She couldn't help worrying though that she had never met his parents, and it was something her mother had mentioned when she told Eileen she was putting the banns up for her marriage.

'What if you don't get on with them?'

'I don't really see what I can do about it. I don't really want to go and plonk myself on the doorstep. Harry said not to worry, he'll sort it out when he gets home. He has told them all about me and that we'll be getting married on his next leave. You don't mind, do you, Mum?'

To Ann's surprise Eileen's only comment had been, 'I expect all mums don't want their chicks to leave the nest.'

While Ann waited for Harry to come home she busied herself getting her wedding dress and accessories. Shirley was to be her bridesmaid and Lucy her matron of honour. Everybody eagerly looked forward to and was getting very excited about the forthcoming wedding – or almost everybody.

'I'm a bit worried about this wedding,' said Eileen to Nell when they were having a quiet cuppa.

'Why?'

'Well, his parents are a bit posh and we can only manage a small do.'

'She's marrying him, not his parents. Besides, they should feel lucky that you'll be doing all the catering.'

'I know, but I'm still worried about it. I'm saving as much as I can from our rations. Mrs Toms has been keeping a few bits back for me.'

'We'll try and give a hand. Any idea when it'll be?'

'No. Ann won't know till he gets home.'

Nell grinned as she stirred her tea. 'You've accepted this one then?'

'Not got a lot of choice, have I?'

'Do you know, you can be a right silly cow at times.'

Eileen smiled. 'I know.'

* * *

Ann was very surprised and happy when Harry's parents wrote and asked if they could meet her. But she was nervous as well.

'I'm terrified,' she confided in Lucy.

'Why?'

'What if they don't like me? What if they don't think I'm good enough to marry their son?' Ann couldn't stop worrying that they would look down on her as she came from a working-class background.

'It's Harry you're gonner marry, not them, and if they're like that then they want their heads examined and they're not worth worrying about.'

But when the Sunday that Ann was going to tea with the Fishers arrived, she was still apprehensive. 'Do I look all right?' she asked for the fourth time, adjusting her hat yet again. 'I've not put too much lipstick on, have I?'

'You look lovely,' said Lucy. 'Now be off with you and enjoy it.'

Ann kissed her sisters and left.

'I do hope they like her,' said Lucy.

'They'd better,' was Shirley's response.

As Ann made her way to Southwark Park Road she admired the lovely big houses. This was always considered the posh part of Rotherhithe. She gave a little gasp at the Fishers' residence as she walked up the path. The garden was full of flowers. Wait till I tell the family about this, she thought. She rang the bell and waited. The front door had pretty coloured glass in the panel. She was very flustered as she watched the outline of someone approaching.

The door was opened by Mrs Fisher who smiled and held out her hand. 'Ann, at last. It's so nice to meet you. Harry's told us so much about you.' She was a tall slim woman who also had brown eyes, her hair was speckled with grey; she had a certain sophisticated air about her.

Mr Fisher was right behind his wife and he too greeted her warmly.

'I feel we know you already,' he said.

'Come into the dining room. When we finish tea you can go and see Harry's room. That way you'll get to know more about him. I'm sure he's told you all about his trophies?'

Was Mrs Fisher trying to make her seem inadequate? Perhaps she *did* think Ann wasn't good enough to marry her son. 'He told me he'd won a few things.'

'He was very good at sport when he was at college,' said his mother with pride.

'I never went to college,' said Ann.

'We know,' said Mr Fisher.

Ann could see who Harry took after. He and his father had the same cheeky smile and deep brown eyes. Mr Fisher's hair was now white, but years ago it could have been dark like his son's. 'Harry's told us all about you.'

Ann blushed. 'Not much to tell really.'

'He's very proud of you, you know, my dear. He said you went to night school to get your diploma in shorthand and typing.'

'Yes I did.'

'It must have been very hard work.'

'It was. But I was determined to do something to get a proper job. And I'm so glad I did, otherwise I would never have met Harry and been his secretary.' Ann began to relax. They knew all about her.

'We were very surprised when Harry told us he was going to marry the girl who used to be his secretary,' said Mrs Fisher as she held a plate of cakes out to Ann.

Ann shook her head. 'No thank you.' She didn't want to be talking with her mouth full as she desperately wanted these people to like her. 'I hope it wasn't too much of a shock.'

'Well, it was at first, but now we've met you we can see he made the right choice.' Mr Fisher patted her hand.

Ann was pleased that they were warming to her.

'Now about this wedding. I think we should talk about it,' said Mrs Fisher.

At first Ann was worried that they might not like going to her parents' house for the wedding reception but they soon put her at ease about that.

'We don't want to interfere and I know it's up to the bride's parents to provide the wedding breakfast, but times are different now with all this rationing and we should pull together,' said Mrs Fisher.

Ann could hear the sincerity in her voice; she was a kind lady. 'We were wondering, if it's at all acceptable and your parents don't mind, that is, whether we could pay for the reception in a hotel as a wedding present. Do you think they would be offended?' asked Mrs Fisher.

'I don't know. Mum can be a bit of a stickler for tradition.'

'Well, have a word with them and let us know, then as soon as Harry can tell us when he'll be home we can get things in motion.'

Ann beamed. 'Thank you both so much.'

'And, Ann,' said Mr Fisher, 'as you won't have the time to have a proper honeymoon we would like you to go to a hotel for a few nights. It can be anywhere you choose.'

Ann was stunned. These were truly lovely people. They seemed quite happy that she was marrying their son.

After they finished tea Ann was shown over the house and the lovely garden that overlooked the park. Harry was an only child and she could see that they were very proud of him. His room had rows of books and she noticed many of his sporting things like a cricket bat and tennis racquet leaning against the wall.

When it was time for her to leave they both gave her a hug.

'It's been wonderful meeting you and you must come again,' said Mrs Fisher.

Ann hugged them back and kissed them both. 'I will, I promise, and thank you.'

She almost skipped down the road. She was so lucky.

She had a man she loved and wonderful in-laws-to-be.

The family had been thrilled at Ann's news and Eileen and Reg were more than pleased with the catering arrangements.

The following morning Eileen made sure to tell Nell about it.

'I bet Reg liked that idea,' said Nell, pulling on her beret.

'Not nearly as pleased as I was,' Eileen confided as she waited for Nell to get ready. 'At least we don't have to go cap in hand to old Alfie Stewart for sausage meat.'

Nell laughed. 'But that was still a good do though.'

'Yes, it was.'

'I wonder what you'll eat at this wedding?'

'Dunno. Hope it ain't too fancy. Some of that stuff can make you ill, so I've been told.'

'Well, if you can find a greaseproof bag don't forget your poor starving neighbours.'

They laughed all the way to the market.

There had been many rows when Shirley first announced that she was going to work in a factory.

'Why on earth do you want to do that?' asked Eileen. 'You know you'll end up looking like the girls in the last war did, all yellow from the gunpowder.'

'Things are different now. They're a lot cleaner. Besides, I want to do my bit and the money's better.'

'Well, I don't like it,' said Eileen.

Shirley didn't argue, she just went and soon

appeared to be very happy making shell cases. She made a new friend, Brenda, who started on the same day she did. Brenda was a year older than Shirley and to Eileen's relief she sounded very sensible. Shirley told them how all the women sang along with the wireless and every week she was pleased with her wage packet and couldn't wait to spend it, although things were getting harder and harder to get. But both Lucy and Ann noticed that their sister was changing. She had grown up.

'I don't like the way she smokes all the time,' said Lucy. 'She smells like an old ashtray.'

'I know – and the way she laughs and tells us those jokes. I like a laugh as well as the next one, but she does go a bit too far at times.'

'I'm afraid our little sister is growing up,' said Lucy.

'I know,' Ann repeated.

They could see Shirley was happy, but they didn't know that one of the reasons was that she had met Vic. Shirley thought Vic was Mr Wonderful. He didn't work in the factory but was always around. He rode about on a motorbike taking messages and parcels somewhere and always seemed to have plenty of money. All the young girls drooled over Vic, but the older ones didn't have a good word to say about him. They thought he was smarmy and a scrounger who should be in the army.

'But what if he's got something wrong with him and can't go in the army?' Shirley said to Brenda when she was showing her the packet of cigarettes he'd given her.

'I still reckon he's no good.'

Shirley knew her friend was jealous because he didn't give her things. 'He might be working for the government and it might be secret.'

'If you believe that, Shirley Wells, then you're more naive than I thought.'

Shirley only grinned and made her way home.

It was almost five thirty on Friday 2nd August. It had been a long hot day and Ann was busy at the filing cabinet when the door to her office opened.

'Could you take a letter, Miss Wells?'

She spun round. 'Harry!' she screamed out and fell into his arms. Tears streamed down her cheeks as he covered her face with kisses. 'How? When?' was all she could utter.

'I got home about an hour ago and I couldn't wait to see you. I knew you would still be in the office so I came here as quick as I could. Ann. Ann, my darling. I've missed you so much.'

'Not as much as I've missed you.'

'Can you get away now?'

She nodded. 'I'll just let Mr Potter know.'

'I couldn't believe it when you wrote and told me they'd brought that poor old devil out of retirement.'

'I know. I'll just get my coat. I won't be long.'

'I'll come along with you.'

Soon Ann and Harry were driving along towards home. Lucy was sitting in the back. She settled down and gently ran her hand over the leather upholstery and let the smell soothe her.

'How long are you home for?' Ann asked Harry.

'Just two weeks. Time enough for us to get married. I know everything is under control, you clever girl. Will Saturday week be long enough?'

'It's fine with me, but what about your parents?'

'Dad's been on the phone: the hotel's booked, as is our honeymoon. We can spend four nights in Bournemouth. Is that OK with you?'

Lucy sat listening. Ann was going to have it all. A white wedding, a proper reception and a honeymoon. But all Lucy had wanted was her Dan to be with her, to hold her and make love to her.

'We can go to the church tomorrow, I've got the licence.'

'What if I'd changed my mind?'

'Then I'd put you over my shoulder and carry you there.'

Ann, laughing, turned and looked at her sister. Her laughter died and her heart filled with sympathy for Lucy. Though she was clearly trying to hide it, her loneliness was plain to see. And Ann couldn't find any words of comfort.

The preparations for Ann and Harry's wedding had gone well. Today, Saturday 10th August, was the big day and everybody was up and about early.

Ann clattered down the stairs with her hair in curlers. 'It's raining,' she wailed.

'It's only a shower,' said her father. 'It'll all be over by two o'clock, you see.'

Ann looked out of the back door. 'I hope so. I don't want me frock getting all wet.'

'Ann, sit down and eat your breakfast,' said Eileen. 'It'll be a long while before you get anything else to eat. It's gonner be a long day.'

'I wonder what we'll have to eat,' said Shirley as she tucked into her egg and bacon. 'This is a real treat, Mum.'

'It's only because I'd saved up some of the rations for the wedding. So don't get too used to it. Where's Lucy?'

'Still reading the letter she got this morning,' said Shirley.

'Give her a call, there's a love.'

Lucy sat on the bed reading Dan's letter over and over again. He'd been hoping to get some leave for the wedding, but it wasn't to be. He told her they were being kitted out and that could only mean one thing, he would be going abroad again. She prayed he'd get embarkation leave.

Lucy wiped her eyes when Shirley called up the stairs for her. 'Coming,' she answered. She had to go down for her breakfast. She wouldn't tell anyone that Dan might be sent abroad; she didn't want to spoil Ann's big day.

* * *

At two o'clock Ann walked up the aisle on her father's arm. She looked serene and lovely. Her long white satin dress clung to her slim body. It had a sweetheart neckline and long sleeves that finished with a point at her wrists. Her dark hair fell on her shoulders and the veil over her face hid her radiant smile. She was so happy she wanted to cry.

Reg stuck his chest out as he glanced about him. Shirley and Lucy were in long frocks, Shirley's pale pink, Lucy's blue; they clutched their bouquets and smiled at the congregation as they followed Ann and their father.

Everybody stood up. There weren't a lot of people in the church, they were mostly neighbours and girls from the office. Ann gave Mrs Conner a smile, pleased that she had left her boys at home with their father. Once again she had brought them back from the country and they seemed more unruly than ever.

Harry, tall and upright, stood in front of the altar; despite his dark hair having been cut short he still looked handsome and his air force uniform gave him an air of authority. He had a fellow airman as his best man. Ann smiled at Harry's parents. Mrs Fisher was wearing a pretty floral frock and a cheeky little straw hat. A fox fur nestled round her neck. She looked very smart. Across the aisle was Eileen. Harry had introduced them outside and they all had a long chat while waiting for the bride. Eileen was wearing the same navy outfit she had worn for Lucy's wedding. She couldn't believe that two of her daughters were now married.

Nell and Fred were in the pew behind Eileen; Nell was so happy to have been included. She really felt she was part of the family now. This wedding was a grand affair, and it made her feel sorry for Lucy; she knew Lucy would have liked something like this. But Nell was just happy that Lucy had married her son and sent up a little prayer for all these youngsters. She closed her eyes and said to herself: Let's hope this war's over soon and they can all start to live their lives.

The wedding reception was held in a very nice small hotel. It was to be a buffet meal and Eileen and Nell were admiring the food that was laid out.

'I ain't ever been in a hotel before,' said Nell as she looked around. 'Look at the curtains, could do with something like that up at my winders.'

'You could do the whole house with one of those,' said Eileen.

'I know. And look at the cake,' said Nell. 'I hope we get to take some home.'

Eileen stood and looked at the single-tier iced cake with a small vase of flowers on top. 'How could they get all this done at such short notice?'

'I expect they've got some ready. What I'd like to know is where did they get the ingredients from and the icing as well,' said Nell, putting a few sandwiches on her plate.

Ann's eyes were shining and she was holding on to Harry's hand when they came up to her parents. 'Isn't this wonderful?'

'It certainly is,' said Reg, who was also putting sandwiches on his plate.

'It's a pity we couldn't have a sit down, but this was all they could manage at such short notice,' said Harry.

'Well, I think it's lovely,' said Eileen. 'And I wish the pair of you all the luck in the world.'

'Thanks, Mum.' Ann kissed her mother's cheek; she knew how hard it must be for her to have two of her daughters married so quickly. But at least they were still at home.

Eileen couldn't believe that this time last year the war hadn't even started, now two of her daughters, one who wasn't even courting at the time, were married to servicemen. She looked across at her three daughters who were laughing together. What would next year bring?

Chapter 14

FOR THREE DAYS Ann and Harry had walked along the sea front gazing across the Channel and the rolls of barbed wire that were strung out all along the water's edge, preventing anyone from having a paddle. They had sat talking about their future and at night they had made love. To have Harry's arms round her all night made Ann feel safe and secure and she didn't want this bliss ever to end. When they were out walking she had been very proud to be at Harry's side and noted that he got a lot of admiring glances from young and old women alike. He did look very handsome in his uniform. But he belonged to Ann and to her it was the most wonderful thing that could ever have happened. Mr Fisher had given his son his petrol coupons so they were able to drive down to Bournemouth on Saturday evening. Now today, Wednesday, they were packing ready to go home.

'I wish we could stay another day,' said Ann as she sat at the dressing table brushing her hair.

Harry came up behind her and, holding her hair to

one side, kissed her neck. 'So do I,' he whispered. He stood looking at her in the mirror. 'I shall hate leaving you. Ann, I'm a bit worried that they've started sending planes over. As you know, according to the wireless and newspapers they've been bombing the airfields around Kent and Sussex. He's trying to knock our fighter planes out.'

'You're frightening me. Do you think you'll be stationed in the south?'

'I shouldn't think so, not as I'll be part of Bomber Command.'

'Do you think this really could be the start of something?'

'I think so. Ann, promise me that you'll take care of yourself.'

She stood up and put her arms round his neck. 'I wish I could go back to camp with you.'

Harry drew her close. 'So do I,' he murmured and kissed her lips passionately. 'Ann, I love you so much. I don't think I can bear to be parted from you.'

'When you're settled in a camp perhaps I can come and stay near you,' Ann said softly.

'That would be wonderful. I'll phone Dad as soon as I get settled and find you a hotel.'

Ann sat on the bed and looked at her husband. For weeks something had been going over and over in her mind. 'Harry, I've been wondering. What if I joined the WAAF? Would it be possible to be stationed with you?'

Harry looked up from folding his pyjamas and after placing them carefully in the suitcase said, 'You can't do that.' He sat on the bed.

'Why not?'

'I don't want you to.'

'But why? You said there were WAAFs on your camp. If it meant I could see you and perhaps be moved around with you, then that's what I want.'

'But they can't guarantee that we would be at the same camp. If I know anything they'll probably keep us apart. Besides, I don't know where they'll be sending me to finish my aircrew training. Some go to Canada.'

'Couldn't you try to pull a few strings? Oh please, Harry. Please.'

Harry pulled Ann to her feet and held her close. 'I shouldn't think so for one moment. Why this sudden urge to join up?'

'I have been thinking about it for a while and feel I should be doing something.'

'But, Ann, you could find yourself in a very dangerous situation. I wouldn't be happy about it. You know the Germans will be bombing targets like airfields.'

'If this war goes on for much longer we may all be called up.'

'That's true.'

'I want to be with you. I love you so much.' Ann snuggled close to him. 'Please, Harry,' she pleaded again.

'When you look at me like that how can I refuse you anything?' He began kissing her. As their kisses became more and more passionate Harry moved her towards the bed and soon they were together as one.

Driving home the thought that filled Ann's mind was that she would be signing on as soon as she could.

They were spending the last two nights of Harry's leave with his parents, then the next day she would be back home and her life would be just the same and, without Harry, just as boring. How would her mother react when she told her she was going to join up? That bridge would have to be crossed very soon but for the moment she was going to enjoy her last few days with Harry.

On Friday Ann, like many other women, stood on the noisy crowded platform and watched her husband's train as it slowly pulled out of the station. In a cloud of smoke and steam it disappeared into the distance. She'd promised him she wouldn't cry, but tears trickled down her cheeks just the same.

As she made her way back to her own home she understood what Lucy had been through when Dan went back and how her sister must be suffering, but at least she was going to do something about it. On her way home she was going to the recruitment office and sign up before anyone tried to talk her out of it. She was going to join the WAAFs.

* * *

The family were very pleased to see Ann and after discussing the wedding and what a lovely time they had had they wanted to know all about Bournemouth. It was when the girls were in Ann's bedroom helping her unpack she told them of her plans.

'You've joined up?' asked Lucy, plonking herself on the bed. 'But why?'

'Well, we might all have to go one day to help the war effort, so I thought that if I went now I might get stationed with Harry.'

'I bet you don't,' said Shirley. 'It's sod's law—'

'Shirley Wells, watch your language. Remember, you're not in the factory now,' said Ann sternly.

'Well, it's true. If he's stationed at one end of the country, you can bet your bottom dollar you'll be stuck at the other end.'

'She could be right,' said Lucy. 'Ann, you shouldn't have gone rushing into this. What does Harry say about it?'

Ann shrugged. 'Couldn't really say a lot as he thinks we might all be called up before long.'

'Well, Mum ain't gonner be pleased, I can tell you,' said Shirley. 'When's the fireworks gonner start? When you gonner tell her?'

'I'll pick me time, so don't you go saying anything, understand?'

'Course.' Shirley picked up her sister's nightie. 'This is a bit of all right. Bet you didn't have it on for long.'

Ann snatched it away from her sister. 'Don't be so crude.'

Lucy was still worried. 'Ann, you should have thought a bit more about this joining-up thing,' she repeated.

'Don't worry, Luce, I have given it a lot of thought and it's what I want to do. I bet if you had the chance to join Dan, you'd be there like a shot.'

Lucy smiled. 'Yes I would.' She looked at her sister. Would she be sent to the same place as Harry? She was concerned that this could start a whole new lot of problems in the Wells' household.

It wasn't till they'd finished their meal on Saturday evening and were sitting at the table having a cup of tea when Ann announced that she was going in the WAAF.

Eileen looked up. 'What do you mean?'

'I've joined up.'

'D'you think that was very wise, Ann?' said her father. 'With him sending all these planes over? That's what he's going for, the airfields.'

'What on earth made you do that?' asked Eileen.

'There is a war on, you know, and I feel I should do me bit. The woman at the recruiting office said she didn't think it would be very long before it would be compulsory.'

'Will they take married women?'

'Yes, Mum, those without babies they will.'

'I see.' Eileen stood up and began clearing the table.

'Is that it?' Ann sat back. She had been bracing herself all day. This wasn't the reaction she'd been expecting.

Lucy looked across the table at her and smiled.

'What do you expect me to say?' asked Eileen.

'I don't know. I thought you'd be angry.'

'Don't seem to matter what I think or feel. As you said, there's a war on, so you'll go off and do whatever you want. After all, you're married now.'

'Does Harry know about this?' asked her father.

'Yes he does. We talked about it before he went away.'

'And what did he think about this hare-brained idea?'

'It's not a hare-brained idea. We've all got to do our bit.'

'I know but there's other things you could do.'

'Me and Harry talked about it and he wasn't very happy at first, but I said that perhaps we could be stationed together.'

'I see.'

Lucy sat watching. She too was surprised at the lack of emotion on her mother's part. Had she accepted that in this war everybody had to help in some way?

'And I suppose you'll be the next,' said Eileen as she took Lucy's cup and saucer from her.

'I don't know. I haven't thought about it.'

'Well, I'm doing my bit,' said Shirley.

'Yes, we know all about you,' said her mother.

'What d'you mean?'

'Leave it, Shirley,' said Lucy.

'What's wrong with me working in the factory? Just because I ain't as clever as you two you've always looked down on me. Well, let me tell you I've got some good mates and I earn more than either of you, so where do all your brains get you, eh? Besides, at least I'm doing something for the war effort that's a bit more than you, sitting in an office typing out invoices all day. That ain't gonner win the war, is it?' She stormed out of the kitchen.

'Well, that's told us,' said her father.

'I didn't mean anything by that,' said Eileen. 'All I meant was that I know she's doing her bit. In fact it's beginning to make me feel that I should be helping out.'

'Don't worry about it, love,' said Reg with a grin. 'You looking after us is more than enough.'

'Well, at least I can queue up all day for a few bits, I suppose.'

'Mum, you're doing a fine job,' said Lucy, going over to her and kissing her cheek.

'I'm sorry, Mum,' said Ann. 'I didn't want to start a family row.'

Eileen smiled half-heartedly. 'It takes our mind off the war, I suppose.' But deep down she did wonder if Lucy would be the next to go.

Shirley sat on her bed. She hadn't meant to shout at Lucy. She was happy at the factory, more so now she was going out with Vic. Although she knew he was a lot older than she was and a bit of a mystery man, and Brenda didn't like him, in some ways that made her more determined to see him. She smiled when she thought about him: he was tall, dark and very good-looking. Shirley couldn't believe it when he first asked her to go out with him. He took her to see a variety show and they sat in very expensive seats. She knew he paid ten and sixpence for them; no one had ever spent that kind of money on her before. Sitting beside him she'd felt very young. When she got home she'd wanted to tell her sisters all about him, but she knew they wouldn't approve.

She could hear Lucy and Ann coming up the stairs so she pretended she was reading. She knew they had things on their minds so they wouldn't bother her.

All through August the dogfights over the south of England and the airfields being bombed were the main topic of conversation. Everybody knew that now France had fallen, Britain was next on Hitler's list.

There had been a few raids on other parts of London and British planes had bombed Berlin as retaliation, Ann was getting increasingly concerned about Harry. She knew he was up north and desperately hoped that he would get leave before she got her posting. She worried about him and thought of him being cramped in an aircraft when he finished his training; she didn't want him to be aircrew – it was too dangerous.

At the end of the month when Ann opened the

official-looking envelope waiting for her on the mantelpiece, she was surprised to find it contained her calling-up papers. She couldn't believe they had come so soon.

'Blimey, that was quick,' said her father when he came home from work.

'They must be desperate,' said Lucy.

Ann was scanning the letter.

'When you got to go?' asked Eileen.

'Thirtieth of August.' She was searching through her papers. 'I've got a travel warrant to go to Innsworth.'

'Where the bloody hell's that?' asked her father.

Ann was pleased he had resigned himself to the fact that one of his daughters was joining up. 'No idea. Let's get the map.'

'Will you be able to get home when you get some leave?'

'I hope so. This is a training camp where they find out what we can do. I expect it'll mean square-bashing as well. Can't say I'm looking forward to that.'

Lucy sat and listened to her sister. It did sound very exciting. Ann had told her that at the recruiting office they wanted to know what she could do and were pleased that she was a shorthand typist. Lucy couldn't do shorthand. Would she be as welcome in the WAAF? And was that what she wanted to do? Did she really want to follow her big sister about?

'It's in Gloucester,' said Ann, looking up from the map that was spread out on the table.

'That's a fair bit away,' said her father.

'Could be nice country. I'll write as soon as I get settled.'

Lucy could see Ann was excited at the challenge that lay ahead. Perhaps, even if it did upset her mother, she too should change her life.

Chapter 15

IT WAS ONLY a week after Ann had gone away but the feeling that she really should do something towards the war effort had overwhelmed Lucy. She missed Ann a great deal; they were very close and the house seemed empty without her. Lucy had been very excited when she got her first letter from her sister; in it Ann told her she was at a training camp. The letter was full of what she was doing and although Ann seemed happy enough she didn't like all the square-bashing and exercise. She had made a few friends but her letter also told her how worried she was that Harry was waiting to be posted. They had talked about this before she left and Lucy had said in some ways the only good thing about being aircrew was that he wouldn't be sent abroad like Dan. But as Ann pointed out it would be very dangerous when he was attached to Bomber Command and flying. Lucy knew he had been hoping to get leave but Ann didn't think they would be able to see each other, not now, as they were miles apart.

'So much for her thinking they would be together,' said Eileen when she read Ann's letter. 'I think she must have been in a dream when she signed on.'

'Or in love,' said Lucy wistfully.

'As she was married she could have got a job that would have made her exempt.'

'For now, but it wouldn't have been what she wanted to do.'

'She still reckons she'll end up doing office work though,' said her mother.

'I know, but she's hoping there'll be other more interesting work later on.'

Lucy thought about her own job; it didn't hold any satisfaction for her these days and everywhere she went she saw women in uniform of all colours. But what could she do?

On Saturday afternoon she went over to Nell's to have a cup of tea and told her how she felt.

'For Christ's sake, Luce, don't let your mother hear you talk like this. She's going mad worrying about Ann as it is.'

'I know.' Lucy twisted her wedding ring round and round. 'I just feel so . . . I don't know. I feel I should be doing something to help the war effort.'

'I know. But think about Dan, he would be worried sick if he thought you might be working with those barrage balloons or even the guns like those that's in the park. You seen 'em?'

Lucy nodded.

'Bloody great things, how d'they reckon young slips of girls will be able to manage them?'

'Those films are just recruiting films.'

'I know, but—' Nell stopped. The wailing sound of the air-raid warning began to fill the air.

'Is this another false alarm?' asked Lucy.

'I don't know, love.'

'I'd better go over to Mum, you know what she's like, she'll be panicking. Shirley's gone out shopping with a mate from work.'

Fred came racing in from the yard. 'Quick, get in the shelter. The sky's full of 'em – there's bloody loads of 'em.'

'I've gotter get to Mum.' Lucy picked up her bag and ran out of the house. Fear overtook her. She felt as if she was in a slow-moving film: her legs were moving as fast as she could make them, but she didn't seem to be getting anywhere. The short distance across the road seemed to take for ever. The droning of the planes filled the air and seemed to be bearing down on her. She looked up. There were hundreds of them. The sky was full of the black monsters.

She ran through the house and out into the air-raid shelter. She fell into her mother's arms and cried, 'What's happening?'

Her father's face was as white as a ghost; he didn't reply at once. It was then the first bombs began to rain down. The whistling then the explosion made them jump.

'I think it's started. I think this could be it.'

'Shirley,' screamed Eileen. 'Where's Shirley?'

'I don't know,' said Reg. 'But she's sensible and she'll go down a shelter.'

'Please God, I hope so.' Eileen was distraught.

'I'm frightened, Dad,' said Lucy.

'We all are, love,' he said softly.

'Are we gonner be invaded?' asked Eileen, her voice trembling with emotion. She winced as another explosion ripped through the air.

'I don't know, love,' said Reg. 'I hope not.' His face was creased with worry.

Everybody sat very quiet listening for the scream of the bombs. They put their heads down and waited. When a bomb hit the ground the earth heaved, shuddered and then slowly went back down again. It was like a living nightmare.

Eileen was holding on to Lucy and murmuring, 'Shirley. My Shirley.'

'She'll be fine, Mum, you wait and see. She'll come breezing through that door grinning and wondering what all the fuss was about.' Although Lucy could hear herself saying these words she wasn't sure she really believed them.

The clanging bells from the fire engines and ambulances broke the silence during any lull.

Then after what seemed a lifetime the all clear went and the Wells family began slowly and reluctantly to leave their shelter.

'My God,' yelled Reg who was first out. 'Look at that.' He pointed towards the river. 'They've well and truly done the docks.'

The sky darkened when the smoke blotted out the sun and its acrid smell caught their breath and lodged in their throats.

Eileen took a quick look behind her when she came out of the shelter and as she followed Reg and Lucy through the house she remembered all the fuss she'd made over the mess the men had made when it was first built. Now she was very grateful that this building was here and could save their lives.

Everybody in Perry Street was standing in the road looking towards the docks. Nell and Fred slowly walked across to Eileen and Reg.

'Looks like he's given the docks a bit of a pasting,' said Fred.

Another plume of smoke rose up as they stood staring at the flames leaping high into the sky; oil drums were being tossed up in the air like toys.

'Certainly does. There was a lot of dry timber in those warehouses,' said Reg.

Mrs Conner came up to them looking very agitated. 'My boys and their father went to see his mother. She lives over Poplar way. I'm ever so worried about them. I should never have brought them back. I won't forgive meself if anything happens to 'em.'

Eileen patted her arm. 'Try not to worry. My Shirley's

gone shopping. I expect they've all finished up in some shelter or another.'

Lucy smiled at her mother. Here she was almost going out of her mind over Shirley but she still found time to console others.

'They'll be all right, missis,' said Fred. 'Old Tommy's got his head screwed on. He won't let any harm come to his kids.'

Mrs Conner gave them a faint smile. 'I hope you're right. Me cats have been going mad through that lot. I don't know what they'll do if we have any more raids.' She walked away very slowly.

'I reckon if those cats get out they'll run a mile,' said Nell.

'I don't know how she manages to feed 'em with everything rationed,' said Eileen.

'I did hear they're putting a lot of cats and dogs down. Stands to reason, got to feed us first,' said Nell.

Fred grinned. 'We might even end up eating 'em ourselves if things get bad.'

'Trust you to say something like that,' said Nell.

Reg was still looking towards the docks. 'Look,' he said very seriously. 'I reckon we're in for a right old night of it. I suggest that we make some tea in the flasks and get a few supplies in the shelter just in case.'

'You really think that, Reg?' said Nell.

'Stands to reason, girl,' said Fred. 'Just look at those

fires, they're gonner be like a beacon tonight. I reckon they can be seen for miles.'

'I suppose we should take some bedding in,' said Lucy.

'We can only try and make ourselves as comfortable as we can,' said Reg. 'That all right, love?'

Eileen nodded. 'I'm so worried about Shirley.' Tears began to trickle down her cheek. 'What if she's been buried somewhere?'

'Where did she go?' asked Nell.

'I don't know.'

Lucy put her arm round her mother's shoulder. 'She'll be all right. She's a survivor.'

'Can we go and look for her?' asked Fred.

'I don't know where she was going,' sniffed Eileen.

'She's probably having trouble getting a bus,' said Reg half-heartedly.

'I wish there was something we could do,' said Nell. 'I feel so bloody helpless standing here.'

'She'll be home as soon as she can,' said Lucy.

'Look, Reg. How about you and me going up the pub as soon as they open and getting a few bottles of beer and something a bit stronger for the women.'

'Trust you to think about the pub at a time like this,' said Nell. 'What if the siren goes off and I'm in that shelter all on me own? I tell yer, if I finish up dead I'll come back and haunt yer.'

Everybody began to laugh.

Fred kissed his wife's cheek. 'I love yer, girl, you

certainly know how to bring a smile to our miserable faces.'

Nell smiled.

'Come on, Mum, we'd better start getting ready for tonight.'

'What if Shirley don't come home?'

'She will.' Lucy went and kissed Fred and Nell. She swallowed hard. 'I hope I see you both tomorrow.'

'You will, love,' said Fred. He held her close. 'You will. Look after yourself for my son,' he whispered.

'I'll try.'

Slowly Perry Street began to empty to prepare for the night, although Mrs Conner was still standing at her door looking up and down the road.

Lucy gave up a silent prayer: Please bring my sister back soon and look after Mrs Conner's family.

'He won't be bombing where Ann is, will he?' asked Eileen as she rinsed out the vacuum flasks.

'Shouldn't think so,' said Reg.

'At least we know she's safe then,' said Eileen.

It was with a heavy heart that the feather mattresses and pillows were taken off the beds and put in the shelter.

'I don't like the idea of them on the floor,' said Eileen. 'They could get very damp and we could all finish up with rheumatism.'

'I think that'll be the least of our worries,' said Reg.

When Fred knocked for Reg he said he didn't want to leave the house in case Shirley came home.

'I can understand that,' said Fred. 'I'll bring you back a couple of bottles.'

'Thanks.'

Flasks of tea were made and sandwiches were being cut.

'Don't think I'll be able to eat any of these,' said Eileen.

'Come on, Mum. I know it ain't easy but we've got to try and look on the bright side.'

Eileen threw the bread knife on the table. 'How can you say that? We could all be killed tonight. And Shirley could come home and find the house flattened and us all dead.' She broke down in uncontrollable tears. Her body shook with emotion.

Lucy called for her father who was standing at the front door looking for Shirley, then rushed to her mother's side and cuddled her. She too was crying, but with anger as well as fear for her young sister. How dare this man come and bomb them? How dare he think he can come to this country and do what he likes? That's it. If I get out of this lot alive tomorrow I'm off on Monday to join up. I'll show the bastard.

When Fred came home from the pub he didn't stop as he could see that Eileen was distraught and Reg – as Lucy had done – was getting angry because he was frightened.

'Don't you think I'd be out looking for her if I knew where to look?' He turned to Lucy and, pointing, said,

'Let this be a lesson to you, young lady. Every time you go out you'd better tell us where you're going and how long you'll be.'

Lucy nodded. She was busy writing a letter to Dan. In it she poured everything she felt, everything that was in her heart. She told him what she planned to do: if she did get out alive. She desperately wanted him close to her.

'Reg, what we gonner do?' asked Eileen.

'We're gonner sit here and wait for the siren to go and then we're going into the shelter.'

'I'll wait for Shirley.'

'You'll go in the shelter,' he said forcibly. 'I'll stay in here for her.'

Lucy watched her mother as she sat wringing her hands. She looked at the clock. It was half past six. How long before it all starts?

The air-raid warden had bustled Shirley and Brenda into a shelter, where they had sat holding on to each other, terrified. All around them women and children were crying as the noise of bombs exploding filled the air and made the ground heave. Shirley was beside herself with fear; she wanted to go home. When the all clear went and they were allowed out she and Brenda made their way home as fast as they could.

The commotion when the front door slammed shut made all the Wellses jump up. Eileen rushed to open the kitchen door.

'Mum. Mum.' Shirley came into the kitchen and threw her arms round her mother. She was crying uncontrollably. 'Mum, I was so scared. I never thought I'd get home. The buses are all over the place. I was so frightened.'

Her father held on to her. 'Where were you?'

'Up West. It was awful. Me and Brenda went down a shelter; the wardens wouldn't let us out till after the all clear went.' She wiped her eyes, smudging mascara across her dirty face. 'And look,' she sobbed, 'I've laddered me best pair of stockings.'

Eileen looked at her daughter's overwrought face. Was this the beginning? 'You're safe home with us now,' she said, wondering how safe they really were.

'Is that the docks that's alight?' asked Shirley.

'Yes. And we've got everything ready for tonight, so put something warm on and take a few clothes in with you,' said Reg. 'And anything that's precious to you.' He grinned. 'Your mother's put the policy bag in first.'

'Well, I ain't been paying it all these years only to lose the papers.'

Lucy gave a little smile at the practicalities. She knew that if the house got bombed in the night, they could finish up with just the clothes they stood up in.

They sat in the shelter waiting. They had cards, ludo and snakes and ladders. Although nobody was in the mood to play games or read they made out they were;

the rustle as Shirley turned the pages of her magazine sounded very loud.

It wasn't long before the siren began to wail. Everybody had fear in their eyes. They knew that the long night had begun.

Chapter 16

ALL THROUGH THE night the Wells family and probably the whole of London sat listening to the sound of the planes droning overhead, bombs falling, guns booming, glass being broken and now and again the sound of a wall crashing down. When the shelter door was blown open the blast sucked out the air and they could see searchlights sweeping the sky. The smell of the hot air, dust and soot clogged their nostrils.

There had been guns in the park for a while, much to the joy of girls like Shirley who loved to go and talk to the gunners. But now when they went off people realised how loud they were; the noise was deafening, making everybody jump.

'That was close,' said Reg when the blast of another bomb blew the door in yet again. He was having a job to hold it shut. 'I'll have to get a proper bolt on this door tomorrow.' He ran his hand over his face and left dirty sooty streaks.

Lucy wanted to cry. Here was her dad talking about

doing repairs tomorrow. Would they all be here tomorrow?

Eileen put her head back and closed her eyes. She was tired and would have loved to be able to sleep but the noise and her thoughts kept her wide awake. Did Mr Conner and the boys get home safe? Was Ann all right? How was Nell coping? She opened her eyes and glanced at her family. Reg, just in the last few hours, suddenly looked old. Even Shirley seemed to have grown up in a day. Gone was that silly giggling girl that left home this afternoon. And Lucy. Sensible Lucy looked as if she had the world's worries on her shoulders. Eileen knew that this was going to be the last straw for Lucy; her daughter would be following her sister off to do her bit somewhere very soon.

Eileen woke with a start. 'What is it? What's happened?'

'Sorry if I woke you, love,' said Reg softly. 'Just been out for a pee.'

'What's happened? It's very quiet?'

'Dawn's just starting to break. It's been quiet for a little while now. I think the all clear will go off soon.'

Eileen began to cry.

'Shh, love. Don't wake the girls.' Reg went and held her close. 'What is it?'

'We're alive. We're safe,' she whispered.

Reg held on to Eileen. 'I know. The house has taken a bit of a bashing.'

'Is it still standing?'

'Just about. I ain't been inside but we ain't got any windows.'

Lucy stirred. 'Mum. Dad. What's happened?'

'It's all right, love,' said Reg. 'I think it's all over.'

Shirley sat up. Tears were streaming down her face. 'We're alive. Dad, we're all alive.'

'We certainly are, girl.'

'I'm dying for a pee. Is it all right to go outside?' asked Lucy.

'Yes, but be careful, there's a lot of rubble underfoot.'

Very carefully Lucy made her way outside to the lav. Although the sky was red with the fires, it still looked incredibly beautiful. The vapour trails from the planes criss-crossing the bright blue added to the beauty. She looked at their house; she could see they didn't have any windows. The bedroom curtains, which her mother had lovingly made, hung in ribbons. What was the inside like? What would they find when they went in? Lucy picked her way over debris and noticed that there were tiles amongst it. Did they have a roof?

The all clear brought the Wellses and every other family out of their shelters.

As Eileen followed Reg through the house she gasped, 'Look at the mess!'

The ceiling had come down in the kitchen, exposing the laths. Everything was covered with white powder; great lumps of plaster were strewn all over the place, mixed with broken glass.

'Careful where you tread,' said Reg as he shoved

some rubble away from the door with his foot to allow him to open the kitchen door.

They all crunched along the passage and standing at the bottom of the stairs looked up.

'I can see the sky,' said Shirley. She went to go upstairs.

'Shirley. Stay where you are,' said her father abruptly. 'It might not be safe.'

They stood and watched as Reg very slowly climbed the stairs, cautiously sweeping each stair with his foot and taking one step at a time. When he got to the top all he said was, 'Bloody hell.'

'Is it bad, Dad?' asked Lucy.

He looked over the banister. 'Well, let's put it this way, if it rains we ain't 'arf gonner get wet.'

'Can we come up?' asked Eileen.

'Yes, but tread carefully.'

As Eileen mounted the stairs she called over her shoulder, 'Shirley, put the kettle on.'

Shirley went into the kitchen and turned on the tap. 'We ain't got no water,' she yelled out.

'That's a bugger,' said Reg. 'I really fancy a cuppa.'

'There ain't none left in the flasks,' said Eileen.

'Shall I go out and see if anyone's got any water?' asked Lucy.

'That's a good idea, Luce,' said Eileen from halfway up the stairs.

Outside Perry Street was full of rubble; Lucy couldn't see the full extent of the damage but most of the houses seemed to be standing. She spotted Charlie the warden up the road with a group of men round him; she hurried towards them.

'Stay back, Lucy,' he yelled out when he caught sight of her. 'It ain't safe.'

Some of the men were busy working round the Conners' house. Slowly she made her way towards them. Lying in the road was what she guessed was a body; it had been covered with a green check tablecloth. Lucy couldn't see who it was. She began to cry and ran back home.

'Mum. Dad. Come quick.'

'What is it?' asked Eileen as she came down the stairs with Reg following on behind.

Lucy put her head in her hands and cried.

'Come on, love. Come into the kitchen and sit down. Shirley, shake the dust off that chair,' said their father.

Shirley quickly did as she was told. 'What is it? What's happened?'

'There's a body outside Mrs Conner's house.' Lucy gave a loud sob. 'It's covered with a tablecloth. I couldn't see who it was.'

'Oh my God,' said Eileen, putting her hand to her mouth. 'The poor devil. I wonder who it is?'

'Look, I'll go and see if they want any help,' said Reg. 'You'll be all right here, won't you?'

Eileen nodded.

'Just be careful with what you do. Is there any water?'

'I don't know, Dad. I didn't ask.'

He patted her shoulder. 'That's all right, love. Don't worry about it. I'll go and tell Fred.' He picked up his fire-watching tin hat and left.

Almost as soon as he left Nell came hurrying through the open door. Eileen and Nell fell into each other's arms. 'You all all right over here? asked Nell.

Eileen stood back. 'Not too bad.'

'Have you heard somebody's been killed?'

Eileen nodded.

'Bloody awful, ain't it?'

'Do you know who it is?' asked Eileen.

'No. It seems a bomb hit the house over the back and as far as they can tell, it ain't any of the Conners. They're trapped in the shelter and they're still digging 'em out.'

Lucy was still crying.

'You all right, love?' asked Nell sympathetically.

Lucy nodded and blew her nose.

'I think it's shock,' said Eileen.

'Not surprised. What a night.'

'What you doing about water?'

'Charlie told Fred that there was gonner be a tanker coming round. But Gawd only knows when that'll be, not with all the damage and blocked roads. Pity we didn't think to fill a couple of pans last night.'

'I don't think any of us knew what was in store for us last night. I hope we don't have many more nights like that one. I don't think me nerves could cope.'

Lucy wiped her eyes and looked all around. 'Mum, shall we start to clear some of this mess?' she asked.

'Well, it'll give us something to do. What's your place like, Nell?'

'Not as bad as this. Got a few broken windows, that's all.' She too looked around. 'It was the bomb at the back of the Conners' place what's done this.'

'Reg was saying he's got to find a tarpaulin to put over the roof. Gawd only knows where he's gonner get one of them from.'

Nell grinned. 'I dare say someone will know. Now, how about getting the dustpan and brush and bringing the dustbin in and we'll make a start.'

'What about your place?'

'When Fred comes back he can find some bits of wood – or I think there's a bit of lino somewhere, he can put that up at the window for now. Mind you, the glaziers are gonner have a field day mending all these broken windows.' Nell laughed.

'What's so funny?' asked Eileen.

'I was just thinking, if you was a winder cleaner you wouldn't have a lot of work to do round here, would you?'

They all laughed. It helped the tension and they all set to and began cleaning away the glass and plaster.

'I could murder a cuppa,' said Nell after they finished clearing up the kitchen.

Ornaments from the dresser and mantelpiece had been put in the drawers for safe keeping.

'We've got to wait for water. Have we got any gas to boil a kettle?' asked Lucy.

'Dunno,' said Eileen. 'Shirley, try it.'

'No gas,' yelled Shirley from the scullery.

'No gas and no water,' said Eileen. 'What we gonner do for dinner?'

'I suppose we'll have to light the fire and use that oven,' said Nell.

'I ain't used the kitchen range for years,' said Eileen.

'Looks like we'll have to start using 'em now,' said Nell. 'At least there's plenty of wood around to keep the fire going. Could put a kettle on it if we had some water. I hope the chimney's all right.'

'Me meat,' yelled Eileen and dashed outside.

Lucy looked at Nell. 'The meat's in the safe.'

Nell laughed. 'Let's hope it ain't been blown away.'

Eileen came in clutching a plate with her precious meat ration still intact. 'Well, that's still there. Mind you, it looks a bit dusty.'

'We still ain't settled what we gonner do for a drink,' said Nell. 'Me throat's as dry as parchment.'

'When Mr Drury come back from the pub last night he brought us back a bottle of lemonade. Is there any left?' Lucy asked her mother.

'I think so.'

'If not I could go up and see if the pub's still there,' said Shirley.

'The pub's still there,' said Nell. 'But if they've got any left is another matter. We'll make do for now.'

'I'll go and get it out of the shelter,' said Eileen. 'At

least it'll be a wet and clear our throats of this dust before we start on upstairs.'

When Eileen went in the shelter she stopped in the doorway and burst into tears. The bedding was strewn over the floor and there, nicely settled, curled up cosily and fast asleep, were Mrs Conner's cats. They were covered with plaster and dust but they seemed content. Eileen didn't have the heart to shoo them away so she let them sleep on.

Perry Street was shocked when they learned that the elderly couple who lived over the back of the Conners' had been killed. When Reg told Eileen she said nothing. Was this just the first? Nobody knew the name of the couple. Their house and shelter had been demolished and had caused the back of the Conners' to be damaged.

All day the people in Perry Street worked together. The Conners had been rescued and apart from shock didn't appear to be badly hurt; with help they were able to walk to the ambulance. The boys and Mrs Conner were crying and very upset, and Mr Conner seemed in a daze as they were taken to hospital.

Tarpaulins arrived from somewhere and the younger men were up ladders like monkeys, pulling the great sheets over the gaping holes in the roofs. All you could hear was the sound of hammering and orders being shouted out as windows were boarded up and as many emergency repairs as possible were done.

Later on in the morning a tanker came round with water and everybody filled everything they had. Those with Primus stoves or those that had managed to get a fire going made tea. It wasn't till midday when the WVS van came round with rolls and tea that everybody stopped work.

'What am I gonner do about these cats?' asked Eileen as she poured out a welcome cup of tea. The WVS lady had filled Eileen's teapot as the fire was taking for ever to boil a kettle.

'Chuck 'em out. Can't have 'em staying in here all night and peeing all over the place,' said Nell as they stood at the door watching them cleaning themselves.

'Where can they go?' asked Shirley, picking up one and cuddling it close to her. 'Listen, it's purring.'

'We can leave 'em for a little while, but they'll have to go back. Has anybody got a key to the Conners'?' asked Eileen.

'You don't need one, their back door's been blown off,' said Lucy. 'So they could go back now.'

'No, leave 'em,' said her mother. 'With no back door they might run away and that'll really upset Mrs Conner.'

Nell smiled. 'Come on, there's work to be done. Always said you was a soft cow.'

Later that afternoon Mr and Mrs Conner were allowed home. The boys were being kept in hospital as they were suffering from shock and young Charlie had a broken arm.

Eileen and Nell went along to see if the Conners needed anything.

Mrs Conner had a lot of scratches on her face. She burst into tears when she was told about her cats.

Her husband put his arm around her. 'Don't upset yourself, love.' He turned to Eileen and Nell. 'We can't stay in our house till they make it safe. They're taking us to some sort of shelter just for the night. They're sending someone to collect the cats.'

'If you need anything,' said Eileen, swallowing hard, 'just ask.'

Silently they walked back and told Shirley and Lucy.

'That's such a shame. Will they put 'em down?' asked Shirley.

'I would think so,' said Eileen.

So Shirley and Lucy, with a heavy heart, took the cats back home.

Chapter 17

ANN, LIKE MOST of the women who weren't on exercise that morning, was taking it easy in the mess listening to the wireless. The announcer was talking about the raid on London last night. Several of the girls came from London and when they heard the news, all the talking suddenly stopped. The silence was shocking.

When the news was over everybody still sat dumbfounded. The sound of someone crying broke the spell.

'Me mum and dad live in London, near the docks,' said one young girl softly.

'So do mine,' whispered Ann, but not to anyone in particular.

'Do you think they will let us have compassionate leave to go and see if they're all right?' asked another.

'Shouldn't bank on it,' said Mary, who over the past week had become friendly with Ann. They had met on the train and finished up in the same billet; they were both married to airmen, which gave them a kind of bond. Mary was tall, slim and very upright. Her dark hair was cut in a short bob. She looked every inch someone who should have been on the recruiting posters. She would definitely finish up an officer; she had that air of authority about her, although her wide blue eyes held their own secrets and fears. Mary's husband Joe was a mechanic stationed down on the south coast. She had told Ann about how the German bombers and fighters had been coming over for the last few weeks trying to wreck the airfields. Mary was a bit brusque, but she had a kind heart and was there when Ann was feeling very lonely and upset. 'It's only if something terrible's happened to them that you'll hear, then you'll get leave,' she continued.

Ann was worried. She wanted to go and see what had happened in Perry Street. This bloody war was disrupting everything. If anything happened to her family . . . 'I can phone Harry's parents. They'll let me know how bad it was.'

'That's if the phone's working,' said Mary.

'Christ, yer're a right bloody Jonah, ain't yer,' said Rosie, who also came from London.

'I know how hard it's been to get hold of my Joe, so I'm only saying.'

'It's all right, Mary,' said Ann. 'We're all upset and worried about the news, that's all.'

After the broadcast one or two of the girls, including Ann, left the mess and went back to their billet.

Ann was sharing with seven other girls and their beds were in two lines, four down either side of the walls. It was a depressing Nissen hut and when it rained at night the noise on the tin roof kept them awake. They had been taught how to make beds air-force style and the discipline was very tough. Most of the girls were really fed up with it and some wanted to leave, but that was impossible. They had signed on for the duration.

'I dunno how you can be mates with that Mary,' said Rosie, sitting down on her bed. 'She thinks she knows it all.'

'Don't forget she's been through quite a bit with her husband being down south. It's pretty bad down there.'

'Well, it sounds as if it's pretty bad in London. Ann, do you think you could try and phone yer feller's parents? Try and find out what part's been hit?'

Ann smiled, trying to keep her fears under control. 'I'll go now.'

As she set off for the telephone box Ann thought about her new life to stop herself panicking about home. This was just a training camp and she would be pleased when she'd finished this training and square-bashing and was actually helping the war effort. Where would she finish up? She was worried that it would be in administration as the board were pleased she was a qualified shorthand typist. She wanted to do more than just sit at a desk. There were so many interesting jobs for women in the service.

Outside it was warm. She hurried to the phone box. Thankfully nobody was waiting. Inside it felt stuffy, almost stifling. By now her hands were shaking and tears were blurring her eyes as she checked she had the right amount of change and dialled the number.

'I'm sorry,' said the operator. 'I'm unable to connect you.'

Ann put the phone back on its cradle and pressed button B to get her money back. Her stomach churned over; she wanted to break down and cry. What if anything had happened to her family, how long would it be before she found out? She would try phoning again later this evening. Mr Fisher was a kind man; he would go and see that her family was all right. As she walked back she silently prayed: Please let them all be safe. She couldn't even bring herself to think of anything happening to her friends and more especially her family; she loved them so very much.

On Monday morning the Wells family emerged from the shelter after another sleepless night with bombs falling all around them. Last night before the raid started they'd got themselves a little more prepared. Buckets and pans were filled with water so at least they could have a wash and a cup of tea if the water main was hit again.

When Reg came in from looking up and down the street he announced that it looked as if once again Perry Street had been spared.

Later on, after Shirley and her father had left to try to get to work, Lucy decided that on the way she would call in to the recruiting office. She still wasn't sure what she wanted to do. The buses were almost non-existent and diversions necessitated by unsafe buildings, gas mains being repaired and unexploded bombs had her walking round in circles. As she picked her way over hosepipes and rubble her mind was turning over and over. Was this what Dan had been through when he was in France? Where was he now? Was he fighting somewhere? She wanted him here with her, she felt so alone. She wanted his arms round her making her feel safe as they had the first time they'd heard the siren and she had broken the milk jug. She choked back a sob and looked round at the devastation; a lot more than milk jugs had been broken now. Whole sides of houses had been blown out, revealing the secrets they'd held for years. What had happened to the occupants, had they been spared? The constant clanging of the ambulances' bells as they raced about told her that perhaps another victim had been found and was clinging to life.

She was amazed at the number of young women hanging about outside an empty shop that had been set up as a recruiting office, waiting to sign on. She stood next to a girl and began to read the many posters inviting women to join up.

'That was another rough night last night,' said the girl.

To Lucy she looked about sixteen. Was she old enough to go into the forces? 'Yes, it was. Do you come from round here?'

'I live over on the Isle of Dogs. Got it pretty bad over there.'

'I think most of London got it pretty bad.'

'What yer gonner do?' asked the girl.

'Don't know. I just feel I should be doing something. I can only type and somehow that don't seem to be enough. My sister's in the WAAFs, but all that square-bashing sounds awful. Puts me off a bit.'

'I know what you mean. I'm gonner join the Land Army.'

'That sounds like really hard work.'

'I expect it is, but they don't do all that exercise sort of stuff and that way you can really feel you're doing something, at least I'll be helping to feed the country.'

Lucy smiled. This young girl sounded like a recruitment poster.

'Always liked the open air when we went down Kent hopping, so I thought this'd be me chance to go to the country.'

Lucy considered what this girl was saying. The Land Army wasn't something she'd even thought about, but perhaps it was a good idea. She really would be doing something useful. She smiled. 'D'you know, that don't sound a bad idea. I think I might join you.'

The girl smiled and held out her hand. 'I'm Janet, named after Janet Gaynor the film star. Pleased to meet you.' Janet's grey eyes were full of expression. Her wavy blond hair touched her shoulders. She was slim but not very tall and Lucy immediately wondered how she would manage to drive a tractor like the young lady smiling down at them from the poster.

Lucy also smiled. 'I'm Lucy. And I'm pleased to meet you. I hope we get to see each other some time.'

'It'll be great if we finish up on the same farm.'

'Yes it would.' Lucy couldn't see that happening but it would be nice. Janet certainly looked as if nothing would ever get her down.

When Reg and Fred finally got as near to the docks as they were allowed they stood and looked at the destruction.

'Can't believe this was a working docks last week,' said Fred, pushing his cap back and scratching his forehead.

'I know.' Reg looked around at the twisted cranes and burned-out buildings. 'It's hardly recognisable. I wonder if anyone was hurt?'

'Would have been if it had been a weekday.'

'I'm surprised he chose a Sat'day to start.'

Slowly Reg and Fred wandered about. They spoke to one or two other dockers they knew well. Most of them had sorry tales to tell of people they knew who had been killed or injured.

After a while Fred said, 'Come on, mate, let's go home. Ain't a lot we can do round here.'

'That's true,' said Reg as they turned away from the docks.

'Wonder if they'll ever be working docks again,' said Fred.

'Wouldn't like to say.'

'Well, a lot of us had better start thinking of going on the dole.'

'Never signed on in me life,' said Reg.

'Nor me. They say there's a first for everything. D'you know, I could do with a drink. Thank God the Beak survived.'

Reg smiled. The Earl of Beaconsfield at the end of Perry Street was still standing, even if, like most of the street, it looked a little battered.

When Lucy got home later that evening she was pleased to hear that Ann's father-in-law Mr Fisher had been to see them.

Eileen was smiling. 'Ann phoned him last night. She was worried about us. That was nice of him to come round to see if we was all right.'

'What about them? Are they all right?' asked Lucy.

'A bit like us,' said Reg. 'Got a few windows missing, but not too bad. That's quite a way for the old boy to walk. He said it was very noisy with those guns in Southwark Park close by.'

'It ain't easy walking anywhere with half the roads closed. Did he say if Ann's all right?'

Her father laughed. 'Not keen on this drill lark. He said they couldn't talk for long as it was late when she finally got through to 'em and she had to get back to camp before lights out. Seems the phone lines have been down all day. She's gonner try again tonight when he had some news.'

The thought that was going through Lucy's mind was that tomorrow the news might be very different.

'You got to work all right then?' asked Eileen.

'Like Dad I had to make a few diversions.' It had been almost lunchtime before Lucy got to the office.

Lucy had just taken her hat and coat off when Shirley burst in. She didn't appear to be very happy. Lucy decided to wait till Shirley calmed down before she told her parents that she'd joined the Land Army.

'It took me ages to get to work this morning and home again tonight,' Shirley moaned, throwing her handbag on the table. 'Good job it's light and I could work out where I was.'

'At least you had a job to go to,' said Reg. 'Don't know what I'm gonner do.'

Eileen looked from one to the other. She was worried that her household, the one place she loved being, would never be the same.

Shirley was told about Ann phoning. 'I wish I was up there with her. Can't say I'm enjoying this life very much. What you been up to today, Luce, did you have trouble getting to work?'

'I didn't go to work till after I'd signed on. I've joined the Land Army.'

'The Land Army?' screamed Shirley. 'What you want to join that for?'

'I felt I would be doing a more useful job than sitting in an office.'

Reg looked over his newspaper. 'You don't know nothing about gardening.'

'Don't be daft, Dad. You can't really call it gardening.'

'Just a joke, that's all.'

Lucy knew her father was upset about the docks; the situation was making him unhappy. The only work that seemed to be available was clearing the rubble away, making the houses safe, and looking for people. He said he'd been out all day and he looked tired through lack of sleep and worry.

'What about milking cows?' said Shirley. 'Can't say I'd fancy doing that.'

'I'll have to learn.'

Eileen sat tight-lipped. Another of her daughters was leaving. She wanted them to be together. She needed them here with her. She needed . . . She stopped her thoughts racing. She knew she was being selfish, but she couldn't help it. She knew she couldn't fight this any more, her daughters had to go and her life was falling apart.

'You're very quiet, Mum,' said Lucy.

'Not a lot to say, is there?'

'No, I suppose not.' Lucy looked around at the kitchen they were sitting in. In just a few days it had been transformed from a happy family haven to a bare and gloomy room. There wasn't any daylight coming in as the windows had been boarded up. There were great holes in the ceiling exposing the laths; the rest of the plaster had come down last night. The glass lampshade had also been broken during the night so the lightbulb just hung on the brown flex. Was this now going to be a morning ritual: cleaning up? All the ornaments had been packed away on Sunday morning. The house looked sad and war worn. But at least they still had a house, not like a lot of people. Lucy wanted to cry. She didn't want to leave her family but knew she had to do something to help the war effort.

'I'll just go over and tell Dan's mum and dad.'

'He won't be that happy about it,' said Eileen.

Lucy didn't answer. She picked up her cardigan. 'I feel like Ann did. I've got to do something positive.' She left the kitchen.

'Get back before the siren goes,' called her father.

'I will.'

'The Land Army?' said Nell. 'Good God, whatever made you want to join that?'

'Dunno. I suppose it was the thought of going on sitting in an office all day. I really do want to do something to help the war effort.'

Fred grinned. 'Well, when this lot's all over you'll be able to do the gardening.'

Lucy smiled. 'Dad made the same joke. What are you going to do about work?'

'Dunno. The docks are in a right mess. Be a while

before any ships get up there. Always do bits of repair work, I suppose.'

'Well, there's certainly plenty of that about.'

'You can say that again, old girl,' said Fred.

'I dunno if me nerves can take much more. It really gets me down.'

Fred tapped the back of Nell's hand. 'You'll be all right.'

'I hope this don't go on for too long. I need me beauty sleep,' she replied.

'Don't we all,' said Lucy. 'I'd better go and get settled for the night. I only hope Dan's all right.'

'So do we, love,' said Fred. 'So do we.'

Lucy made her way back home. Was she right to leave the family? Should she have followed Shirley's example and gone to work in a factory and stayed at home with them? If anything happened to them while she was away, she would never forgive herself. And what about Dan? Lucy stopped her racing thoughts. No, she was sure he would be proud of her.

Chapter 18

NIGHT AFTER NIGHT, all through September, the bombs continued to rain down on London. Every morning, like most Londoners, the residents of Perry Street emerged from their shelters surprised they were still alive and that most of the houses were still standing. Perry Street was beginning to look very war-torn. A huge explosion in the early hours of one morning had almost blown away two houses at one end, leaving a great pile of rubble. Thankfully nobody had been hurt, as the owners had gone away. The kids couldn't wait to scramble over the wreckage to see what they could find. According to Mrs Conner, her boys had the largest collection of shrapnel, despite Charlie's broken arm.

'Don't you worry they might hurt themselves?' asked Eileen as she and Nell stopped to have a word.

'Yer, I do. I want 'em to go away but they won't hear of it. And me old man ain't much help. He reckons we should all be together. He says if we get killed, who'll look after 'em?'

There wasn't an answer to that so Eileen and Nell said they had to go and see if the butcher was still there. They picked their way to the shops ready to join any queue that looked promising.

'I'm bloody fed up with this lark,' said Nell as yet another diversion sent them round in a circle.

'Must be for the best, don't wonner step on a bomb or have a building fall on us. Mind that lump of concrete.' Despite her encouraging words, Eileen wanted to cry. She was so unhappy and with Reg being home nearly every day things were getting very fraught. 'I wish Reg could find some work that pays.' Eileen knew she shouldn't get cross with him; he had tried to keep busy. The shelter now had two bunk beds and a shelf for the essentials like torches and candles.

'And Fred,' said Nell. 'I think helping dig that couple out in Fawcett Road a couple of nights ago took their mind off not having a proper job.'

'Something like that does bring you up a bit short. It makes you count your blessings,' said Eileen. 'Shame the little baby died, though.'

'That upset Fred. He couldn't stop talking about it. He said the poor little bugger didn't stand much of a chance with the wall falling on 'em. It seems the mother was still feeding the poor little mite at the time.'

'I don't know why some of these women want to keep their kids here.'

'Could be like Mrs C. said. I suppose if you're gonner go you might as well all go together.'

'You're cheerful this morning,' said Eileen.

'Hark who's talking.' Nell grinned. 'You seen your face today?'

'No. The bloody mirror in the kitchen fell down last night and broke.'

'You know that means seven years' bad luck.'

'We should be so lucky to last seven years,' said Eileen.

'Come on, girl, cheer up.' Nell put her arm through her friend's and hustled her along.

Nell was as good as a tonic. Eileen wondered what would happen to her if anything happened to Nell. She quickly dismissed that thought.

'Well, he's still here,' said Nell when they turned the corner to see a small queue at the butcher's.

'I like the drawings he's done on those wooden shutters.' The shutters had been put in place of the windows that had been blown out last week.

They stood back and smiled at the pictures of sheep and cows with the words: 'We ain't got much left, only our sense of humour' scrawled underneath.

'Come on,' said Nell. 'Let's see if he can make us laugh.'

They joined the queue in anticipation.

The siren had gone and as usual the Wells family was sitting in the shelter waiting for the night to start. Shirley was watching Lucy writing one of her long, loving letters to Dan. This was now a nightly ritual.

Dan had always told Lucy that it was the letters from home that kept them all going. Shirley knew her sister had told Dan she was joining the Land Army but so far she hadn't heard his reaction. She also knew her sister was pretty certain that Dan was abroad again, because his letters came in fits and starts. She still couldn't believe that Lucy had joined up. Should she follow her sisters and go into the forces? She was happy at the factory doing war work, even though at first she'd thought the girls were coarse. She'd got used to them now: they were a very friendly bunch. Her best friend, Brenda, the girl who'd started with her, was great and then there was Vic. The nightly raids had put a stop to their going out as it had to most things, but she did like him and every morning when she got to work she would eagerly look round for him, hoping he had survived another long night.

Brenda was still cross about him. 'You don't know nothing about him. He's an old man.'

'So? I like someone who ain't all silly.'

'Why ain't he in the army or something?' Brenda had asked for the umpteenth time.

'I don't know. He ain't said.'

'Have you asked him?'

'Yes.'

'And?'

'He laughed at me.'

'You are such a silly cow. You know he could be a conchie.'

'What?'

'You know? A conscientious objector.'

'Don't talk daft.' But that worried Shirley. What would her father say if it were true? Shirley's reply had been: 'He wouldn't be riding a motorbike for a firm that made shell cases if he was.'

'Wouldn't like to say,' said Brenda, tossing her head and making her dark hair swing. 'If you ask me he looks like a bit of a wide boy, always flashing his money about. A lot of the others reckon he's a skiver. Where does he live? And is he married? Well, is he?'

Shirley didn't want to admit she didn't know, she had never thought to ask him. And would he tell her the truth if he were? 'He might have something wrong with him,' was all she could think of to say, as she had done before.

'Shirley, I think you should be very careful,' Brenda had warned her, but when Shirley thought of his kisses, she immediately forgot to be wary. She smiled to herself. His kisses were grown-up kisses, not like those she'd been given round the back of the night school. She wasn't like Ann; she had only gone to night school to learn ballroom dancing and to meet the boys.

Shirley sat looking at her sister and wondered if she should tell Lucy about her feelings for Vic. When she'd told him about Harry and Dan he'd said he wouldn't be like them going off to fight. When she asked him why, he'd kissed her cheek and told her not to worry about it. Was he ill? She hugged herself in excitement at having this secret, but she couldn't help feeling a bit worried.

Over these past nights while they were being bombed Shirley had given this a lot of thought. It was this air of mystery and his charm that had attracted her to him. But how would the family feel about her going out with someone who was a lot older than she was?

On Friday evening Shirley told her parents she was going out straight from work, and was angry when they protested.

'What if the cinema gets bombed?' said Eileen.

'They tell us if there's a raid and we can go down a shelter. Besides, if I go straight from work I'm home before he comes over.'

'That's not the point,' said her father. 'Your mother's worried sick about you.'

'I could just as easily get killed coming home from work. I've got to have a bit of life.' This was the only way she and Vic could be together. Sitting in the back row of the pictures was Shirley's idea of bliss; when he held her close and kissed her, that was sheer heaven.

'It's no good arguing with her,' said Eileen. 'You know what she's like.' But she *did* worry about her daughter every time she went to work; the thought that filled her mind was: Will I ever see her again? Reg would go mad if he knew that, so she kept her thoughts to herself.

Every day Lucy hoped the postman would find his

way to their street. Somehow letters from Dan and Ann managed to get through. It had been a couple of weeks since she'd heard from Dan, though, and she was getting worried. She'd worked out that he might be in North Africa. She'd smiled when he told her his knees were brown.

'I'm surprised we get any letters at all,' said her father. 'I reckon the postmen do a great job, 'specially when half the road's missing.'

It was Saturday and the end of the month. Great whoops of joy went up when the letterbox rattled. Lucy raced to the door. There was a letter from Ann and three from Dan and an official-looking envelope that Lucy guessed were her calling-up papers. She quickly put that one in her pocket. She would open that later. She had been waiting for her papers telling her where she had to report. She knew she was being selfish but in many ways she couldn't wait to get away from London and get a good night's sleep in a bed.

'Ann's waiting to be posted, she's not sure when. She says here she's hoping to get some leave before the move,' Lucy said. She finished Ann's letter then passed it over to her father.

'I hope they're not gonner send her too far away,' said Reg.

'I'll just go up and read Dan's letters,' said Lucy.

In the bedroom she sat down on the bed. She and Shirley were now at the front of the house, in Ann's old room. Although they didn't sleep in here as every night they went into the shelter, their clothes and bits were here. She turned on the light and looked round the drab room; although it was the afternoon it was dark as the windows were boarded up, making it gloomy and uninviting. A tarpaulin covered the roof at the back of the house and when it rained the rain beat on it like a drum and every bit of wind seemed to lift the sheet making eerie noises.

Ann was going to be very upset when she saw her dressing table. Every week she used to polish it till you could see your face in it. Heaven help you if you spilled any face powder on it. Lucy smiled and memories of those happy, carefree days when they'd sit and talk about fashions and make-up came flooding back. They used to experiment with hairstyles and argue about who was wearing whose clothes; life was very simple then. Tears ran down Lucy's cheeks. Those days would never come back again. She ran her hand over the dressing table. Deep gouges from when the window had been blown in spoiled the top and the mirror had been shattered into hundreds of little pieces. Just the wooden frame remained, holding nothing.

She took Dan's letters and began reading them. As usual they were full of love and how much he missed her. She kissed the kiss. This was something they both did: it was the nearest they could get, both knowing their lips had touched the same spot. In these letters he still didn't know she had joined up.

Lucy turned the letter from the Ministry over. This was it. Her life was about to change. She'd had her medical and interview; she had smiled when they asked her if she could ride a bike. With her fingers crossed behind her back she'd said yes, even though she'd never been on a bike in her life. She could learn. She was told to report on Wednesday 2nd October to a depot in Sussex to collect her uniform, then she would be sent to a farm. Lucy was pleased that Sussex wasn't that far away. She was now a member of the Land Army and all she had to do was go down and break the news to her mum and dad.

That same afternoon Shirley was out trying to do some shopping. She held on to Vic's arm and felt very grown up. What would her mother and father say if they knew she had a boyfriend?

He smiled down at her; Vic was head and shoulders taller than she was. His brown hair was always out of control and his laughing brown eyes gave her a thrill every time he looked at her. 'I fancy going somewhere tonight,' he said as they made their way across the road.

'Can't stay out late. Got to be home before the raids start.'

'Shirley, can't we go away for a weekend? Somewhere where we can both get a good night's sleep.' He hesitated. 'Well, after a while we can get some sleep.'

Shirley blushed. 'I can just see me mum and dad

letting me go away for a weekend. They don't even know about you.'

He stopped. 'You're ashamed of me.'

'No. No, I'm not. It's just that my mum don't like any of her daughters going away. Even though Ann and Lucy are both married she still thinks we're all little girls.'

'You know I'm very fond of you, don't you? Even if you are still a kid.'

'No I'm not. I'm seventeen.'

He tilted her head up and kissed her nose. 'And I'm an old man of twenty-eight.'

Shirley looked away. What would the family say? Vic was older than any of her brothers-in-law and she was the youngest of her sisters. And he raced around London on a motorbike. She had asked him many times why he wasn't in the forces, but he only smiled and said that he was wanted here. When he smiled his face lit up. She was so lucky that he chose to take her out when he had the pick of the factory girls. Shirley turned back and smiled up at him.

'Come on, let's see if we can find a shop that's open and sells shoes. My treat.'

Shirley's worries came flooding back. He did always seem to have plenty of money. Did he really earn that much?

'Mum. Dad. I've got me papers.'

'Well, you was expecting them. When you gotter go?' asked her father.

'Wednesday. I shall be in Sussex, so that's not too far away.'

'You won't be here then when Ann comes home,' said her mother.

'No. I'm sorry about that. I would have loved to have seen her. Who knows, we both might manage to get leave at Christmas.'

'Christmas,' repeated Eileen. 'Won't be much of a Christmas this year. That's if we're still here and got somewhere to live.'

Lucy put her arms round her mother. 'Don't talk like that, Mum.'

'Just putting me thoughts into words.'

Lucy looked at her father. He had aged so much in this past month. What did the future hold for them? 'I'll just pop over and tell Mrs Drury.'

As Lucy crossed the road her tears began to fall. What if they were killed or maimed while she was away? She desperately wanted her life to be as it was a year ago, but knew that could never be, not now.

Chapter 19

IT WAS EARLY on Wednesday morning and after all the tears, hugs and goodbyes from the family and some of the neighbours in Perry Street, Lucy was on her way. At the corner she turned and waved, her tears threatening to fall. Like Ann, she hadn't wanted anyone to go with her to the station. Those goodbyes were much too painful. She swallowed the lump in her throat. When would she see the family again? When would the bombing stop? She tried not to think about what could happen to Perry Street and her loved ones.

After fighting to get on the train she managed to find herself a seat and settle down. The train was packed with servicemen and women. She felt out of it not being in uniform. But later today she would be wearing the uniform of the Women's Land Army. Was this what she really wanted to do? Well, it's too late, she said to herself. There's no turning back now.

When she arrived at her station she was pleased to see others getting off the train and making their way towards some women wearing the Land Army uniform.

Lucy looked around hoping that perhaps Janet had been on the train.

'Name?' asked a woman holding a clipboard.

'Lucy Drury.' Lucy smiled to herself. She still hadn't got used to saying that.

'Right,' said the woman, not looking up. 'Go to that building over there and collect your uniform, then make your way to those cars.' She pointed her pen towards a couple of parked cars. 'You're being sent to a farm.'

Gradually, piled high with clothes, including boots, they were put into groups. There were only three in her group. She looked at the other two and smiled. 'I'm Lucy.'

'I'm Trudy.'

'I'm Heather.'

And that was it. They stood watching the lady with the clipboard.

She finally came up to them. 'Right, follow me.'

They trooped behind her to a shooting brake. 'I'll take Mrs Drury to her farm first, then I'll drop you others off.'

Lucy was dumbstruck. She was going to be on her own. She wanted to be with the others. This wasn't what she wanted. Where was the camaraderie everyone talked about?

They drove out into the country for quite a while. Lucy couldn't concentrate on her surroundings. They were in the middle of nowhere; all she could see were fields. They turned off onto a tree-lined drive. At the bottom was a large farmhouse; smoke was slowly curling up from some of its many chimneys. The October evening sun glinted on the windows and it looked very beautiful. The pillars each side of the front door made the house look very regal, but it was also very isolated and lonely.

The woman got out of the car, telling Lucy to follow her. Lucy picked up her uniform and, balancing her small attaché case on top, did as she was told.

The Land Army woman rang the large doorbell.

A tall thin woman with pointed features opened the door.

'Mrs Ayres?' enquired the Land Army woman.

'Yes. You're late. We were expecting you earlier.'

'The train was delayed. May we come in?'

Mrs Ayres stood to one side.

Inside was, to Lucy's eyes, magnificent. There was a large hall with rooms off; she quickly counted three doors. Up the staircase to the right was a gallery. She couldn't see how many doors were up there.

'You won't be staying in the house, you'll be above the stables,' said Mrs Ayres quickly, obviously noting the look on Lucy's face.

Lucy's heart sank.

'I'll be bringing the rest of Mrs Drury's uniform tomorrow.'

'Thank you.' Mrs Ayres almost rushed the woman out and closed the door behind her. 'Follow me,' she said to Lucy. 'And in future you always use the back of the house – through there – if you need anything. Mrs Bennett will see to you.'

Lucy followed this woman and wondered how they would get on. Perhaps the farmer was a bit friendlier.

Mrs Ayres stopped and pointed to a long building across the yard. 'That's the stable block where you'll sleep, up there. I don't look after you. Mrs Bennett will feed you in the kitchen and don't forget to give her your ration book. Mr Ayres will tell you where you will be working.' With that she turned and walked back into the house.

Before Lucy could utter a word she'd gone. Slowly Lucy made her way over to the stables and up the outside iron staircase. There was one large room and although it was sparsely furnished, to her joy she saw there were four beds and two of the beds looked as though they were in use. She put her uniform on a bed that didn't look as if it was being occupied and took her few personal things from her case. She put her picture of Dan on the small table next to the bed. All the beds had a table beside them and two had photos on them. Lucy looked at them. One was a smiling blonde girl with her arm round a sailor. The other was just of a young man in army uniform. There was one wardrobe and when Lucy looked inside she noted there weren't many clothes, just some frocks and two greatcoats. There were a few empty hangers so she hung her coat on one.

This was it. Should she put her uniform on and go

and find out what her job would be? She looked at her watch; it was almost five-thirty. What time would the others be back? She took her ration book out of her case. 'Right. First things first, I'll go and find this Mrs Bennett and see if she's got a cuppa,' she said out loud.

She went to one of the small uncurtained windows and looked out. The stable was at the back of the house and outside was a huge gravel area with a truck and all kinds of machinery dotted about. She pushed open the window; she could hear cows close by. That was something she wasn't looking forward to: milking cows.

Lucy looked at her uniform. She didn't want to put it on just yet; she felt she would look too new. She would wait and ask the other girls what was the right thing to wear.

She crept down the stairs and out into the yard. The wide stable door was open and revealed a mass of farming machinery.

'Hello there,' said a pleasant voice. 'You just arrived?' From behind a tractor stepped the young girl whose picture with a sailor Lucy had just been looking at.

'Yes.' Lucy gave a nervous laugh. 'I feel a bit like a fish out of water.'

'Don't worry.' The girl wiped her greasy hands on a piece of equally dirty rag. 'We all felt like that at first. I'm Emma.' She held out her hand.

'Lucy,' she said, taking the proffered hand and shaking it. 'Are you mending that?'

'Trying to. The spark plug keeps oiling up.'

'I wouldn't know what a spark plug is.'

'You will after a few weeks.'

'Have you been in the Land Army long?'

'About a year. When my Tom joined the navy I thought I'd better do something and as I come from a small village in Somerset I thought I'd join the Land Army. Didn't fancy being stuck in a factory. So, where are you from?'

'London.'

'Thought so.'

'What's it like here?' asked Lucy, looking around.

'Not bad. The old boy's all right but the missis can be a bit snotty – we don't see a lot of her. She does loads of charity work, always on committees doing good. With a house this size she had to help the war effort and she decided she would rather have land girls billeted on her than a lot of evacuees. She couldn't stand a horde of kids running riot.'

Lucy thought about the Conners' boys. They would have a field day here.

Emma disappeared under the bonnet of the tractor again. 'That should have fixed it. Climb up and start her up.'

'I can't get up there.'

'Why not.'

'Look at me shoes! And I've got a skirt on.'

'Hitch your skirt up and I'll tell you what button to press.'

Lucy did as she was told and Emma got behind her and gave her a push.

'Right. See that button there? When I say right, press it.'

Lucy looked down; she was showing her stocking tops and suspenders. She gave a little smile as she waited for Emma to say the word. This was a far cry from sitting behind a typewriter.

When Emma was satisfied the tractor was in working order she took Lucy to the kitchen to meet Mrs Bennett.

'This is Lucy, Mrs B.,' said Emma, sitting herself down. 'She's from London.'

'Pull out a chair, love, and I'll pour you a cup of tea. I expect you're parched coming all the way from London.'

'Yes, I am.' Lucy put her ration book on the table. She looked round the kitchen; it was huge. The whole of their house in Perry Street would fit in this one room. But it did look homely. In the middle stood a large wooden table with wooden chairs pushed underneath it. An old-fashioned range had pots simmering on the top. Whatever was in them smelled good and Lucy suddenly realised she hadn't eaten all day and was very hungry. A cup of tea was put in front of her.

'Is the bombing very bad?' asked Mrs B.

'Yes it is.'

'Have you lost any of your family?'

Lucy shook her head.

'Sorry, love. I didn't mean to upset you.'

'That's all right.'

'See you're married,' said Emma.

'Yes. Dan got back from Dunkirk. Not sure where he is now.'

'Bit like me. My Tom, we ain't married yet, he's on minesweepers. All I know is that he's in the Atlantic somewhere. I do miss him,' Emma said dreamily.

'I know what you mean.' Lucy wanted to get off the subject of Dan and her family and asked, 'Do you know what I'll have to do?'

'Most days at this time of the year I expect you'll be working out in the fields,' said Emma, sitting down next to her. 'That's unless you're on milking duty; then you'll be around here all day cleaning out the cows and seeing to the chickens.'

Mrs Bennett smiled. She looked like the farmer's wife you saw in books, round with rosy cheeks and frizzy white hair. 'That's one of the good things about being on a farm,' she said. 'Always got plenty of eggs.'

'Are there many animals?' Lucy asked tentatively.

'No, not that many. Mr Ayres sends us to other farms where we do all sorts. Depends on the time of the year. We pick spuds and fruit, stack corn, make haystacks, all sorts. It's hard work, but we have a laugh.'

'I'll give you sandwiches and a flask to take out with you,' said Mrs Bennett. 'And you must call me Mrs B., like the others.'

'Thank you. How do we get to the other farms?'

'There's a bike outside for you,' said Emma.

'I've never been on a bike.'

'Oh dear,' said Emma. 'Well, we'll have to teach you. It's a bit like swimming, once you learn you'll never forget.'

'I can't swim either.'

Emma and Mrs B. burst out laughing.

'Looks like we're in for a lot of laughs,' said Mrs B. 'Sorry, love.'

Lucy didn't know whether to laugh with them or cry. Was she going to be happy here?

Although it was October, it was warm and the kitchen door was wide open, so they easily heard the female voice shout from the yard, 'I'm home!'

'That's Trish. She's the noisy one,' said Emma.

Trish appeared in the doorway and took off her hat. A mass of reddish-coloured hair escaped. She ran her fingers through it. 'Hi, I'm Trish, are you one of the new girls?'

Lucy stood up. 'Yes. I'm Lucy.'

'Welcome.' She pulled a chair out and sat down. 'Any tea, Mrs B.? Been driving the cows into that far field. They're such dopey animals. Give me sheep any time. At least you and the dog can get them to go where you want. Mr A. been in yet to tell us what we're doing tomorrow?'

'No. Not yet. I've got the tractor started,' said Emma.

'Good for you, girl.'

Lucy looked at Trish. She was about the same age as herself. She was tall, with a full figure, and looked as if she could lift a cow that wasn't behaving. She had so much confidence. Lucy was worried. She was sure she would spend her time making mistakes and always apologising. Would a townie like herself ever really fit in?

'Have you met the young Mr Ayres yet?' asked Trish.

'No. Is he nice?'

'No,' said Emma. 'He's a right pain.'

'Why ain't he in the army?' asked Lucy.

'Deferred and just because he's got a rich dad he thinks he owns the place.'

'He will one day,' said Mrs B.

'That's no excuse for leering and trying to touch you,' said Emma.

'I told you, Em, you should always try to have a pitchfork in your hand,' said Trish, grinning. 'It's surprising how that keeps them at bay. Don't worry about it, Lucy, it's only Em he looks at and what d'you expect when she goes around in those little shorts and her top tied up. I told her all the old farmers will be having heart attacks at the sight of her.'

Lucy considered Emma. She *was* very pretty. With her blonde hair and blue eyes she was like a doll; she didn't look strong enough to round up cows or drive a tractor.

'That's enough, girls, you're frightening poor Lucy here,' said Mrs B.

Trish stood up. 'Anyway, he's not interested in married women – and he's got a girlfriend.'

'Now, girls, go and have a wash then I'll dish the dinner up.'

'What we got today?' asked Trish.

'Corned beef pie.'

'That's good. I could eat a horse.'

'Let's hope it don't come to that,' said Mrs B., smiling.

Even though it was going to be a very different life to sitting in an office, somehow Lucy knew that when she got used to it, she was going to be happy here.

Chapter 20

THIS DARK, DAMP and drizzly October morning had started early for Ann. She was eager to get home to see the family and had even managed to get a seat on the train. It was crowded with men and women from all the services who, along with their kit, took up a lot of space. Ann was surrounded, too, by the sound of many different languages since so many more countries had joined in the fight. After many stops and starts the train was finally approaching London. It had been a long journey; the carriage was stifling, full of cigarette smoke and body smells. Like most of her fellow passengers, Ann sat in silence gazing out at the destruction. Row upon row of buildings were now just huge piles of rubble.

'Bloody hell,' said one young army lad who since joining the train had had to stand. He was talking to no one in particular. 'Didn't know they'd copped it this bad.'

'Me mum told me it was dreadful,' said a fellow WAAF.

'They all right?' asked the young lad.

'Think so.'

Like Ann's, their eyes never left the window.

As soon as the train pulled into the station, doors were flung open and everybody made a dash for the exit.

It was with mixed feelings that Ann walked towards Perry Street. Her heart was beating loudly, the sound throbbing in her ears. What would she see? Was the house still there? Letters from the family were very spasmodic. Were they even still alive? Had they been injured and not told her? Part of her wanted to hurry on, but part of her wanted to turn back.

At last she was at the top of the street she had lived in all her life. She took a quick intake of breath. It looked so different. There was a huge gap on the other side of the road. Great chunks of wall stood alone and defiant with some of the bedroom wallpaper still intact. The painted roses that must once have been someone's pride were beginning to fade and the rain was helping them to peel away and blow free.

Ann looked towards number thirty-five. Thank God, it was still standing, but it did look a little war torn. There wasn't any glass in the windows and the brass knocker and white step now looked sadly neglected. Her mother had always considered it very important that both be sparkling as it showed what sort of housewife you were. Ann hurried along. She was going home.

'Ann,' yelled her mother, throwing open the kitchen

door when she heard the front door shut. 'It's so lovely to see you, wasn't sure what time you'd get here.' She held her daughter close and let her tears fall.

'The train was all over the place. Oh Mum, I've been so worried about you. Are you all all right?'

Eileen let her daughter go. 'Mustn't grumble. Mind you, a good night's sleep wouldn't come amiss.' She held Ann at arm's length. 'Don't you look smart? Your dad is that proud of you.'

'How is Dad?'

'Fed up not having a proper job. You know the docks got a right pasting?'

'So Lucy said. How you managing money-wise?'

'Him and Fred have had to go on the dole. They ain't that happy about it.'

'It must be hard for them.'

'It's their first time and it dents their pride a bit.'

'But it wasn't their fault. Have you heard from Lucy lately?'

'She seems to be all right. Said she's not so keen on cows, but the girls she's with are nice. She's not that far away. Not like you. How's Harry?'

'He's a fully fledged navigator now.'

'He did pop round when he was on leave. He only had a couple of days but he made time to come and see us. He's a good lad.'

Ann smiled. 'I know. I wish we could have got time together, but it wasn't to be. I've put in for a transfer to his station, but I don't think I'll get it. Harry's tried as well. It would be nice if we were a bit closer to each other, but there you go.'

'Your dad said he's doing a very dangerous job.'

'Yes he is, I worry about him so much.' Ann looked around at the once well-kept kitchen. 'This room is so miserable without any glass in the window.'

'I know. No point in putting it in, it'll only be blown out again in the night.'

'It's that bad?'

' 'Fraid so.'

'Any chance of a cuppa?'

'Sorry, love. I'm that excited at seeing you.' She took hold of Ann's head and kissed her forehead.

'You can tell me all the news over a cup of tea. I've got me ration card.'

'Not a lot to tell really,' said Eileen, coming back into the kitchen and putting the teapot on the table.

'Anybody we know been killed?'

'No. A couple over the back of the Conners' copped it, but we didn't know them.'

'Lucy told me about those. I bet you miss her?'

'Course. Like I miss you. Are you happy?'

'I will be now all that marching up and down's finished. That's something Lucy don't have to do.'

'I think that's why she went in the Land Army. So where're you going to go now?'

'Hereford, wherever that is. For the time being I shall still be doing shorthand and typing. But I'm hoping for something a bit more exciting.'

'I shouldn't wish for too much excitement if I was you,' said her mother knowingly.

They sat talking about everything in general but nothing in particular.

'Is it all right if I go up and put me things away? Lucy said the roof's been mended.'

'You'd be better off putting your kit bag straight in the shelter. We'll be in there again tonight. Dad's made it nice and cosy.'

Ann gave her mother a weak smile. How could a cold, bleak, brick air-raid shelter be cosy? 'I'll just pop up and have a look.' Lucy had told her about her room but it still came as a shook to see her lovely dressing table without its mirror. She ran her hand over the deep gouges; so much had changed. She tugged at the wardrobe door; it squeaked and was a job to open, being all askew and a bit rickety. There were just a few of her and her sister's clothes inside. Most of their bits and piece were in boxes under the bed. She pulled one out. Her mother had carefully folded their clothes and scribbled on the lid what was inside. Ann smiled when she read: 'Ann and Lucy's summer frocks and shoes'. Another box held handbags and hats. It was the one that had 'Wedding dress' written on the lid that made Ann catch her breath. Inside was the outfit Lucy had been married in and underneath, carefully wrapped in tissue paper, was her own beautiful dress. She gently stroked it and all the memories of that wonderful day came flooding back. It would be nice if Shirley ever wanted to borrow it. Perhaps it could become a family heirloom.

'I hope it don't go yellow,' said her mother who was standing in the doorway.

Ann stood up. 'You've gone to a lot of trouble packing all these away.'

'I didn't want anything to get spoiled.'

Ann put the lid back on and pushed the boxes back under the bed. 'I hope they'll be safe under there.'

'As safe as anything can be. Now come on downstairs and put your stuff in the shelter.'

'Will there be a raid tonight?'

'I should think so.'

Ann marvelled at her mother's attitude. 'Don't you ever get frightened?'

'Yes. Every night. But it don't do no good. Your father should be home soon. Him and Fred go out helping do repairs.'

'Mr and Mrs Drury all right?'

Eileen nodded.

'And Shirley?'

'She gets fed up going backwards and forwards to work. Sometimes it takes her quite a while to get there and back. There can be so many diversions, like if they find a wall that might be about to fall down. Then there's the unexploded bombs, or sometimes they're still trying to dig people out.'

'It's awful. I worry about Harry going over and bombing people. He said you mustn't think like that; if you did you'd never do the job you've been trained for. But I know deep down he's not happy about it.'

'I don't reckon the Germans think that.'

'I wouldn't like to say.'

'Will you have time to go and see Harry's parents?'

Ann nodded. 'I've got three days and I told him I would. They do write to me.'

'They're nice people. The old boy's been round a couple of times after there's been a really bad raid.'

Ann went over to her mother and gave her another hug. 'Mum, you're so brave.'

Eileen sniffed. 'Only the same as everybody else.'

There were more hugs and kisses when Reg came in, and when Shirley burst into the kitchen she yelled out in joy and almost smothered her big sister.

'It's really smashing to see you again. And don't you look smart? Poor Mum here's been worrying herself silly about you and Luce. Pity she's not here.'

Ann was surprised at the change in her young sister. She looked so grown up. Her hair was piled high and she was wearing a very bright red lipstick.

'How's the job?' Ann asked.

'Not bad. We have a few laughs.'

'Got a boyfriend yet?'

Shirley quickly looked over at her mother. 'No. All the best ones've been taken.' She still hadn't told them about Vic, she always said she was out with Brenda. She didn't know why she was so worried about telling them – was it because of his age, or was it because he wasn't in the forces that she was keeping him a secret?

The laughter and chatter went on till Reg said, 'Right. Time to get ready.'

'Get ready. Why? Where're we going?' asked Ann.

'Into the shelter,' said Eileen. 'We have to do this nightly ritual. Make sandwiches; fill kettles and saucepans, in case we ain't got no water in the morning. We also fill a couple of flasks with tea. You get really parched with all the dust flying about.'

'Can I do anything?' asked Ann.

'No, that's all right, love,' said her father. 'Got this off pat now.'

Ann sat and watched her father bank up the fire with coal dust.

'Got to try and keep this in. If the gas gets cut off this is the only way we can boil a kettle.' He grinned. 'Gotter have me cuppa first thing.'

Ann was amazed at the calm way her parents had settled into this way of living. When the chores were finished they all trooped into the shelter. And it did look cosy with a bit of carpet on the floor and the bunk beds. There was even a potted plant on the shelf next to the spare candles and hurricane lamp.

'Is being in the forces as great as the posters tell us?' asked Shirley, putting on her siren suit over her clothes.

'No, not really. I like that. It's very smart.'

Shirley stood up and twirled round. 'Mr Churchill wears 'em. They're ever so warm and cosy, but a bit of a pain when you have to go to the lav.' Shirley's all-in-one navy siren suit had a long zip, which she pulled up. 'Right, now, come on, tell us all about it.'

'I'll just turn the lamp down,' said her father. 'We have to save the paraffin, it's a bit hard to get hold of.'

They all settled down and, wrapping a blanket round her shoulders, Ann began to tell them about her new life.

'What're the other girls like?' asked Eileen.

'Not bad. I've palled up with Mary. Her husband's in the RAF. We're both going to the new camp together. Sharing a cold damp Nissen hut with a lot of other women can be a bit daunting. Some do smell a bit. The beds are not very comfortable – you have three small mattresses they call biscuits to lie on – but you're so tired after all the exercise that you don't care. You're in with women who snore and some who talk in their sleep, then there are those that cry. I feel really sorry for them. We spend a lot of time cleaning our shoes and polishing our buttons. One girl reckons we could blind the Germans if we all flashed our buttons at them at the same time.' She stopped as, suddenly, the guns went off, making her jump. 'Is it always as loud as this?'

'Yes, but don't worry,' said her father.

'What's the food like?' asked Eileen, trying to take her daughter's mind off the raid.

'Not good. Half the time you don't know what you're

eating as it all tastes the same,' Ann said distractedly, waiting for the next bang.

'What's the underclothes like?' asked Shirley.

'Don't be personal,' said Eileen.

'I just wonner know if they're pretty.'

Although Ann was scared she welcomed the diversion and laughed. 'I'll show you in the morning. Talk about passion-killers. We've got these long blue drawers, but at least they keep you warm.'

'Can't you wear your own?'

'Not a lot of point. Nobody sees 'em. No, I keep me best ones for when Harry comes home.'

'Thank you for that information, Ann, now settle down.'

'Sorry, Dad,' she said with a grin.

After a while Ann noticed her parents had become quieter.

'Try and get some sleep,' whispered her father after she turned over yet again. 'It could be a long night.'

Ann lay still on the bottom bunk but she knew sleep wouldn't come.

All through the night the bombs rained down and the noise from the guns was unrelenting. Ann was scared. This was the first time she'd experienced anything like this. Shirley was fast asleep. How could anyone sleep through all this racket?

'You all right, Ann?' asked her father softly.

'Yes thanks.'

'When there's a lull you can go to the lav if you want.'

'Thanks, but I'm all right.' Ann wasn't going to leave the safety of the shelter for anything; she had a strong bladder and would wait till the all clear went.

The following morning Ann was surprised that she had managed to sleep and after breakfast she went over to see Fred and Nell.

She was greeted with hugs and kisses. They wanted to know how she was getting on.

She tried to make it light-hearted. 'I didn't like the raid last night.'

'No, they do get on yer nerves,' said Fred.

'I'd love a night in me bed. To sleep all night would be a real luxury,' said Nell. 'Still, we mustn't grumble, don't do much good if we do.'

Ann was amazed at their attitude. It was almost devil-may-care, even though they were all suffering so deeply.

That afternoon she went to visit the Fishers. They were so pleased to see her and once again she was greeted like a long-lost soul. Some of the houses in their road had been bombed, but Ann was surprised at the lack of concern they showed and at the brave face everybody put on. She didn't think she would be like them if she were here now.

That night when she was in the shelter her thoughts went to Harry, Lucy and Dan. Would they ever all be together again?

* * *

When she got back to camp Mary, who lived in Dorset, wanted to know if everyone was all right. Ann told her about the raids and how strong everybody was, putting up with it defiantly.

The following day they were moved to their new base.

Chapter 21

EILEEN WOKE WITH a start. The November air was cold and she huddled down under her eiderdown. She would never get used to living like this; every night she worried that they could be killed or maimed. It was very still and silent, only the sound of Shirley's steady breathing disturbed the air and she guessed it was still dark outside. She lay quietly, straining her ears, listening. There was something wrong. No guns or clanging bells from the fire engines or ambulances. It was uncanny. She sat up. 'Reg,' she whispered. 'Reg. Are you there?'

'It's all right, love,' he answered.

'What's the time?'

Reg picked up the alarm clock and, after fishing for his pencil torch, said, 'Six o'clock.'

'Has the all clear gone?'

'We didn't have a raid.'

'What?'

'Shh. He ain't come over. I reckon some other poor buggers got it last night.'

Eileen lay back down. 'I can't believe it.'

Reg stood up and straightened his back. 'These bleeding chairs cripple me back,' he said in a hushed voice.

'I told you we can take turns on this bunk.'

'No. 'S all right once I get everything moving again. Shall I go and put the kettle on?'

'Yes please. I'll come and join you. We'll let Shirley sleep on for a bit. She shouldn't have so much trouble getting to work if there ain't been a raid.'

Eileen lay for a moment or two after Reg had left. No raids. Does this mean we can go back to our beds again? she wondered. She struggled off the bed and stood looking at her daughter sleeping peacefully. Shirley was a lovely-looking girl and even if at times – like any other mother and daughter – they had their differences, she was a good girl. Despite all her misgivings about Ann and Lucy getting married she sometimes wished that Shirley could find herself a nice, steady young man. Eileen sighed. All the nice ones had been called up.

In the kitchen Reg busied himself making the tea. He knew this lull wouldn't last. Lord Haw Haw in one of his broadcasts had told them that Hitler was going to grind them down one way or another.

Although Reg didn't know it at the time, he was right; many other towns would suffer during November.

* * *

'Shirl, I've got to go away for a bit,' said Vic as they walked to the pictures.

She hung on to his arm and looked up at him. Her heart gave its customary little flutter. 'Oh? Why?' He was so good-looking in a dark swarthy way. He did look a bit like Tyrone Power and she was still in awe that of all the girls he could have had at the factory, he had chosen her.

'Some sort of business.'

'Look at that queue,' said Shirley when they turned the corner.

Now the raids on London had eased up people were beginning to live again.

'Well, we can wait. Did you hear what I said?'

'Yes. How long will you be away?'

'Don't know. Might be away for Christmas. D'you fancy coming with me?'

Shirley was thinking fast. She'd love to go away with him but knew she had to be sensible about it. 'Where're you going?'

'Not sure yet.'

'Ain't even thought about Christmas. I'm hoping me sisters'll be home. It'll be pretty miserable without them. I don't know what to get 'em for presents.'

'Come away with me.'

'Me mum'll have forty fits if I told her I was going away with a bloke for Christmas. When you going?'

'Not sure. Could be the end of next week. So, what about it?'

'I just can't up and go with you. Me mum don't know you exist.' Shirley still always said she was going out with Brenda. She really wanted to be with Vic – that thought of it excited her – but she knew she had to be sensible. 'I can't. Me dad'll have everybody out looking for me.' She was sad that it wasn't to be.

'Can't you tell 'em you're going with that girl, what's her name?'

'Brenda. I don't think so. Besides, where would I get enough money to go away with?'

'Don't worry about money. I'll see you're all right.'

'But you don't know where you're going.'

'I will soon.'

They shuffled along with the queue; finally they were allowed in the cinema. As always, they sat in the best seats. When he put his arms round her Shirley nuzzled close to him. She couldn't concentrate on the film as she kept thinking about him. What did he do that meant he had to go away? It couldn't be very hush-hush if he wanted her to go with him. This war was making people very devious and secretive.

Lucy walked into Mrs B.'s warm kitchen. 'The others not back yet?' she asked, sitting herself down at the large scrubbed table that sat in the middle of the room.

'No. They should be home soon, it's too dark to do much more today.'

'I know Trish don't like driving along these country roads in the dark,' said Lucy.

'I'm always surprised Mr A. sends the girls to collect stuff. Some of it's very heavy. He should send young Bob.'

'Probably thinks he's more useful here and we're supposed to be fit and able.'

'That's no excuse, you're young ladies.'

Lucy wanted to laugh at that. There was no way she thought of herself as a young lady, not after some of the jobs they'd had to do.

It had been a cold and miserable misty November Saturday, the kind of day that never really got light at all, and picking sprouts was the most boring, back-breaking job – well, that was apart from digging up potatoes. Lucy looked at her hands. Her fingernails were broken and her hands chapped; she smiled: they certainly weren't typists' hands. Not any more.

'There's a letter for you.'

Lucy took the letter that was standing beside the clock on the high mantelpiece. 'It's from me sister, Ann,' said Lucy, recognising the writing. 'She was on leave a while back and now she's been posted.' She began reading it.

'Everything all right at home then?' asked Mrs B. as she bustled round putting the knives and forks on the table ready for the evening meal. As usual the smell wafting up from the pans and large cooking range were delicious.

'I hope so.'

'There's tea in the pot if you want a cup.'

'Thanks. Ann says she's settled into her new station but was sorry she missed Harry, he was on leave before her.' Lucy knew how she felt; she desperately missed Dan.

'I feel sorry for you young ones being parted so soon after getting married. Doesn't give you a chance to really get to know one another.'

Lucy smiled. She knew all about Mrs B.'s husband. He had been killed many years ago in a farming accident on this very farm. They'd never had any children and she had been working for the Ayreses before the accident. She said she always felt they kept her on out of duty, but Lucy and the other girls reckoned it was more because she was such a good cook.

This was the first letter Lucy had received since Ann's leave and it was full of how much she'd hated the raids and how she was worried about what the family endured night after night. Lucy didn't have to be told what the Blitz was like; she had been there at the beginning of the raids and now every night felt guilty when she snuggled down in her nice warm bed and thought about her parents and Shirley in the air-raid shelter. She too fretted about them, and Dan's family.

Poor Ann, she had been very upset by the bombing. Lucy was pleased and relieved when the most recent letter she'd had from her dad said they had had a few nights with no raids, but they still slept in the shelter just in case.

Lucy had been here for almost two months now. She knew she was very lucky to have been billeted on the

Ayreses' farm. Emma and Trish were good fun and they all got on very well. They had had plenty of laughs when they tried to teach her to ride a bike, but after plenty of bruises and grazed knees she'd finally managed it and was now very efficient and fast. It was the cows Lucy didn't get on well with: they were so large and mucking out wasn't the nicest of jobs. It took a while but she had learned to do the milking too; that also had brought peals of laughter when she started with milk squirting everywhere but in the pails. Mr Ayres had a lot of patience and gradually she'd mastered it and now did her share, even if on some cold, damp mornings at four-thirty she was still half asleep. Sometimes the girls were sent to other farms to help out. Emma said lambing time was best, even if you were up half the night sitting with some poor ewe. Lucy was looking forward to that. How different her life was now. She was very happy here; she knew she had done the right thing and was very proud when she went to the village in her land girl uniform.

Although Mr Ayres was kind and fair he also expected a good day's work. He was such a contrast to his slim wife, in both build and temperament. He was round and jolly with a florid face and deep blue eyes. Their son Bob was like his mother in build but had his father's temperament. Despite what Emma had said about Bob Ayres she had found him nothing but pleasant and helpful. He was a tall young man of about twenty-five and very strong. Lucy remembered how fascinated she'd been when she watched him and the vet struggle to bring a new calf into the world. That took a lot of strength. Bob had a shock of dirty blond hair that was always falling over his face and his piercing blue eyes seemed to follow you about. He did notice she was married and she told him that her husband was in the army. Perhaps he preferred blondes and thought, as Emma wasn't married yet, he stood a better chance with her even though he was supposed to be courting a girl who lived on a nearby farm.

Lucy looked up when Trish and Emma came in.

'Thought we'd be back before now,' said Trish, sitting at the table. Lifting up the teapot, she shook it. 'I'm dying for a cup.'

'Me too,' said Emma.

Lucy got up and took the cups and saucers from the huge dresser. It took up half of one wall and was full of white china with the cups hanging on hooks and plates and saucers standing in line along the back of every shelf. It was all very orderly.

'I don't know why we had to go to town, I'm sure Mr A. could have got what he wanted over the phone,' said Emma.

'Yes, but how long would he have had to wait for it to be delivered?' asked Mrs B.

Trish, who was sitting with her elbows on the table, shrugged.

'Mind you, it was better than picking sprouts,' said Emma.

'Don't remind me,' said Lucy. 'The next thing I'm gonner do is learn to drive, then I'll be able to run all the errands.'

'Well, let's hope you're better at that than riding a bike,' laughed Trish.

'I mastered it in the end, didn't I? We going to the pub tonight?' asked Lucy.

'D'you know, you're getting to be a right little boozer,' said Mrs B.

'What, on a couple of halves of shandy on a Saturday night?'

'Wish there was something else to do,' said Trish. 'I rather fancy going to a dance or the pictures.'

'Me too,' said Emma.

Lucy had to admit the farm was a bit out of the way and the last bus from town went very early. 'I suppose we could always get a taxi back if we went to a dance one night.'

'That might not be a bad idea,' said Trish. 'At least it shouldn't be that pricey, not if the three of us share.'

'Right, that's settled. We'll find out where the next dance is and we get all glammed up and paint the town red.' Lucy grinned. 'Well, perhaps not red, just a delicate shade of pink.'

Emma smiled. 'Now that's what I call a really great idea.'

That night the three of them went to the village on their bikes as usual.

'Hello, girls,' said Sheila Newman, the landlady,

when they walked into the pub. 'Hope you've wiped the cows' muck off your boots.'

Emma lifted her foot in the air. 'Look, we've got our shoes on just for you.'

Sheila leaned over the bar and looked at her highly polished shoe. 'That's all right then.'

Lucy looked forward to their Saturday night in the pub. She loved the company and often played darts with the old boys. They had great laughs as they cycled back to the farm wobbling all over the road and singing at the top of their voices.

Trish had told her they hadn't been very welcome at first; the old men had said that they didn't like young bits of girls coming in giggling and making a lot of noise and females wearing trousers was sinful. But it seemed Sheila had put them straight and told them that the girls' money was as good as theirs, which was just as well as this was the only pub in the village.

'Going home for Christmas then?' Sheila asked Lucy as she put three halves of shandy on the counter.

'Don't know. I'd like to but I've got to wait and see what Mr A. says and how many of us can be spared.' Lucy looked across at Trish and Emma who were deep in discussion with some of the locals. It would be wonderful to spend Christmas with her family. Perhaps she could broach the subject tomorrow.

Chapter 22

NOVEMBER SLID INTO December and Ann was hoping both she and Harry would get leave at Christmas. She desperately wanted to see him again; she wanted him to hold her and make love to her. At night she dreamed she was in his arms. Ann knew he had been on some very heavy raids over Germany and she worried about him constantly.

The new base she had been sent to was operational. It was very large with many WAAFs and airmen. The planes went constantly back and forth to Germany on bombing raids. To her annoyance she was still a secretary; although she knew her job was important it still didn't stop her from wanting to do more.

Ann had been pleased that Mary had been posted with her; she was in the ops room. Usually when they finished their shift they returned to their billet together.

'Been a busy day?' asked Ann as they huddled round the big black stove that sat in the middle of the room.

'No, not really, not with this weather.'

They sat listening to the rain beating down on the roof of the Nissen hut.

Mary pulled her greatcoat round her shoulders. 'D'you know, I don't think I'll ever get used to trying to put on a brave face when you're tracking a plane and it don't return.'

'Some of them are so young.'

'I know. It's bloody cold in here,' said Mary, holding out her hands to feel the warmth from the fire.

'We could go along to the NAAFI, at least it's warm in there.'

'I don't fancy getting wet again, it's chucking it down out there. What about you?'

'I'm fine just sitting here.'

'Me too.'

Ann found it was nice to sit quietly and mull her own thoughts over, and she knew Mary felt the same.

The NAAFI was usually full of noise and laughter when the young men returned and let their hair down – and they were young men, just lads some of them. When Ann stood and watched the planes take off she knew this was the life Harry was leading. It was perilous and she badly wanted to be with him.

'Have you put in for leave at Christmas?' she asked Mary.

'No, not a lot of point. I'll wait till Joe gets some time off.'

'Thought I'd try. Harry's hoping to do the same. It'll be wonderful if we could spend a few days together.'

'Don't get your hopes up, you know what it's like, you ask for one thing and they give you something else.' Mary paused to take a drag on her cigarette. 'Though I mustn't grumble. I'm doing a job I really enjoy.'

'Don't remind me. I put in again to be in the ops room, but was turned down.'

'Well, you're very important. Not many can do shorthand and typing.'

'It don't seem very important to me.'

They sat and chatted for a while longer then, as some of the others came in shaking the rain off their waterproofs, they went to their beds.

Ann lay thinking about Harry and her family. It would be lovely to see them again. Thank goodness the raids on London had eased up. In his last letter, her father had told her they risked some nights sleeping in their beds and when she made her weekly phone call to Harry's parents they told her the same. Harry did most of his flying at night so they'd arranged that she phone him on a Sunday morning whenever she could. She would stand eagerly in the phone box waiting for him to reply, always relieved when she heard him speak; she knew then that he was still safe. She would hang on to his every word till someone banged on the glass. She adored the sound of his voice and him telling her how much he loved her. She would walk back to the hut sad, but happy at the same time. She turned over and tried to remember how his arms felt when they were wrapped around her. She could be seeing him soon, but she wasn't looking forward to spending nights in the shelter with him surrounded by others. She didn't want to share him.

It was cold and damp as Eileen and Nell made their way to the market to spend hours going from one queue to the next. They started in the butcher's queue as they'd heard he had some sausages.

'Having glass in the windows again is smashing,' said Nell. 'Never thought I'd look forward to cleaning winders in this weather.'

'I'm glad I had plenty of curtains. It gives you a bit of a lift to look out again and not have the light on all day.'

'Reckon we've spent a fortune feeding the electric meter.'

'I know.'

'Don't take much to please us, does it?' Nell grinned.

'I'm really looking forward to Ann coming home. Lucy's still hoping, so I'm keeping me fingers crossed. Look, me and Reg was talking and, well, why don't you and Fred come over and have Christmas dinner with us? We could share whatever we've got.'

'D'you know, that'll be really nice. We can sort out what we want next week, that'll give us a few days to see what we finish up with.'

'That way we'll only have to worry about coal for one fire.'

'I'll bring over a couple of lumps of coal.'

Eileen laughed. 'You gonner wrap it in Christmas paper?'

'Would if I could find any.'

'Mind you, it's decent of them to give us a bit extra tea and sugar,' said Eileen.

'I bet those toffs don't go without,' said Nell.

'Or take lumps of coal to their mates,' said Eileen. 'Can't see any of them queuing up like this for a couple of sausages.'

They shuffled forward. 'I wouldn't mind if they tasted like sausages but they taste more like sawdust.'

'I hope me Christmas pudding's all right. I used that receipt that Lord Woolton gave us. Mind you, Reg didn't like the idea of using carrots instead of dried fruit.' Eileen looked about her and whispered to Nell, 'Mrs Toms let me have a half a pound of dried fruit so it won't be all carrots.'

'She let me have some as well,' said Nell, furtively touching her lips.

'I'm really excited that both the girls might be here together. Mind you, it's gonner be a bit crowded in the shelter.'

'I thought we'd finished with that lark. I must admit that most nights we start off in bed.'

'Thank God the raids ain't as bad. Don't think me nerves could have stood much more of that night after night.'

'I hope Lucy can make it. I'm dying to see her in uniform. I bet she looks lovely,' said Nell.

'It's my Shirley I worry about. Somehow she seems to have lost her sparkle.'

'She'll be all right when the girls get home. Then you won't be able to get a word in edgeways.'

'I hope so. It would be smashing if Dan and Harry was home as well.'

'No chance of that, Gawd only knows where my Dan is, poor little bugger.' Nell gave a sniff.

Eileen patted her friend's arm. 'One of these days we shall all be together.'

Nell blew her nose. 'And what a day that'll be.'

'I should say.'

They were pleased when they managed to get half a dozen sausages. Alf was trying to be fair to all his customers.

'Gonner have a feast tonight,' said Nell grinning as she put her six in her bag.

They continued wandering from queue to queue trying to fill their shopping bags.

'I'm going ho-ome,' sang Lucy as she danced round the table.

'I told you that Mr A.'s not a bad old stick,' said Mrs B.

'Two whole days,' said Lucy. 'I'm so glad the raids on London have eased off a bit. Mum said they spend some nights in bed. Can't say I fancy sleeping in the shelter, not after me warm cosy bed here.'

Emma and Trish smiled at her excitement. They'd heard about the appalling bombing raids on other towns and cities but so far there hadn't been any where they lived so they didn't know what Lucy's family had been through.

'I'm glad we're all going,' said Lucy. 'It would have been awful if one of us had had to stay.'

'I'm sure Bob and Mr A. can manage for a couple of days without you,' said Mrs B.

'Make them appreciate what little gems we are,' said Emma.

'I know, but getting up at half-four on Christmas morning to do the milking . . .' said Lucy. She shuddered.

'Don't let them hear that you feel sorry for them,' said Trish. 'Otherwise they might ask you to stay.'

'No way,' said Lucy, clutching her travel permit and waving it in the air.

Christmas Eve found Ann and Lucy travelling home from different directions. Both were experiencing overcrowded, noisy trains, but neither of them cared. They were going home.

Ann was desperately hoping Harry would be home too. This would be their first Christmas together as man and wife. He wouldn't know till the last minute whether he'd get leave. She could remember every word in his letter and blushed at its contents. He was a very romantic man and she knew that they could have three days of bliss.

Lucy couldn't get a seat and had to stand. Her kit bag was at her feet and she stood guard over it, defying anyone to dare touch it. She smiled to herself in glee at what it contained. There was a chicken, some eggs that Mrs B. had carefully wrapped in newspaper and put in a tin for safe keeping, and also some of the sprouts that she'd been picking for days. But it was the jar of cream that brought back so many memories. The day she broke her mum's jug was the first time Dan held her in his arms. Now she was married to him and he was away fighting and she was working on the land. What stories they would have to tell their children. If only he were here. She wanted him to hold her and make love to her. She blew her nose. It wouldn't do for anyone to see her crying.

Lucy was home first and her hat was knocked askew as she was hugged and kissed by Eileen and Reg.

'I can't believe it. You're home,' said Eileen, holding her daughter close again.

'And don't you look the smart one,' said Reg, beaming with pride.

Lucy cried, she couldn't help herself. Her parents were safe even though they looked tired and older. 'I see we've got glass in the windows,' she sniffed, trying to hide her feelings.

'We've decided to sleep down here now, in the

kitchen,' said Eileen. 'It saves all that dragging the bedding down if we have a raid.' She stopped. 'Let me take your coat.'

'What the bloody hell have you got in this?' asked Reg as he lifted Lucy's kit bag.

'Just you wait and see,' she said, beaming.

Eileen's eyes were like saucers as with a flourish the contents of the kit bag were laid out on the table. 'A chicken and eggs and cream,' she said in disbelief.

'There's some butter that I helped churn as well,' said Lucy proudly.

'A real feast,' said Eileen. 'This is gonner be a fair old Christmas.'

'I don't think these country people even know there's a war on, they don't seem to go short of much,' said Lucy, standing back.

'So they feed you all right then?' asked Eileen.

'I should say so. How are you managing?'

'It can be hard, but we get by.'

'Your mother can perform miracles,' said Reg.

'Nell and Fred are going to spend Christmas Day with us.'

'That'll be lovely. How are they?'

'Like most of us, a bit tired and battle-scarred,' said Reg.

'I'll put the kettle on,' said Eileen.

'Any idea what time Ann will be here?'

'No. It depends on the trains,' called her mother from the scullery.

Lucy sat back. This kitchen wasn't as grand as the farm's: the ceiling had been patched up; the ornaments had been removed; even the mirror over the fire had gone and a small one stood perched on the mantelpiece instead; but this was home, this was where she really belonged. These two days were going to fly by and she had to savour every moment of it.

It was dark by the time Ann turned in to Perry Street. The houses that had been bombed looked frightening. They reminded her of broken jagged teeth, the way they reared up against the dark sky. When she heard footsteps behind her she hurried on.

'Ann. Ann. Is that you?'

She stopped and turned round and Shirley came bounding up to her and hugged her tight.

'It's you,' Ann said, kissing her young sister's cheek. 'I thought I was being followed.'

Shirley laughed. 'Daft ha'p'orth. I thought you was supposed to be a big brave airwoman who was fearless in the face of the enemy.'

'Don't you believe it – I ain't very brave. And not so much of the big, thank you.'

They linked arms and proceeded to carry on to number thirty-five.

'Oh, it's so good to see you again,' Ann exclaimed.

'I wonder if Lucy's home yet? This is gonner be a great Christmas. I've really missed you two,' Shirley replied.

Ann patted her arm. 'And it's good to be home.'

'Will Harry be coming too?'

'I don't know. He has put in for leave, but it all depends if they let them off the base.'

Shirley pushed open the front door. 'Let me go in first. I want to surprise 'em.'

'Don't be daft, they know I'm coming home.'

No sooner had she spoken than the kitchen door was flung open and Eileen rushed up the passage.

'Shut that door,' yelled Reg. 'Or we'll have Charlie coming round shouting at us.'

Shirley and Ann quickly shut the front door and Ann fell into her mother's arms. Lucy came and hugged her sisters.

'I can't believe I've got all my girls here, together.' Eileen dabbed her eyes on the bottom of her pinny.

'Are you lot gonner stay in the passage or are you coming in here?' Reg was standing at the kitchen door.

Ann ran and threw her arms around him. 'It's great to be home. And look at you,' she said to Lucy. 'Don't you look the smart one.'

Lucy twirled round. She was very proud of her uniform.

'What're the cows like?' asked Shirley.

'Big and daft. It's getting up at four-thirty I don't like, especially these cold dark mornings.'

'Look what Lucy's brought,' said Reg, bringing in the chicken. 'And we've got eggs and cream and butter.'

'Wow,' said Shirley, 'this is gonner be a real Christmas feast.'

Eileen sat and admired her daughters. They had grown up into beautiful young women and two of them were married. 'Is there any chance of Harry getting home?'

'He's still hoping although I don't think he's gonner make it. But he'll be here if he can.'

Eileen looked at Lucy. There was no way she would be seeing her husband. 'Wait till you see what your dad's done in the front room,' she said, hoping to lighten the sullen atmosphere.

One by one they trooped up the passage and Reg threw the door open with a flurry.

'You've got a tree!' said Shirley. 'Where did you get that from?'

Reg touched his nose. 'It ain't a tree, it's a load of branches. I went over the park this morning and helped meself.'

'When we got the box of decorations out we found we had a lot of green crepe paper, so we sat and wound it round the branches.' Eileen stood admiring their handiwork. 'It don't look bad now we've put the baubles on it.'

'And we thought we'd put a few decorations up, just to make it feel a bit more like Christmas,' said her father as he put his arm round both Ann and Lucy.

'Not been able to get you a lot in the way of presents,' said Eileen.

Lucy could feel the tears trickling down her cheeks

again. She dabbed at her eyes. 'Don't worry, Mum. Being here all together is enough.'

Ann took her mother's hand. 'I'll second that.'

'Come on. It's cold in here,' said Eileen. 'We can light a fire in here tomorrow. Nell's bringing over a couple of lumps of coal to help out.'

Shirley laughed. 'Is that why you invited 'em, just to get a couple of lumps of coal?'

'This is wartime,' said Reg, grinning, 'and we have to get things any way we can.'

For Lucy this was going to be the best day since her wedding day, even if her Dan wasn't with her.

As for Shirley, she just longed to tell the family about the lovely bracelet that Vic had given her for Christmas. She'd been over the moon when last week he'd been outside the factory waiting for her. She did so want to tell them about him, but what was there to tell? And would her father approve?

All Ann wanted was for Harry to be here.

Reg looked round at his womenfolk and smiled. Nothing was going to stop them from enjoying this Christmas. He had his girls around him and to him and Eileen that was all that mattered.

Chapter 23

LATER THAT EVENING after Lucy had been warmly greeted by Nell and Fred she slowly made her way back across the road. She looked up at the night sky. There was something comforting about the large barrage balloons swaying gently high above her. As usual her thoughts went to Dan. How would he be spending Christmas? It was wonderful when she got his letters. Where was he and how long would it be before she saw him again?

Pushing open the kitchen door Lucy smiled to see the bedding laid out all over the floor.

'Are you fire-watching, Dad?' asked Ann.

'No, love, not tonight. It's me night off.'

'At least it's nice and warm down here,' said Eileen, smiling as she settled down.

'D'you have to wear big knickers like Ann?' Shirley asked Lucy after the girls had got undressed in the scullery. They didn't want to do that sort of thing in front of their father.

'No, the Land Army's not like the forces, but we do

wear them as it can be very cold at four in the morning when you have to do milking.'

'I don't think I could milk a cow,' said Shirley.

'I was terrified of 'em at first, but now I give 'em a slap on the rump and they do what I want. They're soppy things really. It's the mice and rats you have to frighten away.'

'I hope we ain't got mice,' said Ann, suddenly sitting up. 'Can't say I fancy them running all over me.'

'Don't even think about it,' said Shirley. 'I get worried about spiders every time I go to the lav.'

'It's rats in the barns that we have to put up with. They make nests in the haystacks.' Lucy plumped up her pillow.

'Ain't you frightened of 'em?' squealed Shirley.

'Not now. You only have to make a lot of noise and they run. But they do a lot of damage and eat the grain and stuff.'

'Can't say I like the idea of that,' said Eileen. 'Do they make the bread with it?'

Lucy laughed. 'No, it's food for the animals.'

'Now come on, girls, settle down now,' said Reg.

'Will Father Christmas be calling?' asked Shirley.

'Shouldn't think so,' said Ann. 'If he gets caught in a searchlight he'll probably get shot down.'

The giggling went on and Reg told them to be quiet a number of times but the girls couldn't stop talking and chuckling. Eileen was happy to hear laughter in the house again. Even Shirley looked relaxed.

'You won't think it's funny if we all have to troop out to the shelter later on. You'll be moaning you ain't getting your beauty sleep,' said Reg. But he was smiling as he turned over, full of joy, like Eileen, to have his family around him.

After a while they did settle down and silence fell, but the girls were all thinking about Christmas Eves in the past. They had been happy days full of excitement at what the next day would bring. Things were very different now.

Christmas morning arrived and Reg left his warm comfortable spot and, climbing over the girls, made his way to the scullery.

'Father Christmas ain't been,' said Shirley, sitting up and patting the bottom of her bedclothes.

'I'm not surprised,' said Eileen. 'Not with all the racket you three were making.'

'We didn't have a raid last night then,' said Lucy.

'No, thank goodness. I must admit I feel a lot safer sleeping down here,' said Eileen.

'And it's a lot warmer with Dad keeping the fire banked up,' said Shirley.

'When your dad's finished making a cup of tea you girls can take it in turns to have a wash, then I'll get that chicken in the oven.'

When the tea was brought in the girls all disappeared and brought in the presents they had put in the front room under the tiny tree.

Eileen was almost overcome with emotion as she sat and watched her daughters sitting in their pyjamas all laughing and talking at once as presents were handed round. She had been busy knitting socks, gloves and scarves from bits of wool she had unpicked from old jumpers.

'These will be great when I'm mucking out,' said Lucy, holding up a gloved hand. 'Thanks, Mum.'

'I love these socks, they'll keep me little tootsies warm at night,' said Ann.

There were kisses and hugs as Lucy handed out some small bits of jewellery she had managed to find in a second-hand shop. There were small brooches for her mother and sisters. 'I know you can't wear yours with your uniform,' she said to Ann, 'but when Harry's home you can wear it with your civvies.' For her father she had got a new cut-throat razor.

'This is lovely, Luce,' he said, grinning. 'Can't find 'em up here and it's getting a bit of a job to put a good edge on me old one.' He waved his present in the air. 'So listen, all of you, you'd better behave yourselves.'

'Thinks he's Sweeney Todd,' joked Eileen.

Ann had managed to find some second-hand books for all the family. 'I've got a couple for Harry's parents as well.'

Shirley smiled when the presents she gave out were accompanied with lots of oohs.

'You clever girl,' said Ann. 'A new lipstick and a pot

of Bourjois rouge. How did you manage to get hold of this?'

Lucy was tearing the paper off her gift. She scrambled over the bedding and gave Shirley another hug. 'I've got some as well.'

By now Shirley was beaming. When she'd told Vic she didn't know what to get her sisters for Christmas he had come up with the make-up and some chocolates for her mother. When she asked him how he had managed it and how much did she owe him, he told her not to worry. 'Just you and your sisters enjoy it.'

For her father she had bought some cigarettes. Her presents certainly pleased everyone and her mother was intrigued as to where she'd got all these lovely things.

'From one of the girls at the factory,' she said nonchalantly.

'I hope it's all legal,' said her father.

Shirley shrugged. 'All I know is I paid what they asked.'

As the morning went on Ann kept going to the front-room window hoping that Harry would appear.

'If he has got leave won't he want to see his parents?' asked Eileen.

'Mum, I'm his wife. I should come first.'

'I know, but he might not have got home till late last night and be stopping till after dinner.'

'If he's home he'll be round here as fast as he can,' said Lucy.

'Yes, I know. If he's not here today I'll go and see Mr and Mrs Fisher tomorrow; he might have phoned them.'

At last they all sat down to dinner. Lucy and Ann were wearing civvies for the first time in months.

Eileen looked round the table. She felt very proud but upset that two who should be there were missing. She said a silent prayer for Harry and Dan who were now part of her family. She looked across at Nell and although her friend was smiling Eileen knew she was thinking the same.

Shirley had managed to extract a few twigs from the tree and with a few old ribbons and one of the many candles that were always at hand had made a very pretty table decoration.

'That's really nice,' said Nell who was looking very smart in the frock she had bought for Lucy and Dan's wedding. 'You're very clever.'

'And I like these paper hats,' said Fred, adjusting his crown.

Shirley had laughed when they put on the paper hats she'd made out of newspaper. 'You all look really smart,' she said. 'It's surprising what you can do with a bit of newspaper and some flour and water paste.'

Eileen was delighted to see her youngest daughter in high spirits again.

Shirley was thrilled to have her sisters around. If only she could have put on her lovely bracelet but how could she explain where it came from? And where *did* it come from? When she'd asked Vic he'd told her it was a secret. It was lovely and looked very expensive, definitely not the sort of thing you would buy for yourself.

'You're quiet, Shirley,' said Lucy after they'd finished the Christmas pudding and were sitting drinking a cup of tea. 'What dark secret are you hiding from us?'

Shirley could feel herself blushing. 'Ain't got a dark secret. Only wish I had.'

After a while Lucy and Ann decided they would do the washing up and they left everybody in the front room.

'What's this?' asked Ann as she lifted the white enamel bowl up.

Lucy had a look. 'It's a washer.'

'The bowl got a hole in it and as you can't get new ones that's the only way Dad could mend it,' said Shirley, coming into the scullery.

Ann and Lucy burst out laughing.

'This really is make do and mend,' said Ann.

'You all right, Shirl?' asked Lucy. 'You look a bit down.'

'I really miss you two.'

Lucy put her arm round her sister. 'And we miss you.'

'You've both got such exciting lives, mine's just the same. Trying to sleep at night. Not going out much. I'm really fed up with it.'

'Why don't you try and get yourself a nice boyfriend?' said Ann, swirling soda in the water. 'There must be one where you work.'

'There is. In fact we do go out sometimes.'

'Is he nice?' asked Lucy.

Shirley smiled and nodded.

'Well then, bring him home.'

'I don't think Mum and Dad would approve. Look how she was when you two wanted to get married.'

Ann dropped the plate she was washing back in the water with a splash. 'You want to get married?'

'No. I don't know.'

'What's he like?' asked Lucy, wiping the plate she was holding round and round.

'He's a lot older than me. He's not in the forces.'

'Why?' asked Ann.

'I don't know.'

Ann turned and looked at her young sister. 'Is he exempt?'

'I don't think so. I don't know.'

'Shirley, he's not a conchie, is he?' asked Lucy.

'No, I don't think so,' she said again.

'Well, this is a right turn-up for the book,' said Ann, resuming her job. 'You don't know much about him then?'

Shirley shook her head.

'So you don't know if he's married?'

'No, but he would have told me.'

Ann laughed. 'Not if he wanted his wicked way.'

'How old is he?' asked Lucy.

'Twenty-nine a few weeks ago.'

'Bloody hell,' said Ann. 'What's he like?'

Shirley smiled. 'Tall, dark and handsome. In fact he looks a bit like Tyrone Power.'

'I hope he's all right.' Ann frowned. 'And you've not just been swept away by his good looks.'

'Look, Shirley, just be careful,' said Lucy. 'It's a pity we ain't got time to meet him and find out a bit about him. Do you like him very much?'

'Yes I do. You won't say nothing to Mum and Dad, will you?'

'No, course not. But please be careful. You don't want to find yourself in the family way. That would really break Mum and Dad's heart.'

'I won't,' she said as she left the scullery.

'Well, that was a bit of a surprise,' said Lucy. 'What do you think?'

'Dunno. If only we were here to keep an eye on her.'

'I agree. D'you think he's all right? Why ain't he in the forces?'

Ann wiped her hands on the towel that hung behind the door. 'I don't know.'

'You sound like Shirley.'

'Well, I've never met the bloke, have I?'

'What if he's married?'

'I can't answer that. Come on, finish putting these things away and let's get back in the front room,' said Ann.

'It does make me feel a bit guilty, leaving her here looking after Mum and Dad.'

Ann nodded. 'I know what you mean.'

Soon Lucy and Ann wandered back into the front room. Fred and Reg were asleep and Eileen and Nell were sitting talking quietly. Shirley was sitting on her own with the book Ann had bought her.

Lucy's heart went out to her. All the waywardness and liveliness seemed to have gone out of her; she looked so alone and so vulnerable.

All evening they played cards and board games, then all too soon bedtime came.

'Well, let's hope he lets us have a decent night's sleep tonight,' said Nell as she stood at the front door with Fred.

'I'll be over in the morning to say goodbye,' said Lucy as she gave them a hug.

'Pity you couldn't have been here a bit longer,' said Nell.

'Someone's gotter feed the chickens and milk the cows.'

Fred laughed. 'These are funny days.'

Lucy closed the door. She leaned against it and wondered about the future. As Fred had said, these were indeed funny days. Would they ever be right again?

Chapter 24

ON BOXING DAY Lucy woke with a heavy heart. Today she had to go back to the farm. Although part of her wanted to go she didn't want to leave her family. Since joining the Land Army she had got used to getting up early and as she lay listening to the snores of her father she smiled. Her mother was muttering and the only sound from Shirley and Ann was their steady breathing. How long would it be before they were all together again? And what about Shirley? Lucy and Ann had voiced their opinions to each other and both were worried about their young sister. What was this bloke like? What was he doing going out with someone years younger than he was? And why wasn't he in the forces? Shirley said he worked at the factory but surely that wouldn't make him exempt? What if there was something wrong with him? She couldn't bear it if anything happened to her sister over this bloke. On her next leave, she determined, she would try and find out all about him.

Ann turned over and opened her eyes; she was face to face with Lucy.

'Shh,' said Lucy softly. 'Don't wake 'em.'

'I must go out for a pee,' Ann murmured.

Lucy watched her sister carefully ease herself up.

'This floor's hard. Wish we was in bed,' was Ann's whispered comment as she carefully stepped across the row of bodies.

Lucy wanted to laugh. Who'd have thought that they would end up sleeping with their dad? But what about those who had to sleep in public shelters and the Underground? That must be worse, being with complete strangers.

Gradually everybody woke up. The bedding was taken upstairs and a breakfast of scrambled eggs was put on the table.

'When you coming home again, Luce?' Shirley asked, filling her mouth with toast.

'I don't know.'

'Well, I hope it's soon. I love having a breakfast like this.'

'Thanks very much. Is that all I'm wanted for, me eggs and chicken?'

Although everybody laughed they all knew it was going to be sad today when Lucy left them.

When she was ready to leave Nell and Fred came over to say goodbye.

'This is a lot lighter than when you arrived,' said Reg, picking up her kit bag.

One by one Lucy kissed them. She was so near to tears but knew she mustn't break down. When she held Ann she whispered, 'I hope everything's all right with Harry.'

'So do I,' said Ann.

'Now, you've got Mrs Ayres's phone number so if you ever need me you can give her a ring, but make sure it's an emergency. She gets annoyed if she has to come looking for us.'

'Can't see me ever using one of those things,' said Eileen.

'Or me,' said Nell.

So once again Lucy found herself on the train. It had been lovely seeing the family again, but it had gone much too fast. Christmas was all over.

Later that morning Ann got herself ready to go and see Mr and Mrs Fisher. She was pleased she had another day with the family, and she and Shirley were singing along with the wireless.

Suddenly there was a loud rat-a-tat-tat on the door-knocker. Everybody stood still and looked at each other.

'Who's banging like that?' asked Reg as he made his way up the passage.

They listened to the voices at the front door. Then the front door closed and Reg made his way back into the kitchen.

'Ann. It's for you.' He held out a small buff-coloured envelope.

Eileen took a sharp intake of breath.

'It can't be,' said Ann, staring at the envelope in her hand. 'Who knows I'm here?'

'I don't know. D'you want me to open it?' asked her father.

Ann shook her head. 'It might be from Harry telling me he's coming home.' Ann was smiling as she quickly ran her fingers along the envelope. 'No, it's from Mary,' she said as she read out the name before reading its contents.

'What's she doing sending you a . . .' Eileen's voice trailed off as she saw Ann's face turn a deathly white, her hand trembling as she read the paper.

'She says there's a telegram for me to say that Harry's been shot down.' Ann crumpled into the armchair and Shirley began to cry.

'Why's she sending you this?' asked Reg.

'I gave her this address in case anything happened. We all do it.' Ann couldn't take her eyes off the telegram; she couldn't believe it.

'It don't say anything else?' asked Eileen.

Ann shook her head. 'No.' She read out loud: 'So sorry. Stop. Harry's plane been shot down. Stop. Telegram here. Stop.'

'Why couldn't she wait till you got back and saw it for yourself?' asked Shirley.

'She knew I'd rather be with me family and not have the shock of it when I got back.'

'She could have said more,' said Reg.

'Telegrams are expensive,' said Eileen.

'I've got to get over to Harry's parents. I've got to tell them.'

'D'you want me to come with you?' asked Shirley.

'No thanks. I'll be all right.'

'Are you sure, Ann?' asked her father.

'I said I was, didn't I?'

'Dad was only trying to be helpful, love,' said her mother, concerned at her daughter's seeming lack of emotion.

'I know. I'm sorry. I'll be all right.'

She picked up her gas mask and, ramming the telegram in her shoulder bag, was out of the door.

When it closed behind her Shirley wiped her eyes and said, 'She didn't cry.'

'She's in shock,' said Reg quietly.

'She shouldn't be on her own,' said Eileen.

'She don't want us,' said Shirley, sniffing.

'Please God don't let him be killed,' said Eileen.

Reg put his arm round her shoulder. 'He might have been shot down over England. Then he'll be in hospital if he's injured.'

'But what if it was over Germany?' asked Shirley.

'He could end up a prisoner of war,' said Reg seriously.

Ann was in a dream as she got on the bus and off again. Her mind was full of Harry. She had to get back to camp to see the telegram. Mary hadn't said he was dead, but then she wouldn't, that was much too personal. Perhaps he was in hospital. Her mind was going over and over all the possibilities.

Suddenly she realised she was standing ringing the Fishers' front-door bell. She didn't remember walking up the road. The door was opened and Mr Fisher yelled out, 'It's Ann.'

Mrs Fisher came hurrying to the door as Ann was being crushed by her father-in-law.

'Ann, it's so lovely to see you and don't you look . . .' She stopped as Ann's tears began to fall.

She was ushered inside and sat down in an armchair, unable to control her tears.

'What is it, Ann?' asked Mr Fisher.

She took the telegram from her bag and handed it to him. 'This came this morning,' she sobbed.

He read it and then passed it to his wife.

Mrs Fisher sat as if in a trance. 'My boy. My boy,' she whispered.

'She didn't say what was in the telegram?'

'No,' Ann sniffed. 'I gave her my address in case anything happened.'

'Can we phone her and ask her what happened?'

'No, not if she's on duty. I'm so sorry.' Ann wiped her streaming eyes. 'I was hoping he'd phoned you and told you he'd been shot down but the plane had made it back to England. I love him so much.' Her tears were still falling.

Ann could see Mrs Fisher was trying to put on a

brave face as she patted Ann's hand. 'It's so unfair, you've had such little time together.'

'He's your son. This is awful. If only there was something we could do.'

Mrs Fisher's tears began to fall then and Ann quickly put her arms round her mother-in-law. 'I'm so, so sorry.'

'We must try and look on the bright side,' said Mr Fisher. 'Hopefully before long we may hear some good news.'

'I have to go back tomorrow,' said Ann. 'As soon as I can I'll let you know more.'

'This is such a terrible war,' said Mrs Fisher to no one in particular. 'So much killing.'

For the rest of the afternoon they sat talking about Harry. It was heartbreaking for Ann. She wanted him here with her.

She told them that Lucy had gone back to the farm and about what she'd had for Christmas. 'I'm so sorry. I've bought you both a book; they're second hand, I'm afraid, but in very good condition. But I've left them at home.'

'That's all right; we understand. Don't worry about it.' Mr Fisher, a tall upright man, sat slumped in the chair; he had aged in the last hour or so.

Suddenly Ann wanted to leave; she felt like an intruder. She wanted her own family with her. She needed her mum to hold her and make things better like she always had done when Ann was a child. She desperately needed a shoulder to cry on.

Ann said her goodbyes and promised to phone as soon as she could. Then she was on her way home. She sat on the bus trying to erase the horrible thoughts from her mind. Was Harry dead? Fear gripped her. She had to go back to camp tonight. She had to see that telegram. She wanted to scream out that it wasn't fair, she loved Harry so much. If Harry was dead she was too young to be a widow.

Lucy arrived at the farm first. Mrs B. folded her in her big wobbly arms when she walked into the large warm kitchen.

'Did you have a nice Christmas?' asked Mrs B., pouring her out a cup of tea.

'I should say so. Mum and Dad were ever so pleased with all the goodies you gave them. What about you?'

'Went to church for midnight mass and then back here again. Had dinner with them.' She cocked her head towards the door. 'Then went to bed.'

Lucy grinned. 'It's a pity in some ways we weren't here, we could have had a bit of a rumpus.'

'I'm a bit too old to be having a rumpus, as you put it.'

'But we have got the New Year to let our hair down. I wonder what we'll be doing? Wouldn't mind going to one of those dances again. They were good fun.'

Mrs B. laughed. 'Well, make sure you get a proper lift next time.'

They had been along to the next village for a dance,

but only once as getting home had proved a bit of a problem. There hadn't been any taxis and they'd had to hitch a lift on the milk lorry.

'Suppose we could go on our bikes.'

They were laughing at the thought when Emma walked in.

'Hello, Em, had a nice time?' asked Lucy although she could see she didn't look very happy.

Emma sat at the table. 'No, not really.'

'What's wrong?' asked Lucy.

'My gran died over Christmas.'

'Oh Em, I'm so sorry. Was she very old?'

'Ninety. She'd had a good innings.'

'That's a good age,' said Mrs B. 'Would you like a little brandy in this tea?' she asked, pushing a cup in front of Emma.

Emma nodded.

'Purely medicinal,' said Mrs B., taking a bottle of brandy from the larder.

They were having their evening meal when Trisha walked in. It was raining and she was very wet.

'Get those wet things off,' said Mrs B. 'I'll put your shoes next to the fire. There's some stew left.'

Trish sat at the table and grinned. 'This is like being home. You're like a mother to us.'

Lucy looked round. She was very lucky. Although the work was hard she had girls she got on with and Mrs B. was wonderful – she treated them like her own daughters. But she did miss her own family and it had been lovely to be home for Christmas, especially to be with her sisters again. How much longer would this war last – and how would she settle down to being a housewife after it was over? Her thoughts strayed to nights with Dan, cuddling up in his arms; she knew just how happy she'd be with her wonderful husband.

Chapter 25

'ANN, WHAT D'YOU mean you're going back tonight?' asked her mother as she watched her daughter pack her kit bag. 'You don't have to go back till tomorrow.'

'I know, Mum, but I can't sit here wondering what that telegram said. Besides, I'll be better off working.'

Eileen wandered downstairs.

'You can't persuade her to change her mind then?' asked Reg.

Eileen shook her head. 'No. You know what she's like. But then again I can't blame her. It must be really horrible not knowing what's happened to your loved one.'

Reg looked at Eileen. He knew how much she hated to see any of her daughters upset.

It wasn't long before Ann came into the kitchen. 'I'm sorry, Dad, but I really must try and find out what's happened to Harry.'

'We understand, love,' said Reg.

'Will you get some more leave soon?' asked Eileen.

'I shouldn't think so. But I'll write as soon as I get back.'

'What about Lucy?' asked her mother. 'She's got to know.'

'D'you want me to phone her?' asked Shirley.

'No, I'll write to her too. I might have some more news when I've seen the telegram. Now I must go.'

Reg jumped up and held her close. 'Take care, love.'

'I will, Dad,' she said, patting his back.

Eileen hugged her and then Shirley did the same.

'Shirley, write to me?'

'I will.'

'Don't come to the door. You might upset the black-out curtain and we don't want Charlie coming round shouting at us.' Ann left them standing in the kitchen. Eileen stood staring at the closed door. She didn't want her daughter to suffer like this. It wasn't fair.

It was late when Ann silently walked into the Nissen hut. She knew some of the girls were on leave, but most had had to stay. The enemy didn't take time off for Christmas. She fumbled her way to her bed and laid out the three 'biscuits'. She cursed under her breath: she didn't have any blankets; when they went on leave they had to return their bedding to the storeroom and at this time of night the store was closed.

'Ann? Ann, is that you?' Mary, who slept in the next bed, sat up but kept her voice low.

'Yes. It's me.'

'What are you doing back here?'

'I had to see what was in that telegram.' Like Mary, Ann was talking in a hushed tone.

'It's in the boss's office.'

Ann went and sat on Mary's bed. 'Why did they tell you about it?'

'Apparently it arrived on Christmas Eve just after you left. Old Hawkins came here looking for you, she wanted to know where you would be over Christmas. I said I wasn't sure and I asked what she wanted you for; I was worried you might be recalled. Well, after a bit she told me and I managed to persuade her to wait till after Christmas and you were back here as there was nothing you could do. I hope I did the right thing. I thought you'd like to be with your family when you heard about it.' Mary sat hugging her knees, looking anxious.

'Yes. That was kind of you. What did the telegram say?'

'I never saw it. Hawkins only said that Harry's been shot down.'

'So you don't know where?'

'No, sorry. I didn't think you'd come back tonight though.'

'I couldn't stay there wondering.'

'I can understand that. What are you going to do about blankets?'

'I'll sleep in me greatcoat for now. You'd better get back to sleep, you're working in the morning.'

'That's true. Goodnight.'

'Goodnight.' Ann wandered back to her bed. This was going to be a long, cold night.

Ann was surprised when she opened her eyes and in the gloom she could make out Mary and a couple of the other girls moving around. She'd had a good night's sleep despite her worries and the discomfort of no blankets. She sat up.

'Ann. What are you doing here?' asked Freda as she made her way to the ablutions. 'I didn't think you were due back till today.'

'I wasn't.'

'So you couldn't keep away from us then!'

'Something like that.' So not everyone knew about the telegram.

Ann waited till they had all left then she too went to the ablutions hut. After straightening herself out she went along to see Officer Hawkins.

'Fisher. I didn't expect to see you here so soon.'

'I had to come to find out what's in the telegram.'

'How do you—' She stopped and gave a faint smile. 'Godwin?'

Ann nodded. 'She sent me a telegram to prepare me, but she didn't know the contents of the one you have.'

'I see. Take a seat.' Officer Hawkins reached down and took the envelope from a drawer. 'I did take the liberty of opening it in case a reply was required.'

'I understand,' said Ann as she took hold of the

envelope. Slowly Ann read the short message. It only said that Harry's plane had been shot down over enemy territory and that the crew was missing.

'There is every hope that he baled out. He could have been taken prisoner.'

Ann couldn't answer; all she could do was stare in utter disbelief at the stilted words on the telegram. Her dear wonderful husband could be somewhere in Germany. If he was he would remain a prisoner till the end of the war.

She stood up, saluted and left the room.

On Sunday night Reg was preparing to go on fire-watching duty.

'Now remember, you two,' he said, waving his finger. 'As soon as the warning goes off you go in the shelter.'

'Yes, sir,' said Eileen.

'I don't want no waiting till the planes come over, understand?'

'You don't think we're gonner have a raid, do you, Dad?'

'Dunno. He's been a bit quiet over London lately, so anything could happen.'

'Well, you take care,' said Eileen as she began to clear away the tea things.

'See you both later,' said Reg, picking up his tin hat and closing the kitchen door.

'I keep thinking about Ann. I wonder how she is?'

asked Shirley as she helped her mother wash up.

'I don't know. I wish she was a bit nearer then perhaps we could go and see her.'

'I doubt it. Now if we had a phone . . . Look, she might have phoned the Fishers. I could go round there straight from work tomorrow and see. How would that be?'

'That'll be lovely. You miss the girls, don't you?'

Shirley nodded and smiled. 'I don't like being the only child.'

Shirley and her mother settled down on the floor of the kitchen. Shirley was thinking about her sisters. She really did miss them. And what should she do about Vic? She wanted to tell her parents about him but she knew they wouldn't approve. She had missed seeing him over Christmas; tomorrow couldn't come soon enough when she would see him at work. Perhaps they could go out, but not just to the pictures. She wanted to experience love like her sisters. Did they wait till they were married before they did it? She knew that Lucy had as her wedding happened very quickly. But what about Ann? She thought about the beautiful bracelet Vic had given her; it did look very expensive. Shirley smiled to herself. He must really like her. Suddenly the siren slowly started its mournful up-and-down wail.

'Come on, Mum,' said Shirley, getting up. 'We promised Dad.'

'I know, but I'm so cosy here I don't want to go out in the cold.'

'Mum. We promised.'

'I know.'

'Dad'll be very angry if we stay here.'

'Oh all right. You're as bad as your father.'

They collected the bedding and made their way outside.

'It's freezing out here. Quick, shut the door and light the lamp,' said Eileen, clutching the pillows and her policy bag.

'I'll get the flasks and . . .' Shirley's voice trailed off as the guns opened up.

'When that gun in the park goes off it always frightens the life out of me,' said Eileen, looking straight ahead at the closed door.

'They must be right overhead,' said Shirley. 'I hope Dad's all right.'

'So do I. What about poor old Nell? She's over there all on her own.'

'She ought to come over here when Mr Drury's fire-watching.'

'I'll tell her that tomorrow, with just the two of us there's plenty of room.'

Shirley knew that her mother depended on her more and more now. She couldn't bear the thought of Eileen sitting in a shelter on her own on the nights her father was on duty. Somehow they seemed to have acquired a special bond and Shirley liked that.

With the steady crump, crump of bombs falling, Eileen knew that she wasn't going to get much sleep.

She worried about Reg out there. Was he being careful? She also fretted about Nell on her own. Thank goodness she still had Shirley at home. It would break her heart if her youngest decided she wanted to join up. And how was Ann coping with her news? Lucy seemed to be the only one who was happy, even though Dan was away.

When there was a lull they could hear a lot of shouting and there appeared to be fire engines close by.

'D'you think we should look out?' asked Shirley.

'No. I don't want to know what's happening out there.'

Shirley settled herself down again, but not to sleep, as all the noise seemed very close. Then there was shouting right outside and someone started banging on the door.

'Is everyone in the shelter?'

'Yes,' called Eileen, jumping up and standing by the door but keeping it closed. 'What is it?'

'They're dropping incendiaries everywhere and we're just making sure all the families are safe in the shelters,' shouted the disembodied voice.

When the sound of heavy boots went away, Eileen asked, 'How did they get in?'

'The front door must have blown open. I hope they wasn't looters.' Shirley gave a nervous laugh.

'What we got that's worth pinching?' said Eileen. 'He said it was incendiaries. Oh, I do hope Reg is all right.'

'He'll be careful, Mum.'

'Yes, I know he will.'

* * *

When the all clear went Eileen and Shirley left the shelter. The smell of burning took their breath away. They both looked up. There was a rosy glow in the night sky.

'At least the roof's still there,' said Eileen.

They made their way through the house and couldn't see any damage. The front door was indeed wide open and when Eileen looked out she stood for a moment then let out an almighty scream. There was a fire engine in the road and men with hosepipes were all around.

'Nell. Nell.' She ran across the road and was grabbed by a fireman.

'Can't get too close, missis,' said the man whose face was black with soot and smoke.

Shirley was close behind her mother. 'What's happened to Nell's house?' she yelled as she watched the fireman playing water on the roofs of the houses both sides of the Drurys' where there was a gaping black hole.

'One went through the roof and done a bit of damage. Lucky we was just passing through when we saw it.'

'Nell. Where's Nell?' screamed Eileen, looking frantically about her.

'Is that the name of the lady who lives there?'

'Yes,' said Shirley.

'She's fine. They've taken her to hospital.'

'Hospital? What's wrong with her?'

'Just a few burns on her hands. It seems she tried to put the thing out.'

Eileen began to cry. 'She tried to put it out? Always said she was a silly cow.'

Shirley put her arm round her mother. 'Does her husband know?' she asked.

'Dunno, love. Where is he?'

'Fire-watching with me dad.'

'D'you know what post he's at?'

'Up round New Cross way, I think.'

'They've had it pretty bad round there, so I expect they've been kept busy.'

Shirley held back her tears and said a silent prayer: Please let me dad and Mr Drury be all right.

Eileen sat on the coping that ran round her window and just stared at all the activity around her.

'Mum, I'm gonner make a cup of tea.'

Eileen didn't move.

'If you're gonner sit here I'm gonner get a blanket to put round you, otherwise you're gonner freeze to death.'

But Eileen just sat staring at Nell's house.

Inside Shirley put the kettle on the fire as once again they didn't have any gas or water. Thank goodness they'd kept up the evening ritual of filling up things even when there weren't any raids. She took a blanket from the shelter. She knew her mother was going to sit there till Nell and the men came back.

* * *

It wasn't long before the firemen left; they had made sure everything had been damped down and was under control.

'Mum, please come in.'

'No. I'm gonner wait for Nell. It'll be light soon so then your dad should be home.'

'Can I get you some breakfast?'

Eileen shook her head. 'I wonder what state her place is in?' she said, still staring across the road.

'D'you want me to go over and look?'

'No, better wait for Fred.'

Shirley busied herself folding the blankets and tidying up the shelter. She picked up her mother's knitting. It was a standing joke amongst the girls that when the knitting needles went faster she was angry or very worried. Shirley sat on the bunk bed and cried. What was going to happen to them all? How much longer did they have to live? Although she wanted to go to work she knew she couldn't leave her mother. How was Vic? She didn't know where he lived. When she got the chance she was going to tell her mother about him. She wanted him to be close to her and love her. The fireman had told her that this had been the worst night so far for fires. London was burning all over. Was he safe?

It had gone ten when Eileen saw Reg and Fred turn the corner. She ran up to them and threw her arms round Reg's neck and wept.

'What is it, old girl? What's happened?'

'It's Nell,' she blurted out. 'She's in hospital.'

'Oh my God,' said Fred. 'Is she badly hurt?'

Eileen shook her head. 'I don't know. She tried to put out the fire in your house and burned her hands.'

'Silly cow,' said Fred. 'What hospital's she in?'

'I don't know. I didn't see her.' Eileen wiped her tears away with her hand. Her face was dirty with the smoke and her hair was all over the place. She pushed it behind her ear.

'Look, I'll go along to the post and see if they can tell me.'

'Fred, I don't know what state your place is in.'

'Don't worry about it. I've got to find Nell.'

'Would you like a cuppa first?' asked Reg. 'It's been a long night.'

'No, thanks all the same. I've got to find her.'

Reg, with his arm round Eileen's waist, watched him go. 'You and Shirley are all right then?'

She nodded. 'Reg, I don't know what I'll do if anything ever happened to Nell. She's not just a neighbour; she's more like a sister to me. I really love her.'

'I know you do. Now let me have a cuppa then we'll go over and see what we can salvage for them.'

'Dad,' yelled Shirley when Reg walked in to the kitchen. She threw her arms round his neck. 'Phew, you stink of smoke.'

'It's been a rough night.' He ran his hand over his dirty face, leaving clean streaks. The whites of his eyes were bright in his blackened face. 'They reckon that even St Paul's might have copped it. That Hitler's bloody clever. He comes over when the Thames is at its lowest and they've been running out of water.'

'Have many been hurt?' asked Eileen.

'I would think so. Any chance of some tea, love?' he asked Shirley.

'Course. The kettle's been on the boil all morning. Did Mr Drury come home with you?'

'Yes, but he's gone to find out where Nell is.'

'Poor Nell,' whispered Eileen.

'Nell's a survivor. She'll be fine, you'll see.' Reg was sitting in the armchair and he was having difficulty holding his cup: he too had burned his hands when he'd rescued a small boy, but it had been in vain. He put his head back. A great tiredness swept over him, but he knew he had to stay awake and help Eileen. He had promised to help her clear up Fred's house and he wouldn't let her down.

Chapter 26

EILEEN STOOD LOOKING down at Reg. He was dirty and exhausted and how he'd aged in this past year. What sort of night had he had? Eileen's troubled mind was turning over and over. When was this all going to end?

'Mum,' whispered Shirley, poking her head round the door. 'Shall I come with you to try and sort out the Drurys' house?'

Eileen ushered her back into the scullery. 'I don't want to wake your father.'

'I know. So let's go over and see what it's like. Mrs Drury won't be able to do much, not if her hands are bad.'

They quietly left the house and found many of their neighbours – those who weren't busy sweeping out debris – standing in groups talking. Mrs Conner's youngest came running up to them waving a long thin bomb.

'Look what me and Ronnie found. It ain't gone off yet.'

'What?' screamed Eileen. 'Throw it away, you silly little buggers, 'fore you kill yourselves.'

'It's all right. Dad said it was a dud.'

'Come on,' said Eileen, grabbing her daughter's hand. 'Let's get out of here 'fore they blow us all up. Silly little sods. What's that father of theirs doing letting 'em play with a thing like that?'

Shirley didn't comment on her mother's language.

Eileen pushed open Nell's front door and suddenly stopped. Shirley, who was close behind her mother, almost fell over her; they stood mesmerised as they watched the water slowly dripping down the stairs. Like a waterfall it fell from one stair to the next then finished up forming a pool in the passage. The brown lino that Nell always kept so highly polished was curling at the edges, the slip mats were sodden and as they walked in the water was squashed out from underneath.

'What a mess,' said Shirley. 'Where do we start?'

'I don't know.' Bewildered, Eileen carefully picked her way along the wet passage.

'I'll get a broom and go upstairs and sweep the water down,' said Shirley, leaving her mother to pick up Nell's slip mats and throw them outside.

In the kitchen Shirley wanted to weep at the mess. The water had come through the ceiling and had even filled the fancy fruit bowl that was always empty but had pride of place in the middle of the table. The sugar bowl was also full of water. Everywhere was soaked.

Above her the ceiling had a dangerous-looking bulge with water slowly dripping from it. It threatened to come down any minute.

Shirley took the broom upstairs with her mother following on behind. They had learned that when you climbed stairs after a raid you had to feel your way up and only take one step at a time, testing that it was safe.

The bedroom doors were wide open and the gaping hole in the roof looked eerie and frightening. The charred beams were like worn black teeth waiting to pounce.

'What a stink,' said Shirley as the acrid smell of smoke caught her breath.

'And look at the mess. There's not a lot of furniture left up here that ain't been ruined, if not by the fire then by water.' Eileen looked around. 'Can't see much to salvage up here,' she added softly.

'Will they have to move out?'

'I should think they'll have to. They can't live in this place, not now. Looks like all the clothes in that wardrobe have gone up in smoke.'

'And Lucy and Dan's wedding presents,' said Shirley. With her foot she moved what was left of the cardboard box Lucy had proudly showed them which had contained some of their gifts.

Eileen picked up a few of the soggy singed clothes that had been draped over the bed. 'Their bed's had it.' The headboard and the springs were badly burned. 'This is really sad. I think all their bedding must be in the shelter.' Eileen stared at the mess. 'It's such a shame, but there's not a lot we can do up here.'

'I'll sweep the water that's left down the stairs and then perhaps we can see if there's anything worth saving. Perhaps you could find some towels to mop up some of the water off the furniture.'

Eileen marvelled at how efficient her youngest daughter had become.

Downstairs Eileen said it was best they burst the bubble above their heads, so standing well back Shirley poked at it with the broom handle and down the lot came, water, ceiling and all. They then set to and tried to save what they could but it was almost impossible. So much needed to be thrown away.

'Where will they stay?' asked Shirley as she wiped down the dresser. All the cooking ingredients that had been in cardboard boxes were soggy and had to be thrown out.

'They can come over and muck in with us till they know what they're going to do. She'll go mad when she sees her sugar ration,' said Eileen, picking up what was left of the disintegrated blue sugar bag. 'It's almost melted away.'

They toiled away clearing up as much as possible.

'Look, put anything that's of any value in the washing-up bowl and the enamel pail. We'll take them back home.'

'What's Mrs Drury got then?'

'Not a lot. Just any decent crocks or cutlery you find.

I know she's got a couple of nice cut-glass bowls and a cake stand as well. That bowl,' Eileen pointed to the fancy fruit bowl. 'I think that was a wedding present from her mum. We hear so much about people being looted while they're in hospital. Mind you, I reckon people like that should have their hands cut off.'

Carrying the rescued goods, they went home. Shirley, her hands full, closed the door behind her with her foot. It banged louder than she'd planned. 'Sorry, I didn't mean . . .'

The kitchen door flew open. Reg, bleary-eyed, stood up. 'Where have you two been?'

'Over to Nell's to see if we could do a bit of clearing up.' Eileen put the white enamel washing-up bowl she was carrying on the kitchen table. 'It's a terrible mess over there.'

'You should have waited for me.'

'You looked worn out. Besides, there ain't a lot we could do.'

'D'you want a cup of tea, Dad?'

'Yes please, love.'

Shirley went into the scullery and turned on the tap hoping the water was on again. She smiled as the water fell from the tap in spurts. They were certainly getting very efficient at repairing these pipes now. 'We've got water again,' she called out.

Eileen was shocked when she saw Reg's hands.

'They'll be all right. A bit of Germolene works wonders,' he said. 'Don't fuss.'

'I'll just clean them up a bit. I don't think they're that bad,' said Eileen. 'Put a drop of warm water in a bowl, Shirley,' she instructed, getting the Germolene ointment from the dresser drawer.

'How does that feel?' she asked as she gently washed Reg's hands.

'Fine, thanks.'

It was later on that morning, after they'd finished a sandwich, that Nell and Fred arrived.

Eileen welcomed her friend with open arms and felt like crying when she saw Nell's heavily bandaged hands. 'Have you been home?' she asked.

Nell shook her head. 'Fred said we should come here and cadge a cuppa off of you first.'

Shirley was already in the kitchen putting the kettle on; she smiled to herself at the gas being on again. It didn't take much to please them these days: just anything that made life easier.

'What was you thinking about, trying to put that thing out?' asked Eileen.

'Don't you start. I've had enough of him going on at me.' Nell waved her hand at Fred.

Shirley brought the tea in and watched Nell as she tried to pick up the teacup.

'Here, let me,' said Eileen and Fred together.

Nell sat back and let her tears fall. 'I'm like a bleeding baby. How am I gonner get dressed and do me hair?' she sobbed.

'Don't worry, love,' said Fred. 'I'll help.'

'And what about me arse? You won't wonner wipe that for me.' Nell tried to brush her tears away but her hands were big and cumbersome.

Eileen could see her friend was very distressed and her heart went out to her.

'Don't worry, Nell, we'll sort something out. You both can stay here. I'll cook for all of us.'

'Thanks, Eileen,' said Fred.

'I think I'd like to go and see what the place is like.'

'Nell, it's a bit of a mess. Shirley and me's been over trying to have a bit of a clean up. It's the water as well as the fire that's done a lot of the damage. And by the way, we brought over some of your bits, just in case any looters get in.'

'Thanks, love,' said Fred.

'I know what I'd like to do with those blokes that pinch from some poor bugger that's buried alive,' said Reg.

'Like that lot over Deptford way,' said Fred.

'Yer,' said Reg. They were all remembering the story of the young couple who were yelling to be rescued from their air-raid shelter and all the while someone was in their house pinching her fur coat and jewellery.

'Do you want me to come with you?' asked Eileen.

'No thanks,' said Nell as Fred draped her coat over her shoulders.

Eileen sat in the chair after they left. 'How's she gonner manage?'

'I don't know,' said Reg.

'I'll let Lucy know,' said Shirley. 'I still ain't had a chance to finish the letter telling her about Harry. Poor Luce, she's gonner be ever so upset over this lot.'

'I expect she will be, what with Harry and now Nell. They say everything comes in threes, what it's to be next?'

'Don't even think like that, Mum,' said Shirley.

'I can't help it.' They all knew Dan was fighting and that frightened her.

Shirley sat at the table. Her sisters were certainly having their share of this war.

After a while Fred and Nell came back.

'Well, we can't stay there. It's a bloody mess.' Nell, who was on the verge of tears, looked very dejected. 'We'll have to try and find somewhere else to live.'

'I've been thinking about that,' said Eileen. 'Number twenty's been empty for months now. You know that young couple that had a baby? I think they went off to the country, to her mother's. Don't you remember Rose who lives next door to 'em telling us about 'em?' she asked Nell.

'That's only a couple of doors away,' said Nell, brightening up. 'We could move in there. And it's the same landlord so he won't have to worry about the rent.'

'We ain't got a lot of stuff left that's decent,' said Fred.

'Don't worry about that, I'm sure everybody will rally round and help,' said Reg.

'We'll go along in the morning and see Rose, she'll know all about it,' said Eileen. 'After tea we'll sort out the sleeping arrangements. You and Fred can sleep in the front room – I'm glad your bedding was all right – and if we have a raid there's plenty of room in the shelter.'

'Should have stayed with me bedding in the shelter,' said Nell.

'Well, what's done's done,' said Eileen, bustling around.

On Monday evening both Lucy and Ann were listening to the news on the wireless in their separate establishments. The announcer was telling them that there had been a big raid on London and many fires had been started.

Both had the same thought: I hope Mum and Dad are all right. Ann knew she had to phone the Fishers. For her part, Lucy didn't want a phone call, as that would only be bad news.

On Tuesday Shirley said she had to go to work.

'That's if the factory's still there,' she said to her mother, although what she really wanted was to see if Vic was back and safe, for she was worried about him. Where did he live? Did he have any family? Had there been any fires near him? She wanted to tell him that she was going to tell her parents about him and bring him home to meet them, although with Fred and Nell around it would prove difficult. Oh, she had missed him.

Eileen got breakfast for everybody and was sad to see Fred cutting up Nell's toast and helping her with a cup of tea.

'When you gotter go to the hospital again?' she asked.

'Next week. I'm hoping they'll take these bloody bandages off then and let me wear a pair of cotton gloves. Well, that's what the nurse said might happen. Things'll be a bit easier then.'

'Yes, but don't you go doing too much,' said Fred.

'I won't be able to, they'll be too bloody sore.'

'Are you coming over to your place with us later on to try and sort out anything that's left and worth saving?' asked Eileen.

Nell grinned. 'I should say so. But only in the role of supervisor. Got to make sure none of you starts slacking.'

'Cheeky mare,' said Fred.

First they got the key to number twenty, from Rose the next-door neighbour who said the previous tenants wouldn't be coming back and that she'd been told to take whatever she wanted.

'Didn't leave much,' said Rose. 'Not that they had much to start with, poor kids. Gorn to her mother's in the country be all accounts. Anyway, here's the key. And good luck.'

'Thanks,' said Fred.

All day Eileen and Reg set to to give Nell and Fred a hand to move into number twenty. Rose was right, the previous tenants hadn't left much, but Eileen had some curtains and Mr Jacobs in the newsagent's had a couple of chairs he said they could have and Mrs Toms in the grocer's had a card table they could borrow for the time being.

As Nell's scullery, like most of Perry Street, was a single storey building that had been tacked on to the back of the house, it was fine, so Nell's cooking utensils were safe, as was her precious gas cooker.

'Till your hands get better you can come over to me for your meals,' said Eileen.

'I might enjoy this being a bit of a lady of leisure,' Nell replied.

But Eileen knew it was all a show. She knew her friend was just trying to keep her spirits up.

'Fred and me's going to the Sally Army tomorrow to see if they can help with some clothes and furniture.' Nell sniffed her armpit. 'Can't keep these on all the time. I'll stink, and I can't keep wearing yours.'

'I told you it's all right. Got more than enough for what I need,' said Eileen, smiling at her friend, knowing she could never be as brave as she was at the loss of her home.

Chapter 27

LUCY WAS STARING in the mirror but she wasn't really seeing anything as her thoughts were miles away. She felt guilty. Her parents and Shirley were in the thick of it, bombs falling all around them, and here she was getting herself tarted up to go out and enjoy herself. But her heart just wasn't in it. It was New Year's Eve and the three of them were going to a dance in the next village. Lucy shut out the excited babble from Trish and Emma as they got themselves ready. Every night when she was safe in her bed she tried not to brood but couldn't as her mind was always full of the family and Dan. Although his letters were spasmodic they gave her great comfort and she would read them over and over again. It was only because of her sheer physical exhaustion that she managed to sleep. The idea that had been going round and round in her mind lately was, now that Dad didn't have a job in the docks, perhaps they could move down here. But how would Shirley feel about leaving her job and what about this mysterious man that she said she was in love with?

'Come on, Luce, Matt will be here soon,' said Trish, breaking into her thoughts. 'At least it's stopped raining,' she added, looking out of the window.

'That's good,' said Emma. 'Didn't fancy going out in me wellies. They don't go well with this frock.'

Matt, a young man from one of the farms they sometimes worked at, had offered to take them and bring them home from the dance in his van. They didn't care how they travelled if it meant they could see the New Year in at a dance.

'Luce, come on, cheer up.'

'Sorry, Em.'

'We know what you must be feeling, but there's nothing you can do about it, other than go home and find out if they're safe.'

Lucy painted on a smile. 'I know. I'm sorry. I promise not to be a wet blanket this evening. You look nice.'

Emma smiled and did a twirl. Her pretty floral dress with the heart-shaped neckline and short sleeves flared out. 'So do you. It's lovely to get out of uniform and feel like a woman again,' she said. 'Now come on, let's go and enjoy ourselves.'

'Are my seams straight?' asked Trish, turning round and hitching up the black crêpe de Chine skirt she was wearing with a long-sleeved white blouse.

'They're fine and you look lovely as well,' said Lucy, who had on the blue woollen frock she'd worn at Christmas. It wasn't new, but she felt comfortable in it.

'I'll go mad if some burly farmhand treads on my toes and ladders my stockings,' said Trish.

Lucy knew she had to get into the party spirit even though she was worrying about her family. But as Emma had said, nobody had phoned and no news must be good news.

'What time's Matt coming?' asked Emma

'About eight. He had to finish herding in the cows,' said Trish.

Emma sat on her bed and, after peering in her hand mirror, applied her lipstick then spat on the cake of mascara, rubbed it with the tiny brush and skilfully brushed it on to her lashes. She blinked furiously. 'Well, how do I look?'

'Like a film star,' said Trish.

'That Matt's a nice lad,' said Lucy. 'We'll have to buy him a drink.'

'Is he old enough?' laughed Emma.

And so the banter went on. At eight o'clock the sound of the van's horn sent them scurrying down the stairs.

As Lucy climbed into the van she looked up at the stars. What did 1941 have in store for them?

Ann was sitting on her bed waiting for Mary who was just putting the finishing touches to her make-up. They were going over to the NAAFI to see the New Year in. Her heart wasn't really in it, but she knew she mustn't sit around moping. Her thoughts kept going to Harry. Where was he? In his last letter before he was shot down he'd told her how cold it was sitting cramped in the aircraft for hours on end. Had he been injured? Then there were her parents, how were they coping? When she'd phoned Harry's parents they hadn't had any news, but they did say the raid had been a bad one and people were comparing it with the great fire of London. She fretted about her mum and dad and Shirley – and who was this man she said she liked? Was he to be trusted? Were they all safe? Mr Fisher did say he would try to get to see them.

'Right, I'm ready,' said Mary, snapping her bag shut. 'Let's go and see this New Year in.'

Ann picked up her gas mask and followed her friend out of the hut.

When they walked into the NAAFI the chatter was loud and the music blaring and there were couples dancing. Ann was jealous: she wanted to be in Harry's arms. She picked up the drink Mary set before her. 'Cheers,' she said.

'Can't really say Happy New Year, can we?'

'Not really.' Ann looked into her glass. Would 1941 see an end to this war?

Shirley looked at the clock. It was nearly midnight. She guessed her sisters would be at a dance or somewhere seeing in the New Year. She wanted to be with Vic. He hadn't been at work today and she was worried. Her father and Mr Drury were playing cards, her mum was knitting and Mrs Drury was trying to read one of her magazines although she was having a lot of trouble turning the pages. They were in the shelter as the siren had gone, but so far the planes hadn't come over.

Shirley was thinking about her sisters. She had written to Lucy telling her about Harry and her mother-in-law. Many times Shirley had thought about joining the forces and seeing a bit more of life and England. She wanted to get away but there was Vic. She desperately wanted to see him. She would bring him home as soon as it was possible. When her parents saw what a nice bloke he was surely they wouldn't mind about the age difference. They would know she'd be safe with him. Shirley sighed.

'That was a big sigh,' said Nell. 'I bet you wish you was out and about with some of your mates and not stuck in here with us old cronies.'

Shirley smiled. 'Not got anyone to go with, that's if Mum would let me out.'

'That's right, go on, make me out to be a right old tartar.'

'Sorry. But you do go on a bit when I do go out.'

'I know, but it's only for your own sake. I'm that worried about you. Anything could happen.'

'I know,' Shirley said again and looked at the clock. It was now midnight. 'Happy New Year,' she said.

They all looked at the clock. 'Happy New Year,' they replied half-heartedly.

Shirley thought about all those lucky people who

were seeing the New Year in. All the kissing and hugging. Was Vic out enjoying himself? With another sigh she picked up her book: that was all the romance she was going to get tonight.

It wasn't till the start of the following week that Shirley finally saw Vic. She was walking out of the factory when she saw him leaning against the wall. His motorbike was at the kerb. She almost ran up to him – she wanted to throw her arms round him she was so pleased at the sight of him, but she didn't want all the girls to know she was seeing him as there were plenty who wanted to go out with him themselves.

'Hello, love,' he said with the lopsided grin that made her heart skip a beat. He ground his cigarette into the pavement and fell in beside her as she continued walking beyond the gates. 'Did you have a nice Christmas?'

'Yes thank you. Vic, where have you been? I've been so worried about you.'

'Ah, that's nice. So what did you do for Christmas then?'

'Not a lot. Both me sisters come home, so that was good. What about you?'

'Wasn't bad. Mind you, I'm glad I missed that raid. Pretty bad be all accounts.'

'Yes it was.'

'But you and yours were all right?'

'Yes. Vic, I'd like you to come home and meet me mum and dad.'

'Why?'

'I told me sisters about you and they reckon you should meet 'em.'

He laughed. 'So, I've got your sisters' approval then.'

'Well, no. I thought it would be nice to let me mum and dad see you and perhaps if they knew I was with a sensible person they wouldn't be so picky about me going out.' Shirley deliberately avoided saying the word 'man' as it made him sound old.

'Well, that's fine by me. Just tell me when. Look, I've got to be off. Got a package to deliver.'

Shirley stood and watched him walk back to his bike. He gave her a wave as he roared past.

'So, he's still around then,' said Brenda, coming up to her.

'Yes, he is.'

'What's your mum and dad got to say about him?'

'I don't know. I haven't told them.'

'Well, it's up to you, but I reckon they should see him.'

'Why?'

Brenda shrugged. 'If you ask me there's something very cagey about him.'

Shirley was cross. Was Brenda jealous as she didn't have a boyfriend? Shirley tossed back her hair and walked on. She didn't have to answer to Brenda or anyone about whom she went out with.

* * *

It was the end of the week. Lucy, who had just finished the milking, was about to sit down to breakfast when Mrs B. handed her a letter.

'Thanks, it's freezing out there.' She took off her greatcoat and scarf and sat at the table. 'It's from Shirley, me little sister.' For a moment or two she was quiet while digesting its contents, then she looked up, her face white and full of shock. 'It's Harry, Ann's husband, he's been shot down and me mother-in-law's house has been burned and . . .' Lucy had to stop as her voice trembled. 'She's burned her hands.'

'Oh, love. I'm so sorry.'

Lucy now had tears running down her cheeks. 'I don't believe it. What am I gonner do?'

Mrs B. sat next to Lucy. 'Can I help?'

Lucy shook her head and handed Mrs B. her letter.

'What can I do?' Lucy asked again but her voice was muffled with sobs.

'I'm so sorry, my dear. This is a wicked war.'

'I want to go home.'

Mrs B. put her arm round Lucy's heaving shoulders. 'I'm sure that can be arranged. But what good will it do? Your sister won't be there.'

Lucy wiped her nose on the sleeve of her green Land Army jumper. 'I know. But I want to be with me mum and dad.'

'Of course you do. Would you like a cup of tea?'

Lucy nodded.

She was still sitting at the table in a daze when Trish and Emma walked in.

Mrs B. took them to one side and whispered to them.

Trish sat next to Lucy and took hold of her hand. 'We're so very sorry.'

Emma at her other side said, 'Look, why don't you ask for a few days off?'

'Ann won't be there to be comforted, she'll be getting on with her job, and Mrs Drury will have enough of me mum fussing round her.' She stood up and tried to smile. 'I'd better get back to work. Those cows won't muck themselves out.'

As Lucy washed and cleaned the cowshed floor she cried. All the pent-up love she had for Dan and her family came flooding out. Even the cows seemed sad when they looked at her.

Shirley didn't see Vic again until the following Thursday. She'd been hanging behind the other girls when they left the factory as she'd seen his bike and knew he was around. She'd made up her mind, she was going to tell the family all about him and she was going to ask him to come and meet them on Sunday then perhaps they could go to the pictures.

'Hello, Shirl. You waiting for me?'

She nodded and, wrapping her arms around herself against the cold, told him her plan. 'You don't have to stay long, we can go out after if you like.'

'Dunno. I'm going out this Sunday.'

Shirley pouted and looked sad. 'I thought you liked me.'

'I do. You know that.'

'Then why do I have to keep pretending I'm going out with Brenda? I want them to see you and—'

He put his finger on her lips. 'Course I'll come, if it's gonner make you happy.'

Shirley felt her knees buckle and she touched his hand. She wanted to kiss his fingers and have him hold her tight. It was dark and as she moved closer to him she knew he'd kiss her. She looked up and when he kissed her she shivered not only with the cold but also with the thrill of his lips on hers. She desperately wanted to tell him that she loved him.

When they broke apart he said, 'Look, I've gotter go. I'll try and make it on Sunday.' He quickly kissed her again and then he was off.

Shirley touched her lips. She knew then she had to tell her parents.

It wasn't till Friday that she got round to informing them that she was going out with someone and she wanted to bring him home.

'Is he in the forces?' asked her father.

'No.'

'Why not?'

'I don't know.'

'Does he have an important job?' said Eileen. 'What does he do?'

'He rides a motorbike for the factory.'

'I see,' said Reg.

'What's his name?' asked Eileen.

'Vic.' Shirley suddenly realised she didn't even know his surname. But she did know there would be a lot more questions. 'So is it all right if he comes round on Sunday?'

'I should think so. Will I have to get something in for tea?'

'No, don't worry about that. We'll be going out.' Shirley was surprised at how easy that had been. But what would they say when they met him?

On Friday it was well past ten o'clock when Lucy finally arrived in Perry Street. She was pleased she wasn't in the forces and had to get special permission for leave. It was up to the farmer and she couldn't believe how kind Mr Ayres had been when he heard what had happened. He'd insisted that Lucy went home for a few days to see her family. It was very cold and her breath formed little clouds in front of her as she hurried along. Before the moon scurried behind the clouds she caught sight of Dan's old house. It made her catch her breath. The roof had a huge hole in it and it looked so very sad and neglected. She stood for just a moment trying to imagine what Nell had gone through. She turned and quietly pulled the key through the letterbox of her house and went inside.

She rushed into the kitchen and everyone looked up in surprise.

'Lucy, what you doing here?' Eileen exclaimed from her seat close to the fire.

Lucy flung herself at her mother and cried, 'I just had to come home. I was so worried. Are you all all right?'

'How did you manage to get away?' asked Reg.

'When I told Mr Ayres what had happened he said I could come and see you. I've got to be back for Sunday evening milking.' Lucy sniffed. 'He even lent me the money for me train fare.' She blew her nose. 'Have you heard from Ann? Any news?'

'No. But she seems to be coping, so Mr Fisher told us. She phones him when she can.'

'How's Dan's mum?'

'A bit better now they've taken all the bandages off. They look very sore. She has to wear these little white cotton gloves. I've been tearing up some old sheets to make her a few pairs, she get 'em filthy dirty in no time. But you know Nell, she don't complain.'

Lucy looked at the clock. 'It's too late to go and see them now. You said they've moved up the road. Is it all right?'

'Not the same, but at least they've got a roof over their heads,' said her father.

'It's really great to see you, Luce,' said Shirley, giving her sister a hug.

'Shirley's young man's going to call on Sunday,' said Eileen.

'Young man?' queried Lucy. 'So you've not met him then?'

'No. We didn't know she had one. She obviously told you, and I expect Ann knows as well.'

'All right, Mum. It's no big deal,' said Shirley. 'That's awful, Harry being shot down.'

'Yes it is,' said Eileen.

It went very quiet for a moment; each had their own thoughts.

'Any chance of a cuppa?' Lucy asked, breaking the silence. 'I'm sorry, but I haven't got a ration card.'

'That's all right,' said Reg. 'I'm sure we can feed you for a day or two.'

Eileen wanted to smile at Reg saying 'we'. He hadn't queued up for anything in his life.

They sat talking for a while then and Lucy asked, 'Where're we sleeping?'

'In here. I'll get the bedding in a tick.'

'So we didn't get any of those incendiaries then?'

'No,' said Reg. 'We was very lucky this time.'

Chapter 28

THE FOLLOWING MORNING, after exchanging the usual hugs and kisses, Lucy was shocked at the sight of Nell's hands. She could see even through the thin gloves that they were red and sore-looking and her dear mother-in-law was having great difficulty picking things up. Whenever Lucy rushed to help her she was told to sit down.

'And before you say anything I know I was a silly old woman.' She waved her gloved hand at Lucy. 'I couldn't help it. When you see yer home going up in smoke, all the things you've had to struggle all your life to get, well, somehow common sense goes out the window.'

Lucy tried to smile through her tears. 'Good job Dan's not here otherwise he would be very angry with you.'

'I know, so don't you go writing and telling him. He might be worried about what's happening over here and not be looking after himself.'

'I won't.' Lucy brushed away her tears.

'I'm sorry, love, but a lot of your stuff got ruined, if not by the water then by the smoke. Me and your mum, well your mum really, tried to wash the bed linen and stuff like that as best as she could.'

'Don't worry about that. The important thing is that you're alive. Now come on, show me over this mansion of yours.'

Fred laughed. 'It's just the same as our old house.'

'But it ain't got as much furniture,' said Nell. 'Mind you, people have been very kind.'

'We went along to the Sally Army, they were good, helped us a lot with some clothes and furniture,' said Fred.

'It ain't like your own stuff though. Some of it ain't ever seen a bit of polish and as for the clothes, well, some of 'em must'a come out the ark. Managed to pick up a few bits though,' said Nell cheerfully. 'They even wanted to know if I fancied a long frock.'

'You should have seen it, Luce,' said Fred, grinning. 'All covered with sequins.'

'I ask you,' giggled Nell. 'I told 'em that as I wasn't planning on having me dinner at the Ritz just yet, they'd better wait till I can hold a knife and fork properly.'

Lucy sat and laughed and talked all morning. Nell was like a tonic and Lucy was reluctant to leave but she knew that Shirley would be home soon and she wanted to have a talk with her.

* * *

When Shirley came home from work and after they'd finished dinner, she beckoned Lucy to follow her into the front room.

'It's freezing in here,' said Lucy when Shirley closed the door.

'I know, but I wanted to see you on your own. Will you be here when Vic calls tomorrow?' she asked, pulling her cardigan tighter round her.

'What time's he coming?'

'About four.'

'No. I'm sorry, but I've got to leave about twelve.'

'That's a pity. I would have liked you to meet him.'

'Do Mum and Dad know how old he is?'

Shirley shook her head.

'So they'll be in for a bit of a shock.'

'I expect so. Luce, I was thinking of joining up.'

'Why?'

'I'm bored and fed up and I hate me job.'

'But I thought you liked it at the factory.'

'I did at first, but it's noisy and I don't get on that well with the others, mostly because of Vic. I miss Woolies. We used to have a lot of laughs there.'

'Times have changed, Shirl.'

'I know.'

'I don't think being in the forces is all honey and the Land Army is bloody hard work.'

'You and Ann seem happy enough.'

'Well, yes, I suppose we are. But what about this Vic? What will he have to say about it?'

'Dunno. Luce, me mind's in such a turmoil I don't know what to do. I know that if he was to ask me to marry him, I would.'

Lucy swallowed hard. She didn't know how to answer this. 'You're that serious about him?'

'Yes.'

'Are you sure he's never been married?'

'I don't know.'

The thought that was racing through Lucy's mind was: What if he was married and his wife had been evacuated? 'Do you know *anything* about him?'

'Not a lot.'

'What about his friends or his family? Have you ever met them?'

Shirley shook her head.

'Look, Shirley, be sensible, you can't just up and marry him,' said Lucy. 'Has he . . . ? You know?'

'No. But I want him to.'

'Shirley, don't even think like that. I dread to think what Mum and Dad would say if you was to find yourself having a baby.'

Shirley fiddled with the arm of the chair. 'He does want me to go away with him.'

'What can I say? Shirley, please be careful. Just take things one step at a time. Remember he's the first boyfriend you've ever had. What's Mum and Dad going to say about it? And you're under age. Look how she was over Ann and me.'

'But I do love him, Luce. And if Mum carries on

about him, well, I will join up or run away with him.'

Lucy was shocked. 'You can't do that.'

'I can if they won't let me see him again. I remember how you felt about Dan and the fuss Mum made over that.'

'That was different. We both wanted to get married and I've known Dan all me life.'

'I wish you'd be here.'

'So do I. But be careful. See what Mum and Dad think of him before you do anything rash.'

'I know he likes me. Look, this is what he bought me for Christmas.' Shirley took the bracelet from the pocket of her frock.

'This is really lovely,' said Lucy, taking hold of the heavy gold bracelet.

'He must like me to give me something like this.'

'I would think so. It looks very expensive.'

Shirley smiled.

Lucy looked at her young sister. 'Is he well off?'

'I don't know, but we always go in the expensive seats at the pictures.'

It was Lucy's turn to smile. It concerned her that although her sister appeared grown up she was still very young and naive; her eyes were shining with love and that could make her very vulnerable. 'Shirley, take it easy and give it all time.'

'The way things are going have we got a lot of time?'

Lucy held her sister close. In many ways Shirley *had* grown up. She had experienced many things lately, but not affairs of the heart. She was here for their parents and that made Lucy feel guilty. 'I'll try and get home when I can. Even if it's only for half a day, so please, Shirley, let me know what's going to happen and *be careful.*'

'I will.' Shirley kissed her sister's cheek. 'I really do miss you both, you know.'

'I know.'

As the train left the station the same unanswered questions were revolving in Lucy's brain. What was this bloke like? Why wasn't he in the forces? What would Mum and Dad say when they met him? As these thoughts were whirling round and round Lucy's head, Vic was knocking on the door of number thirty-five Perry Street.

Shirley ran to open the door. 'Come on in.'

He took her in his arms and kissed her lips very gently.

It took Shirley a moment or two to recover, then she stood to one side as he stepped into the passage. He looked very smart in a navy-blue pin-striped suit, his tie was a bit bright but she quickly noted that his shoes were polished. She smiled; her father would notice things like that.

'Mum, Dad. This is Vic.'

The welcoming smile quickly disappeared from Eileen's face and her jaw dropped. Although this bloke was good-looking, he looked nearly old enough to be her daughter's father.

Reg stood up. 'Hello, young . . .' He stopped. 'So you're a friend of our little Shirley's then?'

'Yes.'

'Sit down, Vic,' said Shirley, pulling a chair out from under the table. Her heart was beating like a hammer; she did so want her parents to like him.

Eileen and Reg sat down too.

'So what do you do then, mate?' asked Reg.

Eileen had known Reg would get to these sorts of questions right away.

'I run about on a motorbike.'

'You're not taking our Shirley out on a motorbike, are you?' Eileen was horrified at the thought of that.

'No. It's for work.' He smiled, showing his white teeth.

'Not in the forces then?'

'No.'

Shirley was almost praying he would tell them why.

'Does your job make you exempt?' asked Eileen.

'That and a dicky heart.'

Shirley wanted to sing. It was strange but she was overjoyed that he had a bad heart. At least now she knew why he wasn't in the forces.

'Sorry to hear that, mate,' said Reg.

'Would you like a cup of tea?' asked Eileen. She didn't like the look of this handsome chap; to her, with his smart suit and slicked-down hair, he looked very smarmy, but she still hadn't forgotten her manners.

'Yes please.'

Eileen stood up. He had one thing in his favour: he was polite. When she'd got the tea they sat and talked. Or rather, Eileen and Reg asked questions.

'Live locally then?'

'Deptford.'

'Not lost anyone in the bombing?'

'No.'

'That's good. Those incendiaries were pretty bad. Many drop round your way?'

'Dunno, I was away at the time.'

'Anywhere nice?' asked Eileen.

'Not really, had to see some mates down Dorset way.'

Shirley noted that Vic, as always, was very guarded. He never said too much about himself or his family. Where *was* his family?

After half an hour Vic looked at his watch. 'Look, Shirl, if we're gonner see that picture we'd better be off.'

'I'll just get me coat.' Shirley almost ran from the room. She felt sick. She'd known her mum and dad would be curious, but it had been almost like the Gestapo in there.

Outside he took hold of her arm and hurried her along the road. 'Christ, they wanted to know the ins and outs of a duck's arse.'

'I'm sorry. They were like that with Harry – that's my sister's husband who's been shot down – even though she worked for him before he went into the RAF. At least you won't have to go in the forces.'

'Not if I can help it.'

* * *

'What the bloody hell is our Shirley thinking of?' shouted Reg as soon as they heard the front door shut. 'Did you know he was that much older than her?'

'No, course I didn't. Never clapped eyes on the bloke before. He can't be that old.' Although Eileen was angry she was trying to calm Reg down.

'He must be in his thirties. And she's what, seventeen?'

'She'll be eighteen in June.' Eileen was trying to defend her daughter even though she agreed with Reg.

'What if he's married?'

'If he was, he wouldn't take a young girl like our Shirley out, would he?'

Reg gave a cynical laugh. 'Don't you Adam and Eve it. What if he went down to Dorset to see his wife and kids?'

Eileen put her hand to her mouth. 'Oh Reg. Don't say things like that.'

'Got to say what I think.'

'Someone at his work must know all about him.'

'Could be some of them are doing the same and all covering each other's backs.'

'Reg, sit down. If you go carrying on like this in front of Shirley, then she'll be off next.'

'I'm sorry, love, but I don't want anything to happen to her. There's something about him I don't like.'

'I know how you feel. He's got shifty eyes and he didn't look at you when he answered your questions.'

'And what about that bracelet she was flashing about. Have you seen it before?'

'No,' said Eileen.

'So where did that come from?'

'I don't know. As I said, I've never seen it before. It looked very expensive. Reg, you don't think she's going out with him cos he's got a bob or two?'

'I don't care if he's a bloody millionaire. Eileen, I don't like this. I don't like it at all.'

'Nor do I. So what can we do about it?'

'I don't know.'

'If we bide our time it might all blow over.'

'Christ, you've changed your tune. I remember how you carried on about the other two when they wanted to get married, you made your feelings clear enough then to everybody.'

'Yes and look how everyone went on at me, making me out to be the big bad mother. Oh Reg, you don't think she's planning on marrying him, do you?'

'Don't ask me. I'm only the breadwinner in this house.'

'I'll have a talk to her when she gets back.' Eileen went into the scullery to start getting the tea ready. It was only a sandwich on a Sunday these days – high tea with cake, shrimps and winkles was a thing of the past. 'Please God, don't let any harm come to her,' she said out loud.

Shirley and Vic were queuing up for the pictures.

'See you're wearing your bracelet then.'

'It's so beautiful.' Shirley twisted it round her arm. 'You've got lovely taste. I've never had anything so nice before.'

'Play your cards right and you could have a lot more baubles.'

'Two up in the one and nines,' said the doorman, coming out and ushering the queue along.

'We'll take those,' said Vic, pushing Shirley forward.

Shirley wondered what Vic meant. She looked up at him. She loved him but she didn't want to do anything that would upset her mum and dad.

Chapter 29

THAT EVENING WHEN Shirley walked in she knew that there would be questions. So she was more than pleased to see that her father had gone on fire-watching duty and Mrs Drury was sitting in the kitchen.

'Hello, love,' said Nell. 'Your mum was just saying that you've been to the pictures with your young man.'

'He ain't that young,' said Eileen.

'Mum.' She turned to Nell. 'He is a bit older than me.'

'Not in the forces then?'

'No. It seems he's got a funny heart.' Shirley could see her mother was sitting tight-lipped.

'Go to see something nice?' asked Nell, trying to ease the situation.

'Not really, they always have old films on Sundays.' Shirley wished she could go up to her bedroom, but they were still sleeping on the kitchen floor. She wanted to be alone with her thoughts, to go over and over this evening in her mind. She hadn't seen that much of the film because when they managed to get in the back row she had been lost in his long lingering kisses, which had taken her breath away. They were very grown-up kisses. He was wonderful and she loved him. Later, when they stopped in a shop doorway, he'd covered her face with small butterfly kisses. When he slid his hand inside her coat and fondled her small breasts, it was such a thrill. She wanted more, so much more.

'I wish it was warm enough to strip you bare and kiss these wonderful little mounds,' he'd murmured as he kissed her neck. Slowly his hand went up her skirt. He was touching her bare thighs; she was wearing her french knickers: it would have been so easy for him to make love to her. Although she was frightened, she wanted to feel what it was like to be a woman, but not in a shop doorway. She wanted the first time to be perfect and pushed his hand away.

'I won't hurt you,' he'd whispered.

'No, don't. Not here. I want the first time to be perfect.'

'We'll have to get that sorted then.'

Shirley shuddered as she remembered his every word.

'You all right, love?' said Eileen.

Shirley smiled and nodded. 'I think someone just walked over me grave.'

'Oh, don't say things like that, Shirl,' said Nell. 'We don't want any talk about graves.'

'No, sorry.'

'Ann's not heard any more about Harry then?' asked Nell.

'No. Let's hope no news is good news,' said Eileen.

'But *is* no news good news?' asked Nell.

'I don't know.' Eileen was getting cross. There was just no point speculating. They would hear when they heard. 'She's hoping he's just been taken prisoner and not injured. It's such a worry.'

'It must be.'

'Shirley, give me a hand to get the bedding in from the front room,' said Eileen. She didn't want to keep talking about the war.

Shirley followed her mother. At least they were going to settle down early tonight so she had been saved the third degree – till tomorrow.

Although it was cold at least it wasn't raining, thought Lucy. As there weren't any buses on a Sunday she had to walk to the farm from the station and it was quite a trudge. At last, when she turned into the long tree-lined drive and made her way to the back of the house, Lucy felt that in a way she had come home.

When she walked into the warm welcoming kitchen Mrs B. jumped up and put her chubby arms round her. The trauma of the weekend set her off crying again.

'Come and sit down,' said Mrs B., edging her towards the table.

'I'm sorry,' she said, sniffing into her handkerchief.

'Was the news very bad?'

Lucy nodded. 'Ann's not heard from Harry and me in-laws' house is all burned and Dan's mum's got terrible burned hands and there's nothing I can do about it.' It all came rushing out.

'Course you can't, love.'

Lucy looked up. 'Look at the time. That bloody train stopped at every station and a few more unscheduled stops besides. I should be over doing the milking.' She jumped up. 'I'll just go and change into me dungarees.'

'Sit down and don't worry about it. Trish and Emma're doing it for you.'

Lucy sat at the table and let the tears trickle down her cheeks. 'I'm sorry,' she said. 'I'm so sorry.'

'That's all right, love. It's shock; you get it out of your system. It's been a very trying time for you. There's some letters here for you. They'll help to cheer you up, I think they're from your husband.'

Lucy managed a weak smile. 'D'you mind if I go to our room and read these?' she said, picking up the four letters.

'Course not. Take a cup of tea over with you.'

'Thanks.'

Lucy sat on her bed and opened her letters. Every one she read brought more tears, but these were tears of joy. She felt so close to Dan as she read his words of love. She looked at his picture on her side table and tried to imagine his voice, but at times it was hard. She hoped she would never forget anything about him. In his letters he told her that they were pushing the enemy back and said they were fighting with a lot of Australians. He told her what a wonderful place they had made Australia sound. Now, I quite like the sunshine so what d'you think about us settling there when this lot is all over? he'd asked. She smiled; he made her so happy when he was thinking about their future together. She didn't care where she lived as long as she was with him, the love of her life. She kissed all the kisses. 'I love you, Dan, so very much,' she whispered.

Through the following months life for all of the Wells family went on as usual. Ann was still waiting for news of Harry and Lucy's work continued to follow the seasons on the farm. Some nights those in Rotherhithe had an unbroken night's sleep. Despite her parents' disapproval Shirley was still seeing Vic although she'd never brought him home again. He had told her he was going to take her away for a weekend, but so far that hadn't happened. When she did ask him if he was married, he'd only laughed and said, 'Thanks. That what you think? A bloke that plays away? If I was I would have had your drawers off before now. I've got a bit more respect for you than that.'

Shirley's head was spinning. He respected her. 'What about your mum and dad? You've never told me about them.'

'I left home many years ago. I was a bit of a Jack the lad and me dad didn't approve. So does that satisfy you? You're just like your old man. Anything else you wonner know?'

Shirley knew he was getting angry. At times she did wonder what he had to hide but all her doubts were quickly put to the back of her mind when she was with him and her love for him overwhelmed her.

It was the beginning of March that Reg, who had to go to the docks every day to make sure there wasn't any work before he was allowed dole money, came home from signing on and announced that he had some bad news for Eileen.

'They're sending some of us to Cardiff, in Wales.'

'What? They can't do that,' cried Eileen.

'They can. It seems they want dockers and stevedores down there as more and more ships are being sent there. And as there's a lot of us up here with no work they're moving some of us out. Let's face it, love, I can't see the docks round here ever being used again.'

'Is Fred going as well?'

'Yes.'

'What's me and Nell gonner do?'

'You'll be all right, you've got Shirley here with you.'

'I don't want you to go,' said Eileen, swallowing hard to stop her tears from falling.

'I ain't got a lot of choice.'

Shirley was also shocked at the news when she came home. Any ideas that she'd had about joining up or marrying Vic had to be put aside for the time being.

She couldn't leave her mother, not now. 'When are you going down there?' she asked.

'Sunday,' said her father. 'We've got to be at the dock gate be eight in the morning to get the bus to the station and our train tickets.'

'So soon?' said Eileen.

'Those people don't hang about once they get an idea.'

'I bet their families ain't all split up,' said Eileen.

'No. A lot of 'em finished up in America or Canada,' said Shirley. 'I'd love to go to America,' she added, dreamy-eyed.

'I bet that ain't all a land of milk and honey,' said Reg.

'It's only me,' came a voice from the passage.

'That's Nell coming over to have her say,' said Reg.

The kitchen door opened and Nell and Fred walked in.

'What we gonner do?' she asked, looking at Eileen.

'I keep telling her, there ain't much we can do,' said Fred.

Nell plonked herself at the table. 'I was saying that perhaps you and me could go there when they get settled. They could find us somewhere to stay.'

'I can't do that,' said Eileen. 'I can't just go and leave Shirley. What if anything happened to her? I'd never forgive meself.'

'She must be able to get another job,' said Nell.

'I ain't moving. Dad don't know how long he'll be there.'

'Well, I'd like to get away for a bit,' said Nell.

'I reckon it could be a good idea,' said Shirley. 'I'll be all right. Besides, the rest away from these bombs and broken nights will do you all good.'

'Don't talk daft,' said Reg. 'I wouldn't let your mother leave you here on your own. Anything could happen to you.'

'How would you manage?' asked Eileen. 'You couldn't queue up for hours on end for your grub, not while you're at work.'

'I'd manage somehow.' The thought that was racing through Shirley's mind was: If her mother and Nell were away she'd have the house to herself. She gave a little smile. What the eye don't see, the heart don't grieve over.

Eileen looked at the grin on her daughter's face. She could almost read her mind. There was no way she was going away and leaving her daughter to that bloke.

'How long d'you think you'll be there?' asked Eileen.

'No idea,' said Reg. 'A lot depends on how many ships get through. The U-boats are sinking so many of our ships that it's hard to say.'

'Where will you stay?' asked Eileen.

'They'll have to find us lodgings.'

'What about our money?' asked Nell. 'What we gonner live on?'

'Don't worry,' said Fred. 'We'll send you money.'

'I bet some of 'em don't send their old women much.

Probably only too glad to get away from 'em, if the truth be known,' said Reg.

'Well, I don't like the idea of you going away,' said Eileen. 'Have they had any bombs down there?'

'Dunno. Shouldn't think so.'

'Could we be called up?' asked Nell.

'Course not,' said Fred. 'You're too old.'

'They might send you into a factory though,' said Reg.

'Don't say that. I couldn't stand all the noise.'

For the rest of the evening the talk was about the men going away.

Eileen looked round the table. All their married life she had never been apart from Reg. She was devastated. Two of her daughters were away. Now it was her husband who was going. All she had ever wanted was to get married and be a good wife and mother. Now that was being taken away from her. Where would it all end?

Chapter 30

IT WAS LATE spring before Ann had any news about Harry. The letter from the Red Cross told her that he was a prisoner of war. Mary was at her side when she received the news.

'I expect you'll be getting a card from him soon,' Mary said, hoping to cheer her friend up.

'I must phone his mum and dad as soon as I can,' said Ann, brushing away her tears. She gave Mary a weak smile. 'At least he's alive and hopefully well.'

The following morning after Ann had phoned, Mr Fisher went round to see Eileen with the news.

Her face fell when she opened the door and saw Mr Fisher on her doorstep.

He smiled. 'Don't worry, I'm here with good news – well, the best we could hope for under the circumstances. Harry's a prisoner of war.'

'Thank God he's alive,' Eileen said, ushering him into the kitchen.

'How are you managing, my dear? Ann told us that Mr Wells has been sent away.'

'Not too bad. Like any other wife, I suppose. It's hard and I do miss him.'

'Of course you do.'

'Will Harry be allowed to write home?'

'I would think so.'

'How did Ann sound?'

'Upset, of course. But she's a brave girl.'

Eileen nodded. She knew she wasn't being very brave. All she wanted was her family round her. She wanted things to be as they were before this wicked war started.

'Are you all right, my dear?'

Eileen nodded. 'Sorry, but I was just thinking how things have changed in just a couple of years.'

'Yes, they certainly have.'

'I'm sorry, I forgot to ask. How's Mrs Fisher?'

'She's fine. I must admit that we are thinking of going away. These broken nights and all this worry about Harry's not doing her any good. After all, we've got nothing to keep us here, not now. Harry won't be home till this is all over then I expect he and Ann will want to be on their own.'

'Where will you go?'

'To the country somewhere.'

'My Lucy loves the country. The work's hard, but she's very happy.'

'Your girls are very close.'

'Yes they are.'

Mr Fisher stood up. 'I'd better be on my way.' He

patted her hand. 'Just think about when they can all be together again.'

'That really will be a day to remember and it can't come soon enough.'

At the front door they shook hands, then Mr Fisher kissed Eileen's cheek. 'Keep smiling. I don't know when we'll meet again, but I'll write and let you know where we finish up.'

'I'd like that and we'll have to have a real get-together when this is all over.'

After Eileen closed the front door she stood for a moment pondering. Everybody was living for the day when their lives returned to normal. But could they ever be as normal as they were before? The girls had grown up. Two were married and their husbands away. Even civilians like Reg and Fred hadn't been spared horrendous sights and now they'd been moved away from their families. She sighed and moved back to the kitchen.

She reread the letter she'd had from Reg. He didn't say a lot, just that there were ships in the docks and they had to work a lot of hours to turn them round quickly. He said he was having trouble understanding the Welsh. She smiled. A funny language he'd called it. He and Fred were together and their landlady wasn't a bad old sort. It seemed she had been widowed in the first war. When she'd read that Shirley had immediately joked that there was no fear of Reg running off with her then.

Eileen thought about Shirley. She worried about her. She knew she was still seeing this Vic. Why did she have such a bad feeling about him?

At the beginning of May more heavy raids bombarded London. When the siren went Nell, Shirley and Eileen cowered in the shelter silently praying. Bombs fell, guns retaliated and the planes droned overhead. It didn't matter how many times they had been through this same ordeal, it was still hard and frightening: the ground heaving, trembling and falling, the sound of crashing masonry and the familiar smell of cordite mixed with soot and dust filling the air. Shirley made up her mind. If she got out of this alive she was definitely going to let Vic make love to her. But when he had asked her to go away with him a few weeks ago she had made the excuse that it wasn't the right time of the month. Her mind was in turmoil, but was it because deep down she was worried and frightened? What if she found she was going to have a baby? Her mum and dad would never forgive her. Although Vic was patient she knew that he would soon get tired of waiting. He'd never said he loved her, only that he liked her company. Was that love? Another bomb fell close by. Shirley looked at her mother's and Nell's strained, ashen faces. Any night they could be killed or maimed. Shirley knew that she had to know what being a real woman was all about; she wanted to experience real love before she died.

'Fred would go mad if he knew what we was going through.'

'I thought there might have been an end to this before now,' said Eileen.

'Wonder if they're all right.'

'I would think they'd tell us.'

'Would they? D'you know, girl, I've really had enough.' Nell sat back and wiped her face with her hands. Although they had healed they still looked very red.

'If only something nice could happen for a change,' said Shirley softly.

'If only,' said Eileen.

'Now they're gonner ration clothes,' said Shirley.

'And coal,' said Nell.

'Where will it all end?' said Eileen.

'Gawd only knows,' said her friend.

Every time Lucy heard about a raid she panicked about her mum and Shirley. If only there was some way she could get in touch with them. She had to wait for a letter and sometimes that seemed almost like a lifetime.

Ann was also anxious. Now the Fishers had moved away she had no way of contacting them either and she too had to wait for letters.

Everybody knew the war wasn't going well and that peace was a long way off.

* * *

At the end of May Lucy managed to get a weekend off. On seeing her mother she let her tears flow. They stayed locked in each other's arms for several minutes, crying quietly together.

'It's lovely to see you,' said Eileen, dabbing at her eyes with the hem of her apron.

Lucy noted her mother was beginning to look old. 'How's Dad?'

'He's all right. Well, he says he is.'

'Will he be away long?'

'Don't know. Luce, I'm so miserable.'

'Oh Mum. Look, why don't you and Shirley come and stay near me? It'll do you good to have a weekend away.'

'I couldn't leave Nell.'

'I'll find somewhere for you all to stay; at least then you can have a couple of nights in a bed.'

'It sounds very tempting.'

'Then that's settled. Tomorrow when I get back I'll make some enquiries. I'm sure Mrs B. will know someone who'll put you up.' Lucy watched a smile creep back onto her mother's face and she knew she had to do something to help lift her burden.

Shirley was equally pleased to see Lucy, but was a bit put out when she heard her mother's plan.

When she and Lucy were alone doing the washing up she closed the scullery door and said, 'I can't go away with Mum.'

'Why?'

'It could be my chance to be with Vic.'

'So you're still seeing him then?'

'Course.'

'Look, I think Mum and Nell deserve a break and I don't think it would do you any harm either.'

'I must admit the thought of sleeping in a bed is very tempting, but I was hoping it would be next to Vic.'

'He still hasn't had his wicked way with you then?'

'No. Not had the chance. Don't wonner do it in a doorway. I wonner lie in a bed and be pampered and . . . Now, if you take Mum away . . .'

'Don't talk daft. Life ain't all that romantic; besides, Mum ain't ever going to leave you here alone. Not with the raids still going on.'

Shirley looked sad. 'I wish something exciting would happen in my life. I love Vic, but I don't think he loves me. He's never said.'

Lucy took her hands from out of the washing-up water and held her sister. 'Oh Shirl, I do worry about you. I wish I could make nice things happen for you.'

'So do I.'

As usual that night they settled themselves on the kitchen floor. Nell was really pleased at the thought of going away for a weekend.

'Can't wait to see the countryside. We went to Kent once when I was a kid. Me gran used to go hopping. That was really smashing. All the lovely flowers were just growing along the road. Is it like that where you are, Luce?'

'Yes it is.'

'Mind you, we've got plenty of flowers round here now. The bombsites are looking really colourful with all these wild flowers,' said Eileen.

'Makes yer wonder where they all come from,' said Nell.

'Mostly from the birds. They drop the seeds,' said Lucy.

Nell laughed.

'What's so funny?' asked Eileen.

'Well, here we are lying on the kitchen floor waiting for the bombers to come over and perhaps blast us to kingdom come and we're talking about flowers.'

'Just goes to show what a funny lot us British are,' said Lucy, laughing.

At the end of the week Shirley saw Vic again outside the factory and she told him of her sister's plan.

'So, you could be going away?'

'Looks like it. D'you mind?'

'Look, Shirl.' He looked around to make sure Brenda wasn't near. 'I know you don't wonner do it in a doorway but, as I keep telling you, I want you, so I've been giving this a lot of thought. What if I manage to get the key to me mate's place? We could go there one Sunday afternoon.'

Shirley felt her knees buckle. 'Could we?'

He smiled and it made her go weak. 'I reckon it could be arranged.'

'I'm surprised you've waited so long for me to . . . you know? You could have any girl you like.'

'I happen to like you.' He kissed her cheek. 'Besides, I wonner be the first.'

Shirley blushed and looked at her feet. 'Thank you. Not many would keep taking no for an answer.'

He laughed. 'You're a funny little thing.'

'No I'm not.'

He ran his hand down her arm.

She shuddered. 'It's my birthday next week, I'll be eighteen.'

He held her close. 'So I'll have to find something real special for your birthday then, won't I?'

'I didn't say it for that.'

'I know you didn't.'

'But—'

His lips came down on hers and silenced her. Shirley knew this was what she wanted.

The following Friday evening when Shirley turned the corner she was thrilled to see Vic waiting for her. Brenda had gone on ahead to catch her bus.

'Can't stop,' he said, not bothering to get off his motorbike. 'I've got the key to me mate's flat, so I'll see you here on Sunday about two.' He grinned. 'Wear something pretty.' With that he was off.

Shirley stood in a dream. She was going to be made

love to by Vic. She was going to be a woman. This was the best birthday present she could have.

On Saturday morning Shirley knew she was still grinning and being silly.

'You look flushed,' said Brenda. 'You all right?'

'Yes. Just looking forward to me birthday on Monday.' She wanted to tell Brenda that tomorrow she was going to see Vic. What if he wanted to get engaged and was going to give her a ring? The thrill of it all. On Sunday she would know all about love.

When Shirley got home that afternoon Eileen read out a letter that had just come from Lucy. She was grinning.

'Lucy's got a room for us in the village. We can go on Friday the twenty-seventh. That gives me time to answer her letter. So, what d'you think?'

'Sounds a really smashing idea,' said Nell. 'Now we've got these long light nights we'll be able to go to the local and have a drink and . . . Oh, it's gonner really be something to look forward to. She's a good girl, is Lucy.'

'I know.'

'What do you say about it, Shirley?'

'Sounds good.' She was just happy that it wasn't going to interfere with her plans for tomorrow. 'Don't forget I can't go till after work on Sat'day.'

'I know that so we won't leave till then. That all right with you, Nell?'

'That's fine with me,' said Nell.

'Are you sure?'

'Course.' Nell smiled. 'I can't believe it. A whole night in the country in a bed.'

'D'you know, it'll be just our luck for Reg and Fred to walk through that door just as we're leaving.'

'They'd better not,' said Nell.

On Sunday Shirley waited outside the factory gate. It seemed eerie it was so quiet; although some of the women were working they were on different shifts to her and – thank goodness – she didn't know any of them. By half past two there still wasn't any sign of Vic. She began to walk up the road hoping to spot him, but which way would he come? She didn't know where his friend lived. When it got to three o'clock she began to panic. What if he'd had an accident? At four she decided he'd changed his mind. She wanted to cry. She'd worn her very best white camiknickers and best stockings. She had even practised how she would lie on the bed all seductive-looking, just like she'd seen Lana Turner do in one of her films. Tears filled her eyes. She wanted to hold him and tell him she loved him. But where was he?

The next day she hoped he would be outside the factory full of apologies, but he wasn't.

With her sisters and dad away her birthday was a very low-key affair. Tea wasn't anything special and her mother just gave her some money and Nell gave her a scarf. She had cards from her sisters and dad, but nothing from Vic. It was the most miserable birthday she'd ever had.

On the afternoon of Saturday 28th June Shirley hurried home. She was happy that she was going to see Lucy today. They were setting off as soon as they could. Everything was already packed in her small bag. When she left work she'd looked around for Vic as usual; in some ways she was pleased he wasn't there. He'd let her down and hurt her and for two weeks she had been very angry with him.

Back in Perry Street, their bags packed too, Nell and Eileen were having a job to keep their excitement under control. Shirley had just arrived home and they were ready to go when there was a loud rat-a-tat-tat on the front door.

'Who can that be?' asked Eileen.

'Well, it can't be old Charlie complaining about the blackout, it ain't dark yet,' said Nell.

'I'll go,' said Eileen.

'Perhaps he's come round to complain about the sunshine,' laughed Shirley.

'That ain't Charlie's voice,' said Nell when they heard a man talking.

Nell and Shirley stood up and looked at the kitchen door.

When Eileen pushed open the kitchen door they could see that her face had completely drained of all colour. She came silently into the kitchen and Shirley and Nell both gasped when they saw a policeman was right behind her. What on earth had happened now?

Chapter 31

Eileen looked at her daughter.

'What is it? What have I done?' Shirley looked at the policeman.

'Are you Miss Shirley Wells?'

'Yes. Yes I am. Why?'

He took a notebook from his top pocket. 'Do you know a Mr Victor Taylor?'

Shirley nodded and slumped into a chair. 'I know a Vic, but I don't know his surname.'

Shirley heard her mother gasp.

'This was the address we found in his flat.'

'Vic. Is it Vic?' Panic filled her. 'What's happened to him? Is he dead?'

'No, he's at the police station helping us with our inquiries.'

'Why? What's he done?'

'Where d'you want me to start?'

Tears began to roll down Shirley's cheeks.

'We've suspected him of looting and stealing for a while but never been able to pin anything on him. He's very clever. We have found out that he always took the stuff down to his wife in Dorset, and she managed to get rid of it for him. She's there with their kids. You all right, miss?'

Shirley could feel her head reeling. Was this a dream? What was he telling her?

'I'll get you a glass of water, love,' said Nell, bustling into the scullery.

'You said he was married,' Shirley whispered.

'Yes.'

'So what's all this to do with me?' Shirley was numb.

'We think he may have given you some of the stolen goods for safekeeping. Did he?'

'I ain't got nothing.' She looked at her mother's shocked face. 'How did you get my name and address?'

'We went round to search his flat, and his mate, who we've also arrested, told us about you and he gave us your address. It was written in Taylor's notebook. He said Taylor could have passed some of the items on to you. I'm here to find out about that, but it could be that he's only trying to save his own skin.'

'Vic's never given me anything.' Fear was washing over her.

'What about that bracelet?' said her mother quickly.

'A bracelet? Could I see it?'

Shirley picked up her handbag. She kept the bracelet in there because it was so precious to her and she was always worried it might be left in the house if they got bombed. She handed it to the policeman.

'This could have been stolen.'

'I didn't know.'

'You didn't know bugger all about him anyway, did you, you silly little cow? I guessed he was married. Shifty, that's what he was, and you had to go and get yourself mixed up with someone like that.'

'I'm sorry, Mum.'

'It wasn't her fault,' said Nell. 'She at an impressionable age.'

'Impressionable age, my arse. Good job your father's not here. He would give you a bloody good hiding.'

Shirley began to sob. 'Please, Mum. I'm sorry. I didn't know.'

'What happens now?' asked Eileen, suddenly growing strong.

'I'll have to take your daughter to the station.'

'Why?'

'We'll need a statement and she may be able to help us. Are you sure you've not had anything else from him?'

Shirley shook her head. 'No. And why should I go to the police station? I ain't done nothing wrong.'

'You've received stolen goods.'

'I didn't know my bracelet was stolen.'

'I'm sorry. I'm only doing me job.'

Shirley looked at her mother who sat bolt upright. Shirley began to cry. 'I didn't know, honestly I didn't.'

'Of course you didn't, love,' said Nell.

'I wish Luce was here. She'd understand.'

'And I wish your father was here. What a mess. What a bloody mess.'

'If you're ready, miss, we'll be making a move.'

Shirley took her coat from behind the door and ramming her beret on her head silently left her mother and Nell.

At the police station Shirley was asked many questions. All the while she was crying. When they finally said that if she had nothing more to tell them she could go, she felt sick with relief.

'But we might want you back if he tells us anything to incriminate you,' said the policeman who had brought her here.

Shirley began to walk away. 'Can I see him?' she asked.

'Sorry,' he said. 'Would have thought he'd got you in enough trouble with your family as it is. If you take my advice, if he don't get banged up, I'd leave him alone.'

'Will he go to prison?'

'He'd better. We don't take kindly to draft-dodgers and looters.'

Shirley walked out into the bright sunshine, but the sunshine had gone out of her life. She had loved him, but he was married. And how could he rob people that had been bombed? What was left for her now? In place of love she could feel a wave of hatred for him wash over her.

* * *

When she walked into the kitchen she found her mother still sitting in the chair, stony-faced. 'I knew that bloke was trouble as soon as I clapped eyes on him.'

Shirley didn't know what to say.

'What's Lucy gonner say when we don't turn up?' Eileen went on.

'We can still go, can't we?'

'What if they want you back at the police station?'

'They don't. They knew I was telling the truth when I said I didn't have anything to do with whatever he's done.'

'So he was married then?'

Shirley couldn't answer her mother. 'Where's Mrs Drury?' she asked.

'Gone home. She ain't very pleased, I can tell you. She was really looking forward to going away and now you've gone and spoiled it.'

'I'm sorry, Mum.' Shirley burst into tears. 'I wish Lucy was here,' she sobbed.

'So do I.'

'Please, Mum. Let's go to see her.' She wiped her tears away with her hand.

Eileen looked at the clock then at her daughter. She knew she was being unreasonable but she was angry, very angry. Nobody had ever brought any trouble with the police to her door before. Why couldn't the silly little cow see he was trouble? It upset Eileen to hear her daughter crying: she wanted to put her arms round her, hold her and make things better for her, but she had to be taught a lesson.

'If we're not going away then I'll put me things away.'

'I'll go over and see what Nell wants to do.' Eileen stood up and walked to the door. 'I'll have to tell your father about this, you know.'

Shirley hung her head and said nothing.

Nell had persuaded Eileen to go ahead with the planned trip, and it was early evening when they finally got to the station. Thankfully they managed to find a seat on the train.

Nell was trying to make conversation, although even she was finding it hard. 'So how will Lucy know we've arrived?' she asked.

'Got to phone her,' said Eileen.

'I ain't using a phone. They frighten the life out o' me.'

'I'll do it,' whispered Shirley. Those were the first words she'd uttered since they left home.

'She may not be able to get that friend of hers to meet us,' said Eileen. 'It's late. She was expecting us hours ago.'

Shirley turned away and looked out of the window. She couldn't meet her mother's gaze.

It was dusk when the train pulled into the station. Nell jumped up and on opening the door asked the guard if this was Horsham.

'Yes,' he said, looking at her suspiciously.

'I ain't a bloody spy,' she retorted, gathering up her bag and getting off with Shirley and Eileen following.

As they walked away from the train Nell said, 'If you ask me, taking all the stations' names away ain't much help to anyone. I reckon the Germans know more about things than we do.'

'I'll ask where the nearest phone box is,' said Shirley, going off.

'I know it ain't any of me business, but I don't think you should be so hard on her,' said Nell, watching Shirley's slight figure disappear into the gloom.

'I can't help it. What was she thinking of?'

'She didn't know what he was up to. Besides, she's young and these are troubled times.'

Eileen gazed at her daughter talking to the guard who was pointing. Shirley left the station.

Lucy arrived an hour later with Trish driving a lorry. She jumped down. 'You're later than I thought you'd be. Was the train playing up? It's so good to see you.' She held her mother, then Nell. She turned to hug Shirley, who promptly burst into tears.

'What is it? What's wrong? Is Dad all right?'

'Your father's fine.'

'So what's wrong with Shirley then?' The thought that had immediately occurred to her was that her sister was pregnant.

'It's a long story,' said her mother. 'I'll tell you later.'

She looked over at Trish who was still standing by the lorry.

'Come on, I'll show you where you'll be staying.' Lucy took hold of Shirley's arm. 'We'll talk later. Mum, Mum-in-law, this is Trish who I work with.'

They shook hands. Lucy was still holding on to Shirley. 'And this is me little sister.'

'Hello,' said Trish. 'I've heard a lot about you.'

Shirley only managed a half-smile as she nodded. 'Hello.'

'Right, let's be on our way.'

'I can't get up there,' said Nell, looking at the high step.

'It's this or walking and it's a long way,' said Lucy, standing behind her ready to give her a push.

The merriment at getting her mother and Nell in the lorry helped ease the tension, but Lucy was worried: she knew something was very wrong.

After a while they arrived at the village and made their way to a tiny cottage where a Mrs Parish made them very welcome.

'The young lady will have to sleep in the front room on a camp bed.' She turned to Shirley. 'Is that all right?'

'Thank you. That'll be fine, just as long as we get to sleep all night,' she answered.

Lucy was standing beside her sister. 'Don't see any reason why you shouldn't,' she said.

'Now you two ladies are upstairs,' said Mrs Parish, smiling. She was a small thin woman who looked as if one puff of wind would blow her away, but she was agile. 'I did have evacuees, but they went back. Nice little kids, they were. Should be getting some more soon.'

Eileen and Nell followed Mrs Parish as she bustled up the very narrow staircase.

'I'll make a cup of tea, so when you're ready come on down.'

'Thank you,' said Eileen and Nell together.

When the door was closed Nell sat on the bed. She bounced up and down. 'This is gonner be sheer heaven.'

Lucy was in the front room with Shirley. 'So what's happened?'

Shirley turned and tears slid down her cheek.

Lucy took her in her arms. 'You can tell me.'

'It's Vic.'

'Well, I guessed that. He's put you up the spout?'

Shirley shook her head. 'No. It's nothing like that. He's in prison.'

'What?' Lucy closed the door. 'What's he done?'

Shirley told her sister what had happened.

There was a knock on the door. 'I'm just making a cup of tea. Would you young ladies like one?'

'Yes please,' called Lucy.

'And, Luce, he's married.'

'Oh my God. Look, we'll talk about this tomorrow. Trish and me have got to go back soon. And Shirley, don't worry about him.'

After Lucy and Trish left, her mother and Nell said

they'd like to go to bed; it had been a long and eventful day.

Eileen and Nell soon settled down. It wasn't long before Eileen heard Nell's heavy breathing. This was something she had got used to over these past months. Eileen was thinking about Shirley. Why did she have to fall for a bloke like that? Should she write and tell Reg? Would it worry him enough to make him come home? Would he be *allowed* to come home? The silence of the country was disturbing. With no bombs or guns, these people could almost be living in another world.

Shirley, alone in the front room, looked about her. It was very sparsely furnished but had many heavy-framed pictures hanging on thick chains from the picture rail. There was a three-piece suite, but the pristine cushions suggested that it had never been sat on. In the fireplace a bowl of flowers sat in the basket. Mrs Parish must be very fond of flowers, as they were everywhere. Shirley was glad she was on her own: the prospect of spending a whole night with her mother would have been too much. She had so much to think about. How could he be married and a thief as well? She was still crying for him as she got undressed. She stared out of the window. The country was very dark and the strange animal noises frightened and unsettled her. Would she be able to sleep?

The following morning Shirley was woken by the sun streaming through the open curtains. She knew Lucy would be here as soon as she could. There was a faint knock on the door.

'Shirley, would you like some tea?'

She opened the door and smiled. Mrs Parish was standing holding a cup.

'I hope I didn't wake you.'

'No. Thank you. This is a real luxury.'

'Well, you all deserve it after what you've been through. It must be horrible to sleep in an air-raid shelter night after night. And that poor Mrs Drury having her house on fire. Terrible. Terrible. Anyway, as soon as you want I'll do a bit of breakfast. Lucy brought over a few eggs. A boiled egg and toast, how does that sound?'

'Like a feast.'

After she closed the door Shirley went to the open window. It looked so very different now: bright and clean smelling. The sky was a clear blue and the birds were singing their little hearts out. Lucy was very lucky to be waking up to this every morning. This was something she could get used to; it was so much better than Rotherhithe. What did Rotherhithe hold for her now? Did she want to go back to the factory with all its noise and smells, where everybody would soon know about Vic? How could she face Brenda and the rest of them now?

Chapter 32

When Lucy came along on her bike she found them all in Mrs Parish's front garden admiring the flowers. She'd been eager to get away and be with her family. Back at the farm the girls were going to do her chores for her so she could spend the day with them.

Shirley began to laugh. 'Never thought I'd see you on a bike.'

'Never thought I'd milk a cow, but you should see me. That's what I've been doing this morning. Been up since half-four. Anyway, how are you, did you sleep all right?' She parked her bike in the hedge and pushed open the gate, then gave everyone a kiss.

'Like a log,' said her mother.

'I was just saying,' said Nell. 'Ain't this a lovely garden?'

'Yes it is. The cottage looks like the cover of a chocolate box, even got roses round the door.'

'Ain't seen a box of chocolates for a while,' said Eileen. 'I expect that'll be something else on ration soon.'

'So what was it like sleeping in a proper bed?' asked Lucy.

'Heaven,' said Nell. 'Wish I could stay here for ever.'

'You could stay for a few more days, couldn't you, Mum? Would that be all right, Mrs Parish?'

'That would be fine with me,' she said, smiling. 'It's nice to have a bit of company.'

Eileen looked at Shirley. 'I don't know. I must admit it would be nice.'

'What about you?' Lucy asked her mother-in-law.

'I'd like that.'

'What about Shirley?' asked Eileen.

'I'd better go back. Got to go to work.' Shirley looked at her mother. Eileen would have nothing to worry about now that Vic was locked up.

'I don't know. Don't know if I'd be happy about that.'

'That's a shame,' said Mrs Parish. 'But you're always welcome, young lady, if you want to come down for a weekend.'

'I might take you up on that,' said Shirley. 'Why don't you stay, Mum, it'll do you good. Besides, the raids have eased up a bit now. I'll be all right.'

'I must admit it's very tempting. I'll have to think about it.'

'You haven't got long, not if you're going back tonight,' said Lucy. 'What about if we have a stroll to the village, it's not far from here, we could call in the pub and have a shandy or something.'

'I'll get a bit of dinner for you before you go,' said Mrs Parish.

'That's very kind of you,' said Eileen.

The sun was shining and everybody was content and at ease as they made their way to the pub.

'I could get used to this life,' said Eileen. 'Someone cooking me dinner for me.'

Sitting outside, Lucy nodded and passed the time of day with many of the locals.

'You seem to be well known,' said Nell.

'This is where me and the others come on a Sat'day night. Not much else to do.'

'It's so peaceful.' Shirley leaned back and felt the warmth of the sun on her face. 'D'you know, I think I will come back down here again.'

'That's good. Let me know when and I'll try and meet you.'

Shirley smiled. She loved her sisters and it was great being with Lucy again.

All too soon Shirley was on the train heading back to London. Trish and Lucy had taken her to the station. She couldn't believe her mum and Mrs Drury were going to spend a few more days there. Well, her mother was clearly relaxed because Vic was in prison. But Shirley hadn't admitted to them that she didn't like the idea of spending the night alone in the shelter. She told her mother she would go and stay with Brenda, but would she? And did she really want to go back to work?

She envied Lucy and the idea of joining the Land Army was going round and round her head. Could she leave her mother now her father was away? At least Eileen had Mrs Drury and they were like sisters.

That night it was warm and sultry and although there wasn't a raid Shirley decided to sleep in the shelter as it was a lot cooler. However, she couldn't sleep and tossed and turned all night. She was worried being in there on her own – what if a spider came in? She kept hearing noises that weren't there. She wanted her mum with her. She had made up her mind: she was over eighteen now and with Vic in prison she had nothing to keep her here. Tomorrow she was going to find out about joining the Land Army.

It was while her family was away that Ann had a card from Harry. She was over the moon and wanted to tell the whole world. It was in his handwriting so she knew he was alive. He only said he was well, but that was enough. She couldn't even phone his parents now they had moved to the country; they didn't have a phone. She sat holding the card close to her. She loved him so much. How long would they be apart? She sat down to write to both families, but tears kept clouding her vision. She wanted to be with them so much. She wanted someone to hold her tight and make the hurt in her heart go away.

When Brenda caught up with Shirley as they went into work the following morning she didn't mention Vic.

Did she know? They were at their bench waiting for the belt to start bringing them the shell cases that they had to put metal straps round when she told Brenda about her plans.

'So what about lover boy then? What's he got to say about it?'

'I can do what I like. I don't have to ask him.'

'You've changed your mind quick. He's not done a runner, has he?'

'No he ain't.' Not wanting to say more, Shirley was pleased the hooter went for them to start work and the belt jumped into life.

All morning they sang along with the music on the wireless, but Shirley's mind was elsewhere. How was Vic? And should she really join up? She wasn't concentrating when she put her hand out to take a shell case and her sleeve got caught in the belt. She let out an ear-piercing scream and everybody looked up.

Shirley's white sleeve was slowly turning crimson. Someone yelled for the belt to be stopped and for a brief moment the room was silent, save for the loud and intrusive music. Then everybody began running towards Shirley.

Brenda was first to reach her side. Shirley looked at her, before she fainted and fell against her friend.

'You're fidgety this morning,' said Nell to Eileen as they walked towards the village.

'I know. I can't rest knowing Shirley's up there on her own.'

'Well, you know she ain't with that bloke, so what's the problem?'

'Don't know. I can't put me finger on it. Nell, I don't like to ask, but would you mind very much if we went home today?'

'No, not really. A couple of days is enough for me. Can't say I'm that happy with all this quiet and the animals frighten the life out o' me.'

Eileen smiled. 'I know what you mean. I must admit I miss the noise of London.'

'And the shops; not that they've got much, but queuing is a good way of talking to people and having a moan.'

'And what about the pictures? Lucy said there ain't any for miles. Can't say I'd like that.'

'Right then, me old mate, it's off home we go.'

Suddenly Eileen had a spring in her step. She never thought she'd be eager to get back to Rotherhithe and maybe have to sleep in an air-raid shelter again.

Mrs Parish was disappointed to hear they were going back so soon. 'But I do understand. Tell young Shirley she's more than welcome any time she wants to come here.'

Eileen and Nell thanked her and made their way to the farm to tell Lucy their decision.

'What a place. Look at the size of that house,' said Nell as they walked down the long drive. 'Mind you, can't say I'd fancy this walk every day for me bit of grub.'

'You'd have to learn to ride a bike like Lucy.'

Nell laughed. 'I should cocoa.'

'We'd better go round the back. I remember Lucy saying they wasn't to use the front door.'

Round at the side of the house they could see a woman hanging out the washing. 'Hello,' said Eileen.

'You must be Lucy's mum,' said Mrs B., smiling and coming up to them when they pushed open the gate. 'The girls are all over at Moles Farm. They won't be back till tonight,' she added. 'Would you like a cold drink?'

'Thank you,' said Eileen, putting her bag on the ground. 'It's very warm. Is it far, this Moles Farm? Is there any way we could go and find her? We want to say goodbye.'

Mrs B. shook her head. 'Come into my kitchen. The farm's a fair way away and I'm sorry but everybody's out in the fields somewhere. Lucy didn't say you were going back just yet.'

'We wasn't. We've just made up our minds. I miss me daughter, you know, Shirley. I'm worried about her being on her own,' said Eileen as they followed her to the back of the house.

'I can understand that. You've all had a rough time of it up there in London. Look, leave Lucy a note, I'll see she gets it. She'll be very disappointed she's missed you.' Mrs B. smiled. 'She's been on and on about how pleased she is you're here.'

'This is very nice,' said Nell, admiring the large kitchen. She laughed. 'I reckon I could fit the whole of me house in here.'

'How can we get to the station?' asked Eileen. 'Is it very far?'

Mrs B. looked up at the large clock that hung on the wall. 'A bus will be going from the top of the drive in an hour. It'll take you all the way to the station. Would you like a sandwich before you go?'

'Thank you, that's most kind of you.'

Shirley opened her eyes and gave a little moan; she wanted to be sick.

'It's all right, Shirley,' said a kind voice. 'You're going to be all right.'

'Where am I?'

'In the hospital. You've had a nasty accident.'

She tried to sit up. 'Me mum. I want me mum.'

A nurse was standing over her and she gently pushed Shirley back down. 'Don't worry, they've sent someone round to tell her.'

'But she ain't there.' Shirley began to cry when she realised what had happened to her.

'I'm sure they'll find her,' said the nurse.

Shirley looked at her arm. There was a cage over it. Slowly she tried to raise it; it felt heavy. 'What's happened to me arm?' she asked.

'It got caught in a machine.'

'Is it bad?'

'It'll be fine.'

'It hurts.'

'I'll call the doctor.' With that the nurse bustled away.

Shirley lay remembering what had happened. She had seen this sort of accident before. She shuddered. The last girl that did it had to have her arm cut off below the elbow. Tears ran down her face and into her ears. This was her right arm; she couldn't do anything with her left. She started sobbing. She was in pain and she wanted her mum.

It was evening before Eileen opened the front door. 'Shirley? Shirley, it's only me,' she called out, untangling herself from the blackout curtain. She was expecting the kitchen door to open. 'Shirley, where are you? What you doing drawing this curtain? It ain't dark yet.'

Eileen walked through into the kitchen. 'Shirley?' she called again, going out to the shelter. The shelter was empty, but Eileen could see she had spent the night in there. Where was she? The thought that quickly ran through her mind was: Was he out of prison and had she gone off with him? 'I'll kill her if that's where she is,' she said out loud, marching up the passage. Angrily Eileen pulled back the curtain and a letter fell out. Slowly she picked it up and turned it over. It was addressed to her, but she didn't recognise the handwriting.

Chapter 33

EILEEN REREAD THE note from Brenda. Although Eileen had never met her she knew she was the girl who worked with Shirley. The note was brief and all it said was that her daughter was in hospital as she'd had an accident at work. Eileen felt her knees go weak. She sat on the stairs. What could she do? She had to get to the hospital. She wanted Reg. She sat studying the note. Nell. She had to tell Nell.

Eileen ran across the road. 'Nell. Nell,' she shouted as she made her way down her passage.

'What is it? Whatever's wrong? Oh my God, you look like you've just seen a ghost.'

'It's Shirley. She's had an accident at work.'

'Where? When?'

'I don't know.' Eileen thrust the piece of paper into Nell's hand. 'What shall I do?'

Nell quickly read the note. 'I'll put me coat on and we'll go and find her.'

'But it ain't visiting hours, they might not let us in.'

'They'd better not try and stop us,' said Nell, picking up her handbag.

They were unusually silent as they sat on the bus; Eileen couldn't think of anything to say. Her thoughts were full of Shirley. How bad was she? What would Reg say? Eileen stared out of the bus's window, although she couldn't see much as it was getting dusk and the green mesh that covered the windows didn't let you look out.

When they arrived at St Olaf's Hospital, they hurried to the reception and Eileen told them as much as she could.

'Wait here,' said the nurse.

To Eileen she seemed to be gone for hours. When she came back she was with another nurse who asked, 'Mrs Wells?'

Eileen nodded. 'Is she all right?'

'Follow me,' was all she said. And Eileen and Nell quickly fell in behind her.

When she stopped outside a small ward she said, 'Your daughter's in shock. She's had a very bad accident.'

'How bad?' whispered Eileen.

'The doctor has operated and she won't lose her hand.'

Eileen felt faint and she heard Nell take a sharp intake of breath.

'Are you all right?' asked the nurse; this was the first time she'd shown any emotion.

'Yes. It's the shock.'

'You mustn't stay long.'

'All right.' Eileen gently pushed open the door. The room was very dark as the blackout curtains had been drawn; there were also sandbags piled up outside the windows as a precaution against any bomb blast. The smell of disinfectant filled the air and a small light gave off just enough glow for Eileen to see her daughter lying very still. A cage stood over her arm. 'Shirley, love,' she whispered, 'it's me. Mum.'

Shirley's eyelids flickered. 'Mum. Mum? What're you doing here?'

Eileen bent over and kissed her forehead. 'Couldn't stand the quiet. What happened, love?'

'Wasn't concentrating and got me hand caught in the belt.' She closed her eyes again.

Eileen sat in a chair and Nell sat next to her. 'Nell's here.'

'Hello, love,' said Nell softly.

Eileen wanted to gather up her daughter and run away with her, but she could see Shirley didn't want to talk. 'Brenda left a note telling us what happened so it was a good job we came back when we did.'

Shirley didn't reply.

The door opened and a young man in a white coat came in. 'Mrs Wells, I'm Doctor Barker. Can I have a word with you?' He held the door open.

Eileen stood up and followed him out. 'How bad is she, doctor?' she asked.

'She's lost a lot of blood but we saved her hand. It

will be a bit deformed but in time and with long sleeves to hide the scars on her arms it won't be very noticeable.'

'Will she still be able to do things?'

'It will be hard at first, but it's surprising what we can get used to and Shirley will be able to do most things after a while.'

'Will she be badly scarred?'

'She may want to wear gloves, but as I said with long sleeves it won't notice.'

'Thank you.' Eileen watched him walk away.

She wandered back into the room and looked down on her daughter. She was beautiful, but what difference would this make to her life? What could she do to make her daughter's life bearable? First she had to write to Reg, Ann and Lucy. What were they going to say about this?

As soon as Ann received the letter from her mother she put in for leave and now she was on her way home. She knew her dad and Lucy were home already, as they didn't have to go through all the rigmarole she did to get leave. The train had taken for ever and at long last she was hurrying down Perry Street. Was Shirley home? Her mother had said she would only be in the hospital for a week or so. Poor Shirley. Ann was almost running when she arrived at number thirty-five.

The kitchen door was thrown open when they heard the front door slam shut.

'Mum. Dad,' cried Ann as she flung herself at them. Then she looked at her little sister. Lucy was standing behind her combing her hair. Tears ran down Ann's cheeks as she hugged her as tight as she could, careful to avoid her right hand, which was heavily bandaged.

Ann told them she could only get a forty-eight-hour pass, not like Lucy who had managed to get a few days off.

'I've got till the end of the week,' said Lucy. 'I'm so glad I work with girls who are willing to share the work.'

'What about you, Dad? You got to go back to Cardiff?'

'No. They decided they've got a big enough work force for the ships that's coming in. There's talk of sending us somewhere else. Can't say I want to go, don't like being away from home.'

'What about Mr Drury?'

'Fred's hoping to be home next week.'

'That'll be nice for Mrs Drury.'

All evening they sat and talked, but Shirley was getting cross with everybody looking at her and trying to anticipate her every move so that they could help.

'So how are you managing?' asked Ann.

'I'm getting better. Now I know how Mrs Drury felt when she burned her hands. At least I've still got me left one intact.'

'I cut up her food and she can then manage with a fork,' said Eileen.

'I'm trying to write with me left.' Shirley laughed.

'You might have a bit of a job to read it when I send you a letter.'

'I don't mind,' said Ann, trying to put on a brave face. How could she laugh when she must be in pain? 'Does it hurt?' she asked.

'Not so much now. I can't feel me fingers, seems I've damaged the ligaments.'

'You won't be going back to work then?'

'No. Mind you, I'll have to find something to do. I can't stay sitting here all day.'

'We'll worry about that later on,' said Reg.

'I said she could come down and spend some time with Mrs Parish. Me and the others could take her out and about.'

'That sounds a great idea,' said Ann. 'By the way, Mum, did you like it down there?'

'It wasn't bad. Very quiet. And it is miles from anywhere, but it would be nice for Shirley to go, that's when she feels like it, of course.'

'But what about if she has to visit the doctor?'

'Don't worry, that can all be arranged,' said Lucy.

'Excuse me,' said Shirley. 'I've damaged me hand, not me mouth. I can speak for meself, you know.'

'I'm sorry, Shirl. We always treat you like this, don't we?'

'I know. I was always being sent out of the room when you two wanted to talk.'

'So what does Vic – that is his name? – have to say about this? Has he been to see you yet?'

Ann caught sight of Lucy shaking her head.

'What is it? What have I said?'

'I'll tell you later,' said Eileen.

'No, don't keep her in suspense, I can tell her now,' said Shirley. 'He's in prison. He's been had up for looting and he's also married. That's it in a nutshell.'

Ann was taken aback. It was all said so matter-of-factly and on the surface there wasn't any sign of anger or hate at all. This was so wrong. Her little sister had suffered so much.

'So you see, Ann,' said her father, 'he was a bit of a bastard all round.'

'Reg,' said Eileen. 'Watch your language in front of the girls.'

Lucy laughed. 'We hear and say much more than that, Mum.'

'Well, just as long as I don't hear you.'

Ann looked at Shirley who just had a faint smile lifting her tired face. Was she suffering more than she let on?

They were all very upset but pleased in a way when Ann showed them the card she'd received from Harry. At least they all knew now that he was alive. It was very emotional when Ann had to leave; she didn't want to go, but knew she had to. Now she was on her way back to camp. Like most people all she wanted in life was for her and her family to be together again. Tears ran down her cheeks as she looked out of the train window trying to concentrate on happier times.

Lucy too was unhappy when it was time to leave Perry Street. As she made her way back to the farm she knew her first job was to see Mrs Parish. She had told Shirley she would find out about her staying with her. She wanted to get her sister away from the drab depressing sights all around her; surely being in the sunshine and quiet would help her recovery? But how bad was her hand? What would she be able to do with it in the future?

Everybody at the farm was concerned about Shirley. Even Mrs A., who was still aloof, seemed genuinely concerned. Matt, who'd met Shirley in the pub that first lunchtime she was here, also enquired after her.

'That's a shame, she's such a lively person and always laughing.'

'You've only met her once,' said Lucy. She nudged him. 'Here, you ain't fallen for me little sister, have you?'

'Stop it, Luce,' said Trish. 'You're making the poor boy blush.'

Lucy looked at Matt. 'Sorry.'

'That's all right.'

When he walked away Lucy thought that it would be great if Shirley did come here and if Matt did like her at least she would have someone nearer her own age to go out with, and he did drive a truck. For the first time in days she smiled.

Chapter 34

SHIRLEY WAS WORRIED as she sat with her father in the hospital waiting room. She was pleased he'd insisted on coming with her. Today she would see her hand for the first time. She was here to have the stitches taken out and she felt very nervous.

Her father looked at her and patted her arm. 'All right, love?'

She nodded. 'I'm glad you persuaded Mum not to come.'

'She does get in a bit of a state. But then again you can't blame her.'

'I know. Good job she's got Mrs Drury.'

Reg smiled. 'Yer, old Nell's a good old stick.'

'Miss Wells?' asked a nurse, coming over to them.

'Yes.' Shirley stood up. 'Can me dad come with me?'

'Of course.'

Her father held on to her left hand as they followed the nurse.

The doctor was the one Shirley had seen while she

was in hospital. 'Sit down, Shirley. It's good to see you again. Are you keeping well?'

She only nodded.

'Now, let's have a look at my handiwork.'

Shirley placed her hand on the bed as the bandages were slowly removed. She shut her eyes tight and clenched her teeth, giving out a little sound when the bandages stuck. To ease them off gently the nurse bathed them with water.

After a while the doctor announced, 'That's looking very good. Even I must admit my sewing's improving.' He smiled.

Before Shirley could open her eyes she tried to move her hand and couldn't. She panicked. What was she going to see?

'It's all right, love,' said her father. Seeing her tense up, gently he patted her arm.

Slowly she opened her eyes. Her hand was twisted, red and puffy. Big black stitches cobbled it together. She gently turned it over. She looked up at the doctor. 'I can't move me fingers.'

'Some of the ligaments have been damaged. But with use you'll find it will get easier. Now I'm going to remove these stitches. That will make it look a little better.'

Shirley turned her head away. She didn't want to see what he was doing. Among the many thoughts racing through her mind were: Will I be able to do my own hair? What about holding a knife? She wanted to cry, but she knew that wouldn't do any good. If only she hadn't been thinking about Vic. She wanted to blame this on someone and he'd hurt her. Then she thought about all the people who had been injured in the Blitz and that made her determined she too would be brave and would work hard to get her hand moving again.

When they arrived home her mother was talking to Nell at the gate.

'How is it, love?' asked Eileen.

'She was very brave,' said Reg proudly.

'It looks a bit funny, but I expect I'll get used to it.'

'It's surprising how quickly you can start to do things,' said Nell. 'You'll have to get your mum to make you some of those little gloves. I'm sure they helped me.'

'That'll be no trouble. Now I expect you'll both be wanting a cuppa? You want one, Nell?'

'Only if there's one going.'

'I'm sure we can squeeze one out of the pot for you.'

When they were in the kitchen Eileen watched her daughter as she struggled to take her coat off; she kept her gloves on all the time. Although she desperately wanted to see what her daughter's hand looked like, she knew she mustn't rush her. Shirley would show her in her own good time.

'Your mum was saying you might be going to stay with Luce for a bit.'

'I am thinking about it. I really liked it there.'

'Bit too out of the way for my liking. You'll miss the pictures and the shops, not that there's a lot in 'em these days.'

'I shan't mind that. It'll give me something to do. Who knows, I might even be able to help 'em.'

Eileen put the tray on the table. 'How will you manage getting a ticket and all that?'

'I think the stationmasters would help me. After all, think of all the soldiers and others that have lost an arm, they don't let that stop 'em from doing things.'

'That's true,' said Reg.

'D'you wonner see what it looks like?' asked Shirley. She gradually took off her glove. 'It looks a lot better now the stitches are out.' She held out her hand. Her fingers were claw-like. It reminded Eileen of someone with acute arthritis. A deep red scar ran over her wrist. Eileen's heart sank. How would she manage?

'I've been told to use it as much as I can and to keep moving me fingers.' She tried to straighten them, but Eileen could see she was in pain and it broke her heart to watch.

All through the following week Shirley was bored. She kept wandering about trying to do things for herself, but her mother was always there to take over. She even sat on the coping at the front of the house, trying to read and lap up the sunshine, but it wasn't long before someone came along to disturb her. One afternoon after Mrs Conner had been telling her at great length about her boys and what they got up to, Shirley decided enough was enough. She went indoors and said to her father, 'Dad, could you write and ask Lucy if I can go and perhaps stay a few days with that Mrs Parish?'

'Course I will. What day did you have in mind?'

'Dunno. I expect a Sat'day's the best day for her, she might be able to get a couple of hours off to meet me.'

'If that's what you want. Your mother's not going to be pleased about it. She likes fussing round you.'

'I know. But I feel I need to get away. Down there I can wander about where I please.'

Reg smiled. 'Lucy will like it.'

'I know Mum means well, but I'm beginning to feel stifled.'

'I can understand that.'

When Lucy's reply arrived it was full of how Mrs Parish was looking forward to having her and how pleased she would be to have her sister staying close by. It was all arranged for her to go the following Saturday, 2nd August.

As Shirley packed her small case her mother hovered over her. 'Now, you're sure you'll be all right?'

'I hope so, as long as I don't have Lucy and Mrs Parish fussing over me.'

'I expect they will. Get Lucy to write as soon as you get there. I want to know you arrived safe.'

Shirley smiled. 'I will. Please don't worry too much about me. I'll be fine.'

'Of course you will. I'm glad your dad's taking you to the station though.'

'So am I. Now I must be off.'

Eileen picked up her daughter's case. She could understand why Shirley wanted to go, but it was still hard for her to say goodbye. Although Shirley wasn't going into the forces it was still hard. She wanted her to be *here*. She wanted to look after her.

Nell came over and gave her a letter to give to Lucy. 'This is from Dan to us, I know she likes to read 'em.' Nell looked at Eileen. 'That son of mine's still on about going to Australia when this is all over.'

'Him and Luce might change their minds when the time comes.'

'I hope so,' said Nell. 'You take care of yourself,' she said, holding Shirley close.

'I will.'

At the bottom of the street Shirley turned and waved. Then, taking hold of her father's arm, she made her way to the station with him.

'Now, you're all right for money?'

'Yes thanks, Dad. And thanks for the money, you didn't have to, you know. Lucy said Mrs Parish only wants enough for me food and I've got a few pounds in me bankbook. Remember I was earning a bit when I was working and there ain't that much to spend it on.'

Her father patted her arm. He was so proud of his daughter. She was a fighter and would overcome this difficulty in her own time.

* * *

Shirley was pleased and surprised when she saw Matt waiting for her at the station.

'I hope you don't mind,' he said, taking hold of her case. 'Lucy was worried she might not be back from the fields in time, so I volunteered to collect you.'

Shirley smiled. 'No, I don't mind at all. Thank you.'

'It's nice to see you again,' he said as they walked towards his lorry. 'D'you think you'll be all right scrambling up there?'

'It might be a bit of a job in this frock, but I'll manage.'

'I was sorry to hear about your hand. Everybody was so worried about you.'

'Were they? Were they really?'

'Yes. Right, put your good hand on there and I'll push you from behind.'

Shirley did as she was told and fell into the lorry in an ungainly heap. She lay across the seat laughing.

'Are you all right?'

She wiped the tears from her eyes and sat up. 'D'you know, it's the first time I've laughed like that in weeks.'

'Well, we'll have to do something about that then, won't we?'

Mrs Parish rushed out of her cottage when the lorry pulled up outside.

'My dear. It's so lovely to see you again. Here, let me take your case.'

'I'll help you down,' said Matt.

'Thanks. Now, Mrs Parish, I don't want you running

about after me. I want to be able to do things for meself.'

'Of course you do. Would you like a cup of tea, Matt?'

'Yes please.'

As they all went inside the cottage Shirley immediately felt at ease. She knew she was going to be happy here for a few weeks.

'Lucy will be here as soon as she can,' said Mrs Parish. 'She wanted to know if you'll be well enough to go to the pub with them tonight?'

'I can see I'll have to give my sister a good talking to. I came away so that I could be independent.'

'She's concerned about you. She doesn't mean any harm.'

'I know. Will you be there, Matt?'

'I expect so.'

'That's good.'

Matt smiled. He had a lovely tan and his blue eyes sparkled. Shirley hadn't noticed that till now.

They sat and talked for a while. Matt was describing some of the nice places in the area.

'Could I walk to them?'

'Yes. There're some lovely walks,' said Mrs Parish.

'D'you know, I'm really looking forward to being here. It's so much nicer than London.'

'And we like having you, don't we, Matt?'

'Yes. We do.'

'Yoo-hoo. It's me.' Lucy came into the kitchen red-faced and panting. 'D'you know, I'm sure that hill's getting steeper.'

'Could be that you're getting older,' said Shirley, laughing and going to greet her sister.

'Cheeky. Anyway, how are you?' Lucy gave her a big hug. 'I'm really glad you're here. How's that hand?'

'Not bad now the stitches have been taken out, but it'll be a while before I get it working properly again.'

They sat in the garden for a while drinking tea and chatting, then Matt said he had to go.

'And I must get on with the dinner. It's lovely to have someone to look after,' said Mrs Parish as she gathered up the tea things.

'I'll see you tonight,' Matt said to no one in particular as he closed the gate.

'Sure,' said Lucy. 'He's a nice boy.'

'Why ain't he in the forces?' asked Shirley.

'He's a farm worker and they're exempt.'

'Have his parents got a farm or does he just work anywhere?'

'They have got a small one, not as big as the Ayreses' place and like us he goes and helps other farms. You'll have to come and see us when you feel like it.'

'I intend to. Matt was telling me about some of the places I can visit.'

'It is nice here. I really love it. I know Dan wants to go to Australia but I'd like to live here.'

'Yes, that's all very well, but would he find any work?'

'I shouldn't think so. D'you know, you sound like Mum.' They laughed together.

'That reminds me, Dan's mum gave me a letter from him. I've got it in me bag.' She went to stand up but Lucy beat her to it.

'I'll get it.'

'Lucy. I hurt me hand, not me body. I know you mean well, but please don't keep doing things for me. That's why I wanted to get away from Mum. I felt I was being wrapped in cotton wool.'

'I'm sorry. I'm really gonner like having you around.'

'Not nearly as much as I'll enjoy being here.'

Once again they held each other close.

'Now I've got to get back. Mrs B. will have dinner ready for me. We'll pick you up about eight, is that all right?'

'I should think so.'

Shirley watched her sister pedal away. She knew that she was going to be happy here. It was very different to what she'd been used to, but that's what she needed: a complete break. She looked at her hand. Although she hated Vic, if she hadn't done this damage she would still be in the factory. As she went back into the cottage, the aroma of the dinner wafted her way and it smelled good.

Chapter 35

As SHIRLEY WALKED along she began singing, she was so happy the few weeks she had been here; everybody in the village had made her feel really welcome. It was so peaceful here, and Mrs Parish was so pleased to have her to look after, but the problem of not earning any money nagged at the back of her mind. Although her father had sent her some more she knew she couldn't rely on him for ever and her bank balance was slowly dwindling, but she had no idea what work she could do. Would she have to go back home? Then there was Matthew Kendal. She gave a little smile at the thought of him; they had been seeing quite a lot of each other. Whenever he could be spared from his work he hurried over to take her out. He was very handsome, slim and very muscular; he could pick Shirley up with no effort, although he wasn't much taller than her. He was kind and considerate and never mentioned her hand; she felt totally at ease in his company. All her feelings for Vic had left her; it was Matt she liked. Her life was full with him and she was growing very fond of him. This wasn't like being with Vic. Matt was honest, they had talked lightly about the future together and she had met his parents. Although it was early days, she hoped that later on they might even talk about getting married, but what would her parents have to say about that? She had just told them in her letters that she loved this life and the people she had met.

She particularly loved the long walks she and Matt went on together; once they had taken a picnic, but Shirley had been bitten by ants so she didn't think that was such a good idea. Matt called her a townie when he pointed out the names of flowers and birds. Every day she learned something new. Sometimes at the weekend they would just sit in the pub and talk: they always seemed to have something to discuss and laugh about. When they walked home under the stars Shirley felt she was in a different world and when he kissed her goodnight it was a warm gentle caress. She knew she could love him, really love him. She didn't want this summer to end.

During the day Lucy took her with her whenever they were working close by. Trish and Emma treated her like their little sister. Some days, when they weren't busy working or had to go to town for goods, they would take her in the lorry with them.

Getting her in the lorry was always a source of merriment. On those days they would treat her to a cream tea. They'd look in shop windows and talk about clothes before going on to the pictures.

Shirley really didn't want to return to London, although in every letter her mother asked when she was coming home. To her, London with all its horrors seemed a million miles away. How could Shirley tell her parents that she never wanted to go back to the bombs, dirt and confusion? She didn't think she would be able to cope with it – and what job could she get? Shirley knew she had to think about her future, but what could she do? She had told Lucy her fears and feelings and Lucy was going to see if anyone wanted help round here, even if it was only taking little ones to school. That was something she could manage. Perhaps the local school would like some help? When the summer holidays were over she would go along and see the headmistress.

Shirley made her way towards the field she knew Lucy would be working in. She pulled her sun hat down to stop the glare of the sun in her eyes and swung her gas mask in its new Rexine case that Mrs Parish had helped her to make. She was so proud of it; it had been hard work trying to sew with her injured hand but she'd done it and it looked good. Like most fashionable young women she wanted to disguise the cardboard box. Today the hedgerows were alive with chattering birds and bright-coloured flowers and she had a spring in her step. She couldn't believe she had been here a month.

When Shirley got to the field the sun was blazing

down on the girls. They waved when they caught sight of her.

Lucy came bounding over. 'You come to work?'

'If I can be of some use.'

'You can help me stack the corn, will that be all right?' Lucy was still worried about her sister and didn't want to push her too hard.

'Sounds good.' Shirley enjoyed helping her sister.

Lucy looked at her as they worked together. She was amazing; even with her hand that was twisted and not much use she was laughing. Shirley looked so much better; she had lost that pale sad look, she was tanned and the sun had lightened her hair. Lucy smiled: she was so proud of her brave young sister.

In her turn Shirley watched Lucy who was struggling to keep the corn upright. Shirley knew that she would never be allowed in the Land Army now.

Trish came up with some drinks and they stopped work.

'So what are you doing tonight?' Trish asked Shirley, handing her a glass with a straw in it as she found this was the easiest way to drink.

'Me and Matt are going to the pictures,' she said, removing some bits of corn that were stuck in her frock. 'D'you want to come?'

'What, and look at you two mooning over each other all evening? No thank you.'

Shirley grinned. 'Good,' she said. 'But I thought I'd better ask.'

Lucy, who was wearing her hair tied in a turban, came and plonked herself next to her sister. 'Shirking again, I see.'

Shirley pushed her sun hat back from her face. 'D'you mind? I don't get paid for this. This is a labour of love.'

They lay back in the sun looking up at the bright blue sky.

'This is the life,' said Lucy. 'The peace and quiet of it all.'

'Well, it suits me,' said Shirley.

After a while Trish said, 'Right, you two, it's back to work.'

'She's such a slave-driver,' said Lucy, pulling Shirley to her feet.

Shirley began singing. Lucy wanted to hold her. She had never seen her sister so happy. Everybody in the village loved her; in such a short while she had become part of them.

The low drone of a plane made them stop and look up.

'Is it British, is it one of ours?' asked another of the land girls.

'Hope so,' said Trish, waving to the pilot as the plane swooped down.

Lucy shielded her eyes from the sun. Suddenly she let out a scream. 'It's one of theirs. It's a German. Quick, dive in the corn.'

As the girls ran and threw themselves in amongst

the stooks the rat-a-tat-tat from the plane's machine guns filled the air and the bullets hit the ground, sending up small dust clouds.

Shirley turned and saw Lucy stumble. She was in the line of fire as the plane banked to make another pass. 'Luce, quick,' she yelled. She raced towards her sister and threw herself on top of her.

Lucy put her hands over her head as the plane roared overhead with its guns firing. It went quiet and she lay still for a moment or two as the plane turned and went away. Shirley was still on top of her. She had felt her sister's body jump and then slump. She lay motionless, frightened at what she thought could have happened, then suddenly she burst into life, shouting Shirley's name.

'Bloody hell,' said Trish, coming up to them. 'That was close. You two all right?'

Lucy pushed Shirley over and to her horror blood-red stains appeared on the front of her sister's sundress. 'Shirley? Shirley!' she screamed. Lucy rolled over to her and held her sister's limp body in her arms.

Trish knelt beside her. She took hold of Shirley's hand and felt her pulse. 'Bastard,' she called out to the sky. Jumping to her feet she shook her fist and yelled out, 'You bloody rotten bastards. I hope you all rot in hell.'

All the girls in the field came running over to them.

Lucy was holding Shirley tight and rocking backwards and forwards. Her moans were unnerving.

People began running about. Someone tried to take

Shirley from Lucy but she hung on fiercely. 'No,' she shouted. 'Leave her be.'

'We've got to get her away in case he comes back,' said someone. 'We've got to get help.'

'I'll take her.' Lucy gathered Shirley up in her arms; it was only a short distance to the edge of the field. Summoning all her inner strength, Lucy stumbled over the ruts with her sister. Nobody was going to take her away. Lucy couldn't see as her tears had clouded her vision. Someone was holding her arm and leading the way. At the edge of the field Lucy lay Shirley down. Trish took charge and moved everybody back.

'Emma, go and get Mr Ayres. Tell him to phone for an ambulance.'

Lucy knelt on the ground holding Shirley. She knew that life had left her sister.

Men from the other fields came running. Amongst them was Matt.

When he saw Lucy, who now had blood all over the front of her shirt, he fell to his knees. Lucy let go of her sister and it was his turn to hold Shirley close. Tears ran down his face. 'No,' he called out. 'No.' Rocking Shirley's lifeless body back and forth, he cried pitifully.

The following morning when Matt and his father drove Lucy to the station she couldn't tell them what had happened after she had carried Shirley to the edge of the field. It was all a blur. She knew someone had got a doctor, then the undertaker had come and taken her sister away. To her it had all seemed to be happening so fast. Matt and his fellow workers had seen the plane but the shock when he saw Shirley was still haunting him. His sobs were even now disturbing the quiet as they neared the station.

'You will come back?' asked Mr Kendal.

'Yes,' said Lucy softly. 'But I've got to tell Mum and Dad and find out what they want.'

'Yes of course you have. Are you sure you don't want Matt to go all the way with you? We can spare him, you know.'

Lucy shook her head. 'Thanks all the same.'

'Lucy?' exclaimed her mother when Lucy opened the kitchen door. Eileen jumped to her feet. 'What is it? What's happened? Why are you here?'

'Where's Dad?'

'Gone out to the lav. Lucy, what's wrong?'

They heard the scullery door shut and her father walked in with a newspaper tucked under his arm. 'Luce, this is a lovely surprise . . .' His voice trailed off. 'Oh my God. What's happened?'

Lucy let her tears fall. 'It's Shirley.'

Eileen plonked herself down in the chair. The colour had drained from her face. 'What's happened to her?'

'She's dead.'

'Dead. *Dead?*' repeated her father. 'How?'

'We were in a field and a German plane came over.' Lucy had to stop. 'It machine-gunned us and Shirley saved my life. Oh Mum.' She fell to her knees and into her mother's arms and sobbed noisily.

Reg sat at the table. He was speechless. He was trying to let this news sink in. His Shirley. His little girl was dead.

It was a while before Lucy could compose herself. She wiped away her tears and told them the sad story.

'She got through all the bad bombing and now, when we all thought she was safe, this happens,' said Reg. Tears were now rolling down his rugged face.

Eileen couldn't speak. She sat twisting her handkerchief round and round in her fingers.

'Mum, I've got to tell Ann.'

'How?' answered her father.

'I've got the phone number of her camp. We exchanged them the last time we were together, just in case. I'll try and get a message to her. I'll go to the phone box now. Where's the nearest one that's still standing?'

'Don't know, love.'

'Mr Jacob the newsagent's got one. He might let you use it.' Eileen's voice was just a whisper.

Lucy picked up her bag. 'I won't be long.' She left them and hurried across the road. She passed her mother-in-law's house. Telling her would come later; she had to let Ann know first.

Mr Jacobs was more than happy to help when he heard the terrible news. 'Poor Shirley. How's your mum taking it?'

Lucy didn't want to talk about it; she just wanted to get on with telling Ann. 'Pretty bad. I hope I won't be too late to catch Ann, would you mind very much if I asked her to call here?'

'Not at all. Not at all.'

Lucy watched Mr Jacobs shuffle away. Lucy had forgotten how old he was. She dialled the number and hung on to the receiver. Her tears were falling again as she asked for Ann's extension number. Before she was put through she was asked many questions. All she wanted was to talk to her sister. When she told them the reason she was finally put through.

'Hello.'

Lucy called out, 'Ann. Ann, is that you?'

'Lucy! You were lucky to get me; I'm just off. What is it?' Ann was silent as she listened to what her sister was telling her. Lucy kept stopping because the words wouldn't come.

Ann shuddered as she felt a chill run up her spine. 'Shirley. Our little Shirley,' was all she could whisper.

'Do you think you could get compassionate leave?'

'I would think so.'

'This is Mr Jacobs' phone and I'll give you his number if you can't make it.'

'How's Mum and Dad taking it?'

'What do you think?'

'I'd better go. See you soon.'

When Ann put the phone down she burst into tears.

'What is it? What's happened?' asked the WAAF who worked in the same office with her.

'My little sister's been killed. She's been machine-gunned in a field.'

The WAAF put her hand to her mouth. 'I'm so sorry. That's awful. That's not the sister who had the accident, is it?'

Ann nodded. 'I've got to get leave.' She ran from the room.

When Nell opened the door Lucy was immediately crushed in her arms.

'This is a surprise, yer mum didn't say you was coming—' Nell stopped when she saw Lucy's red and watery eyes. 'What is it, love? It's not Dan, is it?'

Lucy shook her head.

'Come in the kitchen.'

Fred stood up when they walked in. He could tell by the look on their faces that something was very wrong.

Lucy sat at the table and told them what had happened. After a while Nell said, 'I'll get me coat. Yer mum might need me.'

Eileen was sitting staring into space when Lucy walked in with Nell and Fred close behind.

'I'm so sorry,' said Nell. She too began to cry.

Eileen looked up. Her face was the colour of chalk. 'Why, Nell? Why my little girl? What's she done to deserve this?'

'I don't know. The one we thought was safe.'

'I don't know what to do. What can I do, Nell?'

'I don't know. I can't answer that.'

Eileen was bewildered. All Shirley's short life suddenly filled her thoughts. Eileen had been worried about Ann and Lucy getting married, but they were happy. Shirley would never know that happiness. She remembered the times she had nagged her about her handbag. It had all been so futile, now she would never put her handbag on the table again. A deep heart-rending sob escaped her.

Lucy looked at her mother. She had brought up three daughters and given them all the love she could. Eileen had never wanted her family to go away but like so many mothers today she had had to accept it. Now she had lost her baby. Shirley had always been the baby.

Lucy knew this was something her mother would never get over. Her mother's sobs broke into her thoughts. How could she comfort her?

After a sleepless night at the camp Ann finally arrived home. 'I've got a week's leave,' she said as soon as she walked in. 'Where is she?'

'Still down in Horsham at the undertaker's,' said Lucy. 'I thought I'd better come up and see Mum and Dad, find out what they wanted to do.'

'We've been having a bit of a discussion about it and me and your mother have decided to have the funeral down there,' said their father, who had aged even further overnight.

'Why?' asked Ann in surprise. 'That was where she was killed. That was where she should have been safe. No, she's got to come home.'

Lucy looked at Ann, bewildered. 'She was happy there. The whole village loved her.'

'I'm sorry,' said Eileen. Her eyes were red and she looked distraught. 'I haven't got the strength to argue with you two. All I know is that I want my Shirley to be where she was happy and, according to her letters, she liked it there.' She stood up. 'Now I'm going to have a lie down.' She left them to go into the front room where they were now sleeping.

Lucy and Ann looked guilty.

'I'm sorry, Dad,' said Ann. 'The last thing I want to do is upset Mum.'

'I know that. But what if she was buried up here and the graveyard got bombed, how would you feel about that?'

Ann began to cry. 'I'm so sorry.'

Lucy put her arm round her sister's shoulders. 'She did like it there and Matt, that's the young man who she's been seeing a lot of, will make sure her grave is kept up. D'you know, all the villagers are so angry at what has happened. They all loved our Shirley.'

The following day the Wells family had to make the sad silent journey they had been dreading. Nobody wanted to speak, they just wanted to sink into their own thoughts. They left the station and made their way to the undertaker's.

'Lucy,' said Mr Baxter, coming up to them and shaking her hand.

'This is me mum and dad and me sister Ann.'

'I'm so sorry to have to meet you in these tragic circumstances. Shirley was such a lovely happy girl.'

Reg gave him a faint smile. 'Thank you.'

'Have you decided where you want Shirley interred?'

Lucy nodded. 'We all thought that as she loved it here she should be buried in the local churchyard.'

'The whole village will be very pleased about that. Now, was there any special dress she liked?'

'She was a bridesmaid when Ann got married and we know she was so proud of that frock. So we thought . . .' Lucy couldn't finish the sentence.

'That's fine,' said Mr Baxter. 'Have you got it with you?'

Lucy nodded and handed him a paper carrier bag.

'Thank you. How are you going to get back to the farm?'

'We'll get Ben's taxi.'

'No. I'll take you.'

Reg looked at Lucy then at Mr Baxter. 'Thank you, sir. Thank you very much.'

It was a warm sunny day when Shirley Wells was buried in St Faith's churchyard. The coffin was covered with a mass of flowers and all the villagers came to the service. Lucy needed no more reassurance that her sister's grave would be well looked after, and Ann had to agree that this was a lovely place, so peaceful.

After it was all over Eileen, Reg, Nell and Fred made their way back to London.

In the church Eileen had prayed for them all. She had lost her daughter and it was something she didn't ever want to go through again. But the war wasn't over yet.

Chapter 36

June 6th 1944 was the day the British people had been waiting for. It had given them hope. The allied forces had landed in France and everybody knew that the end of this war that had dragged on for years must be in sight.

Eileen, along with Reg and probably the whole of Britain, was listening to the wireless telling them what was happening.

'Let's hope it'll be all over soon and Dan and Harry will be back before long,' said Eileen.

'I think you'll find it'll be a while before Hitler surrenders,' said Reg. 'He ain't gonner give in that easily.'

'It hope those boys are all right.' Hope was all they had to cling to and Eileen knew she wanted her two girls to be happy. Since Shirley's death a cloud had hung over this family.

Eileen knew that Ann had received a few cards from Harry and he appeared to be well. Ann had told her parents that officers weren't treated too badly, but she was desperate to know more. She was always in touch with Harry's parents and they were happy enough in the country but eager to get back to London. Mrs Fisher had sent a lovely letter with her condolences after Shirley's death. They had been very upset over that news.

Lucy knew that Dan had been fighting somewhere in the jungle. Eileen and Nell often talked about him, that lad had had a long war, but he always managed somehow to write to his mother now and again as well as Lucy. Whenever Nell got a letter she would hurry over to Eileen and read it out; she was so proud of her son. He told her he didn't like all the creepy crawlies and the noises at night were terrifying, but he was always cheerful.

'And he still wants to go to Australia?' she said, laughing.

'P'r'aps they don't have those sort o' things in the towns,' said Eileen. Although she didn't like the idea of Lucy going all that way away she was pleased Reg had made her see sense about her and Dan marrying. It gave them a future to cling to and work towards.

The war wasn't over as quickly as everyone had hoped and as the allied forces pushed their way through France, London and the south were troubled by Hitler's new menace: flying bombs, or doodlebugs as everyone called them. They were unmanned and came over making a terrible noise, then when the engine cut out they fell to the ground, killing many people.

Rockets followed. These were truly terrifying as they just fell from the sky without any warning.

'When will it all end?' said Eileen to Nell one day after they'd heard that a rocket had fallen on New Cross Woolworth's, killing numerous women and children who had been Christmas shopping.

'I don't know, mate. I really don't know.'

They were sitting in Eileen's having their usual natter over a cup of tea. Over the years it hadn't mattered how many shortages they had had to put up with, they'd always managed to share a cup of tea, even if they didn't have a biscuit to go with it.

'Ann's waiting for news about Harry. The Red Cross said she should hear soon. She's worried he might not be the same. You know, after being so inactive for all these years.'

'He's a sensible lad but I expect like most of us he'll be a lot thinner. Look at this frock, it's hanging on me.' Nell pulled at the front of her dress.

Eileen smiled.

'Where they gonner live?' asked Nell.

'At his parents' home in Southwark Park Road. Thank goodness it's still standing, but she's gotter wait till she's demobbed.'

'It's gonner be hard for these kids to get back to a normal married life.'

'Yes, but what's normal? They ain't known anything different.'

'That's true. What about Luce?'

'She said she's gonner stay on the farm till Dan gets home.'

'Gawd only knows when that'll be.'

'She ain't got nothing to come back here for.'

'That's true, but remember, we've gotter lick the Japs first.'

Eileen sat and played with the spoon. She was thinking about Shirley's grave. Reg and she had been to see it when the headstone had been put in place. Lucy had told her that the villagers as well as she and Matt always placed fresh flowers there.

'Come on, mate, this won't do.' Nell gathered up the cups. 'We've gotter get to the market just in case they've got sides of beef, whole pigs, bananas, oranges and . . .' Nell stopped. 'I was only joking.'

Eileen wiped the tears from her eyes. 'Sorry. I was just thinking about Shirley.'

'Course you was. She'll never be very far from our thoughts.'

September 1945

Eileen stood at her door looking down a war-weary Perry Street. She was remembering six years ago when the Anderson shelters had been delivered and all the trauma that had created. Six years. At times it seemed as if the war would never be over, but now all the hostilities had at last come to an end with Japan surrendering. Everyone's lives had been changed for ever and over these past six years they had endured some terrible things. But to Eileen the loss of Shirley had been the worst. She and Reg would never get over that. People said time heals, but her memory would never die.

Nell and Fred came across the road.

'All right, love?' asked Fred.

Eileen gave him a faint smile. 'As well as I'll ever be. It's good that it's really all over at last.'

Nell sat on the coping. 'Mind you, I don't know if I

like the idea of this new bomb. The doodlebugs and rockets were bad enough but this thing, it's terrible. All those people dead.'

'It was the only way to stop the Japs.'

'I know,' said Eileen, sitting down next to her friend. 'But when we saw what it had done when we went to the pictures last week, it was terrible.' Eileen had been very upset at the devastation and number of lives that had been lost.

'I didn't like seeing it either,' said Nell.

They fell silent for a moment or two then Fred asked, 'Where's Reg?'

'He's gone with Ann to try and find out when Harry might be home.'

'Seems funny seeing her in a frock after all this time,' said Nell.

'The Red Cross are looking after the boys and they might have some news. Lucy will be back home at the end of the month. She wanted to help them finish off the harvesting or something. She really loves that outdoor life. She was saying that Dan could be demobbed soon.'

Nell smiled. 'Thank Gawd he's safe. He's been in the thick of it for years, poor little bugger.'

'As you know, in his last letter he said he reckons their lot will be the first to be moved out,' said Fred.

'Could even be on his way home now,' said Nell, smiling. 'It'll be lovely to see him again.'

'I can't actually believe it's all over,' said Eileen.

'I hope everything works out for these youngsters,' said Nell. 'Mind you, I don't know how I'll feel if all this talk about him and Lucy going to Australia comes off.'

'It's such a bloody long way away,' said Fred, plonking himself next to Eileen.

Eileen swallowed hard. 'Yes it is, but I really can't see Lucy settling down round here again.' Although Eileen knew everybody was elated now the years of war were over, like many, her life would never be the same. She'd lost her dear Shirley. They'd had their ups and downs but she had been a good girl. Look how she'd helped clear up Nell's place. For Ann and Lucy, losing their young sister had taken its toll; they had grown up. Eileen desperately hoped that when their husbands came home they could start their lives afresh and be happy. But she didn't want Lucy to go all that way away.

'I hope Harry's all right,' said Nell. 'We're hearing terrible tales of what happened to some of these poor boys.'

'Ann said as he was an officer they weren't treated too bad.'

'Where're they gonner live?' asked Nell.

'They'll stay at his parents' place for a while till he gets used to being home.'

'It's gonner be real hard for these kids,' said Fred.

They lapsed into silence, each one with their own thoughts.

Eileen looked at the flags hanging from bedroom windows moving gently in the welcome afternoon breeze. They had been out for V.E. day in May; now they had been brought out again for V.J. day. Some of the houses had big 'Welcome Home' signs for the boys that were coming back.

Nell's voice broke into her thoughts. 'Fred's been busy making a banner for Dan.'

Fred's face split into a huge grin. 'We're gonner have a right old knees-up that night, I can tell yer. Thank Gawd the pub's still standing.'

Nell gave a little laugh. 'I'll be that pleased to see him.'

'We all will, Nell. We all will.' Eileen tried to shake off her melancholy, but what was going to happen to her and Reg? The docks would never open again. He had been doing quite a bit of carpentry; perhaps he could do that full time?

Suddenly Fred said, 'I heard that this lot could be pulled down once the government gets itself together. Gonner be called slum clearance.' Fred looked along the row of houses.

'Reg was saying the same thing. But will they?'

'Well, there ain't a lot of point in repairing 'em.'

'If you ask me,' said Nell, 'I think they've got a bloody cheek calling these places slums.'

'It would be nice to move into a new place though. Just think, an inside lav and a bathroom,' said Eileen.

Nell smiled. 'Now I could get used to that. No more filling up the tin bath or going to the public baths.'

'I hate that,' said Eileen.

'I wonder where we'll finish up?' asked Nell.

'Could be anywhere, love, could be anywhere.'

Eileen shuddered. 'It's getting a bit chilly. D'you wonner come in for a cuppa?'

'Why not?' said Nell. 'Well, we've certainly got a lot to tell our grandkids,' she added, closing the front door behind her.

Eileen went into the scullery to fill the kettle. She looked out at the brick shelter: all the nights they'd slept in there . . . She wanted to move away. This house had too many memories. Some were good, but she'd never hear her girls running up and down the stairs again and their laughter filling the rooms. And the times she'd shouted at Shirley for throwing her handbag on the table . . . They had nothing to keep them round here now. Even Shirley was miles away, at rest in her sleepy village.

She let a tear trickle down her cheek. Like her daughters, she and Reg needed to start anew.

Eileen turned the gas out when the kettle began to boil. She dabbed at her eyes with the edge of her pinny. This wouldn't do. They had a new way of life to seize now and there would be other challenges to overcome. Placing the teapot on the tray next to the sugar bowl and enamel milk jug, Eileen pushed open the scullery door and, with a smile on her face, stepped into the kitchen.

Hopes and Dreams

Dee Williams

Dolly Taylor and Penny Watts have been friends all their lives. Growing up in Rotherhithe, they left school at fourteen, and work in a factory making shell cases. Their childhood sweethearts, Tony and Reg, are away fighting and, as World War II rages on, Dolly dreams of escaping to far-off lands.

But, for now, American soldiers provide the excitement, breaking the monotony of factory life and nightly air-raids with music and dancing. Despite her loyalty to Tony, Dolly is attracted to Joe, a handsome GI, and when he proposes, she can't resist. But on reaching America, Dolly is shocked by the cold reception she receives. As she struggles to make friends and understand the man she married, Dolly wonders if she has made a terrible mistake. Will she have to return to Rotherhithe to find happiness?

Acclaim for Dee Williams' novels:

'An inspiring tale, full of surprises, intrigue and suspense' *Newcastle Evening Gazette*

'Flowers with the atmosphere of old Docklands London' *Manchester Evening News*

'A moving story full of intrigue and suspense, and peopled with a warm and appealing cast of characters . . . an excellent treat' *Bolton Evening News*

0 7553 0097 1

headline

A Rare Ruby

Dee Williams

It's 1919, and for fourteen-year-old Ruby Jenkins and her family, life isn't easy. Ever since Ruby's father returned from the war shell-shocked and incapable of working, Ruby and her mother Mary have had to sacrifice all comforts. Amidst the bleak poverty of the Rotherhithe neighbourhood in which they live, Mary earns money doing washing for as many customers as she can cope with.

But when Ruby gets a paid job at Stone's Laundry, a whole new world opens up to her. And as things begin to improve, Ruby starts dreaming of one day having a husband and children of her own. Then sudden tragedy strikes at the heart of the Jenkins family, leaving Ruby distraught and desperate. Will happiness and love only ever inhabit her dreams – or are they much closer than she could dare to imagine?

Acclaim for Dee Williams' novels:

'Flowers with the atmosphere of old Docklands London' *Manchester Evening News*

'A moving story full of intrigue and suspense, and peopled with a warm and appealing cast of characters . . . an excellent treat' *Bolton Evening News*

'An inspiring tale, full of surprises, intrigue and suspense' *Newcastle Evening Gazette*

0 7472 6451 1

headline